The Language of Death

His focus was razor-sharp, his position perfect for listening. He was preparing to shift to a better vantage point when a faint, acrid tang in the air stopped him mid-move.

Weak vinegar.

Salt.

The smell clung like sweat after a long day's labor.

He wasn't alone.

Beyond the pallets, a faint movement caught his eye. Two figures crouched low, hidden as he was—nearly invisible in the dim light. Dressed in all black, they melted into the shadows. The only detail that stood out was their boots.

Strapped leather. Identical to Duwy's.

Rad's stomach tightened.

These weren't random thieves.

Knives gleamed in their hands—long, narrow blades meant for hearts, lungs, or eyes.

Not tools.

Not defense.

Murder.

The assassins were ten feet away, their wicked blades glinting in the dark.

And they hadn't moved—not even when the stray cat scattered a rat nearby.

The realization hit him like a bucket of cold water.

They don't know I'm here.

"Magic is not an invention. It is an inheritance—woven through the stones, the trees, the waters, and the blood of living things. It hums beneath the feet of mortals and whispers through the old forests. It can be bent, bound, and broken—but it can never be wholly tamed. Those who thought they could died fools."
— Miralon of Haddensack, Archsage of the Bright Age, *Treatises on the True Currents, Vol. I*, RH5

"The Age of Rising Kingdoms lasted four centuries—four hundred years of wars, strife, alliances, and ambition, measured more often in broken crowns than golden ones. Emerging from this chaos was Orlath of Haddensack, who, with his sword Falconclaw, treaty, and the most formidable host seen since the Bloodlords, forged the western duchies into a single realm. Thus began the present era—the Reign of Haddensack. Also termed, the Bright Age."
— Historian Varlen of Ornst, *Annals of the Unification*, RH15

"The Age of Rising Kingdoms ended when one man put a bigger sword to the map than the rest."
— Scholar Jaspen Greyvine, *The Kingdom Born of Swords*, RH16

Leskaré da-nater dormitas. (Leskaré never sleeps.)
— Graffiti found scratched on tavern doors, merchant houses, and temple stones

"True magic is not found in the earth, the sky, or the heavens. It lies within the pages—waiting for those brave enough to read."
— Merrow Keff, Ornst Library Founding, RH223

"I stand corrected. True magic isn't in the pages—it blooms the moment someone is sent to me for help. No, young lad, I don't know where there are sketches of dryads."
— Merrow Keff, Assistant to the Assistant Head Librarian, RH225

"The year of the Eclipse Wine, Maitrasse Cru Bonnage, was RH389. Sonner boasted its vineyards were a thousand years old, planted by Elves. Nonsense. Everyone knows the Elven vines were burned during the Mage Wars. Still, it is a very fine wine."
— Erolin Tyne, *Wines of Elarandor*, Volume V, RH391

"Two Elf brothers smuggled cuttings from the Elven vineyards—grapes said to be the finest known to Elf, Man, or god. They barely escaped the fires of the Mage Wars and found fertile soil west of Thariel, where they took root in secret. That land is now known as Sonner."
— Scribe Superior Halric Danorin, *Heroes of the Mage Wars*, RH255

"The notion that a wizard nurtured these grapes with spells—or that the eclipse imbued them with cosmic essence—is absurd. Just like the idea that Elven vines survived the wars. And yet... this is the finest wine I have ever tasted. Maitrasse Cru Bonnage—buy every bottle you can find."
— Erolin Tyne, *Wines of Elarandor*, Volume VI, RH392

The Servant

Paul Heisel

ISBN: 978-1-969376-08-5
Cover design and illustrations © 2025 by Paul Heisel. Generated using artificial intelligence tools under the author's direction.
Map illustrations by: Ryne Callahan—
www.rynecallahan.com/commission
Manufactured independently via print-on-demand.
First Edition

Visit www.books.by/books-by-paul
For more works by Paul Heisel, visit: www.paulheisel.com

The Servant

Keeper of the Deer
Book One

Also by Paul Heisel

First Frontier

Tale of the Catstaff

<u>An Emperor's Fury Series</u>

Book One—Most Favored
Book Two—The Frayed Rope
Book Three—Warlord of Pyndira
Book Four—Legion

<u>Keeper of the Deer Series</u>

Book One—The Servant

To Comrade,
You know who you are.
Smash evil.
Tilt one to the west.

Pelt
NORTHERN REALMS
Thalraya
DARRIEN
FANN
STORM ISLANDS
COLLETH
City of Colleth
City of Haddensack
Abyssal Bastion
HADDENSACK
APP
VORTEIL
Withering Pass
Leafy Forest
Caliss
WICKTON
Leafhold
ATARIN
Needle Forest
NORLMIBEU
Tower of Knekora
Sigin
Arboretum
ICHING
CANTER
MARVIN
GREVIN
Bacani
ORNST
SMYTHE
SON
THROM
PENDLETON
City of Ornst
Rasmus
CONWICH
WESTMERE
ISHOLME
BIGGS
City of Throm
BUCK
Grew Ocean
GRELSHORE
Saltfell
RICHARDSON
The Great Sea

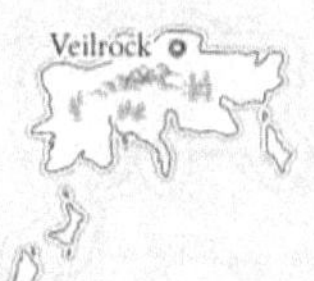

Veilrock

Sea of Ice
Kaldaraya
HALSTEAD
Tralina
Veilspire
STENGA
Golden Wood
THARIEL
Mallin
Wintermourne
Mist Fens
JECLEN
NER
Curow
Cherish
PEHRONE
ATRUA
Shadowfang Citadel
Pehrone City
FLAUX SMYA
Virdaya
Hollowkeep
TROASIA
Gateb
Lyrom
SCURIA
Aridaya

Infernal Sanctum
Herveen
Kaalnaes
FAUSTRON
Dreadwood
Maldrithar
The Deep
WACRAIT
GRAYL
Achivum Maledictum
Elarandor
The Known Lands
aker
undless Tides
Capital Cities
Cities & Towns
Points of Interest
Unknown Point of Interest
Realm Boundaries

CHAPTER ONE

∞

Tethered

Radcliffe crouched on the floor of his spacious but stark bedroom, carefully positioning his pillow a short distance from the fancy old wooden chair. The evening sunlight slanted through the tall window, illuminating the pale, undecorated walls. His room always smelled like wood polish. The housemaids used way too much of it.

He glanced at the shadow creeping toward the faint smudge he'd marked on the wall long ago. When the shadow touched the mark, he'd have just enough time to get to the bath before the governess sent someone to fetch him.

The chair wobbled as he tilted it back, and Radcliffe adjusted its position with his small hands, eyeing the landing place—the pillow. He didn't need strength to outwit Tristin—he needed leverage. He remembered one of the servants removing a crate lid with a long metal bar—a thing called a prybar. This was no different.

He pushed the top of the chair with his hand, noting how easy it was to teeter. With a single finger, he guided it to the tipping point. A smile crossed his face. *This was going to be easy…*

The chair wobbled sharply, the legs screeching. It twisted to the side when he pushed it too far, missing the pillow and crashing to the polished wood floor with a deafening *thud*, like a serving tray dropping in the kitchen.

Radcliffe froze, his breath catching.

This would be the third time in three days.

If he got in trouble again, he wouldn't get another chance until next week. Muffins were tomorrow…

Scrambling, he righted the chair and tossed the pillow onto his bed as heavy footsteps pounded up the stairs. The seconds ticked off. Radcliffe knew it would take Wilkins a bit of time to get to the third floor.

Silent in his stockinged feet, he slid next to his bed, pulling the covers around the pillow and tucking it in as if nothing had happened.

The door creaked open, revealing Wilkins's gaunt face, pale and sharp. His thin lips twisted into a sneer, the faint scent of soap and bourbon preceding him.

"What mischief are you up to now?" The venom in Wilkins's tone made Radcliffe flinch.

"I—I just banged the chair!" Radcliffe stammered, his voice high-pitched and strained.

Da's valet stepped into the room, his sharp eyes scanning every corner. "Don't test my patience," he said as he came close to the small boy. "I heard something hit the floor."

Radcliffe waved his hand across his nose to waft away the bourbon smell, then caught himself and quickly diverted to rubbing his face. Radcliffe fidgeted, his small hands curling into fists. His instincts screamed to shout, *Don't touch my things!* But he knew better. Wilkins would only find a way to twist his words and get him into more trouble.

"It was the chair," Rad said. He had to be calm… the muffin.

Wilkins's gaze lingered on the desk, then drifted to the closet.

Radcliffe watched him, a pang of fear rising.

Wilkins moved with purpose, opening drawers, shifting books, and tugging open the closet door. The sight of Radcliffe's neatly arranged uniforms and stacked toys amused him.

"Still pretending to be well-behaved, are we?" Wilkins said mockingly, bending down to inspect the crate of old toys. His fingers brushed the edge of the pile, and Radcliffe's stomach turned.

He held his breath. The chamber pot was hidden beneath the wooden blocks and tin soldiers—exactly where he'd placed it. If Wilkins found it, he'd take it away.

Wilkins shut the closet door with a sharp snap and straightened, brushing off his hands. "Another peep out of you, and your father will hear of this nonsense. And you know how that will end."

Radcliffe swallowed the lump in his throat, his gaze fixed on the floor, not wanting another beating. "It's not fair," he mumbled under his breath.

Wilkins offered a knowing smile, one reserved for those convinced the game was already won. "Life rarely is, especially for little boys who don't learn their place."

With a final, lingering smirk, Wilkins turned and strode out, the door snapping shut behind him.

Radcliffe let out his held breath, waiting until the sound of footsteps faded before he moved. He slid to his desk, pulling open the drawer and removing the false bottom. Relief washed over him. The sling and the worn book on magical swords were still there, untouched. He rubbed the rough leather of the sling's pocket, wondering if there was a way to make it softer. Oil? Radcliffe longed to fit a rock into the sling, twirl it around, and let it fly—it would go halfway across the city.

He closed the drawer and turned to his closet. Beneath the stack of folded towels, he retrieved his sketchbook, which was too fat to fit in the desk drawer.

He flipped through the pages—crude drawings of traps, maps of the estate grounds, and a half-finished diagram of a chair in the breakfast nook.

Tristin's chair.

His fingers hovered over the page, then traced the circled 'T' at the top, his mind already playing through the scenario.

It was going to work.

The high back of the chair would give him the leverage he needed against Tristin. All he had to do was wait for the right moment.

The sun dipped lower on the horizon, and Radcliffe noted the time—bath time. He stowed the sketchbook underneath the towels, then took one in his left hand and a washcloth in his right. He spun the towel and it landed on top of the chair, settling exactly where he thought it should go. Radcliffe tossed the washcloth, and it landed on top of the towel. He wanted to celebrate, but he might make too much noise.

Slowly, he undressed, putting his clothing in a wicker hamper for collection by one of the servants. For a moment, he admired his scrawny body in the mirror and wondered when he would get bigger and stronger, like Tristin. He donned his white robe, which swallowed him, cinching the sash.

Before leaving for his bath, he picked up a feather quill from his desk. The leather grip felt smooth beneath his fingers, worn from use. He swung it lightly through the air, mimicking the movements from an illustration in the book of magical swords.

"Ha, I have you now!" he whispered as his feet silently pattered on the floor. He sliced at an invisible foe, then a second, then stabbed a third.

An errant elbow landed on the wooden chair, sending a wave of agony that almost made him cry out. He stifled the pain, grimacing as he slithered toward the mirror.

The ache in his elbow dulled to a throb, and his mind drifted to the stories he had overheard from the kitchen servants. They spoke of bandits ambushing one of his father's caravans on the road to Haddensack. But the rumors hadn't stopped there. Some swore a fey creature—a guardian of the woodlands—had appeared, aiding the thieves of all things. A forest creature… could that be real? As real as the ones in Da's artwork collection?

Radcliffe swished the quill again, imagining himself slaying the bandits, saving the caravan, and gaining his father's favor. Perhaps his good deed would lift the curse from the fey creature, who was forced to do bad things for the bandits. And the fey forest king would reward him handsomely with a magic sword for saving the fey princess.

He paused, resting the quill on his shoulder like a sword. "Tomorrow," he whispered, his eyes narrowing. "Tristin's going to get what's coming to him." He stabbed at the fluffy monster in the mirror, expecting the white robe to turn crimson.

Radcliffe stared, doubt etched across his brow. It was now or never. Muffins were tomorrow.

The trance broke. He slid the quill back into place, grabbed his soap basket, and headed for the bath.

For Radcliffe von Schule, it was another day at his family's opulent estate in the Duchy of Ornst. At the age of ten, he already knew the monotony that awaited him: get up and dress properly, eat a sumptuous breakfast prepared by expert cooks, endure tedious studies with the governess, and partake in forced playtime devoid of enjoyment.

After a simple lunch, more studies followed, capped by a lavish dinner fit for royalty. Next came the compulsory bath and an early bedtime, staring at the ceiling for hours before waking to do it all over again.

Counting how often he saw his parents had become a habit, and this week's tally wasn't much: only twice for Ma and once for Da. His older siblings said Da was busy working with foreigners, making deals that brought in piles of gold—or so they claimed. Tristin had once called those deals 'lucrative,' a word Radcliffe didn't quite understand yet, but figured it meant something good. Whatever it was, those mysterious foreigners were important to his father's work, even if he couldn't grasp why.

This morning, he had one focus: the muffin.

Descending two flights of the broad, circular stairs in a rush, his shoes untied and his formal shirt hastily tucked, Radcliffe was drawn by the irresistible aroma of breakfast: spiced ham drizzled with honey, fresh eggs from the estate's farms, and buckle-berry muffins made with berries from brambles near the outer walls.

He sprinted through the empty dining room, past the butler's pantry, and leapt down five steps into the breakfast nook. He ran not out of fear of being late but to beat his older brother Tristin's mischief. If he didn't get there first, his muffin would be gone.

Years of practice had made Radcliffe adept at running in silence through the house, a necessary skill to avoid breaking rules.

There were too many rules.

Despite his efforts to behave, trouble always found him.

As Radcliffe turned the corner with speed at the bottom of the stairs, he was met with the familiar sight of the breakfast nook. Desperate to maintain his balance, he clutched the door molding, tumbling into the space like a playful, undisciplined acrobat.

Though it was called a 'nook,' he couldn't help but think it was more like a full dining room in any other house in Ornst. The square wooden table dominating the space could easily seat fourteen or fifteen guests, reflecting the von Schule family's insistence on nothing less than extravagance.

By comparison, the formal dining room he had rushed through could host forty or fifty people with ease, and if needed, extra tables from the cellar could be added to accommodate more.

Turning the final corner, he skidded to a halt at the sight of Tristin, who already had the muffin. Clutching it like a dragon guarding its hoard, Tristin smirked, victorious.

"You're too late," Tristin said, tearing into one of the muffins.

Despite his youth, Tristin's hardened features and self-assured posture gave him the presence of someone far older than sixteen. He already towered over their Da, broad-shouldered and as strong as a bull.

Radcliffe's sisters, Bella and Marie, burst into mocking laughter, delighting in his misfortune. Abigail, however, stared at Tristin, her expression cold and disapproving. Her hands clenched in her lap as if willing him to stop.

Radcliffe stepped forward, his chin tilted up. "I'd like my muffin, please."

Tristin set the muffin on the table, resting it just out of reach. The bite he had taken left it crooked, crumbs scattering across the pristine linen tablecloth.

Radcliffe's stomach fluttered, but he held his ground.

"Please," Tristin said, his nasally voice dripping with false sweetness. "What are you, a beggar? Heading to the streets of Ornst to plead with peasants? They'd laugh at you. Scrawny little brat. Little *merred*."

Bella and Marie gasped, their laughter faltering. The word *merred*—'shit' in High Ornst—was forbidden in the household, joking about it was no exception.

Radcliffe kept his eyes on Tristin, refusing to rise to the insult. His voice was steady, his words practiced for days in the mirror. The flutter inside him vanished, replaced by calm resolve. "Hand me the muffin and save yourself from further embarrassment. This your only warning."

The girls dissolved into laughter again, but Abigail's face tightened. She shook her head, a silent plea for Radcliffe to let it go.

Tristin leaned back in his chair, crossing his arms. "You're the embarrassment, runt."

Radcliffe lunged—not for the muffin, but for the high-backed chair. He threw his weight against it, angling his shoulder into the polished top stick. The heavy chair tipped over, dragging Tristin with it.

A loud crash filled the room as Tristin hit the floor, arms flailing to break his fall. The tablecloth jerked, sending plates and food clattering and bouncing.

In the confusion, Radcliffe seized the muffin, taking a triumphant bite before leaping onto Tristin's chest, his knees knocking the wind out of his brother. With the last remnants of the muffin in hand, he smeared sticky crumbs and honey across Tristin's face and into his combed hair.

Chaos erupted.

Bella and Marie screamed in unison, their high-pitched cries filling the room.

Abigail stepped away, her hand covering her mouth in disbelief. She stared, frozen, fear tightening her features as she realized the punishment he would face.

The cook wailed over the overturned plates and desecrated food, and the governess spilled her steaming tea as she rushed toward the commotion, her eyes filled with panic.

Suddenly, everyone stiffened.

Da's strong hands grabbed Radcliffe, yanking him backward and shoving him hard against the wall. His head hit the unyielding surface with a dull thud, stars bursting in his vision. Dazed, he barely registered his father's lean frame as it closed in, dark and fast as a storm cloud.

The room fell silent as Da grunted, a guttural sound that sent waves of dread through everyone.

Bella and Marie's shrieks stopped instantly.

The cook fell quiet.

The governess halted mid-step.

All eyes snapped to Da, whose jaw was clenched so tightly the muscles in his face twitched.

"What are you doing?" Da bellowed, his voice reverberating off the walls. His face was twisted with rage, his presence suffocating. "What has gotten into you? This is no way to behave in this household!"

Radcliffe straightened, stiffened, despite the pain exploding from the back of his skull. "He took my muffin," he said, his voice sharp and unyielding. "I warned him there were consequences. I won't be bullied!"

Da growled again, rooting everyone in place.

The sharp sting of a backhand slap cracked through the air, sending Radcliffe sprawling against the wall. His cheek burned, tears welling in his eyes as he slumped to the floor.

"If you're going to behave like a thug," Da thundered, his voice shaking with fury, "then you're going to be treated like one!"

He hauled Radcliffe upright with a single, crushing grip, shoving him into the waiting arms of the hovering vulture, Wilkins.

Radcliffe's stomach turned at the valet's smug expression, the faint scent of soap clinging to him.

The breakfast nook stilled.

"Lock him away until supper," Da ordered, his words cutting deep. "I'll deal with him properly tonight. You've gone too far this time, Radcliffe. Too far!"

"Yes, sir," Wilkins said, his voice like velvet. His grip tightened as he took Radcliffe away.

"Tristin, get cleaned up!" Da snapped, his anger flaring anew as he turned to his eldest son. "Curse that boy! I can't have you looking like this today..."

Radcliffe caught one last glimpse of Tristin's face before Wilkins forced him out of the room. His brother's expression was a mix of shock and... something Radcliffe couldn't quite place.

The door slammed behind them, cutting off the sounds of Bella and Marie's shrill complaints and Da's furious commands. He thought he heard Abigail...

Wilkins steered him forward with an iron grip, fingers biting into Rad's arm. "Enjoy your little rebellion?" Wilkins hissed under his breath as they went to the stairs. "You've only made things worse for yourself."

Radcliffe clenched his jaw and stayed quiet. His cheek stung, but the unfairness of it burned deeper.

They passed through the dining room and the foyer, climbing the stairs to the third floor. As they went up, the sounds of voices and footsteps from below faded into silence. Unlike his siblings, whose bedrooms were on the second floor, he had been exiled to the third—a place for the unwanted in the von Schule family.

His room, though generous in size, felt like an afterthought: unfinished, barren, and unnecessary. The stark walls and sparse furnishings mirrored how he often felt in his family—out of place and overlooked. He'd crept through every hallway and peered into every hidden corner of this enormous manor. This was the only room left untouched. The only one. Even the storage rooms had more character.

Wilkins guided him into the room with a grip that allowed no resistance. Radcliffe tripped over his own feet and fell to his knees.

Without a word, Wilkins crossed the room and opened the closet. The hinges groaned as the door creaked wide.

"Get in," he said—not a shout, but a command wrapped in quiet authority.

Radcliffe hesitated, staring at the darkness like it might swallow him.

"Get in," Wilkins snapped, voice sharper now.

His hand found Radcliffe's shoulder again, guiding him into the cramped, airless space. Rad stumbled forward, his knees brushing the floor as the heavy door swung shut behind him.

The latch snapped shut with a heavy click.

Radcliffe flinched.

It was dark. Really dark. The kind that pressed in on you, like the air got thicker.

"You know the rules," Wilkins said through the door, his tone dry. "If you soil yourself, your father doubles the punishment. And you'll be the one cleaning it up."

Radcliffe didn't say a word. Talking back would only make things worse.

He sat down hard on the cold floor and curled up by the wall. It was too dark to see anything. He touched the bump on his head, wincing a little. It hurt, but not as much as his stomach, which felt tight and awful.

Da said the real punishment would come tonight. Rad didn't know what that meant, not exactly. But he knew it would be bad.

The quiet was the worst part. It made the bad thoughts come back again. Why was it always like this? It didn't matter what he did—good or bad—they still acted like he didn't belong. Like he was just... extra.

His brothers and sisters didn't have a hard time like he did.

Tristin worked with Da now. He was strong and sure of himself—everything Da liked.

Bella and Marie got whatever they wanted. People were always fussing over them.

Even Abigail, the only one who stood up for him, had that warm way about her. Everyone liked being around her.

But Radcliffe? He was the one sent off to the edge of the house. Forgotten until he messed up.

His chest felt tight, and his eyes stung with tears. He didn't want to cry, but it just kept building up. He wanted his family to notice him. Really notice him. Not only when he got in trouble.

Just once, he wanted to feel like he belonged.

But here, in the dark and cold, he felt the truth sink deeper than ever.

He was alone.

Unwanted.

Suffocated by the shadows of his own flesh and blood.

CHAPTER TWO

∞

The Servant

The hours dragged on in the dark closet, lit only by the faint glow seeping under the locked door. Radcliffe shifted on the wooden floor, the cold seeping through his thin trousers. His legs ached, but he stayed as still as he could, listening for any sound from outside. The house was quiet now, but Wilkins's threats lingered in his mind, keeping him alert.

Quietly, he reached into the crate of toys tucked beside him. His fingers found the familiar shapes of carved wooden figures—a soldier, a cart, a horse. He laid them out, arranging them by touch alone. The faint light barely illuminated their outlines, but he didn't need to see them; he knew each one by heart.

Radcliffe picked up the soldier and turned it over in his hand. It was one of his favorites, its edges worn smooth from years of play. In his mind, the figure wasn't merely a toy; it was him—a hero, a leader, someone who could fight back.

The caravan rolled through the dark forest, its wheels creaking under the weight of stolen goods. Radcliffe crouched in the shadows, waiting. The guards didn't see him, they were watching the path ahead. An ambush was all it would take.

He moved the soldier, tipping over the cart with a careful nudge of his finger. Blocks he had stacked earlier became toppled crates, spilling imaginary treasures. His breathing was slow, quiet. He'd played this scene so many times, his hands just knew what to do as the whole battle played out in his mind.

"Surrender your goods," the bandit demanded in a firm whisper, his voice commanding but quiet enough not to give him away.

The guards froze, their swords shaking a little as they faced him.

But the leader of the caravan—his father—stepped forward. His face was set like stone. "You'll never win, boy," he said, his voice echoing in the stillness of the forest. "This is no way to behave in an ambush!"

Radcliffe's hand hovered over the soldier, his lips pressed into a tight line. His thoughts scrambled, and the imagined victory slipped away.

He couldn't beat Da. Not in his games. Not in real life.

The soldier tipped onto its back with a soft thud, its painted face staring up at the ceiling.

"I'll show you," he whispered. His fingers curled around the wooden figure, its face chipped and scuffed. "One day, I'll get you. I'll shove a muffin in your face, just like Tristin."

The thought stuck with him, sharp and a little scary.

Was it all the rules? The way people acted like he wasn't even there? Or just the way Da seemed to fill up the whole house, like no one could breathe right when he was around?

He would get out. One day, he'd be gone, and Da's precious von Schule name would mean nothing.

He leaned against the wall, the toys scattered around him in the darkness. For a moment, he closed his eyes, picturing a world where he wasn't locked away, ignored, or cast aside.

One day, he thought again with a firm grip on the soldier. *One day, I'll be the one in control.*

His stomach growled, sharp and mean.

He imagined what lunch would've been—thick slices of dark bread, smelly cheese, sweet strawberries, and green grapes cut into little pieces.

He could almost taste them.

The cheese made his mouth water, even if it stank.

Downstairs, his sisters were probably stuffing their faces and laughing about him. The kind of laughter that made your ears burn. His stomach twisted even more.

His gaze shifted to the narrow shelf at the back of the closet. Tucked beneath it lay another secret—a small knife, its thin blade perfect for slipping the latch. The thought of it called to him from the darkness. He ran a finger along the seam of his trousers, a nervous habit he couldn't quite stop, and toyed with the idea.

It would be easy. A quick twist, and he'd be free.

But his mind kept going back to Wilkins.

The valet was probably nearby, boots thumping the floor, waiting for a chance to catch him. If he tried to get out and got caught, things would only get worse. And tonight… Da was going to be angrier than ever.

Radcliffe let out a slow breath, his head falling back to rest against the wall. The knife would remain hidden—for now. His stomach grumbled again, but he forced himself to ignore it, staring into the darkness and biting the inside of his cheek until the urge to break free went away.

Light footsteps broke into his thoughts—too soft to be Wilkins, and not Ma or the governess either. His ears pricked at the sound, a gentle rhythm he knew right away: Abigail. She was the only one who still gave him hope. The closest thing he had to a friend.

The footsteps stopped outside the door. Then came the faint sound of fabric shifting. He pictured her crouching, her stiff blue dress making that crinkly noise as she moved. It was the same kind of plain uniform he had to wear during lessons—reading, writing, history, and learning fancy High Ornst words. But his favorite was arithmetic. Numbers and patterns made sense, even when nothing else did.

"Rad, I don't have much time," Abigail whispered through the door.

Rad.

The sound of it filled the darkness with a rare warmth. Ma and Da forbade nicknames—strict rules against shortening their proper names or using pet names like 'Bubba' or 'Sissy.' Abigail was the only one bold enough to defy them, calling him Rad. It was their shared secret, a small act of rebellion.

"I understand, Abby," he whispered, using her forbidden name in return. Saying it was freeing.

"I brought you some bread. It's squished—I had to hide it from Wilkins. I think he suspects I'm helping you."

Radcliffe didn't know why she never opened the door when she came to him. They always spoke through the crack, their voices muffled by the wood between them. He thought it was her way of staying within the rules—or at least bending not breaking them.

A small gap under the door let her slide a piece of bread into the dark. It was warm from being tucked away and a little squished, but to

Radcliffe, it felt like a feast. He grabbed it fast, his stomach twisting with hunger. It wasn't much—he could've eaten ten pieces, especially with that stinky cheese his family loved—but it was enough. Enough to know someone still cared.

"Thank you," he whispered.

"Da was furious with you," Abigail said, her voice trembling. "I mean extra mad. I don't want him to beat you again. Please, Rad. Don't make him angry... don't fight back! I'm begging you!"

Her words hurt more than the thought of the belt. She meant well—she always did—but hearing her say that made it feel worse. Abigail always tried to protect him. She was the only one who did.

"I'm trying," he said, his voice faltering. "I can't. Maybe Da's right. Maybe I'm no good. I'm rotten. Even when I stand up to bullies, I'm wrong. I'm bad."

"Don't say that," she protested, her voice cracking. "He doesn't mean it! You're not bad, Rad. Apologize to Da. Say you're sorry, be sincere. Don't be so defiant. Please, just this once."

"I'll try," he lied.

But deep down, that stubborn fire inside him was still burning. Every failure, every punishment, only pushed him further away. He couldn't stop thinking about the whipping—how it was coming, how it would hurt. He braced for it, knowing the welts would sting for days. The belt left marks, sure—but the worst part was how it made him feel. Like he didn't matter.

"I warned Tristin. I was more than fair..."

A muffled voice came from the first floor.

Abigail cut him off, her words quick and hushed. "I'll talk to you tomorrow. The governess is looking for me! Oh dear, oh dear!"

Radcliffe heard her shuffle away, her footsteps fading down the hall and down the stairs. He pictured her hurrying to her room on the second floor, slipping in quiet like nothing had happened. She didn't want anyone to know she'd been talking with her troublemaker brother. Even his best friend didn't want to be seen with him.

Alone once more, Radcliffe ate the bread, enjoying each bite and ensuring no crumbs would be left as evidence of Abigail's kindness.

Minutes crawled by in the dark. Radcliffe sat there, dreading the sting of the belt. It didn't matter what he did—big mistake or small—the punishment was harsh. It just wasn't fair.

His fingers found the small knife hidden in the closet, and he began twirling it without thinking, passing it between his hands as if it were a toy. He didn't realize how easily he could do it with both hands—just to keep himself busy.

Before he even realized it, Rad had made up his mind. He slipped his small knife into the gap under the door and pried the latch open. The heavy lock gave way with a soft click. Rad pushed the door open and crept into his room. Pale sunlight crept in through the tall window, and he stopped to blink, his eyes slowly getting used to the light.

The room stood unchanged from the morning—spacious yet barren, its emptiness a stark contrast to the extravagant rooms of his siblings. No paintings, no rugs, no personal touches adorned the space. It was less like a bedroom and more like a prison cell, a reflection of how he often felt: insignificant, trapped, and out of place.

Radcliffe crossed to the solitary window and gazed out over the sprawling estate. The land stretched endlessly before him, a sea of green beneath the midday sun. A bright sky and a soft breeze stirred the treetops.

Below, his sisters strolled through the gardens, their parasols bobbing as they tried to keep the sun off their faces. The governess followed close behind, walking stiff like always. She was probably giving one of her boring lessons about how to act like a lady, and Radcliffe was glad he couldn't hear her at this distance.

Fancy that.

Radcliffe smirked, mocking their parasols, their gowns, and the governess's endless talking.

On days when he wasn't confined or punished, he liked the freedom of the open grass. Simple exercises were his attempt to build muscles. He didn't grasp what 'constitution' meant, but he assumed it had something to do with not being scrawny anymore.

Tristin, of course, knew what it meant. He was old enough to train with the guards, learning swordplay and doing all the things Radcliffe wished he could do.

Strong. Skilled. Respected.

People looked at Tristin like he belonged.

Radcliffe dreamed of joining them—standing tall with a sword in his hand, maybe even a magic elven blade. In his head, he wasn't just a child—he was a hero, slicing through bandits to save a caravan, his sword flashing in the sun.

The guards would cheer.

Even Da might nod, just once, like he was proud.

But that was just pretend. In real life, they always said the same thing: too young, too small, not worth the trouble.

His gaze roamed across the estate, his mind slipping into daydreams of exploration. Though he had never gone far beyond the central grounds, he had memorized every detail he could observe or imagine.

The manor was the center of attention, its towering shadow dominating the landscape. To the south were the stables and carriage house, their slate roofs glinting in the sun. Farther out lay the blacksmith's workshop, the barracks, and a small warehouse buzzing with activity.

Scattered around the estate were sheds and small buildings, their use a mystery. Some probably held tools or animal feed, but others made him wonder. Their locked doors almost looked like they were hiding secrets, just waiting for him to figure them out.

The estate was always busy—more than sixty people working to keep the von Schule family living like kings. Radcliffe still couldn't believe it. *Sixty!* Just to cook, clean, sweep, and do whatever else wealthy people needed done.

Wilkins, that awful valet, ran the staff like he was king of the world, snapping orders and acting like everyone was beneath him. The governess handled the rest while Ma and Da were off doing... whatever it was they always did.

Gabrielle, the governess, was pretty and graceful, and smart enough to teach them all their lessons. But Radcliffe still found her annoying. She was always there, reminding him to sit up straight, speak properly, and keep his room neat.

Sometimes he thought about running away. Just getting on a horse and leaving. If only he had a magic sword... he'd ride across the countryside, fighting bandits and helping people, and no one would boss him around ever again.

He'd have to learn to ride a horse first...

But for now, he stayed where he was—watching a world that felt just in front of him, like he could almost touch it... but not quite.

Radcliffe leaned on the windowsill, staring out and wondering why they never went to the city. Why did the family stay stuck here at the manor all the time? He wanted to see Ornst more than anything. Just thinking about it made his legs feel jumpy. He pictured the busy streets, full of shouting, clattering carts, and the smell of pies and cookies drifting out of bakeries. He imagined the sound of coins clinking while people argued over prices.

And the blacksmiths.

He could almost smell the hot metal and smoke. He'd walk right in and ask for a sword—his sword. It would be shiny and sharp, made just how he wanted. He'd call it *Bandit Crusher*. With it, he could beat any enemy, just like the heroes in his stories. Maybe he'd even find a wizard to enchant it, make it magic—strong enough to cut through stone.

He craned his neck, angling his view to catch a glimpse of the distant spires on the horizon—most of all, the famed Ornst Library.

The governess always said the library had more books than all the people in the city—maybe even more than the whole Duchy. Radcliffe loved reading, though not as much as Abigail. Still, the size of the library amazed him. He imagined wandering through endless rows of old books until he found a secret one, full of ancient spells he could learn. Maybe there'd be a spell to turn Tristin into a toad who ate flies instead of muffins. Or better yet, a spell to make *him* grow bigger and stronger.

He snapped out of his daydream at the sound of heavy footsteps in the hall.

Wilkins.

The sound of his boots grew louder, each step bringing Wilkins closer to catching him out of the closet.

Acting quickly, Radcliffe darted back into the closet, clutching his small knife. He slid the blade into the latch, locking himself inside, and returned it to its hiding place. As he stepped deeper into the cramped space, his usually sure feet caught on his untied laces.

He stumbled backward into the hanging clothes, flailing for balance, and hit the floor with more force than he intended.

"Stop messing around in there," Wilkins barked from the other side of the door. "One more sound, and I'll recommend additional punishment. Do you want more?"

Radcliffe froze, his heart pounding in his chest. He stayed silent, knowing from the past that any answer would only provoke Wilkins further.

"Did you soil yourself?" Wilkins demanded.

Radcliffe didn't respond.

"Answer me," Wilkins growled.

"No, sir," Radcliffe replied, his voice steady. "I can hold it all day if I need to."

"You better."

Wilkins stomped away, the echo fading into the distance, leaving Radcliffe alone.

Radcliffe listened intently, waiting for any noise—anything that would tell him Wilkins was coming back. He shifted and twisted on the floor, trying to find a comfortable position that wouldn't make his legs numb.

Frustration bubbled up—he was locked away *again*. He was angry, mad at Da, Wilkins, and Tristin.

He grabbed his toys. They gave him hope.

One by one, he lined them up in the dark, arranging them for inspection. Scooting back, Radcliffe found the far wall of the closet and leaned against it. He shifted his hips, trying to change the angle of the light under the door, hoping it might help him see better. Then he sat still, watching, waiting… always waiting.

How was he supposed to get back at them for punishing him?

He couldn't. Revenge just meant more punishment.

Radcliffe leaned his head back, and it thumped against the wall.

It sounded odd.

He did it again.

Thump.

Hollow.

Radcliffe pivoted on his knees, using his hands to feel the wall behind him. The surface of the wall was rough, unfinished in his closet, yet he felt a seam where no seam should be. He traced it with his finger from the floor up to as high as he could reach. He stood, finding the seam extended up to his height, across for two feet, then down again.

It was a door.

Inch by inch, his fingers moved—right, left, up, down—searching for any other strange bumps or seams.

Then he felt it.

Another seam—a rectangle about two fingers wide and twice as long. Poking and prodding, it finally shifted with a snap, like it had been stuck for a long time.

It hit him—this was a secret door.

But to what?

Maybe a hidden storage room no one remembered… packed with old treasures. Maybe even gold.

His fingers curled around the latch. All he had to do was pull.

Radcliffe froze.

What if this got him in trouble too? What if Wilkins found out, or Da? He was already in enough trouble just for fighting back.

But still… what if there *was* treasure behind it? Or maps leading to treasure? Or an old sword, left behind and waiting to be used again?

He tugged, but the door didn't move. Bracing his feet, he pulled harder. With a groan, the door creaked open.

A dark gap opened in front of him.

He paused, listening for Wilkins.

Nothing.

His breath came faster as he waited—just a little longer—before moving another muscle.

In the darkness, he pulled open the door and looked into the void. There was a tiny light coming from somewhere, but not enough to see by. He didn't know what was in front of him—a fall to his death?

He dropped to his knees and crawled forward, using his hands to guide him along the rough planks. The prodding and probing told him there was open space at least for a foot of more, and off to his right and left was the same. Except to the right was the mysterious pinpoint of light.

He took a deep breath, noting the stale air, and crawled forward, hands searching. He was on a platform, with nothingness on both sides.

A squeak in the distance halted him mid-crawl, his head cocking to the side to figure where the noise came from. Was there someone else here?

He heard a muffled, distant voice coming from the same direction as the faint light. Groping with his hands, he encountered two upright pieces of wood and a rung—a ladder.

Then came two different muffled voices—two people talking in hushed tones.

He rotated on his knees, searching for the ladder with his hands. When he found it, he tested the first rung. He lowered himself down the ladder, pausing as each creak echoed in the darkness. His feet found solid floor after four rungs, and he stopped, listening for the muffled voices ahead.

With cautious steps, Radcliffe moved toward the sounds and light, his hands skimming the wall studs to guide his path. He tested each step before putting his weight down, moving slow and careful. The faint glow and murmuring voices drew him forward until he reached a narrow peephole.

He wasn't sure if he felt excited or scared. Maybe both.

"I do hope Ma will let us go in town to shop," Marie said.

Radcliffe pressed his eye to the peephole. He was looking into Marie's room, decorated in bright pinks and light yellows. She was sitting on the soft bed, with Bella sitting on the floor at her feet. Marie was brushing Bella's long auburn hair.

"We need more dresses," Bella said.

Rad was surprised by how well he could hear them. He could see Marie's eyes go wide in agreement. It felt strange… his stomach turned.

This was wrong.

"I know, we are so out of style. Maybe we can get permission for Gabrielle to take us shopping."

"Better yet," Bella said, "we should make it Ma's idea."

Marie stopped brushing her hair and clapped her hands. "That's a splendid idea. If Ma can suggest it, then Da will allow it. I can't wait…"

Radcliffe backed away, and her words were muddled. At the peephole was a cover, which he decided not to touch. He retraced his steps, the air around him was oppressive. It felt... hot. Sweat rolled off his forehead as he climbed the ladder.

Who built these passageways? Were they made to protect the family... or for something worse? Radcliffe didn't know. But the thought of Wilkins sneaking around in them made his skin crawl.

Radcliffe slipped back into the closet and pushed the secret door shut, his mind full of thoughts. The passageways were not only hidden—they were secret, and secrets in this house were never safe. Da knew everything, didn't he?

But... what if Da didn't know? What if no one else knew?

What if it was only him?

What if this was *his*?

What if this could really be *his* secret?

Radcliffe pulled his knees to his chest and rocked gently in the dark. The idea of spying on his own family made his stomach twist. He loved them—even if they locked him away like he didn't matter.

But the thought that he was the *only one* who knew about the passageways? That lit a spark inside him. A feeling he couldn't name, but it made his fingers curl and his breath come quicker.

This is mine now, he thought.

And maybe secrets weren't just for keeping. They were for doing.

The dark felt thicker now, like it was pressing in. No matter how tight he shut his eyes, he still saw peepholes.

Shadows.

The idea that nothing in this house was ever private.

He stayed quiet, thinking.

Next time, he'd go farther.

He had to know where the passages led—and what else they could show him.

Radcliffe woke with a start, his throat parched and his limbs stiff from hours spent huddled on the floor. The restless sleep had done little to soothe his exhaustion. The sound of boots and polished shoes clopping against the wooden floor echoed. He sat upright, his legs folding beneath him, as the heavy latch on the closet door rattled, then clicked open.

The orange glow of sunset slipped through his small window, stretching long shadows across the floor. It was past bath time. His stomach tightened with hunger as his eyes adjusted to the dim light—and the shapes standing in front of him.

His Da stood in the doorway, tall and stern, looking at him the way only a father could—he was scary without speaking one word.

Wilkins didn't say anything either, but his face said it all: *Of course it's you. Of course you messed up... again.*

Tristin came last, hands clasped in front of him, eyes cold—but not angry. More like... nervous. Like *he* knew what was coming.

Rad glanced past them, hoping to see Ma. Or his sisters.

But no one else was there.

That made it worse.

Radcliffe pushed himself to his feet, knees shaking as his heart dropped. He didn't dare hope for a reprieve—there never was one. This was just another punishment he couldn't avoid.

But the fire in his Da's eyes burned straight through him.

It wasn't just anger.

His face held a weight Radcliffe had seen before.

It looked final—like the time Da sacked the old governess for saying he drank too much.

She said it right in front of everyone, calm and steady, like she was doing him a favor.

Da didn't yell.

He just stared at her.

And Radcliffe remembered thinking: she's finished.

She was gone the next day, and no one talked about it again.

"I'm sorry, Da," Radcliffe said, his voice trembling as hope drained away. "I apologize for my behavior earlier today."

"Speak when you are spoken to," Da barked, his words cutting deep. After a tense silence, he added calmly, "You may speak."

"I'm sorry, Da. It won't happen again," Radcliffe repeated, though the words were hollow.

"I have grown weary of showing you the belt," Da said, his voice cold. "Clearly, it hasn't been effective in altering your behavior. You leave me no other choice but to do what I should have done years ago."

Radcliffe swallowed hard. What did that mean? *Years ago…*

Hunger, thirst, and exhaustion clouded his mind, making it difficult to think. He feared his legs might give out. "I'm sorry, Da," he whispered.

"Starting tomorrow, you are no longer a child of this household," Da said, clearing his throat and adjusting the cuffs of his burgundy smoking jacket. "You will work as a servant—cleaning stables, tending the grounds, scrubbing floors, running errands for the blacksmith. One way or another, you will earn your living here and find your place. But it will not be as a von Schule. Not as one of our children."

Radcliffe's chest tightened as the words sank in. His vision blurred—he thought he might pass out.

"You will eat with the servants and live among them until you are sixteen," Da continued. "At that age, you will be cast out into Ornst as a nobody. Best forget the von Schule name unless you want to die with it. Do you understand?"

Radcliffe nodded, eyes blinking, barely hearing his own voice.

"I'm sorry, Da," he whispered again.

"Your apology is not accepted," Da said, his voice sharp, each word landing like a slap. "Do… you… understand… what… I… just… told… you?" He paused, letting the silence settle. "Do you understand what this means?"

Radcliffe's head swam. Blood pounded in his ears. His throat felt tight, and his stomach flipped so hard he thought he might throw up. The room tilted sideways, just a little.

"Yes," he whispered.

"Repeat it back to me," Da said.

"I'm a servant," Radcliffe said, his voice thin and shaking. "And when I'm sixteen, I'll be turned out into the streets."

He swallowed hard.

His eyes burned, but he wouldn't let the tears fall. "And I'll forget my name," he whispered.

"About time you listened and obeyed," Da said.

Tristin stepped forward, arms crossed, chin high. "Maybe you'll learn some discipline working in the stables."

Radcliffe hesitated, glancing between Da and the imposing figure of his older brother. His voice came out small. "Can I keep my room?"

"Absolutely not," Wilkins snapped. "He is a servant now."

Radcliffe looked to his father, unsure if the sharp glare Da shot was meant for him… or for Wilkins.

"Let him sleep in the stables for all I care," Tristin added. "Putting him in the west wing with the other servants is a luxury he doesn't deserve."

Da's expression, hard as granite moments before, shifted. Just slightly. He looked at Radcliffe, then back to Tristin, as if weighing the comment.

"Servants don't live with the family," he said at last. "They serve the household. They don't belong in it."

Radcliffe's heart kicked. He felt the floor slipping from under him. "I'll behave," he said quickly, voice cracking. "I promise. Da, I'm sorry. Please—please give me another chance. I don't want to scrub floors. I don't want to be a servant. I don't want to lose my room. I *love* my room."

"Stables," Tristin said again, like it was a judgment.

Da cut the air with a flick of his hand—sharp and final.

"My decision is final," he said. His voice had lost all warmth. "Tomorrow morning, you will report to Hadley in the stables to see if you can be of use there. You will take your meals with the servants in the west wing and wear servant's clothes."

He paused, just long enough for Radcliffe to feel the weight of it.

"I will allow you to sleep in this room."

His eyes locked with Radcliffe's.

"Disobey… and you'll lose it. And you'll face a punishment far worse than the belt. Do you understand?"

Da turned to Tristin.

"Take his uniforms. Have them burned."

Tristin gave a single nod, his face unreadable. He crossed the room, opened the closet, and began removing Radcliffe's neatly folded clothes one by one.

Radcliffe's mouth opened, but nothing came out. He watched as Tristin carried his life away in silence.

Da didn't even look at him.

"Take him to the west wing," he said. "Let him eat a late supper with the servants."

Wilkins stepped forward and seized Radcliffe by the collar. "Move it," he growled. "Pick up your feet or I'll drag you down the stairs."

Radcliffe didn't fight. Resistance would only make things worse. His body went limp as Wilkins dragged him toward the door.

He glanced back once.

Da stood beside Tristin, a hand resting on his eldest son's shoulder, speaking in low tones. Tristin held an armful of Radcliffe's uniforms, his face hard, unmoved, like the clothes meant nothing. Like *he* meant nothing.

The realization hit—this was really happening.

"It's for the best," Da said, his voice already fading as Radcliffe was pulled into the hallway.

Radcliffe didn't resist. He couldn't.

The weight of his father's words crushed the last piece of him, leaving only silence.

He wasn't Radcliffe von Schule anymore.

He was nothing.

Chapter Three

∞

Hadley

The next morning, Radcliffe was roused from sleep by a persistent poke. A servant boy named Jamie stood over him, holding a lantern that cast flickering shadows across the room. The darkness outside made it impossible to tell if it was early morning or the middle of the night.

"Up," Jamie said, poking him again.

Radcliffe groaned but obeyed, pulling on the coarse servant's clothing Wilkins had so gleefully provided the night before. Gone were his polished leather shoes; in their place, he slipped on stiff, unwieldy work boots that pinched his feet. The boots were stiff and awkward, rising almost to his calves and full of too many holes to lace up properly. He hated them already.

As they left his room and headed to the stables, Jamie set a brisk pace along the cobblestone path, his lantern bobbing in the predawn gloom. Radcliffe struggled to keep up, his steps clumsy in the unfamiliar boots. The air was damp and sticky, the sky a weird gray that made everything feel off.

He wasn't used to being outside this early—wasn't even sure what time it *was*.

"The sun isn't up," Radcliffe said, stifling a yawn. "Breakfast…"

"We start work in the early morning, before the sun is up," Jamie replied matter-of-factly, glancing over his shoulder. "We've got to finish everything before Mister von Schule needs the horses—whether he actually needs them or not. Every day's the same, so you'd best learn to live with it. Breakfast is later."

He motioned ahead with the lantern to the stables in the distance before continuing.

"Once we're done with the morning work, we can eat. I'll show you the ropes until Hadley gets up. It's not so bad—I'll teach you."

Inside the stables, Jamie lit the lanterns along the wall, casting light over rows of wooden stalls. The glow revealed about thirty enclosures, housing twenty horses of different sizes, ages, colors, and temperaments.

The air hit Radcliffe like a wall—dried grass, old leather, and the sour, sweaty stink of animals.

It smelled like trouble.

Like the kind of stink that clung to your clothes and got you scolded. The kind that proved you'd been somewhere you shouldn't.

"These are the basics," Jamie said, gesturing to the horses lined in their stalls. Their ears twitched, tails swishing idly as they shifted on their hooves. "Work horses, carriage horses, show horses, riding horses—they all need care. Feeding, brushing, mucking stalls. Hadley will tell you if there's more to do, but we start with the same routine every day."

Radcliffe's nose wrinkled at the sharp mix of dried grass, sweat, manure, and a dampness he couldn't name. The stink wrapped around him, thick and warm, crawling into his servant clothes.

He could hear the horses breathing—loud and wet—their hooves shifting in the straw, tails flicking, snorting like they were annoyed he'd walked in.

Every part of this place was loud and messy and wrong. It smelled like *punishment*.

This was the place you got sent when you were bad.

This had to be hell.

At least with the belt, it was over quick.

This was a punishment that didn't end. Every day was going to be like this…

Until they changed their minds.

He tried not to let Jamie see his hesitation.

Jamie chuckled, catching the sour expression.

"It'll get easier in time. Now, the first thing you do is let the horse know you're there. Always approach from the front or the side, where they can see you. Never from behind. You don't want a hoof to the gut, do you?"

Radcliffe rubbed his tummy, swallowing hard. "No."

"Good. Watch." Jamie moved to the first stall and opened the gate, stepping inside with calm confidence. The horse—a dapple-gray mare with intelligent eyes—shifted her weight but didn't move away as Jamie approached.

"You keep your voice low," Jamie said, patting the mare's neck in slow, steady strokes. "And your movements steady. They don't like sudden jerks or yelling. Spook them, and you'll have a mess on your hands."

Radcliffe mimicked the motion on his own arm, trying to get a feel for it.

"Here." Jamie handed him a curry comb—a round tool with short, firm teeth. "Start with this. Press it against her coat and make circles, like this." Jamie showed him on the mare's shoulder, dragging up loose hair and dust into little piles. "It loosens dirt and keeps their skin healthy."

Radcliffe hesitated, then stepped closer, holding out the comb as if it might bite him. The mare flicked her ears back toward him, her tail swishing again.

"Go on," Jamie urged. "She won't hurt you if you're gentle."

Taking a deep breath, Radcliffe pressed the comb against her side and began moving it in small circles. Dust rose in the air, tickling his nose, but he kept at it. His strokes were uneven at first—too hard, then too soft—but Jamie reached over, adjusting his grip.

"There, better. Not bad for a first try."

Radcliffe glanced up, a flicker of pride warming him. "What next?"

"Next, we use the stiff brush." Jamie pulled a bristled brush from a nearby bucket. "Follow the same areas you just groomed with the curry comb, but brush in the direction of the hair. It smooths it out and gets the rest of the dirt off."

As Jamie worked on the mare's side, Radcliffe copied him, his strokes growing more confident. The mare leaned into the brush slightly, and Jamie grinned. "See that? Means she likes it. A proper brushing's like a massage for them."

Radcliffe let out a small laugh. The mare hadn't kicked him. Jamie hadn't scolded him. For the first time in days, *he hadn't messed up.*

The tight feeling in his shoulders started to fade.

Maybe this wasn't going to be so bad after all.

"Once they're brushed, you check their hooves. Come here."

Jamie crouched beside the mare, running his hand down her leg. "This part right above the hoof? That's the fetlock." He leaned in and gave it a gentle squeeze. "Most of the time they'll lift it for you. If they don't, a little nudge helps."

The willing mare lifted her hoof, and Jamie held it steady. "You take the hoof pick and clean out the dirt and rocks," he said. "Be careful not to dig too deep, or you'll hurt them."

Radcliffe watched, surprised by how careful Jamie's hands were. Each movement was calm, steady—gentle.

Jamie hummed softly as he worked, like this was the most natural thing in the world.

The mare trusted him, and now Rad understood why.

This wasn't just a job. There was a *way* to it. A rhythm.

And if you got it right, the horse listened.

When Jamie handed him the pick and pointed to the mare's other hoof, Radcliffe swallowed hard and crouched down. His hands trembled as he gripped her leg, but the mare didn't pull away. She stood still. She *trusted* him.

He moved carefully, mimicking what he'd seen. Jamie stepped back, giving him space. "That's it. Keep at it."

By the time they finished, Radcliffe's arms ached and his knees were covered in dirt.

But he'd done it.

He had done it.

And deep inside, a spark lit—the thrill of getting it right.

"Not bad for your first time," Jamie said, clapping him on the shoulder. "Remember what I showed you, and you'll be fine."

Radcliffe nodded, brushing the dust off his tunic. "Thanks, Jamie."

"Don't thank me yet," Jamie said. "Wait until you've mucked your first stall."

Radcliffe offered a strained nod but didn't answer. His arms ached, and his eyes felt heavy.

He wanted to lie back down. Just for a minute.

He thought of his bed—soft blankets, the warm weight of them. The smell of his pillowcase after the maids had changed it. And breakfast. Fresh rolls, butter, warm tea…

He blinked hard, forcing the thought away.

"When Hadley gets up," Jamie said, his voice dropping, "he'll check our work. If anything's wrong, we'll have to do it all over again. Trust me—you don't want that. Just do your best to keep him from noticing us."

Radcliffe straightened, blinking toward the stable doors.

He hadn't even met Hadley, but he imagined a giant with arms like tree trunks and a stick for smacking anyone who looked at him wrong.

His stomach turned.

Jamie didn't give him time to dwell on it. The morning moved fast—cleaning up leftover feed, scooping out old bedding, and hauling fresh hay. Radcliffe followed along in a fog, each task more unpleasant than the last.

Then came mucking the stalls.

"First rule," Jamie said, handing him a pitchfork, "you start with the worst of it." He pointed to the wet, soiled hay piled in the corner. "Shovel it all out and dump it in the barrow. Don't leave any behind. It can make the horses sick."

Radcliffe's stomach growled. His arms ached.

He wrinkled his nose and jabbed the pitchfork into the mess. The sour stink was so strong it chased away what little hunger he still had.

Sweat prickled at the back of his neck.

"How can horses live in this?" he muttered, tossing another heap into the barrow.

Jamie chuckled. "They don't care as long as they're fed and groomed. But we care. Hadley cares. Mister von Schule cares the most. A clean stall keeps them happy and healthy." He pointed to a nearby bale. "Once you've cleared the muck, spread fresh hay evenly across the floor."

Jamie demonstrated how to fluff and spread the new bedding with long, easy strokes.

Radcliffe copied him, but his pile came out crooked and lumpy.

Jamie stepped in and adjusted his grip on the pitchfork.

"Like this. Let the fork do the work. And don't stab it like you're fighting a dragon—you'll wear yourself out."

Once the stalls were clean and fresh hay was down, Jamie led him back to the horses.

"Next, we brush their manes and tails. Always start from the top and work your way down. Keeps them calm and stops tangles from turning into knots."

Jamie handed Radcliffe a soft-bristled brush and led him to a tall, reddish-brown horse with a glossy coat.

"This is Finch," Jamie said, patting the horse's neck. "But I call him Flinch—he's an irritable gelding."

Radcliffe gave him a puzzled look.

"Gelding," Jamie added, catching the confusion. "That means he's male, but calmer than a stallion. Usually, anyway."

He grasped Finch's mane and started brushing.

"If you hit a snag, don't yank. Work it loose with your fingers first, then brush again."

Radcliffe nodded and tried to follow the motion. Finch snorted softly, tossing his head when Radcliffe tugged too hard.

"Easy," Jamie said, steadying the horse with a firm hand. "Be gentle, but confident. Horses can feel your nerves, so stay calm."

It took a few tries, but Radcliffe found a rhythm, smoothing the mane until it was flat and neat.

"Not bad," Jamie said. "Now the tail. Same rules, but keep your body off to the side, so you don't catch a kick if the horse spooks. You'll see why I call him Flinch."

Radcliffe hesitated, buried his fear, and stepped to the side of Finch, brushing the tail with slow, careful strokes.

By the time they finished brushing manes and tails, Radcliffe was surprised his arms hadn't fallen off. His back ached, his knees were filthy, and dirty sweat itched under his collar.

Surely they were done.

He looked to Jamie, hoping for a break. Maybe breakfast.

"After that," Jamie said, already moving, "we clean their faces."

Radcliffe blinked. "There's more?"

How can there be more?

Jamie didn't answer—just grabbed a bucket of water and a soft cloth from a nearby shelf.

Radcliffe rubbed his eyes and noticed, for the first time, that sunlight was pouring in through the stable windows.

"We clean their faces," Jamie said, showing Radcliffe a bucket and cloth. "Use the cloth to wipe their eyes and noses. Horses get dust and dirt in there, and if you don't clean it out, it can make them sick."

Radcliffe frowned as Jamie gently wiped Finch's face. "Do they like this?"

"Some do. Others will try to bite your hand off," Jamie said, grinning. "Flinch is the biting type."

He passed Radcliffe the damp cloth.

Radcliffe hesitated. He couldn't imagine what a horse bite felt like—but it couldn't be good.

Still, he stepped forward, speaking softly like Jamie had shown him earlier. He dabbed the cloth over Finch's eyes, then wiped his muzzle.

The horse shook his head, but didn't snap or back away. In fact, he seemed to lean slightly into Radcliffe's touch.

Jamie raised an eyebrow. "Huh."

"Finally, we refill the water buckets," Jamie said, nodding to a row of empty pails. "Fresh water every morning, without fail. You don't want them drinking old, dirty water. Check them again during the day—some of these guys go through it fast. Especially Vanguard."

Radcliffe grabbed one of the pails. The handle dug into his fingers, and the empty bucket still felt heavy.

He trudged behind Jamie, legs dragging, arms aching like they'd been carrying bricks all morning.

At the well, Jamie worked the winch, hauling up a bucket of clean water with ease.

Radcliffe leaned against the side, head dipped, his breathing shallow. His shirt clung to his back. He barely noticed the sunrise now, just the heat building and the dull pounding in his legs.

Jamie handed him the filled pail, and Rad nearly tipped it trying to lift it. Together, they carried the buckets back to the stalls and set them in place.

Radcliffe wiped his brow and glanced down the row of horses.

That was just one round.

There were more.

By the time they finished, Radcliffe's shirt was drenched, and his arms felt like dead weight.

Jamie clapped him on the shoulder with a smile. "Not bad for your first morning. Now let's split up and finish the rest before Hadley shows up."

Radcliffe's head dipped.

Of course there were more.

At this point, he was too tired to care. They could've asked him to polish every floor in the manor and he might've just nodded.

"But don't rush to finish fast," Jamie continued. "Do it right, or Hadley will murder you. He loves these horses more than his own mother—if he even has a mother. Can't imagine anyone claiming him as their son."

Radcliffe stared blankly at Jamie.

Jamie chuckled, though his body went a little rigid. "No rework," he said. "Remember that—no rework."

Radcliffe nodded, picking up his tools and slogging toward the next stall like a sleepwalker. His arms ached. His back screamed. The stink of manure clung to everything. This was punishment—*Da* had made that clear. But still...

Flinch hadn't tried to bite him.

Jamie hadn't mocked him. Hadn't called him "von Schule" like a joke or treated him like a servant.

Just a boy doing a job. Like him.

I'm not a failure.

He didn't know where the thought had come from, but it stuck.

He glanced across the stable. The way Jamie checked each stall, the way water was measured, hay spread just right...

The horses were treated with more care than most people gave his sisters—and they were adored.

A weary Radcliffe tackled the next stall while Jamie worked across the way. Without Jamie guiding him, he realized how much slower and clumsier he was. By the time he finished, Jamie was already halfway through the next one.

The hollow ache in his chest deepened as his thoughts began to spiral. He hadn't seen his sisters since yesterday, or Ma since earlier in the week—but it already felt like a lifetime.

Surely they still cared for him. *Didn't they?*

If they did, they wouldn't let him stay out here long…

Right?

But the longer he thought about it, the more the doubts crept in. Maybe they weren't coming. Maybe no one was.

His throat tightened.

He bit his lip and blinked hard, willing the tears away. At least he hadn't cried in front of Da. That would've made it worse, so much worse…

A sharp, unkind voice cut through his thoughts. "You there. The new lad."

Startled, Radcliffe turned toward the voice. A man stood at the entrance to the stables, rough-looking and mean-faced. This had to be Hadley—the horse-master. The one Jamie said loved the horses more than his own mother.

Hadley's servant uniform had been through as much as he had—faded, patched in places, and sagging on his lean frame. Over it, he wore a scuffed brown leather coat couldn't close in the front. His face reminded Radcliffe of an old tree stump, with deep cracks and creases, telling a story Rad wasn't sure he wanted to hear. His hands were rough and thick with calluses, coming from years of hard work.

Under a battered straw hat, tufts of coarse gray hair stuck out at odd angles. His beard was patchy, and his wiry mustache curled down at the edges, making him look even grumpier. And that scowl—Radcliffe couldn't tell if it was aimed at him or just the world in general.

"Yes," Radcliffe replied, his voice trembling as he sniffled.

"No crying," Hadley snapped. "You keep at it, I'll knock your teeth out. Do a poor job? Same thing. Cause rework?"

He leaned in just a little. "I'll break those little fingers. *Comprere?*"

Radcliffe recognized the word from the High Ornst language, which his family often used during formal occasions. Ma and Da spoke it fluently. His sisters too. Radcliffe lagged behind—less confident, slower to pick it up than Tristin or the others.

Still, he straightened, forcing down the lump in his throat. He took a deep breath, then another, blinking fast to stop the tears.

"*Wi matrisse*," he said, offering a slight bow.

Hadley snorted and brushed past him with a wave.

"Don't show off."

The horse-master led Radcliffe and Jamie to the stalls they had finished for inspection. Hadley scrutinized every detail—the bedding, the horses, their manes, tails, and hooves.

"Who did Shadow?" Hadley asked, stopping at a stall.

Jamie eagerly pointed in Radcliffe's direction.

"Look here, lad," Hadley said, crouching beside the horse and lifting a hoof. "See this grit? You need to clear it out—all of it. Be careful around the white line and don't damage the frog." He jabbed a finger toward a soft, V-shaped section near the middle of the hoof. "Now, Shadow's a healthy horse—but if you ever see black in the frog, or the hoof smells bad, you come get me. It means there's an infection. And if anything's stuck in there that won't come out easy, you fetch me right away. It takes a practiced hand to handle punctures. *Comprere?*"

Radcliffe paused. He nodded and asked, "What's the frog again?"

"This." Hadley jabbed again at the spongy section near the back of the hoof, his tone sharp. He dug out a small pebble and continued inspecting the rest of Shadow's hooves with quick, precise movements. "Not bad for your first time," he muttered.

Radcliffe paused, unsure if he should thank him or stay silent. A polite *merci matrisse* in High Ornst felt appropriate, but Hadley's warning held fast. Instead, he kept quiet and gave a slight nod of acknowledgment.

Radcliffe returned to his stall, picking up the brushes and picks again. His fingers ached. The skin along his knuckles and palms was rubbed raw, stinging with every movement.

He winced as he flexed his hands, already planning to ask Jamie for gloves in the morning.

Surely they'd let him rest tomorrow—just a day to heal.

That was how it worked when you were injured.

Right?

He kept working, slower now. But he didn't stop.

As he toiled, a quiet determination took root.

He would endure.

He had to.

The servants' morning meal was at nine—nearly five hours after Radcliffe had started work. He sat in silence with a bowl of porridge cooling in front of him, his arms limp at his sides, his eyes half-closed.

Around him came the clatter of spoons, the scrape of benches, the low hum of voices.

He didn't look up. He didn't have to.

He could feel the stares.

They were whispering about him. Of course they were.

Spreading rumors, twisting what little they knew.

This is only a test, he told himself. *A temporary trial.*

He would prove himself.

He'd return to the house soon. To Ma. To Abby. To better breakfasts.

When the meal ended, Jamie led him back to the stables.

The rest of the morning was spent assisting Hadley with exercising the horses.

Radcliffe watched in quiet awe as Jamie and Hadley guided the sleek animals through their paces, muscles rippling beneath glossy coats, hooves thudding in rhythm against packed earth.

"You'll be mucking stalls again if you don't keep moving," Hadley barked—his voice sharp, but not cruel.

Radcliffe sighed and dragged another bucket toward the trough. As he passed, his eyes caught on a stall at the far end of the stable.

A dark bay stallion stood alone, dark brown coat almost like polished obsidian, four white socks, and a diamond-shaped mark bright on his forehead.

But it wasn't just the markings.

It was the way he stood—head high, eyes alert, like he knew the world was watching him.

Radcliffe stopped in his tracks.

"That one's Vanguard," Jamie said, catching Radcliffe's gaze. "Beautiful, isn't he? But don't let it fool you—he's not easy to handle. 'Quirky,' Hadley calls him."

"Quirky's a polite way of saying he doesn't like most folks," Hadley added, stepping up behind them. "Shadow's the one I'd trust with anyone. Vanguard is... particular."

Radcliffe moved closer to the stall, drawn by the stallion's steady gaze. Vanguard nickered softly, lowering his head.

"Careful, lad," Hadley warned, his brow creased with concern. "He don't usually take to strangers."

Radcliffe stood still for a breath, then slowly reached out. His fingers brushed Vanguard's muzzle, gentle and unsure.

The stallion huffed, then lowered his head and leaned into the touch.

Hadley tilted his head, arms folding across his chest. "Well, I'll be," he muttered. "Reckon he likes you."

He studied them both a moment longer, eyes narrowing—not with suspicion, but something closer to recognition.

"Want to see if he'll let you ride him?"

Radcliffe's mouth fell open. "Really? I've never—"

"Bareback," Hadley said, already waving Jamie over. "No sense saddling him. If you're going to learn, might as well do it the hard way."

Jamie grinned and gave Radcliffe a boost onto Vanguard's back. The stallion shifted beneath him, ears flicking back—but he didn't bolt.

"Sit up straight," Jamie said. "Grip with your knees, not your hands. Hold his mane—light. Don't yank it, or you'll regret it."

Radcliffe's heart thudded in his chest as Vanguard stepped forward.

The horse's stride was smooth and strong, like he knew exactly where he was going. Radcliffe clung with his legs, trying to move with him, not against him.

His nerves started to fade, replaced by a surge of confidence.

This massive, powerful animal was moving because of *him*.

He wasn't just riding—he was in control.

And it felt incredible.

"Pressure with your knees," Hadley called from the side. "Guide him with your weight. He'll feel it—he's smart."

Radcliffe leaned to one side, and Vanguard followed the shift like he'd read his mind.

It wasn't just luck—it *felt* right, like they already knew how to move together. A grin spread across Radcliffe's face.

Hadley's expression didn't give much away.

"Vanguard doesn't take to people," he said. "Lad must've done *something* right."

When Radcliffe slid down from the stallion's back, Vanguard turned his head and let out a soft nicker.

Hadley shook his head, a faint smirk tugging at his mouth.

"Don't let it go to your head, boy. Vanguard's picky—not perfect."

Then, almost too quiet to catch, he added, "But he might've found himself a new friend."

By the time the horses were cooled, groomed, and returned to their stalls with fresh food and water, Radcliffe's muscles were numb, but he felt an unfamiliar sense of accomplishment.

And he got to ride Vanguard.

"Jamie, excellent work as always," Hadley said, his gruff voice echoing through the stable. "Be back two hours after lunch, or you'll get the back of my hand."

Jamie dashed off toward the manor house, eager for food and rest, or time to play with the other boys.

"Radcliffe, you stay here," Hadley said.

Radcliffe froze. He had no idea what Hadley wanted, and the older man's harsh presence unnerved him. Was he in trouble? What did he do wrong?

"Let me see your hands, Radcliffe," Hadley said, his normal gruff tone softer.

Radcliffe exhaled, unaware he'd been holding his breath. For a moment, a flicker of defiance rose within him—a smoldering rebellion against Da's control.

"Call me Rad," he said, breaking another rule.

He held up his hands for inspection.

Hadley snorted but didn't argue. He examined Rad's hands, his rough fingers brushing over the soft skin. "Those soft hands will harden soon enough. I'm not cutting you any slack because you're *Monsur* von Schule's son. He told me you've got a harsh lesson to learn, and we're going to make sure you learn it."

Rad nodded.

"What else do you know how to do?" Hadley asked, his sharp eyes watching Rad with interest.

Rad hesitated, unsure how to answer. "I guess I can draw stuff. I'm good at math."

Hadley's weathered face cracked into a grin. "Math, eh? Not much use for numbers in the stables, but I'll keep it in mind if I ever need my coins counted." He nodded toward the horses. "You rode well today on Vanguard, decent for your first time."

"Riding was fun," Radcliffe said, his smile bright. "I like Vanguard."

"Well, he's taking a liking to you, so you keep taking care of him and Shadow. Those two are your priority, got it?"

"Got it," he answered.

"Well, for your first day, you're better than Jamie was after two weeks. I think you've got a future with the horses." Hadley crossed his arms, his grin fading back into a stern expression. "I'll try to keep you here instead of sending you off to do dirtier work, but if you want to stay, you'll have to work—and work hard. You slack off, and I'll knock your teeth out. *Comprere?*"

Radcliffe nodded, swallowing hard.

"You'll be up before the sun and finishing when it goes down," Hadley continued. "By the end of the day, you'll be so tired you won't want to eat. Your hands will crack and bleed, but they'll heal, and you'll get stronger. Scrawny boy like you needs some meat on those bones."

Hadley's voice softened as he added, "Do you have any questions before I let you go?"

Rad nodded, curiosity flickering. He hesitated, a question burning in his mind. "I heard someone call you 'Hadley the Pillager'—why would they call you that?"

The air in the stable shifted in a heartbeat. Hadley's expression darkened, his jaw tightening as if he were biting back sharp and bitter medicine.

"Who told you?" he asked, his voice raw and dangerous.

Rad shrank under Hadley's glare. "I—I didn't mean anything by it," he stammered, the words catching in his throat. He'd just made a mistake—a bad one.

"*Who?*"

"My Da."

Hadley took a slow step forward, his boots scuffing the hay-strewn floor.

When he spoke again, his voice was quiet—dangerous—but it sliced through the stable like a blade. "Listen here, lad. You don't ask about that name, and you sure as hell don't *use* it. Ever. Understand?"

Radcliffe nodded, his throat dry and scratchy, like he'd swallowed dust.

Hadley stared at him, eyes hard, fingers stroking his beard. Then, with a sudden motion, he shoved Rad's shoulder. Not hard—but sharp. Enough to send him stumbling.

Rad tripped and landed flat, pain shooting up his back as the breath whooshed out of him.

He looked up.

Hadley stood over him, his face shadowed, jaw tight, chest rising and falling.

For one terrible second, Rad thought he might yell—or worse.

Stomp him to death.

The fear hit him all at once—like the time Tristin shoved his head into a snowbank. Cold, sudden, and stealing the air from his lungs.

But Hadley didn't move.

Instead, he straightened, ran a hand down his face, and finger-combed his beard again.

"Be back two hours after lunch," Hadley said. His scowl remained, but his voice had gone flat—like nothing had happened.

Radcliffe stayed frozen on the ground, heart thudding in his chest.

Hadley turned on his heel and strode off, boots thudding against the stable floor.

Rad swallowed hard and forced his voice to work. "Where do I go after I eat?"

Hadley didn't stop walking, but he barked over his shoulder, "Hide or nap. I don't care. Just don't let Wilkins catch you snooping, or he'll work you to the bone until I call you back."

Then he turned, his glare sharp again.

"Now go! Get out of my sight! *Go!*"

Rad scrambled to his feet, his eyes drifting toward the manor house. From here, he could almost make out the spot where his room sat, high on the third floor.

How tempting it was to crawl back into bed.

To sleep.

To pretend none of this had happened.

But that wasn't an option. If he went back, he'd never wake in time to return to the stables.

"I'll be here after lunch," he said, his voice trailing off. He nodded toward the stables. "It'll keep me out of trouble."

"I don't care," Hadley muttered, already walking away.

He disappeared into one of the nearby sheds—*his* place. The slate roof was mottled with patches of moss, the lone window fogged with grime.

Radcliffe couldn't imagine a place more plain or empty than his own room.

But somehow, he'd found it.

As he walked off, he glanced back once more.

The shed. The man who lived in it.

Hadley the Pillager.

Maybe he wasn't the only one Da had sentenced to this life.

Two misfits.

One small, one fearsome.

Both trapped in Xavier's world, made to serve the horses.

Radcliffe felt a strange flicker of understanding.

He shoved it down before it could grow into anything more.

After a lunch of dried meat and mushy, tasteless vegetables, Rad returned to the stables, clutching a small piece of day-old bread he had saved.

It wasn't much, but it would do for a snack.

The quiet surroundings of the stables felt like a break from everything, and he climbed into the hayloft, weaving his way between the bales until he found a hidden corner where no one would spot him.

He leaned against the stacked hay, nibbling on the bread and wishing he'd thought to grab butter from the kitchen. Still, it wasn't terrible—better than the soggy vegetables he'd forced down earlier.

Below him was an empty stall, ensuring no horse would disturb him. He arranged two small piles of hay, knocking them down with strikes of his imaginary sword. After a time, he grew bored defeating the bandits and arranged the hay into a makeshift bed and pillow.

Satisfied he was safe from prying eyes, he rested his head on the hay and let his exhaustion take over.

His muscles ached—arms, legs, even fingers he didn't know could hurt. He wriggled into the hay, the rough strands prickling his skin, but it didn't matter. It was warm, dry, and soft *enough*.

Better than the floor.

Better than standing all day.

Not his bed, but close enough to pretend.

Sleep crept in, stealing over the pain, tugging him under.

Jamie would wake him when it was time to work again. Radcliffe was sure of it.

Jamie might be the only friend he'd have for a long time.

Hadley?

Not a chance.

Voices woke him with a start.

Low and urgent, they weren't Jamie's or Hadley's.

For a moment, Rad thought he heard men plotting murder, but as he listened closer, the words came into focus. They were chirping numbers back and forth, making agreements, exchanging coins, and muttering about 'bones.'

He shifted quietly, peering down from his hidden perch in the hayloft.

Four house servants were in the empty stall below. The straw had been cleared from the floor, and the men squatted, small stacks of coins and dice spread between them.

They were gambling, rolling the dice.

Dice games and playing cards existed in the household, but gambling was forbidden for family and servants alike.

Now in the past, Da did have men over to smoke pipes, drink smelly bourbon, and play cards in the cellar—but it was like an informal party, not like the galas they held every so often.

Rad wondered why these servants would take a chance on getting caught. This didn't seem like fun—not even a little.

They exchanged coins and celebrated in muted whispers, their movements slow to avoid drawing attention.

The dice knocked against the wall, spinning to a stop with double sixes on the hardpacked dirt.

One of the servants scooped up the pile of coins in the middle. Each put down more coins and the next man gathered the dice.

"You lads get caught using my stable to roll the bones, I'll break off your fingers and shove them up your arse," Hadley's gruff voice said from the entrance to the stall. He removed his battered straw hat, revealing his balding head and bleach-white scalp.

"Bugger off," one of the servants snapped. "I'm not scared of Hadley the Pillager. More like Hadley the Villager! The village idiot!"

Rad braced for an explosion of anger.

Hadley's response was steady, his voice calm and cutting. "Lads, I was raping and whoring before you were born. One of you could be my son for all I know. Pay your dues to me, and I'll let this go. Use my stables again to roll the bones, and I'll make good on the bit about your fingers. Pay up. Now."

"Old man," the servant said, flicking a worn copper coin into the air.

The tarnished coin spun several turns before landing in Hadley's left hand.

"Get out of here before you have an accident."

Hadley let his hat slip from his head, discarded like it might get in the way.

His right hand moved faster than Radcliffe could track.

A flash of polished steel—then a blade sank into the dirt between the servant's fingers.

"I can hit a raven's eye at fifty paces with my knife," Hadley said, his voice ice-cold. "Get your arses out of here. Now."

The four servants froze, their eyes fixed on the blade. They scrambled to gather their coins, dice, and purses before hurrying out of the stables.

The dagger remained planted in the dirt.

Hadley retrieved it without a word, wiping the blade clean on his sleeve before sliding it back into a hidden sheath. Without another glance at the stall, he turned and disappeared deeper into the stables, whistling a tune.

Rad let out a soothing breath.

He didn't move—not a twitch—afraid Hadley might sense him up in the loft.

But his mind replayed the scene again and again.

The dagger had landed perfectly—right between the servant's fingers.

No blood. No hesitation. Just precision.

A strange excitement buzzed in his chest.

Could I learn to throw knives?

The idea burned through him—clean, focused, sharp.

Knives didn't scare him. Not in the dark, not in his hand.

He'd always liked the feel of one, even before he knew why.

Hadley had thrown his like it was part of him. Rad wanted that.

The thought lit a spark in him.

Not fear. Not dread.

Just the urge to know what Hadley knew—to do what he did…*and more.*

Chapter Four

∞

Château Saignoral

The stables were quiet in the afternoon heat, with only the faint rustle of hay and the occasional stomp of a hoof breaking the silence. Radcliffe stood by Vanguard, brushing the dark brown stallion's glossy coat in slow, steady strokes.

The horse leaned into the attention, but when the stable doors creaked open, Vanguard's ears flicked back, and he turned his head to see the visitor.

Rad glanced up, his grip on the brush tightening.

Abigail stood in the doorway, a basket tucked over her arm. Her simple yellow dress fluttered in the faint breeze, and her dark hair, usually so neatly braided, had a few loose strands framing her face.

"Abby?" Rad asked, his voice breaking in surprise.

She smiled, stepping inside. "Hello, *Rad.*"

Before he could say anything more, Vanguard nudged his shoulder with a soft huff. The stallion turned his attention to Abigail, reaching his long neck toward her, clearly interested in the basket.

Rad scowled and swatted Vanguard's nose. "Stop it, you big oaf. She's not here for you."

Abigail laughed, stepping closer. "I think he knows I brought something."

Vanguard nudged Rad again, this time harder, and Rad stumbled. "Quit it! You're like Marie when she wants everyone to notice her dress."

Abby giggled, setting the basket on a nearby bale of hay. "I see he's got personality. What's his name?"

"Abby, this is Vanguard. Vanguard, Abby. Don't give me that look," Rad muttered, brushing harder. "You're jealous, aren't you? Big baby."

Vanguard snorted and nudged him again—gentler this time, like he was saying, *Come on, you're not really mad at me.*

"Need help with him?" Abigail asked, watching Rad work.

Before Rad could answer, Jamie appeared at the end of the stable. He wiped his hands on a faded rag tucked into his belt, careful to keep the hay dust from clinging to his shirt.

"Afternoon, Miss Abigail," he said with a smile, tipping his head in greeting.

"Hello, Jamie," she replied with a polite nod.

Jamie turned to Rad. "I'll finish up with Vanguard. Go on, spend time with your sister. You're lucky to have visitors."

Rad hesitated, but Jamie waved him off. "Go. Hadley will be by soon enough to bark at you if you're slacking."

Rad set the brush down and followed Abigail out of the stables, squinting in the bright afternoon sun.

Hadley was waiting outside. He smeared the mud off on his trousers without blinking—his pants were already filthy, and he didn't seem to care.

He straightened when he saw Abigail and gave a respectful nod, tucking his dirty hands behind his back.

"Miss Abigail."

"Hadley," she replied, offering a faint smile.

His eyes shifted to Radcliffe. "Take a walk with your sister," he said, gruff as ever. "Be back in half an hour. Not a minute later."

"Yes, sir," Radcliffe replied.

Hadley's eyes narrowed. "If you call me 'sir,' you may as well call the horses 'sir' too. Drop it."

Radcliffe blinked. "Yes—Hadley."

The two siblings started down the path toward the orchards, the scent of ripening fruit drifting on the warm breeze. The trees were heavy with blossoms and small, growing apples, their branches casting broken shadows over the ground.

Abby glanced sideways at Rad. "How are you doing?" she asked.

Rad shrugged, holding up his hands. The skin was raw and calloused, blisters dotting his fingers. "I'm fine. What about you?"

"I'm fine too," Abby said with a tightlipped smile. "I miss you. It's not the same without you at the house."

Rad looked away, his jaw tightening. "Do you think Da will let me come back?"

Abigail hesitated, her gaze dropping to the ground. "I don't know. I wouldn't get your hopes up."

Rad swallowed hard, nodding. "What about Ma?"

"She's... sad," Abigail said, her voice quiet. "She only comes out of her room for dinner, and she and Da shout at each other. I think she blames him for..." She trailed off, shaking her head. "It's hard. I think she's trying to get you back in the house."

Rad nodded. "And Tristin?"

Abigail sighed. "Busy with Da. He was mean to Gabrielle the other morning—called her a spoiled brat—and nothing happened. No punishment, no belt, nothing."

"Tristin never gets in trouble," Rad muttered, kicking a loose rock off the path.

"What about Bella and Marie?" he asked.

"They won't stop talking about new dresses," Abigail said with a faint smile. "That's all they care about right now."

Rad glanced at her, remembering what he'd overheard through the secret passageway. "Yes... sounds about right."

He hesitated, then added, "I've learned a lot about horses. I can groom them, muck stalls—even ride Vanguard bareback."

Abigail's eyes widened. "Bareback? Really?"

"Yes. It's not as hard as it sounds. But..." He trailed off. There was more he could say—but not today. Not about Hadley, or the work, or what it felt like to be forgotten.

Abigail slowed, her steps falling quiet on the path. She looked at him—just looked.

Rad shifted and muttered, "It's fine."

She gave him a small smile, soft and knowing, but didn't press. Then she reached for the basket she'd brought. "I have something for you."

Inside were blocks of cheese, fresh bread, cured meats, jars of jam and jelly, and two books—one on the history of Ornst and the other an adventure story about a pirate captain.

Tucked into the corner were three bars of chocolate.

"For me?" Rad asked, his voice brightening.

"Of course," Abigail said. "You can share the chocolate with Jamie and Hadley, if you want. Or keep it all to yourself. I won't tell."

Rad grinned and closed the basket with a snap.

Real food.

When they returned, Hadley was standing near the doors, watching the two of them approach.

Abigail gave Rad a firm hug, wrinkling her nose as she stepped back. "You smell awful," she teased.

Rad laughed, a bit of color returning to his cheeks. "It's part of the job."

"Take care of yourself, Rad," she said, turning toward the house.

He watched her go, his chest feeling both lighter and heavier at the same time.

Back inside, he shared the basket with Jamie and Hadley, pulling out the cheeses and chocolate.

Jamie's eyes lit up, and Hadley allowed himself a rare smile.

"Don't start without me," Hadley said. "Old Hadley will be back before you know it."

He disappeared into his shed and returned with two brown, stoppered bottles of ale, handing one to Jamie and Rad, and keeping the other for himself.

"Split it," he said. "And don't ask for a single drop more."

The three of them ate and drank together, the weight of the day fading into quiet contentment.

Maybe this isn't all that bad after all.

A week had passed—seven sunrises, seven sunsets—and Rad sat with his sore hands and a head full of thoughts he didn't feel like sharing. He wandered the manor grounds, exploring, avoiding where his family would be.

He didn't want to see them.

Well, except for Abby, maybe Ma.

His hands were raw, the skin cracked and sore despite the greasy ointment they used on cows' udders. It helped a little, but not enough.

Without bandages, the cracks bled—a constant reminder of the toll his new life was taking.

Hadley worked him hard, each day piling on more tasks and responsibilities for him and Jamie to share. At times other boys from the household helped, but Hadley preferred to keep his stable running with a lean crew of two reliable hands.

Rad hadn't seen the gamblers again, nor had he worked up the nerve to ask Hadley about knife-throwing. The thought lingered, but it shriveled every time he remembered Hadley's offhand remarks about 'raping and whoring.' Rad understood how terrible those acts were—people went to the gallows for crimes like that.

Why would Da hire a man like that?

Wasn't it dangerous for the family?

But the more Rad watched Hadley, the less he believed he was a bad man—at least, not anymore. He worked hard, and the horses were always clean, healthy, and ready to go. Whatever Hadley used to be, he'd left it behind.

Rad's thoughts drifted to Abby. Seeing her had felt good—but it also made his chest hurt. She hadn't said he was stuck here forever, but she didn't say he'd be coming home either. Still, she brought books. She brought chocolate. She made him laugh. She hadn't forgotten him.

As the days passed, Abby's words stuck with him. Maybe this wasn't temporary. Maybe Da really meant for him to stay with the servants until he turned sixteen—and then get kicked out.

Whatever he'd done, he couldn't fix it.

Running away wasn't an option. Not yet. He didn't know what was out there.

But he was pretty sure it wasn't anything like *Château Saignoral.*

He still held out hope for Ma's influence—maybe she could talk Da into changing his mind. That had to be why they were arguing. It was nice, thinking she might be fighting for him.

For now, a quiet defiance simmered in his chest. If they didn't want him, then he didn't want them either.

All except Abby—she still loved him enough to bring chocolate.

And Ma, who hadn't given up.

The grounds felt endless—like the deck of a great ship rolling on the sea or a forgotten battlefield. Rad wanted to ride Vanguard along the high stone walls, wind tugging at his hair as they raced past buckle-berry brambles and the grim-faced guards.

But he didn't. Not yet.

Getting caught would mean a lecture, a punishment… or worse.

Hadley.

Rad wandered along the edge of the tall stone wall, his feet crunching the gravel path. Every crack, every chunk missing from the old stones seemed to stick in his mind, even if he wasn't trying to remember. Thick vines crawled up the sides like ropes, and up top, sharp iron spikes poked at the sky. He spotted little dark spaces near the corners—maybe hiding spots, maybe not.

A guard passed by, eyes sharp and hand resting on his sword. Rad opened his mouth to ask about the blade, but the man gave him a look and tapped two fingers to his temple—then pointed at Rad's head like he was lining up a punch.

Rad scurried off without a word.

The mercenaries roamed in pairs, patrolling on foot or horseback, their presence a constant reminder of the estate's security.

As Rad ventured further, the landscape began to change. Behind the manor was a whole other world—gardens that went on forever, fields full of crops, pens packed with noisy animals, and little farms scattered everywhere. Workers moved among them, brushing past him with curt nods or ignoring him.

Was this where their food came from?

Rad stopped, eyes wide. He'd never been this far south on the property.

It was like a secret city.

Tiny homes, gardens, workshops—people moving around, working, talking. It was its own place, hidden inside the walls. Still part of *Château Saignoral*, but almost like its own little town.

The guarded gates along the roads caught his eye next. Well-traveled paths led in and out, offering the farmers a way to come and go without disturbing the manor's daily life.

When he spotted the vineyards, he squinted. Were those grapes? He hadn't known they grew those here.

Did they harvest grapes for snacks and making wine?

He remembered poking around the wine cellar when he was younger—huge tanks, wooden paddles, rows of empty bottles, and the sharp, sweet smell of old oak barrels. The place had felt like a maze.

Did Da make wine?

It was a weird thought. He'd never seen his father near the vineyards, and nobody really talked about wine like it mattered.

Except when guests came over. Then there'd be trays of glasses, lots of sniffing and sipping, and people saying strange things like '*notes of plum*' or '*earthy tones.*' Whatever that meant.

But Da liked bourbon. Always had a bottle nearby—on his desk, in the dining room, wherever.

Rad looked at the vines again. He liked grapes. Especially the red ones.

When he was sure no one was looking, Rad slipped between the rows of vines and wrestled a cone-shaped bunch of grapes off the stem. They were dark purple, smaller than the kind served in the kitchens, and felt firmer.

He plucked one off and popped it in his mouth.

Crunch. Seeds—lots of them.

Then came the sweetness. *Way* too sweet. His face twisted.

"Yuck," he muttered, spitting it out. He kept spitting until all the pieces were gone.

Rad tossed the bunch at the base of the vine and wiped his hands on his trousers as he crept out of the vineyard.

As lunchtime crept closer, Rad started the long walk back to the manor. He planned to eat with the servants, then poke around the front grounds. He'd passed through that part of the estate plenty of times, but he'd never really looked at it.

Seemed smart to know every inch of the place. If he was stuck living here, he might as well figure out the layout.

Lunch was simple: bread, cheese, and leftovers from the family's meals, plus some boiled potatoes. At least they peeled them. The food didn't taste like much, but Rad didn't care. It filled his belly, and that's what mattered.

As he neared the front of the estate, Rad looked up at the big wrought-iron sign over the entrance: *Château Saignoral.*

Beneath the letters was the von Schule family emblem—a black half-moon wrapped around the green *VS*. He spotted the same design on round signs posted along the walls.

The front grounds made him stop for a moment. They were huge—neatly trimmed hedges, stone paths, flowers planted in perfect rows. It looked even grander than he remembered.

At the gate was a little guardhouse, where visitors and delivery wagons could be told where to go. Rad watched as a person with a huge satchel walked up and dropped a folded piece of parchment through a slot in the wall.

That's how they got messages from outside?

Rad stared, wide-eyed. What a brilliant idea!

A cobblestone road ran from the gate all the way to the manor. Green hedges lined both sides, trimmed perfectly straight. Tall iron posts stood between them, each with a lantern on top—probably really bright at night.

Pine trees flanked the road, one after another like they were standing guard.

Rad frowned. Why didn't they just build a fence? It would be easier than cutting back trees and trimming hedges all the time.

Smaller roads split off from the main one so carriages could pull over and drop people off without blocking the way. On the left was the carriage house—big and fancy, with space for all the wagons and coaches.

Up ahead, the manor rose like a mountain. It was huge, with two long wings and towers that reached almost to the sky. The towers were four whole stories high, except for the east tower that was taller!

Rad stared up at the manor, walking through it in his head.

His small room sat way up high—on the third floor, right in the middle. The only thing up there, except for the twisty stairs leading into the tall spires. From there, he pictured going down to the second floor.

Bella and Marie's rooms were right near the stairs, one on each side. They had a landing between them where you could look down into the giant foyer. That spot had a balcony too, with a view of everything.

Across the hall were Tristin's and Abby's rooms. They faced the back of the estate and had their own balconies, which he always thought was unfair.

There was also the quiet room—an extra study with desks and shelves where they did lessons and reading.

One of the most impressive parts of the whole estate was the east tower. A spiral staircase wound all the way up—six stories high—ending in a round glass room at the top called the lantern room. On clear days, you could see all of Ornst from there—rooftops, hills, and even the river in the distance.

The city stretched out like a giant maze—red and gray roofs packed close together, winding streets too narrow to count, and tall temple towers poking up like needles. Right in the middle of it all stood the Ornst Library. It took up a whole block and was even taller than the east tower—eight stories high, with a big spire in the center and smaller ones on the corners. Its stone walls and rows of windows made it look like a castle built for books.

Farther off, the duke's keep sat on a rise, dark and heavy, like it had been there forever. Smoke rose from chimneys and melted into the morning mist, wrapping the rooftops in quiet.

Rad wandered up to the second floor of the west wing, where four small bedrooms circled around two bigger guest rooms. He always thought those rooms were strange—they even had tiny kitchens in them. Why would guests need their own kitchens? Maybe they were for families who stayed a long time and didn't want to bother anyone.

Still, he was sure the maids polished those floors every week, even if nobody used them.

He crossed to the east wing and found three more bedrooms, plus a sunroom, a sitting room, and the long upstairs library. Big windows let the light pour in, but the room still felt stiff—like the kind of place where kids weren't supposed to touch anything.

The first floor of the west wing was where the servants slept. Rows of bunks, side by side, like a barracks. Next to that were the kitchens and the noisy washrooms, where everyone always seemed to be scrubbing or hauling laundry.

The east wing was different. That's where Ma and Da had their fancy guest rooms, meeting rooms, and the small wine cellar. Da also had a vault back there, hidden behind a thick door. No one was allowed to touch it—just him.

Rad remembered it clearly. One time, a servant tried to sneak one of Da's special bourbons, and Da had him whipped. Just for a bottle.

Both wings had full basements. Most of it was boring stuff—extra furniture, crates, piles of supplies no one used.

But the east wing basement was different.

That's where Da kept his wine. Racks of bottles, big barrels, metal tanks with tubes. The whole place smelled like wet wood and old fruit. No windows. No light. Just dark and quiet. Rad always thought that was weird—why keep drinks in the dark?

Nobody was allowed down there. Da's voice echoed in his head: *"Some of those bottles are worth more than a year's wages for a working man."* Rad didn't know how much that was, but it sounded like a ridiculous price for a drink.

He remembered being down there once. The word *SONNER* was printed in big letters on a bunch of empty crates and bottles. Sonner was another duchy, like Ornst—and a family name too. Maybe *they* made the wine using Da's grapes. Could that be how it worked?

The thought stuck with him. If Da really was making wine… what would he name it?

Would it be called *von Schule* wine?

The whole first floor was where the family mostly lived. At the front of the house, near the big front doors, was a long hallway full of fancy things. Paintings in gold frames, old vases with dragons or flowers on them, and statues that looked too fragile to even breathe on. Rad used to run his fingers along the marble or tap on the glass cases when no one was looking. Now he kept his hands at his sides. He wasn't sure he was even supposed to be here anymore, and he didn't want to get scolded for leaving fingerprints.

Rad lingered by a painting of a dryad—a real one, not just a made-up story kind. She was standing next to a red tree with her green hair tumbling over one shoulder, smiling like she was teasing someone. She didn't have any clothes on. At all. Rad's eyes flicked over the painting, trying not to stare but also kind of staring. He knew he shouldn't be looking—definitely not this long—but it pulled at him. Was this really what dryads looked like?

When people came into the manor, the first thing they saw was the giant front hall. It stretched up two stories high, with shiny floors and tall windows that filled the space with light. To the left was the library. Rad had been in there plenty of times before, but now he paused and really looked at it. The shelves climbed all the way up the walls, packed with books and old scrolls. The air smelled like ink and dust. There were ladders on wheels, thick rugs, and heavy chairs that looked too serious to sit in. He used to curl up in a corner and read whatever he could reach. Now he wasn't sure if Wilkins would stop him for even poking his head inside.

On the right was the dining room, with its long table and high-backed chairs and more forks than anyone could possibly need. That was where the family had their formal meals, the kind where Rad had to sit still and not fidget, even if his nose itched.

Straight ahead, the twin staircases curled upward like ribbons, meeting at the landing above. Rad had once dreamed of sliding down the rails, but he never did.

Past the stairs was the grand ballroom. Rad hadn't any reason to step farther into the great room, as it was large and empty. Now it just looked too clean. Too shiny. Like no one had ever really lived there. It was where they held parties.

Da and Ma calling these parties 'galas,' though he didn't know why they couldn't call it a party. Some fancy word.

A wide hallway led from the ballroom to Da's study, and beyond that was the master bedroom—his parents' room. Rad hadn't been in there in a long time and didn't remember what it looked like. Just past it, stretching across the back of the manor, was the biggest deck he'd ever seen.

The deck was huge—wide enough to fit a whole army. From there, you could see the entire back lawn, neat as a chessboard, with flowerbeds, trimmed hedges, and trees that looked like they'd been trained to stand still. Guests used to play lawn games out there or stroll around pretending they were royalty.

Near the middle of the grounds stood the gazebo. It had a pointed roof and narrow columns. Rad had sat in it once, ages ago, during a summer picnic. He didn't remember what was said, but he recalled the sound of the wind rattling the leaves overhead. Now, it looked like the kind of place people went to whisper things they didn't want heard.

Tucked nearby were the bathing rooms and closets. These were full of coats, shoes, and fancy clothes for Ma and Da. Enough to dress a hundred people, he thought.

On the far side of the ballroom, past the double doors, the kitchens were always busy. They were as big as the ballroom itself, with clattering pans and shouting cooks and the smell of roasting meat or fresh bread drifting into the hallways. Rad used to sneak in there to snag a cookie or two when the cooks weren't looking.

Next to the kitchens was the family room. It wasn't fancy like the rest of the house—just soft chairs and warm rugs where people could sit and not worry about crumbs. Past that, a covered terrace looked out over the gardens. He'd seen Da take his tea there.

There was also a morning room, meant for Wilkins and the governess. Rad had never been inside, but he imagined they drank tea and complained about the children.

Near the dining room sat the breakfast nook—the site of one of his finest and worst moments. He could still picture the look on Tristin's face, muffin crumbs stuck in his perfect hair. The mess, the yelling, the way it all exploded so fast. That was the day everything changed.

The last part of the manor was its massive basement, a maze of odd spaces. Directly beneath the master bedroom was replica of the room above, reserved for important guests—but he had never seen anyone stay there.

There were closets, pantries, and mechanisms for heating the grand estate in winter. Below the grand ballroom stretched a similar room, complete with a stage and podium. While Rad wasn't sure of its purpose, he imagined it might be used for speeches or meetings. It remained unlocked and unused.

Beneath the kitchens and dining rooms were additional gathering spaces, each designed for practicality or leisure. Another art gallery occupied this level, dedicated to one of Da's biggest pieces. Rad wasn't sure why these were down here and not upstairs with the other artwork.

The centerpiece was an enormous white marble statue of a rider on top of a rearing horse, its greatness both inspiring and overwhelming. Rad was astonished by its sheer size—it must weigh thousands of pounds. Yet, like the room with the podium, this gallery was seldom visited, he assumed for the most important guests.

As Rad's mental tour finished, he found himself ascending the stairs back to his room. His scuffed boots dangled from his hands, his stockinged feet making no sound against the polished wood steps. Being quiet was one way to avoid unwanted attention.

Halfway up, Bella descended, chin high as always, brushing past him without so much as a glance. A moment later, Marie followed. Her eyes met his for a split second—just long enough to show disapproval. Cold, but at least it was something.

He waited a moment longer, hoping Abby might come next. She usually did. Her presence had a way of settling the ache in his chest. But she didn't appear.

Once inside his room, Rad shut the door and set his boots aside. The bed wasn't much, but it was better than what the other servants had—and that still felt like a reward.

He lay back, staring at the ceiling, but the worry wouldn't go away. It had only been a week. Six more years stretched out in front of him, long and uncertain. Too many ways to mess things up. Too many chances to lose what little he had.

What comes next? he wondered. *Will they cast me into the streets before sixteen?*

The thought chilled him, but he clung to the faint hope that time might grant him the opportunity to prove himself. He needed to keep from messing things up any further.

He tossed his outer shirt toward the closet, planning to hang it later.

He might've been cast out, but the rules still applied to him: hang your clothes, stow your shoes, keep things neat. As his gaze lingered on the closet, something tugged at the edge of his mind—a faint tickle of a forgotten thought.

His eyes fell on the lantern sitting on the floor. It had become a necessary companion during the early mornings in the stables. After a week of practice, he had mastered its operation: trimming the wick to the right length, using the correct oil, and lighting it on the first try. He felt a small swell of pride in his newfound skill. But the lantern's presence now...

What am I forgetting?

His gaze returned to the closet, the tickle forming into a memory. The lantern hovered at the edge of his vision, and it clicked.

The secret passageway!

His tiredness vanished, replaced by a spark of excitement. A bold idea took hold. With the lantern, he could explore the hidden passage—find out where it went, and maybe even what secrets it was hiding.

Rad didn't hesitate. Grabbing the lantern, he lit the wick, adjusting the flame to a soft, steady glow. It cast flickering shadows across the closet walls as he stepped inside. Opening the concealed door, he crouched and peered into the dark recess beyond.

This won't take long.

Radcliffe slipped into the passageway from his closet, his lantern casting flickering light along the rough, narrow walls. The space smelled of dust and old wood, with an occasional whiff of dampness that made him wrinkle his nose—it smelled sour, like old stockings.

Shadows danced as he descended the ladder to the platform below, his bare hands gripping the cool, lightly splintered rungs. The air was stale, heavy, and the cramped space made his breathing sound louder than it was.

As his feet touched the wooden platform, the creak echoed through the passage.

He froze, heart pounding.

The silence following stretched long enough for him to steady himself.

He lifted the lantern higher, its glow barely reaching the shadowy corners. These passageways weren't a mistake or an afterthought—they were built this way on purpose. Someone had designed them for one thing: spying.

Rad turned down a narrow corridor, the lantern light revealing more panels and faint cracks in the walls where peepholes had been drilled. He stood by one he recognized from his first venture into the passageways and peered through it. Marie's room came into view, bathed in soft afternoon sunlight.

She was sitting at her vanity, humming to herself as she brushed her hair. Rad watched for only a moment before sliding the cover back over the peephole. He wasn't interested in her fussing over her hair and didn't want her to sense anything was amiss.

He moved on, feeling a little odd. It was strange, watching them like this—like he was both in the house and outside at the same time.

On the opposite side, Rad found Bella's room. He pressed his eye to the peephole and saw her standing before a long mirror, holding up a shimmering green dress with gold embroidery. She smiled, turning to admire it from every angle.

Rad rolled his eyes but kept watching.

She began to undress, and Rad yanked his head back, heart leaping into his throat. He shoved the slider over the peephole, heat rising in his cheeks. The thought of spying on his unclothed sister made his stomach churn.

He leaned back, shaking his head to clear the awkwardness of spying on Bella. Then he noticed the faint black marks scratched into the wall beside the peephole—seven thin charcoal lines—counting. But seven *what*? Days? People? Times?

The corridor twisted, leading Rad to another peephole, this one overlooking the grand ballroom. He crouched and pressed his eye to the opening. The view was expansive; the whole room stretched out below, the crystal chandelier casting fractured light onto the polished floor.

Rad let out a soft whistle, impressed despite himself. Whoever had designed these passageways had planned for someone to watch everything happening in the house. The thought sent a small thrill through him, softened by unease of private moments not being private.

He continued deeper into the maze, passing through increasingly narrow passages until he came to a spot overlooking the kitchen and dining area. A peephole framed the space below, where a pair of maids were cleaning up after lunch. Rad noted the warm glow of the hearth and the clatter of dishes being stacked.

His stomach grumbled, and he thought next time he explored, he should bring food and drink. Sitting here for hours could be tempting—the entire house was his to observe.

Further along, Rad found a peephole that gave him a view into Da's study. His father and Tristin were bent over a table, a map of the city of Ornst spread between them.

Rad leaned against a stud, listening while he stared down upon them.

"We need the warehouse closer to the docks," Da said, tracing a line on the map with his finger. "We can offload goods from the ships directly. Efficiency is profit, Tristin."

"And it costs twice as much," Tristin replied, resting his hands on the table. "The western fringes are half the price. It's better to transport the goods by wagon than pay for prime real estate and your efficiency."

Rad's eyes flicked between the two of them. They weren't arguing or shouting—their voices were low and steady, trying to convince each other they were right.

Routes, cost, convenience. It was a business conversation, and Rad found himself fascinated by how calm they were when they disagreed. He slipped away before they reached a decision, feeling as though he had glimpsed another side of both.

The next peephole led to the master bedroom. Rad held his breath as he peered inside. His mother was lounging on a chaise, dressed in comfortable house clothes, a book resting in her lap. The soft flicker of sunlight through the curtains made the room feel calm, but Rad felt like an intruder.

A knock at the door broke the quiet, and Marie entered, her voice animated as she described the dresses she and the others had found in town. "This one had lace all along the collar, Ma, and the fabric was so soft! You should come with us next time—you'd love it! We should go soon!"

Rad listened, a small grin forming on his lips as Marie tried to convince their mother to arrange another trip into the city. Ma tittered, closing her book. "Another time, Marie," she replied, though her tone held no real promise.

The dramatic Marie pouted, tossing herself onto the end of the chaise. "You always say that! We met some women at the dress shop who want to have afternoon tea with us, all of us. Can we go? Please?"

Rad grinned at the familiar back-and-forth and quietly stepped away. He let the slider fall back into place and turned to continue, but another peephole caught his eye. This one was positioned over the bed.

He hesitated, the uneasy memory of Bella's room bubbled up. Still, he knelt down and raised the lantern, its light revealing a small ledge near the peephole. Sitting there was a stoppered bottle of bourbon and a dusty tin cup—left behind, but not by accident.

Rad's stomach turned.

Someone had sat here, watching his parents sleep.

It made his chest tighten, though he couldn't articulate why. He didn't know the word for it—but it felt wrong, like he'd stumbled on a horrible aspect of these secret passageways. Without another glance, he moved on, his pace quicker now.

The air grew cooler as Rad descended another ladder, this one leading to the basement and cellar.

The damp chill prickled against his skin, and the faint smell of crushed fruit and yeast mixed with the woodsy scent of aging barrels. He stopped at several peepholes along the way, each offering a view of rows of wine barrels and vats. It was a surprise to find the space clean and organized, and a pair of long tables stood nearby, freshly arranged. There were no workers in sight, but the area wasn't abandoned. It made him wonder, was Da getting ready to make wine?

At the far end of the corridor, the passage narrowed and the construction changed from the familiar raw wood and plaster to solid stone. Rad stopped in front of a stout metal door unlike anything he'd seen before. It had no handle or lock—merely a five-by-five grid of engraved wooden panels set into a frame. One square was left empty, the design incomplete.

Rad stood on his tiptoes, holding the lantern closer. His fingers brushed over the swirling black and gold patterns etched into the panels. The engravings shifted in the dim light, almost as if they were alive.

He hesitated, then reached for one of the pieces, sliding it into the empty slot. It moved with ease, snapping into place with a faint hum that made the hair on the back of his neck rise.

His heart raced. *It has to be magical.*

A magical puzzle.

He stared at the puzzle, his mind spinning with possibilities. What could it be hiding? Treasure? Jewels? More secrets? The idea formed in his mind, irresistible. He imagined gold coins piled high, glittering swords and enchanted blades, or perhaps a secret Da was hiding.

And he would be the one to discover it.

Rad bit his lip, his pulse quickening with anticipation. "I'll figure you out," he whispered to the door.

The puzzle pieces weren't simple, and the intricate patterns made no immediate sense. He decided to bring paper next time—to draw the grid, map it out, and figure out what it meant later.

Whatever was behind this door, he would find it.

Climbing back up through the bowels of the manor, Rad found himself outside Abby's room. Through the peephole, he saw her sitting at a desk, a stack of books beside her. She picked one up, running her fingers over the embossed leather cover. The warm glow of her lamp lit her face, and a small smile crossed her lips.

"Oh, Rad will love this one," she murmured, setting the book aside.

Rad's chest tightened, a strange mix of gratitude and longing welling inside him.

Abby's gifts weren't just kind gestures—they were lifelines, windows to a world he might not otherwise reach. He backed away without a sound, his mind already buzzing with plans.

I'll read every word, he thought. *Every book she gives me. I'll read them all.*

Knowledge was power.

For sure he couldn't rely on Hadley to teach him everything. Abby's books would be the key, each one unlocking his brain, shaping him into a person who could make sense of the world around him.

He crept back through the passageways, his thoughts racing ahead of him. If he worked hard in the stables by day, and read by night, perhaps he could turn this punishment to his favor.

Returning to his room, Rad collapsed onto his bed, the extinguished lantern set by his side. His thoughts swirled, still caught in the maze of passageways and the secrets they held. The sheer complexity was amazing. Whoever had constructed the manor—certainly not his father—must have designed it with spying in mind. It was the only explanation making sense.

These hidden corridors granted him glimpses into every room of the house. He could spy on Ma and Da as they slept, observe guests dining, or listen in on Da's private business discussions in the study. His siblings' activities, from the mundane to the secretive, were all within his reach.

The power this knowledge offered made him pause, a chill creeping up his spine. He couldn't ignore the thrill of it, but the thought of someone else holding this same power terrified him.

He had to make sure no one else found out.

The passageways—and their secrets—were his alone.

Settling into bed, Rad felt the weight of exhaustion from the day. He knew he would drift off well before sunset, his body aching from his work in the stables. Tomorrow would be filled with the same toil.

Staring at the ceiling, Rad's thoughts lingered on the past week. He had proven himself through hard work. Hadley had acknowledged his growing talent with horses, treating him as Jamie's equal. Vanguard had taken a liking to him, too—a small but welcome victory.

As for the servants, their early whispers and curious glances had faded within days. After a week, they barely looked at him. They didn't ignore him exactly—just treated him like any other servant: present, but unimportant. He was an oddity—a child of the household turned servant, a status that left everyone unsure, including him.

Rad didn't mind now that he thought about it.

If anything, their wariness made things easier. The younger servants watched him from a distance, their eyes filled with curiosity, but they never approached to talk or to play.

Only Jamie offered him company. The others treated him with cautious politeness, like an object to avoid.

As fatigue overtook him, his thoughts dimmed. The faint glimmers of his plan to solve every riddle in the passageways unfolded in his mind. He would find the truth behind the puzzle, the passageways, and the secrets lingering in the shadows of the manor.

CHAPTER FIVE

∞

The Vintner

A month had passed, and Rad had all but faded from his family's thoughts except for Abby. They found a way to exchange books, and he promised her he would read every word he gave to her. It was their own little game, where he would put the books in a hidden spot, then she would exchange them for new ones, and he would gather them later. It became so important to Abby that she convinced Ma and Gabrielle, the governess, that she needed to get books from the renown Ornst Library.

Rad had become another thread in the servant tapestry, caught in the grind of identical days punctuated by occasional days off. Today was one of those rare breaks, and he found himself at the stables in the morning. Jamie was on duty, with his own day off scheduled for tomorrow.

Rad had managed to borrow a few knives from the kitchen and now stood in an empty stall, hurling them at the wooden walls.

The clamor of clinking metal filled the space as blade tips struck—or bounced off—the intended target. Only one in ten stuck, and the angle was usually off. They were butter knives—not meant for throwing—but they were all he had to practice with.

Gathering the blades, Rad surveyed the scratches and slight warping. He would have to return them once he had straightened them out in the vise near Hadley's shed, but the damage was obvious. With any luck, no one would discover the additional wear of the household utensils.

A sudden rush of air passed his ear, followed by a metallic blur. A polished throwing knife embedded itself in the wooden wall with a resounding *thud.*

Rad spun around, clutching the kitchen knives close to his chest.

Hadley stood behind him, arms crossed, his grizzled face unreadable.

Rad braced for the slap he was sure was coming, but it didn't. Hadley smiled.

"Listen well, lad," Hadley said, his tone harsh. "Those are for spreading strawberry jam over buttered toast." He pointed at the knives with a gnarled finger. "Not for hurling at walls. You'll bust them up so bad, you'll have no excuse for why they're bent. And in case you didn't know, those are solid silver. Get caught with them and accused of stealing? You'll lose more than your breakfast—you'll lose a hand. Thieves aren't tolerated."

Rad flinched, trying to hide the knives in his small hands. One slipped from his grasp and fell toward the ground. With a quick flick of his boot, he kicked it upward, catching it.

"Sorry," he muttered.

Hadley's weathered face didn't soften, but neither did it harden further. His head cocked to the side. "Been watching you," he said, stepping forward and wrenching the throwing knife from the wall. It took three solid yanks to free it. "You're nimble for a nine-year-old..."

"I'm ten!"

"Ten, it is," Hadley said with a curt nod. "Well, ten or not, you've got no business wrecking knives meant for fancy tables." He held out his hand. "Give them here. I'll see they're put back before anyone notices. You have my word, and I won't tell."

Rad hesitated but handed the knives over, one by one, his movements reluctant.

"Good lad," Hadley said. He pressed the throwing knife into Rad's hands. Its weight and balance were far better than the utensils Rad had been using. "Hold onto this until I get back. And don't cut yourself. If you do, I'll leave you to bleed out—make no mistake about it."

The throwing knife rested in Rad's small, calloused hands, its weight grounding him in a way that was both unfamiliar and thrilling. The balance was perfect. For a moment, he imagined he could send the blade sailing clear across the estate, piercing any target with ease.

Testing his confidence, Rad flipped the blade into the air. It arced gracefully, and as it descended, he caught it in a smooth motion. Again, he sent it skyward, the rhythm of steel and motion felt right. It felt like the blade belonged to him, like they were meant to be together.

Eager to test his skill further, he shifted the knife to his left hand. It was awkward at first, but he persisted, noting his left and right were the same. As he had done with the right, he flipped it up and caught it, twirled it without fear of being cut.

Hadley's return snapped him out of it, but the feeling didn't go away. In his hands, Hadley carried a round wooden target, worn and scarred from years of use. Without a word, he hung it on the wall, its weathered surface still bearing traces of a faded red center.

"Before I let you throw your knife, you need to learn about it. Understand?"

Rad's eyes lit up as he nodded.

"Put it in your palms, like you're begging for food."

Rad did as asked. Hadley's bent finger pointed. "This is the handle, guard, cheek, and tip. They all have different sizes, depending on what you want to do with it. Go on, grip it, like a hammer."

Rad's fingers curled around the knife's handle, the grip felt familiar and was comforting.

"Hammers point upward lad," Hadley said. "That grip is for stabbing, not throwing."

Rad reversed his grip so the tip was aimed at the roof.

"Show me how you throw," Hadley said, his voice rough but not unkind. "Go on. We'll fix your mistakes as we go. Hit the target—show me what you got."

Rad took a breath, feeling the knife's balance once more. With a flick of his wrist, he let it fly.

Thunk.

The blade didn't find the red center, but it lodged into the battered wood target. Rad's chest swelled, his eyes widened, and he said, "I hit it!"

"Terrible! The only thing you got right was keeping your body relaxed. Stand up straight. You throw right-handed, keep your right foot forward. Left-handed, left foot forward. It feels awkward now, but there's a reason for it." Hadley handed Rad a second throwing knife. "Show me—stand correctly."

Rad fidgeted, trying to find what he thought was the proper stance. Hadley's strong hands quickly corrected him, aligning his shoulders and positioning his feet. Rad adjusted, his grip firm as he flicked the knife. It struck the target, this time landing much closer to the red center.

"Still terrible," Hadley grumbled. "Watch my feet. This is why we start with our lead foot forward." Hadley stepped into position with unexpected elegance, tossing the knife where it *thunked* into the target dead center. He retrieved the knife with two yanks. "See that? Get your feet right, and the rest will follow. Later, when we work on power, you'll see why it matters. Got it?"

"I got it," Rad said. "I can do it."

Hidden in his sleeve, Hadley pulled out two gleaming throwing knives. "A hundred throws a day, each hand, until you can hit the red dot from across the stables. Footwork first. When you can do it, come find me, and I'll teach you more."

Rad didn't respond. He cradled the blades as if they were treasures.

"I'll get you a sheath," Hadley said as he rolled up the long sleeve of his shirt. There, nestled along his forearm was a black leather band with space for two throwing knives. "This one won't fit you." Hadley scratched his head. "I may have smaller ones in my shed. But for now, stow them away here in the stables, not on your person. Understand?"

"Yes," Rad answered.

"Those knives stay here, no taking them to your room or into the manor—got it?"

"Got it."

Hadley paused a moment, his face became stone and his rough hand gripped Rad's shoulder. "Don't let anyone see them. They're not toys—no playing around, no bragging to the other boys or showing off to the pretty girls or mentioning this to Miss Abigail. This stays between us. You brag about this, and you'll wish for your Da's belt instead of mine. Got it?"

Rad's imagination ran wild for a moment, his eyes sweeping over the leather harnesses hanging on the stable wall. The thought of those striking his back instead of Da's belt sent a chill down his spine.

His restless feet shuffled against the straw-covered ground, and he resolved then and there—he would never give Hadley a reason to prove his threat. "What... what about Jamie? He'll see me practice."

"He knows how to keep his mouth shut," Hadley said, brushing off the concern. "I'll deal with him. Your only worry is making sure no one else catches you. We'll work together on this, me and you. Partners?"

Rad squeezed the knives. "Partners."

Three weeks of relentless practice—marked by aching arms, blistered fingers, and more than a few nicks—had transformed Rad's fumbling throws into confident precision.

His hands, once clumsy with the twin knives, now sent them sailing into the red dot on the target, though its once-bright hue had faded beneath the countless strikes.

Pride swelled within him.

Today, he would prove to Hadley the lessons hadn't been wasted.

He still wondered, though, why Hadley had allowed him to learn to throw knives. He was sure it broke some household rule.

What fascinated him more was Hadley's *lack* of interest in his progress.

He didn't ask about how he was doing, his sole focus was on the stable and keeping it running efficiently.

Under the warm glow of an afternoon sun on his rare day off, Rad lingered in the stables, his sanctuary.

The knives twirled in his hands, their polished steel catching the light as he flipped, spun, and tossed them with ease. Each motion had become second nature, a seamless rhythm honed by hours of focus. He waited, knowing Hadley would appear soon, as he always did when least expected.

The stables were quieter than usual.

With his Da and Tristin away on business, the house breathed easier, its bustling routine subdued and relaxed.

The horses were fewer in number, granting a rare tranquility to the day.

Jamie had long since finished his tasks and was off somewhere playing with the other boys.

Rad had no such inclination.

The boys' indifference toward him echoed the distance of his own family. He found no comfort in their company. The only relief he found was the gleam of the throwing knives and thoughts of his improving skills.

Hadley was the exception, as he did pay attention to him and his work in the stables. Though gruff and guarded, the puzzling horse-master protected Rad from the others' indifference. His name alone—'Hadley the Pillager'—carried weight, an unspoken warning that kept curiosity at bay.

Yet, for all the stories whispered among the servants, Rad wanted to know the truth. What lay behind his menacing title? What life had shaped the man who now taught him to throw knives?

When Hadley finally appeared, his crooked grin broke the tension lingering while Rad waited. It wasn't a warm or open smile, but it was Hadley's—a unique gesture he reserved for those he considered worthy.

"Smiles are for ladies," he had once said with a shrug.

Yet here it was, a quiet acknowledgment of the bond they shared.

"You been practicing?" Hadley asked, his pipe clenched between yellowed teeth. He removed it, tapped the ashes out against the stall wall, and brushed the remnants into the straw with the toe of his boot.

"Every day." Rad juggled the two blades in a hypnotic rhythm, their polished surfaces catching the light. "I can hit the middle of the target."

"Show me."

Rad caught the knives mid-air, pivoting toward the familiar target halfway across the stables.

The distance wasn't daunting—he'd done this a hundred times.

Probably a thousand.

"Not there," Hadley said, his hand firm on Rad's shoulder. He pointed upward. "See the knot on the crossbeam? Up yonder. It's your mark. Hit it."

Rad's gaze shifted to the beam, spotting the knot—a dark, distorted spot against the smooth wood, like a swollen grape. His practice didn't involve targets so high, but to him, a target was a target. What was the difference?

With a steadying breath, Rad adjusted his stance.

His right foot edged forward, toe pointing at the beam, his grip on the knife relaxed but precise.

In a single fluid motion, he released the blade.

It sliced through the air, spinning once before striking dead-center, cleaving the knot cleanly.

The faint sound of wood splintering marked the success of his throw, but Rad wasn't finished.

He shifted the second blade to his left hand, aligning his feet for the throw.

The motion was smooth, his body moving as if the knife were an extension of his will. The blade flew true, embedding itself into the wood a hairsbreadth from the first.

The faint scrape of metal against metal punctuated the success.

Rad thought he'd get praise, but instead, Hadley smacked the back of his head and made him stumble forward.

"You showing off, lad? Trying to make a fool of me?"

"No! I was only—"

"You show off like that again, and I'll crack your skull in two. This isn't for show—it's for killing." Hadley's voice was sharp, cutting deep. "In six months, you'll be a dangerous lad if you listen to me. If you don't? Deaf or dead."

Rigid, Rad held back the fear—Hadley was angry. He was one offence away from smacking him again. "I'll listen." Rad's voice was steady. "I'm sorry. I thought you'd be pleased with my progress."

Hadley didn't answer right away. "I am pleased with your skill. But today's lesson is this—don't show off. Your throw would've killed a man if it hit him in the eye. You don't kill a man twice, and you sure as hell don't waste a fine blade on a corpse. You need it for the next kill if you're in a desperate fight."

The thought made him shiver; killing a person had never crossed his mind while practicing.

The cold truth hit him—these knives were made for killing.

And he was learning how to use them.

Rad didn't know how to respond to Hadley.

Hadley stuffed his pipe into a weathered leather pouch and slid it into his battered coat pocket. Moving to retrieve the knives, he raised a pitchfork and tapped them free from their lofty perch.

A groan escaped him as his body spasmed in pain.

The pitchfork slipped from his grasp, but before it clattered to the ground, Hadley snatched it mid-fall with a sharp motion of his right hand.

He rolled his left shoulder as if to loosen it.

"Are you hurt?" Rad asked with genuine concern for the horse-master.

"Of course not! I'm still standing, aren't I?" Hadley barked. "You'll know when I'm hurt because I'll be flat on the ground, dead."

He handed the retrieved blades back to Rad, then reached beneath his coat, withdrawing a different weapon from a sheath. The knife gleamed in the light, its long, tapered point measuring eight inches—built for piercing, not slashing. It had a sturdy, well-balanced design, and Rad could feel its weight in the air, even before it touched his palm.

The handle, crafted from polished dark teakwood, bore a stark contrast to the sharp steel. At the base of the blade, an inscription caught Rad's eye.

DARTER.

"This is *Darter*," Hadley began, his tone reverent.

He held the blade aloft, letting the light catch its tapered point.

"This blade is meant for puncturing lungs, plucking out eyes, piercing hearts. It's not the first *Darter* I've had. There's a long line of *Darters*—lost, broken, or left behind in a fight."

He turned to Rad, his expression hardening, eyes sharp with meaning.

"Always name your important blades, lad. They're your family. When no one else will have you, your blades will. Remember that."

The notion wasn't lost on Rad. His family had abandoned him, but these knives wouldn't. Rad hesitated, glancing down at the throwing knives in his hands.

"I should name these two?"

Hadley hissed through his teeth, the sound sharp enough to make Rad flinch.

"No, you dolt," he snapped. "Those are throwing knives—disposable. I've got dozens hidden in my cottage and eight on me right now." He tapped his chest, both forearms, and belt for emphasis. "What I mean is, name your distinct blades. The ones that matter. *Darter* matters."

Hadley offered *Darter* hilt-first to Rad, his expression didn't soften. "Now, take this and hold it. It is like a small sword—do you know what the parts are?"

Rad nodded, recalling the book on magic swords he had stashed in his room. "Uh, pommel, guard, grip, blade?"

"From here to here is hilt," Hadley said, his finger pointing. "From here to here is the blade. The hilt is made up of the pommel, grip, and cross-guard."

"Cross-guard," Rad echoed.

"The blade has a tip, an edge, and a central edge. *Darter* is meant for stabbing, not slashing."

"Is that why the blade is so thin?"

"Aye," Hadley answered. "But's thick, so you can throw it when you need to. Now, handle it, tell me what you feel."

Rad, as he'd done countless times before, flicked both throwing knives into the nearby wall with ease. They *thunked* in unison, the sound reverberating through the stable.

He cringed, bracing for a slap to the head from Hadley.

No backhand came, no sharp lecture followed.

"Go on. Handle it," the old man said, his voice rough. "Get the feel for it."

Rad hesitated for a moment before taking the dagger. Its balance was extraordinary, its weight solid and reassuring.

He turned it in his hands, letting his fingers explore every nuance and imperfection. Despite the blade's formidable length and sharp tip, it spun with a flick of his wrist.

He glanced at Hadley, uncertain if his fascination would be deemed disrespectful.

"You can show off," Hadley said, nodding. "That's how you learn."

Encouraged, Rad let the blade twirl again. He flipped it, caught it, rolled it across his knuckles, and cradled it in his palm.

He inspected it closer, noting the fine scratches and subtle blemishes giving it character.

Another flip, and the dagger balanced on the tip of his index finger, its weight heavy yet thrilling.

"Where'd you learn to do that?" Hadley asked.

Rad shrugged. "It feels right." With a smooth motion, he let the blade drop into his waiting hand, gripping the hilt lightly.

Hadley gestured toward a column across the stable. "See the column? Put it right in the middle. Gentle throw—this one's got more weight."

Rad nodded, squinting at the spot and taking a deep breath to steady himself.

He aligned his feet as Hadley had taught him, exhaling slowly as he flung the dagger.

It spun once, slicing through the air before embedding in the column with a satisfying *thunk*.

No vibration, no wobble. It sat still, buried in the wood like it belonged there.

A rush of exhilaration surged through Rad, tingling in his chest. *Darter* wasn't just a knife—it felt sharp and dangerous, like it could do anything.

It wasn't the thought of what it could do, the lives it could take.

It was the mastery of it, the sense of holding a dangerous weapon and knowing he could command it.

He didn't expect to enjoy it so much—it made him feel strong and full of wonder. Yet he hesitated. *Darter* wasn't just sharp; it was meant to end lives.

"Your throw sank two inches into solid wood. What do you think it'd do to a man's flesh?" Hadley asked, his voice quiet, dangerous.

Rad thought for a moment. "Go deeper?"

"Only if you missed bone," Hadley replied with a wry smile.

He yanked *Darter* free with a few deliberate tugs and turned back to Rad.

"This time, throw it harder. More force. You've got the accuracy—no doubt you're a natural—but power's what'll make you dangerous. Right now, at ten, you're not knocking men off their feet. When you're fourteen, older and stronger, you'll be able to send a blade like *Darter* through a man's skull. Watch closely. Follow my movements."

Hadley's stance shifted, fluid and precise.

His movements weren't practical or easy—they were calculated, artful.

Rad was fascinated, as the older man executed a series of steps and pivots, every motion purposeful. Hadley transferred his weight, his body generating momentum.

It was like a dance—but not the fancy kind with music and spinning.

Every turn and twist served dual purposes: evasion and power.

When Hadley let *Darter* fly, the dagger became a silver streak, slicing the air with a deadly hum before sinking halfway into the column.

"Four inches," Hadley said with a note of satisfaction, gesturing to the embedded blade. "What did you see?"

Rad nodded, still stunned. "You were... dancing."

"You dance with pretty ladies and devils," Hadley said, his tone dry and edged with a trace of humor.

He paused, considering Rad's analogy.

"If you want to call it dancing, fine by me. You're starting to understand. Now try it—do what I did. And don't forget your footwork."

Rad stepped toward the column, intent on retrieving *Darter*, but Hadley's firm hand stopped him. "Leave it. Use these instead."

From his belt, Hadley pulled two sleek throwing knives, their edges catching the light. He handed them to Rad. "Your knives are dull from your practicing. *Darter* will end up the same way if we keep burying it in wood. Let's see what you can do with these baby blades, they are a bit heavier than your throwers. I'll take your little ones, and I'll teach you how to sharpen them later."

Rad took the knives, feeling their balance. They didn't have *Darter's* weight, but they would suffice. Practice was practice, and he was excited to see what he could do.

Under Hadley's gruff but steady guidance, Rad mastered the art of throwing knives. The three key techniques—spin, bounce, and crow hop—required a combination of precision, body control, and rhythm.

Each throw demanded full focus, using his body's momentum to drive the blade with deadly accuracy. At first, Rad's arms ached from the relentless practice, but over time, his movements became instinctual, fluid.

Throwing knives started to feel normal, even though most nights he was so tired he fell asleep with one of Abby's books still in his arms.

The latest book, *Chronicles of the Great Kingdom*, was about Haddensack, Ornst's formidable northern neighbor, and the sprawling duchies of Faustron, Halstead, and Pehrone. Rad devoured the tales of ancient alliances, border conflicts, and the quiet maneuverings keeping politics intact. The stories of rivalries between noble houses, secret treaties, and grand battles were distant but thrilling, offering him a glimpse into the complexities of a world he was beginning to understand.

As spring melted into summer, the days slipped by in a blur of stable work and knife practice. Thoughtful Abby marked his birthday with a basket of chocolates, a small indulgence more precious than any grand gesture—he shared the delights with Hadley and Jamie.

He and Abby continued exchanging books in secret, though Rad suspected no one cared about it. Where was the harm in letting him read?

Over the summer, Rad turned his attention to *Arcane Foundations: A Study of Practical Magic*. The book's descriptions of simple enchantments captivated him: merchants conjuring blocks of ice to cool goods, street wizards enchanting lanterns to burn forever, and farmers using magic to draw water from deep underground. These were practical, everyday magics, not the world-shaking sorcery of legends. But it fascinated Rad regardless. If such wonders existed, what else was possible?

Another book, *The Tactician's Manual*, proved a much harder challenge. Its dense prose and advanced concepts frustrated him, the language often sailing far above his grasp. Several times, he was tempted to toss the book aside and never look at it again, but the intricacies of the logic drew him back. The complex strategies, the careful balance of deception and anticipation, and the sharp insight into Human behavior fascinated him. He found himself reading certain sections again, trying to understand how the legendary generals thought and acted.

His current obsession was *Heroes of Haddensack*, a collection of tales about knights, rangers, and other bold figures who had shaped the kingdom. He pored over accounts of giants defeated in the northern wilds, Gnoll tribes driven from Human lands, and daring campaigns waged over disputed territories. The stories were thrilling, but what struck Rad most was how each hero faced more than monsters and armies—they dealt with political intrigue, impossible odds, and personal struggles.

To Rad, these books weren't just stories. They were tools. Each one unlocked a spark of ambition in him, a sharpened sense of observation, and the quiet realization knowledge could cut as deeply as any blade.

Whether it was magic, strategy, or history, Rad soaked it in, his hunger for understanding growing with every page.

As summer gave way to autumn, the leaves turned vibrant hues, and a crisp chill crept into the evenings. The looming harvest brought a hum of activity to the manor, but Rad's world remained focused on the stables, reading books, and training under Hadley's sharp eye.

The passing months were far from idle.

Rad's mastery with the throwing knives became undeniable; Hadley declared him a natural. He could strike a target from any stance— stationary or in motion, even in tight quarters—and his ambidexterity made him all the more formidable.

Hadley expanded his lessons to include combat with piercing weapons like *Darter*, teaching Rad to wield a blade in a fight rather than only throwing it.

Their bond grew stronger during these lessons, forged through companionship and discipline. It wasn't fatherly affection, but Hadley's stern guidance carried a weight Rad had come to respect.

The occasional boxing of his ears tempered Rad's youthful arrogance, though secretly, those moments of reprimand brought him pride. They affirmed his knifework was worth noticing.

Today marked a break from routine as Rad finished his chores early and retreated to his room.

The puzzle he had transcribed was on the verge of revealing its secrets, its solution tantalizingly close. The mechanism involved sliding panels into place, aligning them to unlock a door promising untold treasures—gold, gems, and answers to mysteries he could only imagine.

The image on the puzzle showed two crossed knives, accompanied by an inscription in High Ornst: *Leskaré da-nater dormitas.*

The phrase both intrigued and unsettled him. 'Leskaré' was a name shrouded in infamy, whispered in fearful tones. It referred to a shadowy organization of assassins and thieves whose influence extended across the entirety of Eldor—the known lands.

Within the sanctuary of his room, Rad bolted the door and sat with the pilfered High Ornst dictionary clutched in his hands. The phrase was a riddle demanding to be solved. He pored over the words, translating them into the common tongue, eager to grasp their meaning.

Leskaré never sleeps.

Rad's head swam with questions.

What could the phrase mean? A password, perhaps? Or did these assassins and thieves wield some dark sorcery that kept them forever vigilant, fueling their wicked deeds?

He collected his scattered notes and slipped on soft leather shoes to muffle his steps. With his lantern casting a faint glow, he ventured into the hidden passage behind his closet. His previous ventures into the manor's secret depths had uncovered little of value—only fragments of lives he wasn't a part of.

From the safety of his hidden peepholes, Rad observed the household, catching bits and pieces of lives he couldn't understand.

Wilkins marched through the estate like he owned it, barking orders at the other servants. He treated them like dirt, snapping commands with a sharp tone. When Da was nearby, Wilkins got louder, acting like he ran the whole house and wanted everyone to know it.

Da spent most of his evenings in the study, surrounded by papers and maps. Rad often watched him through the tiny hole. Sometimes, Gabrielle came in, her blue dress neat and perfect like always. They hugged for too long, and once, Rad saw Da's hand resting on her hip, rubbing the fabric. They whispered quietly to each other, and Gabrielle left soon after, smoothing her dress and smiling a little as she walked away.

In the master bedroom, Ma sat at her vanity, absently combing her hair. Sometimes she wiped tears from her cheeks, other times she stared into the mirror like she didn't recognize herself. She and Da didn't spend much time in the same room.

His siblings were just as strange.

Tristin stood in front of his mirror, flexing his arms and tilting his chin, as if he were trying to impress himself.

Bella sneaked cookies into her room, nibbling on them as she twirled around in her stockinged feet.

Marie fussed over her countless dresses, holding them up and muttering about how she needed more clothes.

Abby was different. She sat on her bed, reading books, her face calm and focused.

Rad longed to talk to Abby more than he dared to admit. Her quiet smiles and thoughtful gestures—like the books she continued to slip him—were his salvation in a world determined to isolate him. But talking to her openly, even for a moment, was out of the question. If Da or Wilkins caught them together, there'd be trouble—for both of them.

At first, they had found a way to cheat the rules.

Abby, brilliant and thoughtful, had tucked small notes into the pages of the books she gave him. Tiny scraps of parchment, folded and hidden between chapters, filled with quick thoughts and questions.

"Are you well? Are your hands still hurting?" one note had read, the ink slightly smudged, as if she'd written it in a hurry.

Rad had replied in the same way, his handwriting cramped and uneven in the margins of the next book he returned to her. *"I'm fine. Hands are better. How's Ma?"*

The notes became their secret conversations, passed back and forth under the cover of shared books. They wrote about everything—how much they missed each other, the daily frustrations of life in the manor, and the small jokes made the loneliness more bearable.

"Wilkins looks like he's been chewing lemons all day. Did someone steal his bourbon?" Abby had written once. Rad's grin had lingered for hours after reading it.

But the game had come to a halt one afternoon when Wilkins had almost caught them.

Rad still remembered the way his heart had hammered in his chest as he flipped through the book Abby had left in the hayloft. The familiar folded scrap of parchment he had expected was missing. His fingers hesitated on the pages, then he checked between the pages again.

Something was wrong.

The answer came the next day, when Abby darted into the stables late in the afternoon. Rad had been brushing Vanguard when the sound of quick, light footsteps made him glance up. She stood at the entrance, nervous, clutching the doorframe and glancing over her shoulder.

"Abby?" he whispered, setting the brush down. "What are you doing here?"

Her face was pale, her expression tight. "No more notes," she said whispered. "Wilkins almost caught me. He flipped through the book— I thought for sure he'd find your message."

Rad's stomach sank. "What happened?"

"Nothing. He didn't find anything, but it was too close. If he had..." Abby shook her head, her hair falling into her face. "We'll have to stop the notes. It's too risky. If Da or Wilkins find out, they'll stop the books altogether—or worse."

Rad opened his mouth to protest, but she cut him off. "I mean it, Rad. We'll figure out something else, but no more notes. Not now."

Her gaze darted to the stable doors again, her nerves palpable. "I have to go," she said, already stepping back, "before anyone realizes I'm here."

She was gone, her footsteps fading as quickly as they had come.

Rad stood still for a moment, his head full of thoughts.

No more notes.

The words echoed in his mind, sharp and heavy. Their small conversations—those scraps of connection had carried him through the loneliness—were gone. The books would remain, but they'd be silent now, no longer the threads tying them together.

He picked up the brush again, his grip tightening.

Vanguard nudged him, as if sensing his frustration, but Rad ignored the horse's questioning eyes. He couldn't let himself dwell on what they had lost. Abby was right—if Wilkins or Da discovered their secret, the consequences would be far worse than losing the notes.

Still, the hollow ache in his chest refused to fade.

Guided by instinct, Rad snuck through the hidden passages of the mansion. In his hand, he clutched a single page bearing the correct combination for the puzzle—a key to unlock its mysteries. He intended to head straight to the door, convinced the panels would slide into alignment with ease.

But as he neared the cellars, distant voices reached his ears, drawing him to a halt.

Curiosity overcame him.

Peering through a concealed opening, he saw his Da speaking with an unfamiliar man amidst the rows of wine barrels, mixing tanks, and racks of bottles.

The stranger's appearance caught Rad's eye. He was dressed like someone important; a navy coat with shiny gold buttons and a folded silk scarf in the pocket. His long mustache matched his gray, bushy eyebrows, giving him a stern look. His black boots gleamed, and his trousers were spotless, like he'd never worked a day in them. In the soft lantern light, the man stood straight and stiff, as if he were waiting to be praised—or scolded.

"Mister Bazalgette," Da began, his voice cordial. "Your reputation precedes you. I've heard of your experience with wine and spirits—particularly your fondness for Sonner vintages."

"Please, call me Gaspard," the man replied, his voice was like velvet. "And yes, I am the best at what I do. You will not be disappointed."

Da's expression darkened, his tone hardening. "The last man I hired made promises like yours. He failed me. I had to dump hundreds of barrels into the ocean and send him out of Ornst—without his fingers."

Gaspard's composure wavered, a flicker of uncertainty as he straightened his collar, but it vanished in an instant. "A dreadful fate. Believe me, I understand the stakes. Failure is not in my nature."

"I like your confidence," Da said, tapping his thigh. "But remember who you work for. You answer to Xavier von Schule. My reputation, my reach, and my expectations are unmatched. I won't tolerate incompetence or anything less than perfection."

Gaspard inclined his head, adjusting his posture. "Understood, completely. Now, what is the task at hand? What are we replicating?"

Da reached for a small crate with the word *SONNER* painted in white across the front. Stamped beside it was a white circle overlaid with an offset black one. Inside, cushioned in straw, nestled six bottles of dark red wine. He pulled one free and handed it to Gaspard.

The man accepted it with quiet reverence, as if it might shatter under too firm a grip. His fingers brushed the green glass the way Rad had seen Hadley stroke Shadow's muzzle—soft, slow, full of memory. Gaspard turned the bottle, studying the ornate label and the familiar eclipsed symbol.

"The Eclipse Wine," he murmured.

"You believe that nonsense?" Da asked.

Gaspard nodded slowly. "As part of the appeal—yes. I believe the vines were elven. That a wizard coaxed magic into their growth. And the eclipse that year… that much is certain."

"It's part of the mystique," Da said. "But I won't overplay it."

"You won't need to," Gaspard replied. "Once people know it's *The* Eclipse Wine, they'll want to believe it all. Every word."

"That bottle is your first payment," Da said, his tone heavy with expectation. He gestured toward the other five bottles cradled in the crate. "Five siblings for you to claim—if you succeed. Along with the rest of the coin I promised. The formulation must be perfected within two weeks. In three weeks, I'm hosting a gala here at the manor to unveil the wine. It *must* be ready."

Gaspard studied the bottle before placing it with care on the table. "You have worthwhile stock to work with, I trust?"

Da pointed to the rows of barrels lining the cellar wall. "Every barrel is full. Same vintage, same fermentation period. It's a fine wine on its own—worthy of mention if served alone. It is like this vintage in taste and color. How much can you make?"

Gaspard's sharp eyes flicked to the barrels, his mind calculating the numbers. "I can produce six thousand bottles. I'll need one barrel for testing, leaving five thousand seven hundred. Perhaps more if I achieve the proper formulation early. I must remind you, though, this process will involve trial and error."

"You're allowed one barrel," Da said. "Anything more is wasteful."

Gaspard's lips parted, a protest forming, but he thought better of it, nodding with reluctant acceptance.

Xavier's hand swept through the air, dismissing further objections. "Open it. Let's share a part of your reward now."

Gaspard moved with the elegance of a noble as he drew a leather kit from within his coat. From it, he produced a small knife with a polished white bone handle. He sliced through the wax covering the bottle's top, each motion measured and clean. He reached for a silver corkscrew, its handle matching the knife's bone material, and inserted it into the cork with a deft twist. He extracted the cork with a soft puff of release.

With bottle in hand, he and Xavier moved to a nearby table. Upon it rested a rounded glass container and two generous, round glasses.

"Definitely worth decanting," Gaspard said. He tilted the bottle over the container, a decanter, with a steady hand. The dark liquid streamed forth. Halfway through the pour he paused, frowning.

"I see sediment," Gaspard remarked as he placed the bottle on the table. Reaching for a quill, he dipped it into an inkwell and made a quick notation on a piece of parchment.

"We have lees," Xavier said with a dismissive wave. "It won't be an issue. Note the amount, and we'll ensure the same goes into each bottle before corking. Simple."

Gaspard nodded and continued decanting the wine, pausing periodically to manage the flow of sediment. When he had poured to his satisfaction, he tipped the bottle and emptied the sludge onto a small plate. He leaned in close, scrutinizing the sludge before murmuring, "Half a spoonful." He marked it on the parchment, then stole a fond glance at the SONNER bottle before adding another note.

The scene stirred memories of his Da hosting similar wine-tasting events. Those gatherings were rigid, formal affairs filled with rules, protocols, and endless discussions about fruity notes—whatever those were supposed to be.

The importance baffled him.

He'd once stolen a sip of wine from the kitchen and found it revolting. Why had Da gone to the trouble of hiring Gaspard? To make the wine taste better?

Gaspard swirled the decanter gently before pouring a precise amount into one glass. He handed one to Xavier, then poured an identical measure into his own. Gaspard tilted his glass back and forth, holding it up to the lantern's glow.

"Deep ruby bordering on purple," he mused. "Beautiful. Simply beautiful." He jotted more notes on his parchment. "The color alone may defeat us. It only comes with age. These are mature wines."

"The base wine is similar enough," Xavier assured him. "The color won't be an issue. I've been waiting years for these barrels to mature."

Gaspard's features tightened as he lowered his sharp face into the glass. He inhaled deeply, his long nose quivering as it absorbed the aroma.

"Burnt cedar," he announced with satisfaction. "Ah, yes, unmistakable." He jotted it down, muttering as he worked. "Ripe mulberries. Fresh mint." Closing his eyes, he drew another deep sniff. "Sweet pipe tobacco… druid smoke, if you've ever had it. Yes. Tobacco."

Xavier mirrored Gaspard's movements, sniffing his glass with visible focus, though he left the notetaking to the expert. Watching them, Rad marveled at the nonsense of men praising drink that smelled like charred wood and Hadley's pipe.

Gaspard swirled the wine again, tipping it to his lips. "No spitting this out," he declared as if making an oath. "Not on your life."

He took a sip, swishing and gurgling the liquid before swallowing with an audible smack of his lips. "Bitter dark chocolate," he uttered. He scribbled more notes before he repeated the tasting ritual. "Silky. Polished. Balanced acidity. Burnt sugar raspberries. Cedar… yes, more cedar."

He paused to sniff his glass again, closing his eyes and nodding to himself. "This will be a challenge to replicate. Many subtle notes and flavors to introduce."

"You claim to be the best vintner this side of Sonner. Prove it." Xavier's tone carried the weight of expectation.

"I'll need the agreed coin to acquire the finest raw materials," Gaspard replied, his voice steady but resolute. "And the stipend for my assistant."

Xavier reached to his waist, extracting a pouch and dropping it onto the table with a heavy *clunk*. The soft leather sagged under its weight.

Gold.

"This should suffice. You have two weeks to perfect the formulation. Earlier would be better. Logistics to consider."

"You've secured genuine labels? Proper green bottles?"

Xavier scoffed. "Naturally. The labels come from the same print house Sonner uses and have already been aged. Six thousand, ready to go. The bottles are sourced from the same family supplying Sonner. If you need extra hands, I can assign more servants to assist."

"Perhaps for manual tasks," Gaspard said, his fingers drumming the tabletop as he thought about it. "But the formulation will remain for me and my assistant's eyes only. It's safer—less chance of loose tongues."

"As you wish. Anything you require, my valet Wilkins can procure."

"Certainly."

Xavier took another swig from his glass, savoring the wine as he leaned back. "Are your quarters to your liking?"

"Yes, I appreciate the generous space. It will suit me well when I'm not working here." Gaspard's gaze swept across the cellar before settling back on Xavier. "On second thought, could you have beds brought down? It would be more efficient for my assistant and I to sleep here."

"Wilkins will see to it." Xavier rose from his chair, pinning Gaspard with a sharp stare. "Two weeks," he said, his voice firm. He pounded the table once for emphasis. "Two weeks."

Da took his leave, disappearing behind the towering barrels and winemaking equipment.

Gaspard, now alone, indulged in the remnants of Xavier's unfinished glass, savoring it. He settled at the table with the half-full decanter and his round glass, his features softening into quiet satisfaction. By the time Rad slipped away toward his original destination, Gaspard sat with his eyes closed, rolling the glass between his hands. He looked like he was dreaming and didn't want to wake up.

When Rad reached the hidden door, he realized solving the puzzle was far more difficult than he'd anticipated. He slid the pieces back and forth, attempting to align them to complete the image.

Leskaré da-nater dormitas.

The phrase nagged at him, its meaning as elusive as the puzzle's solution. Frustration mounted with every failed attempt, and at last, he relented, deciding to try again another day when his mind was fresh.

The hour was growing late, and he needed to retreat to his room to record the day's events in his secret journal. The journal held every observation, thought, and discovery he deemed significant.

Tonight, it would take time to detail the secret meeting between Da and Gaspard, but Rad resolved to capture every moment while it was still vivid in his memory.

If the gala was in three weeks, soon the house would be dipped into chaos and the preparations. He made a note to get the evening off so he could watch the festivities.

Chapter Six

∞

The Gala

By trading two days off to Jamie, Rad had secured the day of the gala for himself, leaving Jamie, Hadley, and the other servants to handle the madness of the arriving guests and their carriages. Rad had expected Hadley to be furious, but the horse-master's reaction surprised him.

"You're a slippery one, I'll give you that," Hadley muttered, adjusting the fit of his stiff formal coat—the pompous thing he was forced to wear for galas. The dark blue coat was too tight around his broad shoulders, the brass buttons gleaming so brightly they reflected the lantern light from the carriage house. "You've wriggled out of the worst of it. Meanwhile, the rest of us get to prance around like fancy boys in these damned outfits."

He tugged at his collar in frustration.

Rad grinned despite himself as he rubbed his shoulders. It was cool this evening and he didn't bring his coat. It didn't matter, this was going to be a short visit.

Hadley caught the expression and shot him a warning with a sideways glance.

"Don't think you've won anything, lad. When the guests roll in, and we're busting our backs parking carriages and keeping the horses calm with all the racket, you'll be the one with an extra day of work waiting for you after the gala's over. Just watch, you'll see."

Jamie came running up, his formal blue uniform too tight, and the trousers were too short. "Where do you want me to go?"

"By the lamppost," Hadley snapped. "Carriages staying, line them along the side drive. Drivers can wait in the carriage house. If not," he twirled a finger, "turn them around and send them out the side."

"Got it," Jamie said, turning toward the lamppost.

Rad laughed.

"And don't think I didn't notice how cunning you think you are. Scheming always comes back to bite you in the arse."

Rad tilted his head. "It's not scheming. It's... strategy."

Hadley snorted, shaking his head. "Strategy, is it? Well, your strategy leaves the rest of us sweating while you get to sit on the top of the stairs." He pointed a finger at Rad, his tone gruff but not unkind. "You owe me and Jamie a favor for this, lad. And don't think I'll forget."

"I already traded two days off to Jamie so this could be my day off," Rad said, his confidence building. "That's all I owe him, nothing more. And I don't owe you anything, old man."

Hadley suppressed a grin, then he smiled. "Good lad," he said. "This old man's still got a few tricks. Just watch."

Rad waved and sprinted toward the side of the manor, knowing he couldn't go in the front with all the commotion.

He circled around the massive deck, came to the back entrance, and went up to the door. Inside he slipped by the lounge room and into the ballroom, where preparations had ended, and he headed toward the stairs. He found a suitable spot on the second-floor staircase overlooking the atrium, where he could watch everything unfold.

The manor buzzed with an air of heightened anticipation, the staff swept up in last minute arrangements as the hour of the gala approached.

Da and Ma emerged in their finest attire, their carefully chosen outfits reflected their status.

From his vantage point, the household transformed, his watchful eyes lingering on his elder brother.

At seventeen, Tristin had only grown more striking. Memories of their confrontation six months earlier flitted through Rad's mind, a victory that felt distant now. Tristin descended the staircase with confidence. His black coat and matching trousers, complemented by a formal hat, made him a picture of polished elegance.

Not once did Tristin glance Rad's way as he went by, his focus consumed by the impending arrival of the guests.

For Rad, the lack of acknowledgment was no slight—it gave him the freedom to observe unnoticed, to exist on the edges where he found himself most comfortable these days.

In the entrance, long tables stood adorned with tall, slender glasses filled with a sparkling drink, its pale color was the same as the straw in the stables. Servants moved with care, adding slices of strawberries to each glass. The fruit's arrival sent the bubbles spiraling upward, a lively dance beneath the flickering candlelight.

Overseeing the entrance was Wilkins, his expression twisted into a self-satisfied sneer as he barked commands and directed the staff like an obsessed general. Rad recalled Wilkins's many private boasts about being the true authority of the household—a claim the valet carried with unshakable arrogance.

Rad froze as Wilkins's sharp gaze found him, pinning him like a cat spotting a mouse. A slow, deliberate gesture followed, his hand cutting through the air—a silent order for Rad to retreat to his room.

Obedient in appearance but defiant in spirit, Rad dipped his head and shuffled out of Wilkins's line of sight, ducking into a shadowed area where he could continue his quiet observation.

The creak of a door on the second floor drew his attention.

Abby emerged, glowing and poised, the girl was becoming a young woman. Almost fourteen, her transformation over the past six months had been impossible to forget.

The knee-length white lace dress swirled around her like wind-caught snow—a style Rad had heard his sisters call 'the latest fashion.' It suited her perfectly, but it was her eyes—bright, unguarded, and full of hope—that made her unforgettable.

When their gazes met, Rad couldn't help but smile, warmth and admiration spilling over in his expression.

Abby's cheeks flushed a rosy crimson, her lips curling into a shy but delighted smile. She went to him, bent down, kissed him on the cheek, and hurried down the stairs, a cascade of white lace trailing behind her.

Bella and Marie emerged moments later, their movements slow and elegant. Their dresses mirrored Abby's in color but were bolder. The designs revealed toned arms and more defined silhouettes, the fabric falling just above the knee to expose lean thighs. Their outfits were completed with white box hats matching Abby's.

Rad could see their beauty—the delicate balance of youthful vibrance and refined elegance—but his smile was met only with smirks.

They descended with arrogance, a stark contrast to Abby's kiss lingering on his cheek.

Observing his family gathered in the hall, a wave of unease swept over Rad, threatening to consume him.

As he studied each family member, the distance between their world and his was insurmountable, an invisible barrier weighing heavily on his mind.

He wasn't a son tonight—only a servant, a ghost amidst the splendor.

Da stood at the center of it all, commanding the room with a distinguished black uniform adorned with gold buttons that gleamed under the chandelier's light. His smile was reserved for the girls, brimming with pride as he praised their beauty.

Nearby, Ma fussed over Tristin, straightening his coat to ensure it fit properly across his broad shoulders. Her dress, cut in the same style as Marie and Bella's but rendered in elegant black, shimmered with subtle style. A matching black box hat, adorned with white feathers, crowned her arranged hair. Pearls as rare as they were beautiful adorned her neck, wrists, and ears—she was the matriarch of the von Schule household.

Rad's gaze shifted to Gabrielle, the governess. Her sleek black dress clung to her lean body, its low-cut neckline both elegant and bold. She wore no hat or jewelry—adhering to the unyielding rules prohibiting servants from displaying wealth—but her natural beauty made jewelry unnecessary.

For a heartbeat, Rad thought Gabrielle had to be the most beautiful woman he had ever seen.

"You were dismissed. And yet, here you are."

Wilkins spoke in a low, sharp whisper as his iron grip clamped down on Rad's arm. Before Rad could react, he was spun around and marched toward the stairs leading to his third-floor room.

The movement lit a spark of defiance in Rad.

Pivoting on the balls of his feet—a reflex sharpened by hours of knife practice—he twisted and knocked his arm against the railing.

"Watch it," Wilkins said sharply, tightening his grip.

Rad clutched his arm and winced, pretending it hurt. Wilkins didn't flinch. He guided Rad up the stairs with firm, unrelenting pressure.

Rad cursed his eleven-year-old body for being too small, too weak. But his resolve was steel.

One day, he swore, *when I'm grown, I'll take his finger and toss it in the mud for the pigs to fight over—just like Hadley said.*

"If I see your sorry face downstairs tonight, I'll lock you in your closet. Not even your dear friend Hadley will get you out. Stay put, or I'll wipe that smirk off your face."

Rad raised an eyebrow. "Hadley's not my friend," he said coolly. "But he does have a way of remembering who messes with the horses."

Wilkins exhaled sharply through his nose. "Stay. In. This. Room." He closed the door with force—less a slam, more a verdict—and the sound carried down all three floors.

Rad's hand moved in a blur, one of his throwing knives flying from its concealed sheath. The silver blade struck the wood near the handle, quivering before going still.

As the vibrations settled, the door creaked open.

Wilkins' menacing face reappeared, his sharp eyes scanning the room. "What are you playing at?"

Rad's expression was an unflinching mask. "I don't know what you're talking about. You're the one slamming doors."

Wilkins' hand gripped the doorframe, mere inches from the embedded knife.

Rad's heart thudded in his chest, but he kept his face calm, waiting for Wilkins to decide if tonight's punishment would escalate further.

"Not a single peep out of you for the rest of the night."

Wilkins glowered before shutting the door again—less forcefully this time.

Rad exhaled, relieved, then retrieved the knife and inspected the blade.

Hadley's lessons on keeping a sharp edge came to mind as he ran a thumb along the steel.

His knives were hidden in the forearm sheaths, snug beneath his sleeves. He had leg sheaths too, but tonight he'd brought the blades anyway—despite Hadley's warning to leave them in the stables.

If he could have a double sheath on each hip, a double sheath on each forearm, and a double sheath on each leg, he could have twelve throwing knives on him.

Twelve.

But he only had two.

Why only two?

The question troubled him as it often did, but Hadley wouldn't relent.

Still, he couldn't shake the longing for a blade like *Darter*—a weapon with weight and presence. He'd asked Hadley over and over to take him into Ornst to find one, but the response was always the same: someday, but not today.

Rad arranged his clothing under the covers, creating a convincing outline of his sleeping form. He extinguished one lantern and took the smaller one with him into the closet.

Slipping through the secret door, he sealed it behind him.

His curiosity propelled him forward.

The mystery of the gala, intertwined with Gaspard's work over the past several weeks, refused to leave his mind. Something important escaped his understanding—a piece of the puzzle he couldn't yet picture.

Navigating through the dim, narrow passageways, Rad made his way to one of the many viewing stations overlooking the grand hall below.

He had overheard snippets of conversation among the cooks, servants, and Wilkins: over a hundred guests were expected, most hailing from Ornst, though some had traveled from distant duchies and the kingdom of Haddensack.

He recalled tidbits from an old book Abby had given him, its pages yellowed and its information from another era. It explained how the collective lands were nominally ruled by Haddensack, the most populated kingdom, with an army unmatched by any other.

Its influence stretched across the duchies and regions, shaping trade and diplomacy alike. Places like Faustron, Halstead, and Pehrone, though similar in size and wealth, lacked the military strength or political unity to rival Haddensack's dominance.

Rad found it fascinating, even if much of it was beyond his understanding. The tangled alliances, subtle rivalries, and shifting loyalties between the rulers were a puzzle he couldn't quite piece together.

The book made it sound as though the duchies were content to play supporting roles, but Rad wondered if it was still true. The book was older, written long before he was born, and he couldn't help but think the current political landscape might be different. Still, the idea of kingdoms interacting like players in a grand game intrigued him.

This knowledge deepened his assumptions.

His Da must wield considerable power to draw such a crowd, nobles from great houses, duchies, and kingdoms. Like other galas, he assumed the event would showcase extravagant food, loads of wine, and celebrations, but the exact purpose remained a secret.

How did it connect to Gaspard, his odd assistant, the cellar, the wine, and the mysterious preparations?

From his elevated perch, Rad had a sweeping view of the grand hall. The front section and the doors to the kitchen were visible. Tables and chairs were arranged, though not nearly enough for all the guests to sit; many would be left standing.

At the room's forefront there was a makeshift stage constructed from wooden crates. Draped in pristine white linen, it stood out as the center of gala. Beside it, a pedestal held an object obscured by a white cloth, its shape suggesting a box.

The tables themselves were adorned with decorations—an indulgent display of crisp apples, juicy plums, and peeled citrus arranged in intricate patterns. The citrus, rare this far north, must have come from the southern provinces—sharp-scented and shining like jewels under the candlelight.

The excess spoke of great expense—wealth meant to be not only savored but seen.

Rad's gaze lingered on the details, and his thoughts turning to Gaspard. The peculiar man with his sharp features and a sharper palate had spent, what, two weeks in the cellar. What role did he play in this grand affair?

What *was* his Da planning?

As the guests began to arrive, they were greeted with gracious smiles by the von Schule family. Da and Tristin escorted the elegant ladies to their preferred seats, while Ma and the girls guided the handsome gentlemen with equal grace.

Rad recognized several of the attendees from past gatherings at the estate.

Names like Hogarth, Frederickson, Regenbogen, Fairmont, and Ruud came to mind, each tied to the shared wealth and status mirroring his father's position in Ornst.

Their attire was equal to their affluence: jackets adorned with gold buttons and jewelry glittering in the lantern light. Everyone was so elegant and dazzling, like they belonged in one of Da's paintings.

The women displayed an array of styles, from modest to daring, their dresses showcasing rich colors and intricate designs. Hats with sweeping brims or dainty veils adorned their styled hair, while their jewelry competed for dominance.

Amid the clinking of glasses and bursts of lively conversation, the gathering swelled with energy. The noise grew, a hum of wealth and celebration, rendering individual words garbled to Rad from his concealed vantage point.

Rad remained there in awe of the joyous occasion.

Servants soon began weaving through the crowd, bearing silver trays laden with tantalizing appetizers.

Rad's stomach tightened with longing as he spotted two classic Ornst delicacies: *bouffes,* savory pastries stuffed with spiced meats, and *porcene frita*, crispy strips of pork skin fried to perfection.

Other trays carried an assortment of delicacies—plump oysters from the Bay of Ornst served with horseradish and lemon wedges, long green peppers oozing melted cheese, wedges of pungent *epoisses* cheese his family adored, and golden sweet rolls dusted with raw sugar and cinnamon.

Rad's mouth watered.

The food was a distant echo of the bland meals he had endured as a servant over the past six months. For a fleeting moment, he yearned to be among the guests, sampling the indulgent food and enjoying the splendor of the gala.

The festivities rose to a climax, the laughter and clinking glasses filling the grand hall with an infectious energy.

As the last of the sparkling wine poured into upraised glasses and the trays of delicacies retreated to the kitchens, Xavier von Schule stepped onto the makeshift stage with a commanding presence.

His polished black coat shimmered under the lantern light, and his silver ring gleamed as he tapped it against his empty round glass, the same ones Rad had seen in the cellar.

The crystalline notes resonated, rippling through the air.

One by one, the guests followed suit, their own glasses chiming until the grand hall grew still moments later, anticipation thick in the silence.

Servants darted forward, refilling every glass without being obtrusive.

One such glass didn't simply find its way to Xavier—it was delivered. Gabrielle approached with effortless poise, her sleek black dress catching the light with every step. She carried the crystal flute like it was meant for royalty, her movements smooth and unhurried.

Without a word, she offered it to him, her eyes shining—not with flirtation, but with triumph. This was her moment, and she knew it.

Then she turned and walked away, each step measured, deliberate. A faint smile played at her lips as she basked in the weight of every gaze.

Conversations faltered.

All eyes followed the elegant lines of her body.

Everyone noticed.

Ma noticed.

Rad frowned. It was strange—he would've expected Ma to hand Da the drink, or maybe one of his sisters.

But it was Gabrielle. The governess.

He glanced at Ma. Her expression was cold, tense with dread.

In Da's study… his hand, resting on Gabrielle's hip, rubbing…

The long hugs…

The private smiles…

Rad didn't understand everything.

But he understood enough.

Xavier raised the glass high. With his other hand, he set aside his empty tumbler, took a measured sip of the sparkling wine, and let the moment stretch—heavy with meaning, and power.

"Ladies and gentlemen," he began, his voice resonated to every corner of the room, "my esteemed guests and cherished friends, I bid you the warmest of welcomes to this night of revelry and grandeur. I am, as you well know, your ever-gracious host, Xavier von Schule!"

The crowd erupted into applause, cheers interspersed by whistles and the stamping of feet.

Xavier spread his arms as if embracing the compliments, his smile broad. With a playful tap of his glass, he brought them to silence. The audience, charmed and captivated, obeyed, their sparkling glasses raised in friendship.

"Tonight," he continued, "we are not merely gathered to indulge in the splendor of fine wine, exquisite food, and unparalleled company—though indeed, we shall enjoy all these delights to their fullest! Tonight, we celebrate the enduring legacy of Ornst, our beloved city of light and wealth. Let us bask in her majesty, for she is a jewel among jewels, a beacon of prosperity shining across all Eldor!"

A murmur of agreement rippled through the crowd, and Xavier seized the moment to press forward.

"Let us also pay tribute to the noble families who form the bedrock of Ornst's greatness. To the illustrious von Schule lineage,"—here he bowed his head with dramatic humility—"and to our dear compatriots: the Hogarths, the Fredericksons, the Regenbogens, and all others whose steadfastness and ambition have woven a tapestry of strength and prosperity."

Polite applause followed, but Xavier wasn't finished.

His tone softened, growing more personal, more reflective.

"Yet, my friends, let us not forget amidst the glories of wealth and power, the truest treasures of life lie not in gold nor land, but in the warmth of our loved ones. They are our anchor in the storm, the stars that guide us. Tonight, I am deeply honored to stand before you alongside my most precious treasures: my beloved wife, Justine, whose wisdom and grace are the cornerstone of this house; my son, Tristin, whose strength and resolve make me proud beyond words; and my daughters, Bella, Marie, and Abigail, each radiant and poised, the picture of elegance and virtue."

The hall broke into polite, approving applause, the kind reserved for a family perfectly presented, perfectly polished.

Rad, watching from his hidden perch, felt his stomach tighten. His father's words echoed through the ballroom, and the absence of his name was sharp—deliberate.

A lump rose in his throat, a bitter knot of shame, anger, and longing.

He had been erased. No longer a son beneath the lights, just a servant tucked into the shadows.

"And so," Xavier continued, lifting his glass high, "as we raise our glasses in celebration, let us also raise our voices in gratitude—for the blessings gracing our lives, the wealth of this grand city, and the bonds of kinship uniting us. Tonight, we toast not only to the enduring legacy of Ornst but to the rare and exquisite wine that graces our tables. Let this evening stand as a testament to our shared splendor and the boundless possibilities of the future."

The crowd erupted into applause, their cheers and clinking glasses filling the air.

Xavier let the noise increase, basking in the energy of his audience.

When the commotion subsided, he raised his voice once more, his tone warm.

"Cheers, my friends! To Ornst, to family, and to the joys of life!"

The hall roared with approval, a cacophony of cheers as every guest lifted their glass in unison. They sipped their sparkling wine, savoring the bubbly delight.

Xavier drained his own glass in a single gulp, setting it aside with a flourish before reclaiming the round wine glass he had discarded earlier.

As the crowd settled into a hum of excitement, Xavier called out, "My friends!"

The tinkling of glasses resumed, a call for silence.

When the room quieted, Xavier's voice softened, drawing in the crowd.

As if compelled by his tone, the partygoers shuffled closer to the stage, their steps subtle but unmistakable, creating a tide of eagerness.

"When I sent out the invitations months ago," he began, his voice calm and assured, "I must admit, I wasn't certain what kind of response I would receive. After all, I could not divulge the true purpose of this gala—not yet. It is not often a man like me has the chance to share one of his deepest passions, not only with his closest friends but with the nobles of Ornst and the distinguished guests who have traveled far to be here tonight."

He paused, his expression softening, his gaze sweeping the room as though addressing each individual personally.

"This evening," he continued, his voice brimming with emotion, "is dedicated to a passion dear to me. To the appreciation of a rare gift I received twenty-two years ago. Yes, my friends—twenty-two years! In many ways, this gala has been twenty-two years in the making."

Xavier paused again, letting the weight of his words settle over the audience, the anticipation palpable.

The room leaned forward as one, hungry for the revelation of what this long-kept secret might be.

At that moment, the governess Gabrielle gathered the three girls and quietly ushered them out of the room.

There were no protests, no objections—only silent compliance. Rad presumed they were retiring for the evening, though a question lingered in his mind.

Was this message not for their ears? Or was it simply time for them to go?

The servants began collecting the sparkling wine glasses, empty or not.

The clinking of glass against silver trays filled the air as the remaining attendees watched, murmurs of curiosity rippling through the room. It took several moments for the servants to finish their task, and when the last of the glassware disappeared through the kitchen doors, Da stepped forward.

"Now for the main event," he announced.

The hum of conversation faded, replaced by a hushed murmur of anticipation.

Rad felt it too—the tension building like a coiled trap ready to snap shut.

Both men and women leaned in, their gazes locked on Da, hanging on his every movement, his every word.

Rad scanned the room—there were no servants left in attendance—though he suspected a few were lurking in the corners. The absence struck him as odd, though his focus shifted to Tristin, who stood stiff and disinterested, as if already privy to the revelation.

Ma stood off to the side, a smile fixed on her face that never reached her eyes. Rad saw the strain behind it—how she blinked too quickly, as if she'd just been stunned.

She looked pale, stiff, like she might be sick.

What's wrong? he wondered. *Was it Gabrielle?*

His thoughts swirled with questions, each one heavier than the last.

He wanted to know the truth—about Gabrielle, about Ma—and more than anything, he wanted to help her. If he could do that, maybe things would shift. Maybe he could find a way back in.

He pictured himself standing beside them with his head held high, dressed in a uniform like Tristin's, greeting guests like he belonged.

I have to make it happen, he told himself. *Ma must be the key. If I can earn her favor, maybe Da will see me differently. Maybe… next time… I'll be announced as Radcliffe von Schule—the youngest son.*

"My friends, esteemed colleagues, and honored guests," Xavier began, his voice commanding the room's attention. "You are undoubtedly aware twenty-two years ago marked a truly historic moment in the world of winemaking. From the fertile duchy of Sonner and from the heavens came the *Maitrasse Cru Bonnage*, a vintage so extraordinary the likes of it comes only *once in a lifetime*. Let me emphasize that—*once. In. A. Lifetime.*"

"The Eclipse Wine!" someone shouted.

A ripple of excitement passed through the crowd, their anticipation building.

"Rumor has it," Xavier continued as he leaned toward the crowd, his voice lowered, "only a thousand bottles of this legendary wine were ever produced. A thousand bottles. A number so small, it has haunted collectors and connoisseurs alike. Tell me, my friends, has anyone here had the pleasure of sampling The Eclipse Wine, *Maitrasse Cru Bonnage?*"

A few tentative hands rose among the guests. Others shot up in earnest.

"And tell me," Xavier said with a grin, "would any of you like the chance to acquire a bottle? Perhaps two? Three? Six?"

A wave of cheers erupted, echoing through the hall.

Noblemen and women shouted with enthusiasm, their voices blending into an uproar of anticipation.

It took a few moments for the clamor to subside.

"But surely…" called out a man from the crowd, "surely there can't be more than a handful of bottles left! Most of them are long gone!"

Xavier clasped his hands together and swayed back and forth. "What if I told you," he began, his voice softening, "far more than a thousand bottles were made? What if I told you Sonner themselves would deny this? That they would vehemently insist only one thousand bottles ever existed?"

The crowd fell silent, their collective breath held as murmurs and whispers began to spread.

"What if I told you," Xavier continued, his voice rising in triumph, "more than seven thousand bottles of *Maitrasse Cru Bonnage* were crafted? Seven thousand!"

Gasps of astonishment rippled through the room.

"Now, you may ask—what became of the rest? Where are those elusive six thousand bottles of The Eclipse Wine?"

Silence gripped the crowd, the air thick with interest as speculation buzzed.

Xavier raised his empty glass in a sweeping gesture. "My friends, the answer is simple. Those six thousand bottles have been here, *with me,* aging in the cellars of *Château Saignoral.* For twenty-two years, they have waited, tended with meticulous care while I built my empire, settled into family life, acquired this estate, and nurtured it into grandeur. Tonight, I am here to share these bottles with the world."

He paused, allowing the weight of his words to settle over the captivated audience.

"Months ago, I opened one of these bottles—an indulgence, a personal treasure. And I tell you now, it is perfect. It has reached its zenith. There will never be a better time to savor this incomparable wine. *Maitrasse Cru Bonnage* is ready to grace your palates once more."

Xavier's stepped forward to the edge of the stage. "But don't take my word for it! Those among you who have had the privilege of tasting *Maitrasse* before—share your thoughts! Speak of what you remember!"

"Cedar!"

"Chocolate!"

"Tobacco!"

"All of those sumptuous notes and more," Da declared, his voice rising over others to command the room once more.

With a grand flourish, he reached for the linen-draped pedestal beside him and, in one sweeping motion, unveiled an aged crate.

The wood bore the patina of time—faded, scuffed, and weathered as if it had been unearthed from the deep recesses of a forgotten cellar. Across its sides, faint white letters spelled out 'SONNER,' their edges softened by years of wear. Stamped on it was a representation of an eclipse.

The crowd leaned in, fascinated.

Da worked the lid free with a prybar, and the creak of wood was timely.

He donned pristine white gloves, then from within the crate, he tenderly drew forth a single dusty bottle. Its label, a stark white script that whispered of exclusivity and mystery, caught the lantern light and sent a ripple of whispers through the audience. He turned the label toward the crowd.

"I'm going to open this bottle," Da announced, holding it high for all to see the Sonner label. "So we can experience what all the fuss is about."

Cheers broke out, triumphant at first, then fading to a murmur.

Among the crowd, the wine experts exchanged glances of awe, their eyes betraying both disbelief and hunger.

To them, this was no mere show.

This was the promise of tasting history.

Others, enchanted by Xavier's theatrical unveiling, hung on his every move, caught up in the spectacle of wealth and power on display.

From his hidden perch, Rad marveled at the excitement generated by the dusty bottle. It made him curious—what was going to happen next?

With a steady hand, Da drew a knife and expertly broke the lead seal at the bottle's neck. Rad recognized the technique, recalling how Gaspard had performed it with ease.

Da's method lacked the same skill, but the moment was no less exciting.

The cork came free with a soft *pop,* and Da held it aloft, revealing its stained purple end like a trophy.

The room fell silent, every pair of eyes fixed on the bottle in Da's hand.

Rad found himself captivated too, not by the wine but by the sheer charm of his father's performance. This was a man who commanded the room, who could weave a story so compelling it made six thousand fabricated bottles feel like genuine treasure.

And yet, Rad knew the truth.

Below this room, in the cellar, lay rows upon rows of bottles—Gaspard's meticulous copy.

As he watched his Da bask in the admiration of the crowd, a knot tightened in his chest. This was no mere celebration; it was a risk, one in which their family's name and fortune were at stake.

It hit Rad, the realization seeping into his bones and shaking him to the core.

Was this a scam? Some scheme?

Those bottles weren't twenty-two years old.

They were three weeks old.

Da intended to sell the fakes—that's why Gaspard had spoken with such exactness about the formula. They had taken those barrels of common wine and turned them into fake bottles of the Sonner vintage.

But why?

Rad's mind spun with calculations. How much could a single bottle sell for? Ten gold crowns? Sixty thousand gold crowns in total? An enormous sum by most measures, yet to his father, it was insignificant.

He was certain a single painting from the gallery was worth more.

So what was Da's true purpose? Why risk the honor of their name for an insubstantial sum compared to the vast wealth he already had?

"Who would like to be the first to taste this rare vintage?" Da's voice broke through Rad's thoughts. "Any takers?"

Hands shot up across the crowd.

Then the excited jingle of purses filled the air.

Volunteers clamored to be chosen, their enthusiasm mounting.

"I'll pay one hundred gold crowns for the first taste," a stately man declared, stepping forward with a leather pouch raised high for all to see.

His voice carried above the murmurs, firm and strong.

"Ah, Lord Fairmont," Da said, inviting the man toward the stage. "Ever the slave to your indulgences, aren't we Alden?"

"As are you, Xavier," Fairmont replied, his face alight with joy.

The tall man strode with purpose, parting the crowd as though they were his subjects. His long-tailed black jacket flowed behind him with each brisk step, its polished buttons gleaming under the chandeliers.

At the stage, Fairmont handed over the pouch and gave a bow, its weight in gold clinking audibly as it exchanged hands.

Da pocketed it.

Taking the first glass of wine from Da's hand, Fairmont raised it with ceremonial flair.

Rad was mesmerized as Fairmont performed the ritual he had seen countless times before.

The man sniffed the glass, his sharp inhalations accentuating the moment. He swirled the purple wine with energy and held it up to the light of the chandeliers. With precision, he tilted the glass and took a sip.

With a more indulgent swig, he gurgled the wine and smacked his lips.

His eyes closed as he stood still, a serene expression overtaking his features, as though he were transported to a realm of pure bliss.

"Magnificent," he proclaimed, his voice booming.

The word reverberated through the hall, met with a ripple of admiration and approval from the assembled crowd.

Da poured him another taste, his charming smile widening.

"Lord Fairmont, the honor is yours. Choose four others to share in this exquisite moment. We shall *empty* this bottle before unveiling the true purpose of tonight's gathering!"

A wave of cheers and applause erupted, the sound echoing through the grand hall.

Lord Fairmont, glass held aloft in triumph, rotated, his sharp eyes scanning the sea of eager faces.

The room pulsed with anticipation as guests leaned forward, their jeweled hands extended as if reaching for an invisible prize, their expressions alight with hope of being chosen.

Soft whispers floated through the crowd, each person promoting their unspoken case for selection, while others stood frozen, their gazes locked on Fairmont's every move.

The rustle of fine fabrics mingled with the faint clink of glasses, a subtle chorus of anticipation.

Rad, watching from above, could almost feel the tension like a physical weight, the collective desire of the crowd for a taste of the rare wine.

Fairmont, as natural as breathing air, surveyed the crowd and made his selections.

His first choice was his wife, Celeste, who came forward with a calm elegance. She was a delicate woman, though not frail, her thin frame clad in a gown of soft silk. Her long, golden-brown hair was styled in flowing waves, framing a lovely, warm face. Her pale green eyes sparkled with mischief.

Fairmont selected another noble couple with striking ginger hair, their matching attire reflecting their unity, and the last one, a portly man whose jovial demeanor contrasted with the others' grace.

Da provided each with a glass, evenly distributing the prized wine among them.

For Lord Fairmont, the final remnants of the bottle were reserved, poured into his glass with ceremonious flair.

As they stood together at the forefront, the five figures basked in the crowd's admiration, their smiles beaming like rays of sunlight piercing a cloudy sky. They sipped the wine as though it were perfection. They basked in triumph, their excitement elevated by the knowledge of the wine's rarity and the extravagance it represented.

Rad did the math, it was easy, six thousand times one hundred gold brought the total value of the collection to six hundred thousand gold crowns.

A tidy sum.

Audience members whispered in awe, some stepping closer to the crate housing the remaining five bottles, their gazes heavy with longing.

From his vantage, Rad could see Da scanning the room with an expression of controlled delight.

As the murmurs swelled into a chorus of rising anticipation, Xavier tapped the empty bottle with his silver ring, the crisp sound cutting through the growing noise.

All at once, the room quieted, all attention shifting back to the stage.

"As I have said, I have six thousand bottles of *Maitrasse Cru Bonnage* to sell tonight and tonight only. What I don't sell, I will keep in my glorious cellar, and I'm sure I will consume them... one by one... until the day I die a happy, wealthy, drunk man."

A cheer flowed through the crowd, interrupted by scattered laughter.

"Many of you know how much these are worth; how much you can buy them for on the open market. If you can find them."

Numbers rang out from the partygoers, shouted in speculation and excitement, each one higher than the last.

Rad, perched in his hidden spot, calculated every figure in his head. If Da sold all the bottles, it would mean millions of gold crowns. *Millions.*

Could there be that many coins in Ornst? In all Eldor? *Millions,* for wine?

Da raised his arms, commanding silence. "I know for a fact these sell for three hundred and fifty gold crowns—if you can find someone willing to part with one!"

Applause thundered in agreement.

"These are for sale tonight, exclusively at this gala, for four hundred gold crowns each," Da continued. "Payment terms can be negotiated, but the price will not. Four hundred gold crowns."

The applause faltered.

Some protested with boos and muttered complaints, their discontent moving through the room.

Others shook their heads, disappointed but still calculating their options.

The murmurs swelled into unintelligible chatter.

Da raised the empty bottle, tapping it with his silver ring. The sharp sound cut through the noise. Before he could speak, another voice rose from the side of the stage.

"You have to be joking," Lord Fairmont declared, pausing only to sip from his glass of wine. "Three fifty is what they're worth. With so many extra quantities, you should sell them for three hundred or less. At a discount!"

"No one is going to profit from these wines but me," Da said, his voice cool but unyielding. "No one but me. The price is set at four hundred gold crowns. Twenty-four hundred for a crate of six. If you came here hoping to buy wine and resell it for profit, you will fail. This wine is meant to be enjoyed, not auctioned off at a markup. Four hundred is the price. If you're unwilling to pay it, I'm confident others will. Believe me, these bottles will not last long, no matter how much you complain."

A hushed murmur swept the room, growing louder as opinions diverged. Some nodded in agreement, eager to secure their bottles despite the cost. Others grumbled, weighing the offer with skepticism. A few remained still, contemplative.

The tension mounted, interspersed by bursts of muted conversations.

A voice, loud and firm, broke through the rising clamor.

"I want assurances! Before I spend a fortune, I want assurances!"

The room became quiet, the collective weight of attention shifting toward the speaker.

An imposing man emerged from the crowd, dressed in a striking burgundy suit adorned with gold tassels at the shoulders. A tall black hat perched atop his head, and in his gloved hands, he gripped an ornate cane.

The crowd parted before him, creating a path to the stage.

Trailing close behind was a gaunt man clad in a gold-and-blue-striped jacket, paired with a billowy white shirt and matching blue pantaloons.

A third figure followed at a languid pace, cloaked in deep purple robes with a hood obscuring his face.

The man in burgundy ascended the stage with a determined stride, his cane tapping rhythmically against the wood. The tasters retreated into the crowd, clearing the space for him to take center stage.

"I am Duke Vesy, from Haddensack," the man declared. "My house may not be well-known in Ornst, but I have traveled at ruinous expense to be here. And I demand assurances!"

He swept an arm toward the crowd, then turned his full attention on Da, his voice rising with righteous indignation.

"Sonner has whispered rumors—*rumors!*—of additional *Maitrasse Cru Bonnage* bottles, but now you claim... six thousand? Six thousand? The Eclipse Wine?"

He let the number hang, scandalized.

"It defies reason! A miraculous surplus, conveniently unearthed just in time for your grand offer?"

He stabbed a finger toward the table.

"I demand proof! Proof of your offer's authenticity, or I walk— and every noble here should walk with me!"

The room buzzed with unease, whispers spreading from corner to corner.

All eyes turned to Da, whose composed demeanor faltered slightly to suggest doubt. His brow furrowed and he glanced at the weathered crate beside him, as if gauging its ability to withstand scrutiny.

He smoothed his expression, replacing the hint of worry with the faintest trace of a practiced smile.

"I'm an astute businessman," Da spoke in a calm voice. "You know I have many arrangements with Haddensack, duchies, and earldoms throughout the known lands. I didn't acquire these bottles twenty-two years ago by chance or illicit means. I acquired them properly through my hard work, negotiating, and paying for them with the last of my precious earnings. Twenty-two years ago, I saw this as an opportunity to invest. I merely held onto my investment until the time was right."

Vesy scoffed, loud enough for the room to hear. "An *investment?*"

He turned slowly, as if addressing the assembled nobles, not Da.

"A man buries gold, not grapes. Wine does not wait. It breathes, it ages, it spoils. And you would have us believe that this—" he motioned to the crate, "sat untouched for two decades, and now emerges in perfect condition? At the very moment you wish to sell?"

He raised his voice. "Gentlefolk, I ask you—does this sound like foresight... or fabrication?"

Polite applause rippled through the room, though pockets of doubt lingered, evident in the skeptical murmurs spreading among the guests.

Duke Vesy struck his cane against the polished floor, silencing the rising noise.

He raised his chin, his expression unyielding.

"When I learned you were selling a mystery vintage, I sought out one of the finest sommeliers alive—at immense expense to myself. *Immense.* I have brought with me Damien Édouard," Vesy declared, his tone rich with authority.

He gestured to the tall, lean man beside him, whose golden-striped jacket shimmered in the lamplight.

Vesy continued. "I too am an astute businessman. He is renowned for his expertise with rare wines. Do you know of him—and his flawless reputation?"

Gasps and nods swept through the crowd.

"Yes, of course," someone muttered.

"I've heard of him," another said. "He can tell you where the grapes are from—down to the hill."

"They say he once tasted a vintage blind and named the barrel cooper by scent alone," someone said, awestruck.

A nervous ripple passed through the guests.

Eyes turned sharply toward Xavier von Schule.

Da's lips twitched.

"Indeed… indeed, I've heard of *Monsur* Édouard," he said, his tone carefully measured. "A man of singular reputation."

But his fingers fidgeted at his side, brushing the edge of the crate. Just once.

The smug Vesy lifted his chin as his incredulous smile broadened, voice rising with practiced gravitas.

"But that is not all."

He stepped aside, gesturing with a flourish toward the hooded figure beside him. "I have also retained a representative from the Wizards of Arcana—to verify the truth of what's been claimed here tonight."

The figure in deep purple offered a shallow bow, his face shrouded beneath his cowl. The fabric shimmered faintly, as if resisting the light.

A ripple passed through the room.

Shined shoes shifted.

Breath was held.

The air stilled.

The mention of the Wizards of Arcana was not taken lightly.

Magic was rare. Expensive. Dangerous. And never neutral.

Whatever doubt remained among the nobles had now curdled into heavy anticipation and… fear.

Rad's pained heart thudded against his ribs. Every muscle in his body screamed at him to run, to vanish before everything exploded—yet he remained rooted in his hidden perch.

This was spiraling. Fast.

Out of control.

Would the sommelier see through the counterfeit? Could a single whiff unravel everything? And what of the wizard? Was truth a thing magic could pull from cork and glass?

Vesy's voice shattered Rad's thoughts.

"Xavier," he said with a velvet edge, "my associates and I simply wish for transparency."

He turned slightly, letting his words roll over the audience. "Surely, as a man of business, you understand the importance of trust."

Da inclined his head with practiced calm, though his feet betrayed him—shifting, uncertain. "Naturally," he said. "We all seek the truth. In everything."

"And yet," Vesy continued, his voice rising with righteous momentum, "I would feel more assured if this esteemed sommelier and our arcane friend were permitted to examine a bottle—right here, right now. Publicly. For all to witness."

Vesy smiled faintly. "A single sip should suffice to prove the authenticity of your claim."

Gasps punctuated his words, and the murmurs grew louder.

For the briefest moment, Da's polished mask cracked.

He hesitated at the challenge.

"If this will ease your concerns, Duke Vesy, then I shall be happy to oblige," he said. "A bottle from this crate you see here shall serve to demonstrate my integrity."

He lifted the lid with a flourish, revealing another dusty bottle of *Maitrasse Cru Bonnage*. He held it aloft, the label catching the lamplight like gold.

"Shall we proceed?" he asked, his tone carefully light.

"No!"

The word cracked through the hall like thunder.

Vesy's cane struck the stage, sharp and with purpose.

"I want a random crate from your cellar," he declared, his voice brimming with indignation. "One chosen at random. By your staff. In full view of these assembled nobles. One you would sell to us—not one handpicked for this *charming little performance*."

Gasps broke like waves across the room, followed by a rising tide of murmurs.

Heads turned, eyes sharpening.

"Let us see the truth, Xavier," Vesy pressed, lifting his voice for the room. "If what you've said is real, then let fortune decide. Surely a man of integrity has nothing to fear from a random bottle."

Da's polished composure wavered for an instant, his lips thinning into a hard line.

With an angry snap of his fingers, he summoned one of the servants stationed discreetly near the curtains. The man flinched before shuffling out, his expression drawn and wary, as if already bracing for the storm to come.

Da stepped close to Vesy, his voice cold. "You, sir, have gone too far. This accusation is not only absurd, it is *insulting*."

Though his words were aimed at Vesy, their sharp edge sliced through the murmuring crowd, stilling it.

Straightening, Da let his voice rise. "After the wine is proved, we will have words, Duke Vesy. And you will beg for my forgiveness."

He paused, letting the words settle like dust. "I may not sell you a single drop of this vintage—despite your wealth, and whatever influence you pretend to wield among our northern neighbors. Your accusation is… *unwise*."

Vesy didn't blink. He remained still, composed, the very picture of cool authority. Then, after a beat, he said simply: "If the wine is proved," his voice smooth, "you may speak to me as you wish—in private."

Vesy raised his cane and swept it toward the assembled nobles, commanding the hall—not with law, but with presence.

"I want witnesses," he said, voice ringing with authority. "Let the truth be seen by more than just your servants."

He pointed with measured confidence. "You. And you—go with him. See everything for yourselves."

Then, with a turn of his wrist, he singled out another man near the wine table. "You will personally select the crate. Make your choice carefully. You carry the eyes of every house in this room."

Gasps and hushed words rippled through the crowd as Vesy took control.

The will of the room would pass judgment.

He turned back to Da, voice lower now, all edge. "I know you, Xavier. If this vintage were real, you would've sold me every bottle before tonight. You'd never let a treasure rot in dust if it were real. A gala… preposterous."

Da stiffened.

His jaw clenched.

Then, with a sharp gesture, he signaled the servant.

The chosen men followed the servant as the crowd shifted to let them pass, their footsteps vanishing into the cellar like the beginning of a sentence no one wanted to finish.

CHAPTER SEVEN

∞

Revelations

While they waited, muted whispers swirled through the crowd like a gathering storm. Rad's heart pounded in his hidden perch, the enormity of the moment made him nervous. This was danger, real and immediate. If Da's deception unraveled, it wouldn't only tarnish his name; it could doom the entire von Schule household.

Questions and fears came to the surface. Why did he still care about them? Was it the shred of hope somehow he might regain their favor?

His thoughts darted to Ma, her smiles growing hollower in recent months, and to Abby, whose kind words lingered like warmth in a cold room. Her books and messages kept him going while his family had cast him aside.

The thought of their disgrace filled him with unease.

He was certain everything would come crashing down tonight.

Would Da's exposure lead to the militia storming in, shackling him before the assembled nobility? Would they all bear the stain of criminality, the von Schule name crushed under the weight of scandal and ruin?

Rad's fingers tightened on the edge of the viewing portal, his breath shallow as he waited for the servant and men to return.

This was not going to hold up to scrutiny.

The dreaded moment arrived.

The servant and his chosen witnesses returned, bearing a crate that carried the fate of the von Schule name upon its weathered planks.

Dirt-streaked and aged, it bore the weight of decades and the scent of dust and judgment.

From its depths, the servant lifted a bottle—dusty, sealed, unmistakably *Maitrasse Cru Bonnage.*

Or so it claimed.

Every eye turned to Damien Édouard.

The acclaimed sommelier stepped forward like a high priest of Unara, his movements fluid, reverent. Compared to Da's earlier efforts, his hands made an art of every motion.

He uncorked the bottle with a single twist and a soft, dignified *pop*. The sound, faint as it was, cut through the murmurs. He poured only a sip into a crystal glass, just enough to judge.

With ritualistic calm, he began a slow, mesmerizing swirl.

His sharp gaze followed the liquid's motion as though reading prophecy in its movement. Then came the inhale—deep, precise, and unhurried.

And finally, he raised the glass to the chandelier's golden glow, the light refracting through the wine like a blade suspended in air.

The room went still.

The nobles held their breath, Vesy watched with smug certainty, and Da... Da was wary of exposure.

The wizard stepped forward.

Clad in deep purple robes that shimmered like stormlight, he raised a hand and traced a glowing arc through the air.

A rune sparked, hovered, then vanished.

His voice, when it came, rang with power and warning.

"If truth is spoken," the wizard said, "the glass will change. If lies taint these words, the glass will shatter—its shards biting deep."

The final word of his incantation thundered through the silence, leaving a hum in the floorboards and a pulse in every chest.

Even the chandeliers trembled.

The sommelier began his evaluation, his voice a rich, melodic cadence that glided through the room like silk.

"Deep, deep ruby color," he declared, holding the glass high with reverent flair. "Oh my. Lovely. Just lovely."

But the voice was not Damien Édouard's.

It was Gaspard's.

Rad's breath caught in his throat.

The timbre—the rhythm—was unmistakable.

The words pierced through his stunned thoughts.

"Burnt cedar," the disguised sommelier continued, swirling the glass with a flourish, his voice sensual. "Ripe mulberries. Fresh mint."

He inhaled, eyes fluttering closed. "Sweet pipe tobacco."

Rad's heart thudded painfully.

Gaspard. What does this mean?

He darted a glance at the wizard.

Hood lowered.

Cowl tilted just enough to reveal what Rad already feared.

Gaspard's assistant. The entire scene—scripted.

A sleight of hand, dressed in velvet and authority.

Gaspard took a sip.

The audience leaned in, rapt.

He swished, savored, then swallowed with a soft exhale. "Bitter dark chocolate," he declared. "Silky. Polished. Balanced acidity. Burnt sugary raspberries. Cedar."

The crowd sighed in appreciation, as if the wine itself had spoken through him.

He held the glass aloft. A crude etching shimmered into existence along its side: **SONNER.**

Magic.

The wizard gave a solemn nod, his voice deep and reverberant. "He speaks the truth."

A collective gasp rippled through the room.

Gaspard raised the glass higher, letting the etched name gleam in the chandelier's light.

"No doubt," he declared, voice rich with conviction. "This is genuine. This is *Maitrasse Cru Bonnage*. It could be nothing else."

The room erupted.

Applause roared to life, crashing over the grand hall like a tide of jubilation.

Shouts of affirmation mingled with cheers, their echoes dancing off the gilded ceiling.

The energy surged—palpable, contagious.

Nobles who moments ago had whispered doubts and calculated risks now broke into spontaneous celebration.

Hands clasped in firm, congratulatory shakes.

Others embraced, laughter rising, skepticism swept away in the storm of shared relief.

The transformation was stunning. These people hadn't just accepted the truth—they had *willed* it into being. Their faces glowed with triumph, as if the wine's validation were their own personal victory.

They wanted it to be true.

Needed it to be true.

This wasn't just a bottle of wine.

It was *the* wine.

Maitrasse Cru Bonnage—legendary, unattainable—now, at last, within reach.

The steep price, once a source of tension, faded into irrelevance. What was four hundred gold crowns, or twenty-four hundred for a crate, compared to the allure of sipping history? This was no longer about wine—it was about status, exclusivity, and being part of the momentous occasion.

To taste it was to join a rarefied circle, a privilege worth any cost.

A portly man in a green velvet coat slapped his neighbor on the back, exclaiming, "Worth every crown! Every crown, I say!"

Nearby, a lady with cascading auburn hair pressed her hands to her chest, her eyes glistening with tears as though witnessing a miracle.

Another man, visibly shaking with excitement, turned to his wife and declared, "We must have a case. No, two!"

The crowd surged closer to the stage, a living wave of opulence and ambition. They jostled for position, some craning their necks to catch another glimpse of the etched glass, while others thrust their purses into the air, gold coins jingling in an unspoken promise to secure their share. Those who had initially balked at the price now leaned in, their eyes alight with desire.

A metallic clang rang out—Da pounded his ring against the empty bottle in his hand, the sharp report slicing through the noise.

"Patience, my friends!" he called, his voice rising above the clamor. "There is wine enough for all!"

The crowd stilled, though the buzz lingered beneath the hush—like sparks beneath ash.

Da raised the bottle, letting the light catch its gleaming label one final time. "Let this be a lesson to those who doubted," he proclaimed.

His gaze swept the hall, pausing—just long enough—on the space Vesy had occupied moments before. "Honesty," he said, tone rich with self-satisfaction, "and integrity will always find the light. Always!"

A few nobles cheered.

Others nodded, already convinced.

Vesy had vanished into the crowd, his purpose fulfilled, and Da stood at the center, basking in the glow of vindication.

To the side, Gaspard and the wizard made a quiet, efficient exit—their roles played with precision, their lies sealed in gold and applause.

Rad stared in disbelief, not quite understanding what he had witnessed.

In defiance of fate, Da had pulled it off—turning doubt into belief, suspicion into awe.

Now, the pieces aligned.

Vesy, with his theatrics and sharp demands, hadn't been an adversary.

He was part of it—a plant.

An accomplice.

His role was to provoke, to cast the seed of doubt... only so Gaspard, disguised as the famed Damien Édouard, could rise as the savior of the wine's reputation.

And the wizard—Gaspard's assistant, cloaked in false Wizards of Arcana robes—had sealed the illusion with magic.

Rad's mind replayed the moment: the runes traced in the air, the hushed chant, the glowing etching on the glass. It hadn't been for show.

Magic had been woven into the lie—not just to authenticate it, but to enhance it.

Gaspard's formula alone hadn't been enough. His father had resorted to both alchemy and illusion to mimic the qualities of the legendary vintage.

The realization landed hard.

This was all a lie.

And Da had done it with precision, skill—and the full force of the family's reputation in jeopardy.

Shame twisted in his gut, but so did wonder. *Was this how Da made his fortune?* Profiting off fake goods, playing on the aspirations and vanity of the wealthy. It was no wonder Da kept his dealings shrouded in secrecy.

Tristin, so confident in the family's legitimate standing, had to be an innocent participant in this web of deceit.

Rad wrestled with the implications—how many other trades or deals carried this same taint? Could it all collapse with the uncovering of a single lie?

Below, the grand room buzzed with activity.

Nobles surged toward the front to place their orders, some clutching bulging purses while others gestured frantically toward servants, obviously lacking enough funds on hand.

Two separate tables had been set up to manage the chaos: one where names, quantities, and deposits were recorded in an order ledger, and another where an inventory ledger tracked the dwindling supply of crates.

Servants worked with swift efficiency, noting details for those who placed deposits, with assurances their accounts could be settled later.

Rad watched with detached fascination as the efficient system operated. The line of buyers ebbed and flowed, but the number of reserved bottles climbed at a steady rate. Gold coins clinked into lockboxes, while diligent scribes worked to ensure no detail was missed.

Da's scheme had succeeded.

Rad marveled at the deception's scale.

Not only was Da selling the counterfeit wine for an astronomical price, but he was also securing future payments that would keep the illusion alive for weeks to come.

As the line thinned and the night wore on, Rad's gaze flickered to the inventory ledger. Servants marked off each crate brought up from the cellar, their chalk-streaked hands betraying the strain of carrying such precious cargo.

Only those who paid the full price in coin on hand were permitted to take their crates with them, their wealth granting them the immediate gratification of possession.

For others, their preference for delivery or later pick-up was noted in the order ledger, ensuring no request was overlooked.

Soon, it would all be accounted for, and Rad realized Da's promise of exclusivity—*this night and this night only*—was as calculated as the rest of the scheme.

It had been reaffirmed throughout the evening—through Da's proclamations, the murmurs of eager buyers, and the servant's whispered reassurances—tomorrow, no further orders would be taken, no offer entertained, no matter how extravagant.

Tonight was the sole opportunity, and Da would see to it the illusion of rarity remained unbroken.

Rad's attention drifted to the concealed passage he had hoped to explore earlier.

The timing was wrong now.

Too many people lingered, and Wilkins was prowling about, barking orders at the servants who cleared glasses and gathered debris.

Tomorrow, he resolved as he headed to his room. The puzzle door would have to wait.

Back in his room, sleep eluded him.

His thoughts spun, relentless—Vesy and his calculated outrage, Gaspard's performance beneath a borrowed name, the shimmering etching on the glass.

The deception had layers.

Every moment had been coordinated, every reaction manipulated by his Da.

He lay in restless silence, eyes fixed on the ceiling, mind turning over Da's scheme and the weight of what it meant. Finally, unable to shake the questions clawing at him, Rad rose and slipped back into the passage, drawn to witness the aftermath of the night's grand deception.

When he returned to his vantage point, the party was winding down faster than he expected. Unlike the gala affairs of his memory, where party goers lingered until dawn, this one tapered off well before midnight. Only a few privileged guests remained, milling in intimate groups.

The servants, led by Wilkins, moved with precision as they cleared the tables and rearranged furniture.

Rad's gaze sought out Da, and when he found him, his heart sank.

Xavier von Schule stood near the front, triumphant, with a quiet smugness carved into every line of his face. His hand rested on the small of Gabrielle's back, the governess leaning into him as she laughed at something said within their circle.

Her movements were elegant, intentional, the curve of her lips and sparkle in her eyes drawing attention from everyone close by.

The laughter of their small group carried across the near-empty room.

Rad's understanding deepened.

He remembered the way Gabrielle had carried the sparkling wine—graceful, sure of herself, her fingers wrapped around the glass like it belonged to her… and not the von Schules.

His Da, Gabrielle… Ma hadn't been there. Gabrielle had stood in her place, shining and animated.

He searched for the right word but nothing sharp came to mind, nothing that fit how he was feeling.

She was… *annoying.*

Having searched in vain for Ma among the crowd, Rad navigated the concealed passageways until he reached the master bedroom. His intuition proved correct—he found Ma in the sitting room, slouched in a wingback chair.

Tear tracks marked her reddened cheeks, her eyes puffy and bloodshot. The black dress she wore was wrinkled from sitting too long in one position, and her box hat lay discarded on the floor.

From the peephole, Rad watched in silence. He didn't need words to understand.

Her heart wasn't just hurting—it had given up.

It was broken.

And he began to wonder… had all the smiles been real? The laughter, the soft touches, the way she used to hum to herself in the garden—had she just been pretending all along?

Maybe she'd been sad for years.

Maybe getting kicked out hadn't just broken him.

Maybe it had broken her too.

He didn't fully understand what was happening between Da, Ma, and Gabrielle—but one thing was clear: something big had happened tonight.

"You shouldn't carry on like that in front of our guests," Da said as he entered the sitting room, his voice raised. "It isn't ladylike. It is beneath you and beneath a woman of your station. You went to a proper Ornst finishing school, and they taught you how to be a gracious, obedient wife. You should remember what you were taught. You should remember your place in this household."

The room, though luxurious, felt oppressive and stark.

The intimate fire in the hearth cast flickering shadows.

Rad found he was holding his breath, waiting for Ma's response.

Ma lifted her pale face to gaze at Da, her eyes searching for answers, traces of her tears lingering on her cheeks.

"And what is my place, Xavier?" she asked, her defiant voice trembling. "To smile while you humiliate me? To pretend not to notice while you flaunt that *girl* in front of everyone? Or is my place simply to be forgotten?"

A growing sense of unease filled Rad.

Da became visibly angry. "Your place? You are to behave as the matron of this family," Da said, his voice like iron.

Ma smoothed her rumpled dress, drawing in a deep breath to steady herself, though her tears threatened to spill anew.

"I won't tolerate this, Xavier. This has gone on long enough." Her voice wavered, but she didn't stop. "You presented her to everyone— as if it were official. As if I no longer mattered. Your hands were all over her… in front of our friends. Our neighbors."

Rad saw it on Da's face—that look, cold and dangerous.

A mix of rage and disappointment.

He'd seen it before.

Dozens of times.

Always right before the belt came down.

Da's expression hardened, his voice growing stern. "Justine, do you think speaking about my private activities to our guests is appropriate? No matter how you whisper, my faithful will always hear you and report your insubordination to me. These actions are beneath you. You are the woman of this household. Start acting like it. My interactions with Gabrielle have no bearing on your responsibilities as the woman of this house. None whatsoever."

"Responsibilities!" Ma snapped, her furious voice quivering. "I'm supposed to stand there and watch as you take liberties with the governess? In full view of everyone? She is a servant! She's not much older than Tristin, your son! She is an innocent *girl!*"

"She is my mistress whether you like it or not," Da replied, his anger simmering beneath his words. "Gabrielle is twenty. She's old enough to know what she's doing and not as innocent as you must think."

"Am I supposed to feel better now?" Ma's voice trembled. "I'm supposed to accept this situation, quietly, without protest? Xavier, how could you?"

"You have no other choice, Justine. This was the arrangement you agreed to, and I told you one day this was going to happen. I told you one day I would take a mistress, and you would not interfere. You accepted it. Remember, you accepted it willingly. Besides, your hands are as dirty as mine. There are no innocent parties here."

"I was terrified," Ma said, her voice breaking. "I feared for my life. How can you hold me to a coerced promise I made eleven years ago? You forced me!"

"I've kept my word, as you will keep yours," Da said, his voice full of venom. "This was your choice, remember—your choice to sire the bastard boy you call a son. I endured eleven years of shame and regret. Every day reminded me of your decision to lie with him—that repulsive man. A man, must I remind you, who abandoned you in the end. Disappeared. Vanished. Didn't have the decency to see the face of his newborn son." He took a deep, calming breath. "For a time, I thought of Radcliffe as my son, but as he grew, we discovered his true nature. He's rotten through and through. Like his father. Like his father was."

Rad felt lightheaded, as if his soul had peeled away from his body and was floating above, watching from a distance.

His hands were numb.

His legs, too.

The peephole blurred before his eyes, and for a moment, he thought he might be sick.

Ma scoffed, her defiance cutting through her pain. "You used to be friends with his father, and you're one to talk about being bad. Look at what you do. Tonight—what was this? The entire evening was a contrived show! To do what, pilfer thousands of coins from our neighbors and friends? You lie and deceive in one week more than I have done in my entire life. And for what? Thousands of coins? Don't you have enough?"

"Millions," he corrected her. "Don't judge my various means of income while you live under this roof and enjoy a carefree lifestyle. Legitimate or not, you are here and have station because of me. You are alive because of me. I could have thrown you and your bastard into the streets eleven years ago. I let you stay because of your promise to me—when the time came for me to take a mistress, you wouldn't object. You promised, and I'm holding you to it."

"How can you do this? What about us? Don't you love me? How can you love that skinny little *chenne*?"

Da's hand shot out, striking Ma across the face. Her head snapped to the side, hair whipping across her cheek.

The crack echoed through the room, sharp and final.

She didn't move.

For a long moment, Ma and Da were motionless.

The room was still—dead still—as if even the fire dared not crackle.

Ma slowly turned back toward him, eyes wide, her breath caught in her chest. She cowered and whispered, "What about us?"

"This isn't about *us*. It never has been," Da said, his voice unyielding as Ma gently touched her reddened cheek. "This is about *me*. The last sixteen years have been about *you* and the children, about my business, my efforts to build an empire I can pass on to Tristin. But now? Now it's my time. My time to enjoy life on my terms. If I choose to spend it with Gabrielle, I will. And you will not object. Do you understand?"

He leaned in, his voice low and menacing. "Unless you're ready to find a new home—and make no mistake, I won't hesitate to throw you into the gutter—I suggest you accept your place in this family. Be the dutiful, loyal, loving wife you once pretended to be. And move on from this nonsense."

He straightened, his eyes cold. "Otherwise, I'll turn you out into the streets of Ornst. You won't last a week. The filth in the alleys will walk past your rotting corpse—and I'll make sure of it."

From his hidden perch, Rad's heart pounded so loudly he feared they'd hear it. The truth unraveling below was more terrifying than he'd imagined. None of it made sense.

"What about Radcliffe?" Ma's voice trembled but didn't break. "Don't you think six months is punishment enough?"

Rad froze.

Punishment.

Not a lesson. Not a test of his worth.

Punishment.

And then it struck him—not just the word, but everything behind it.

He wasn't Da's real son. Not by blood.

The truth unraveled in his mind, each thread weaving a story of sorrow and rejection.

It all made sense now—the constant criticism, the cold distance, the way Da looked at him like a horse with a broken leg. He wasn't part of Da's bloodline. He was the result of another man's brief union with Ma.

A man who had vanished before he had even drawn his first breath.

This wasn't punishment for what he had done.

It was punishment for who he was.

A bastard.

The clarity stung. His stomach fluttered, hollow and uneasy.

His Ma—his kind, grieving Ma—was the only truth in a house built on false smiles and buried lies. Her sorrow wasn't weakness; it was the weight of guilt and shame she had carried for years, hiding the truth to protect him as best she could.

Who is my father?

The question burned inside him—unanswered, agonizing.

Who was the man who'd made Da hate him so deeply?

Who had abandoned Ma, leaving her to carry the weight of it all alone?

The truth shifted everything.

The stables, the punishments, the endless scorn—they weren't just about discipline or disappointment.

It wasn't just what he did.

It was who he was.

His very existence was the offense Da could never forgive.

As the truth settled over him, Rad didn't collapse beneath it—quiet resolve rose in its place.

Better the stables than the streets. Better to be with Hadley and the horses than lost in Ornst, nameless and alone. His work, his growing skill with knives, the quiet lessons Hadley shared—they weren't scraps. They were a beginning.

It wasn't the life he'd imagined. But it was his. And it was better than being discarded.

He still had Ma, even if she was breaking. Maybe he could find a way to protect her too.

And he had Abby.

Abby, who broke rules to sneak him books and messages.

Abby, who stayed close even when Da told her not to.

When Da didn't answer, Ma repeated, "What about Radcliffe?"

"Radcliffe will remain in his quarters and continue working under Hadley," Da said, his voice cold and precise. "He'll learn a trade— horse work suits him. When he turns sixteen, he can go out into the world and make his own way. Just as I did."

He paused, letting the weight of his words settle.

"But understand this—if *you* step out of line again, Justine, if I so much as suspect you're stirring up trouble… neither of you will have a place here. I'll see you both out on the streets."

Ma stiffened.

He straightened his jacket like the matter was settled. "Hadley says the boy works hard. I believe him. The man has a talent for obedience, and he knows how to instill it in others."

Da glanced back toward her, voice cutting. "Let the bastard earn his keep. Better that than wasting space."

"I don't trust Hadley with our son," Ma said, her voice trembling. "He's a... murderer! Why do you keep him on our staff?"

"*Your* son," Da said, each word forcible and cold. "Whether you trust Hadley is irrelevant—he stays. I trust him. I pulled him from the gallows, and he's never forgotten it. He is dangerous, yes—but loyal. Unshakably loyal. And that's what matters, Justine. More than love. More than blood."

"All the terrible things he's done..." Ma's voice faltered, her face gone pale. "And you would put that kind of fate on me? On the woman you claim to love—the one who bore your children?"

Da's expression didn't change. "What Hadley was before me doesn't matter. Since I brought him in, he's been loyal—more than I can say for you." He leaned closer. "Hadley will do whatever I ask. Without hesitation. No matter how grim the task."

"I have been loyal and faithful," Ma wept, covering her face with trembling hands. "How can you say that?"

Da let out a sharp, humorless laugh. "Having a bastard isn't faithful, Justine."

"Since then," she choked, lowering her hands to meet his steely gaze. "We all make mistakes, Xavier—but Radcliffe is not one of them. He's a good boy. He's smart, and he's resourceful."

"He's the bastard of your despicable lover. That will never change."

"Promise me," she begged, her voice cracking with desperation. "Promise me again that Radcliffe can stay until he's sixteen. I need to hear you say it. One more time. Please, Xavier. *Promise me.*"

From his hiding place, Rad felt his stomach twist.

The promise she begged for—it wasn't law. It wouldn't be written down.

If Da gave it, it would be quiet, buried, and his alone to break.

Rad knew Da loved his daughters. He treated Tristin with respect. He had to love Ma, how could he not?

But when it came to him, there was nothing.

No warmth.

No pride.

For the first time, Rad wondered if Da's hate for him had poisoned everything else too.

Maybe it wasn't about what Ma had done. Maybe it was just about *Rad*—what he was. A reminder Da couldn't forget... would never forget.

"He can stay here until he's sixteen," Da said. "*If* he behaves. He may keep his room—again, if he behaves. But I will hear no more talk of him rejoining this family. He is a servant. Nothing more, nothing less."

"Abigail misses him," Ma whispered through her sobs. "She asks me when he can come back to us."

"I don't want Abigail, Marie, Bella, or Tristin speaking to him. Ever," Da said, his voice like a drawn blade. "I've made myself clear, and I'll say it again: he is a servant, not their brother. He is beneath their station and no longer part of this family. There will be consequences if that line is crossed."

"They miss him," Ma said again, her voice trembling. "They won't admit it—but I've asked them, each one. They do. Can't you reconsider? I know he understands now. Let him reconnect with his siblings. Let him back into the household. Show me the man I once loved. The man I married. Please, Xavier... be kind. Think of what he's going through."

Da's gaze flickered with icy contempt before settling on her. He didn't pause to consider her plea.

"No."

His tone was flat, resolute.

"He stays where he is. I don't care what our children have said to you in private. Radcliffe is not part of this family—and he never will be. My decision is final."

He leaned forward in his chair, just enough to close the space between them. His voice dropped, each word spoken with emphasis.

"Do we have an understanding? Gabrielle. Radcliffe. Or must I cast you out into Ornst to fend for yourself?"

He let the silence hang, his eyes locked on hers.

"You wouldn't last. A woman of your station, abandoned and disgraced, would find no protection—no mercy—beyond these walls."

From the darkness, Rad clenched his fists.

Part of him wanted Ma to fight back—to throw Da's words back in his face, to show him she wasn't afraid.

But another part—quieter, colder—hoped she wouldn't.

Let her stay. Let her survive.

Once he was gone, she could live out her days on the estate, untouched by Da's wrath, unashamed by his presence.

He would carry the punishment. He always had. And now, he always will.

Ma took a deep, measured breath, steadying herself. She wiped her tear-streaked cheeks and squared her shoulders, tilting her head to reclaim a shred of dignity.

"Yes. We have an understanding," she said quietly. "I will abide by our arrangement—for Radcliffe's sake."

Her voice grew stronger.

"And you will abide by your promise. You will honor it—no matter what. When he turns sixteen, you will let him go. Free to make his way in the world."

Da kicked back his chair and rose, one knee creaking as he straightened to his full height. He adjusted his jacket and rolled his shoulders, towering over her.

He offered a thin smile—devoid of warmth.

"Yes. We have an understanding."

He leaned in and placed a kiss on her cheek—the one he'd struck.

Then, with a patronizing pat to her shoulder, he turned and left the sitting room.

Da paused to rub his knee, then strode away, out of Rad's line of sight. His gait was brisk, purposeful—like he had somewhere important to be.

Ma sat trembling, teetering on the edge of tears.

Rad ached to comfort her—the yearning almost unbearable—but he knew better.

Such a gesture wouldn't mend anything. It would shatter everything.

If he revealed himself now, the hidden passageways would be exposed. The small sanctuaries he still possessed would vanish.

He'd be cast out of his room—maybe even onto the streets of Ornst—once they discovered just how much he had heard and seen… and how long he had been listening and watching.

Amid the whirlwind of emotions, a flicker of clarity broke through. If redemption existed, it came in the knowledge that his siblings missed him.

For too long, he'd let resentment fester, secretly wishing misfortune on them—everyone but Abby, who had always held a place in his heart.

Now, he saw it differently. Their coldness had been a shield, a way to survive under Da's rule. That realization steadied him.

A new resolve took root—quiet but fierce: to protect Ma and his siblings from Da's cruelty, and from the lies that kept them in his grasp.

Da loomed in his mind—a towering villain, and not his true father. Rad filled in the gaps as only a child could: his real father must have been a good man. Noble. Brave. Driven away by Da's cruelty and greed.

The story spun itself—clean, simple, and comforting.

It gave shape to the emptiness.

And for a moment, that was enough.

Rad moved like a shadow through the concealed passageways, retreating to the refuge of his room. Each time, he half-expected to find Wilkins waiting—ready to catch him, punish him, and cast him out with Da's approval.

But the room was quiet. Untouched.

He slipped into bed and closed his weary eyes, though his mind refused to rest.

He was no longer his Da. He was Xavier.

And Xavier would pay. Somehow.

For Ma.

For the siblings Xavier had turned against him.

For all the indignities Rad had endured.

Wilkins…

Rad didn't trust Xavier's loyal valet and he never would.

For now, Tristin, Bella, and Marie remained exempt.

They were victims too—though that reprieve might not last forever.

As slumber crept in, a thought took root—sharp, defiant, and dangerous.

He didn't know how yet. But he would find a way.

Five years to learn. To grow. To watch.

To become more than a servant. More than a mistake.

He wouldn't hide from the name von Schule. He would wield it.

And when the time came, Xavier would know—without question—that the bastard boy he tried to erase was the one who rose above them all.

CHAPTER EIGHT

∞

The Journal of Rad and Abby

Since passing notes in the books became too dangerous, Rad devised a scheme where they could write to each other using a shared journal.

On the second-floor landing was an old accent table which hadn't moved in ages. It was made of cherry wood and stained a dark color, had two empty drawers with silver pulls, and was ignored as far as he could tell. Rad was sure he'd walked by that table a thousand times and never once paid attention to it.

As Rad approached Abby's door, he thought this would be the most dangerous part of the shared journal—telling Abby how it was going to work.

He tapped on her door.

It opened and Abby gasped, "Radcliffe, what are you doing here? If Wilkins see you, you'll get in trouble."

Rad showed her an empty journal, on the inside cover were 'R' and 'A' in big letters. He motioned toward the table on the landing.

Abby poked her head out, wary. "What am I looking at?" she asked.

"The accent table," Rad whispered as he waved the journal. "We can write to each other. I get up early to work in the stables, so I can pick it up in the morning and put it in my room and read your notes. I'll respond, put it back in the evening, and you can take it on your way to bed or your bath. We don't have to do it each day, just make sure we hide the journal when it's in our rooms."

Abby's smile was bright. "When do we start?"

"Now," he answered handing it to her. "We'll work out the kinks later."

Abby kissed him on the cheek, retreated into her room, and shut the door.

The spine creaked as Rad cracked open the ledger, stiff from disuse. It groaned like old wood in a cold wind, reluctant to come alive again. The scent of aged parchment and ink rose sharply, mixed with the faint tang of leather and dust.

Not paper—proper parchment, pressed and lined for trade inventories, notes on barrels, orders for shipments and wine sales. A business journal. One of Xavier's, swiped from a shelf in the study when no one was looking. Rad had taken it because it was blank, and because it wasn't meant for him. That made it feel right.

It felt… important. Heavy. Like words meant for this thing should matter.

He turned to the inside cover, dipped the nib of a borrowed pen, and scratched out the title in slow, perfect letters:

The Journal of Rad and Abby
(Keep Out or Face Certain Death—Especially You, Tristin)

So, I'll start. Abby, you were so beautiful at the gala in your white dress! Like someone straight out of one of those stories about princesses and queens. Everyone was watching you—everyone was impressed! Sorry I couldn't be part of it, Wilkins tossed me into my room—that no good snoop. I hope you had fun.

Beautiful? Ugh. The dress was so itchy I thought I'd go mad by the end of the night. The ridiculous hat kept falling off. I don't think anyone was watching me, they were watching Gabrielle! I had fun, but we had to go to bed early before the party got started. I heard Da sold some of his wine. Maybe the next gala I can stay up past bedtime. I hope this works.

This is much easier. I'll make a false bottom in the drawer just in case—we have extra wood in the stables from repairs. The way you pull it up is from one of the corners. You'll sort it out I'm sure.

The false bottom is a pain. It takes too much time, and it's suspicious if I'm lingering around the table. The journal is hardly in there—do we need to use the false bottom?

I guess not. I thought it was smart in case Wilkins snoops or one of the housemaids discovers it accidentally.

Perhaps you are right. Wilkins might start snooping and open a drawer, or one of the housemaids might find it when cleaning, I didn't think of that. We should use it. Don't eat the chocolates!

Why not? You are letting a hunk of chocolate go to waste. I ate it anyway.

Let's leave a chocolate in there, in case Wilkins sees me. He can think I'm sneaking chocolates to you. We can leave other stuff in there if we want to throw him off. So don't eat the chocolates!

I ate the chocolates. More please.

You are incorrigible.

I don't know what that means.

Rad was excited to read the next entry from Abby and opened the journal, his eye catching the inside of the cover.

"What?" he asked aloud.

The title of the journal had a line through it and a new title inscribed just below the grim warning to keep out.

The Secret Letters of a Disobedient Chocolate Thief and His Long-Suffering Sister

(Don't eat the chocolates!)

He flipped the pages to find out what 'incorrigible' meant.

It means you are a corrupt rascal who can't be trusted!

First off – I didn't steal it! You gave it to me. What do you mean? Can't be trusted? You're being silly. I need time to think about a better title.

Abby, you won't believe what I saw when Hadley took me into the city! It's massive—bigger than I ever imagined. There were these enormous buildings with banners fluttering from the rooftops, and the streets were full of people shouting and laughing and selling everything you can think of. We stopped at a little shop selling meat pies, and I swear it was the best thing I've ever eaten.

The noble part of the city was quieter but more impressive— huge houses with gates and carriages everywhere—but not as big as *Château Saignoral*. I can't stop thinking about how much fun it was to go into the city—it was amazing. Do you ever get to go into the city? What's it like for you?

The new title is perfect, so don't you change it!

I've been to the city a few times, but not like you saw it. Ma keeps us in the nicer areas—straight to the shops or someone's house and back again. Guards go with us. I'm jealous you got to walk through the markets; they sound so exciting! Gabrielle says markets are for commoners, but I think she's afraid of getting mud on her shoes."

Is Ma doing well?

I think so. She is spending more time with me, Bella, and Marie that's for certain. Gabrielle comes with us sometimes, but her and Ma don't talk to each other.

I wish I could talk to her, but it would only get her in trouble probably. Wilkins tripped on the stairs today. Best thing I've seen all week. He blamed the rug.

I wish you could talk to all of us!
I heard! He's been grousing about his knee all afternoon. Did you have anything to do with it?

Me? No. But if I did, I would gladly take the blame. I hope he limps.

He also fell in down in the cellar getting a bottle of wine for Da. Surprised you didn't hear him screaming all the way in the stables.

The wizards are here, Abby. There are four of them in the basement, putting up permanent lights. I wish I could watch how they do it. Do you know why Da wanted the lights? Was it because Wilkins tripped in the cellar?

Partly. Wilkins still complains about his arm, even though it's fine now. But Da told Ma he wanted the lights to keep the servants safe—and the wine, too. He didn't say it, but I think he's worried about someone stealing those extra bottles and his bourbon collection. The lights aren't going everywhere, though. Only the cellar and outside along the walls. I heard him talking with Wilkins about the cost. Fifty gold per light! Can you believe it?

Happy Birthday—I put a present in your room.

Thanks for the chocolates. I shared them with Jamie and Hadley.

Wilkins was sniffing around again. He saw me near the landing, and I think he's onto something. The chocolate was gone—did you see him take it? Either way, we should be more careful. Maybe we can leave the drawer empty for a week or two, just in case. What do you think?

I didn't see him, but he didn't find the journal of course—he's a lunkhead. I'm sure he thinks you are leaving sweets for me. Let him think that. I'll make sure he doesn't catch on, but you're right—let's stop sharing for a while. I'll see if I can find another hiding spot for the journal if it gets worse. And don't worry, Abby—we'll figure this out together.

"Looking for something?" Wilkins' voice cut through the air, sharp and cold.

Rad flinched, his calloused hand jerking away from the drawer as if it had burned him. He turned, guilty, molding his expression into one of feigned surprise.

"No," he lied, his voice steady but his heart hammering.

He relaxed and leaned against the accent table, pressing his hip against the drawer to shield it from view.

Wilkins stepped forward, slow and watchful, his beady eyes flicking between Rad and the table. His boots made noise until they hit the woven carpet runner.

"What's in the drawer?" Wilkins asked, his tone steel-edged.

"Nothing," Rad replied, his response too quick.

Wilkins tilted his head, his hand reaching into his jacket pocket.

"Nothing, is it?" He pulled out a small, wrapped chocolate, holding it aloft like a hunter displaying a fresh kill. His expression was… victory.

Rad dug at the floor with his toes, his nerves getting the better of him.

"This what you're looking for? Contraband from your sister?" Wilkins asked.

His fingers peeled back the wrapper, slow and taunting, the rustle of paper loud in the silent hallway. He popped the morsel into his mouth, chewing with exaggerated satisfaction.

Rad shook his head. "I wasn't—"

"Don't bother lying." Wilkins stepped closer, towering over him. "I know Abigail's been leaving chocolates for you in the drawer. Did you think I wouldn't notice? I wouldn't find out? You fancy yourself a mastermind, skulking around the shadows like a parasite?"

Rad looped his thumbs into his belt pockets and kept his mouth shut. He knew better than to argue or answer.

Wilkins leaned down, his face inches from Rad's. His breath smelled of the chocolate he'd devoured and bourbon.

"This is your only warning," he growled. "I will speak to Miss Abigail about her poor choices. And if I catch you loitering here again—you will regret it."

Wilkins gripped Rad's shoulders—firm, not harsh—his fingers pressing just a bit too long, just a bit too low. It wasn't painful, but Rad felt the pressure through his ribs, a quiet warning masked as correction.

Before either could speak, hurried footsteps approached, soft shoes tapping over the polished wood.

A housemaid rounded the corner, arms stacked high with linens. She froze, her eyes darting between Rad and Wilkins. A top sheet slipped from the pile, landing in a gentle puff.

Wilkins straightened at once, his hands rising to adjust Rad's collar—too precise, too casual. A friendly act, too late.

The maid's gaze shifted from Rad's uneasy face to Wilkins' hands. Her posture wavered.

"Pick it up," Wilkins said.

She bobbed her head and murmured an apology, fumbling with the fallen sheet.

"I'll leave you to it," Rad muttered, stepping past the valet.

He didn't look back as he descended the stairs. His shoulders' discomfort eased with each step, but the echo of that grip—too familiar, too knowing—lingered in his chest.

I know it's been a while. I've had the journal for weeks now.

I got in trouble for leaving you chocolates—Wilkins yelled, and Gabrielle said she was disappointed I broke the rules. I wasn't even allowed to go to afternoon tea with Ma, Bella, and Marie. I guess we have to be more careful if we want this to last.

Did you find a better place to hide the journal? I had to keep it tucked under my mattress like a thief. I half expected Wilkins to sniff it out like a hound.

Sorry you got in trouble because of me. It's my fault, but I did it to throw Wilkins off the scent of the journal. When you take your walks in the morning, put the journal under a loose board under the center bench of the gazebo—I have it all rigged. There is a waterproof canvas bag you can slip it in so it doesn't get wet. I started carrying things to and from the house for no reason, so I should be able to hide the book, and no one will notice I'm carrying it. You can start walking with a book in your hands; no one will think twice.

On second thought... the reason we got caught had nothing to do with the plan and everything to do with *you.*

You're not sneaky.

I bet you were humming to yourself while hiding the chocolates, and when that maid passed by, you probably chirped, *"Not hiding chocolates for my brother here! Just opening the drawer of a table that has absolutely no use!"*

Honestly, I'm amazed you weren't caught sooner. You're about as subtle as a trumpet in the library.

Not surprised Wilkins didn't sniff out the journal under your bed. I can smell your stinky socks up here on the third floor.

Abby opened the cover, noticing immediately her title was crossed out and a new one put there.

The Disobedient Thief and His Useless Partner in Crime

(A true tale of chocolate theft, betrayal, and deeply flawed family members whose names start with the letter 'A')

I do NOT have stinky socks. YOU are not funny.

Your title is stupid. Go ahead, look at the correct title after you read this. I fixed it; enjoy.

The reason we almost got caught is because you had chocolate smeared all over your face like a starving troll who normally eats garbage.

Besides, if anyone stinks, it is you! You smell like horse and epoisses cheese that's been out in the sun for two weeks!

The gazebo works fine, unless it is raining or the weather is too cold, Gabrielle won't let us go outside.

(Us girls are so delicate if you haven't noticed.)

Rad flipped back to the inside cover to see how Abby had fixed it. The title wasn't crossed out, and it looked like nothing had changed.

Then he saw it—a scribble.

(A true tale of chocolate theft, betrayal, and deeply flawed family members whose names start with the letter ✸ '*R*')

You crossed out my *subtitle*?! That's against the rules. You can cross out the title—but the subtext is sacred.

Your amendment is rejected.

And for the record, delicate ladies don't have smelly socks. Gabrielle would let you out in a lightning storm because you're so rugged and robust, you'd probably scare the weather off.

Title has officially been retired. Go see for yourself.

I'm not answering that last comment.

Instead, maybe we should write more—longer entries, real thoughts. A journal isn't just for fighting and food crimes. Each one of these takes us a day or two, and you never know how long we'll have if we get caught.

It's hard to say everything I want in a few lines. Besides, it feels like we don't get to talk much anymore after Wilkins nearly caught us. What do you think?

Don't worry, I won't tell anyone you smell like wet leather and Hadley's straw hat.

The title made him laugh. Abby had to be the smartest person he knew.

I'm Thinking

(About how much better this journal would be if I were corresponding with something smarter than you—like a tree!)

You know, I should probably admit this:

You're the only person I know who could outwit me using nothing but ink and a tree joke.

It's annoying.

And a little impressive.

But I feel obligated to remind you that there is this ancient creature of the forest called The One Tree, the magical tree that all druids worship and bow down to.

That sounds EXACTLY like me.

I'll write more as long as you write more and keep comparing me to legendary creatures.

We got a new horse, Moonsilver is her name. She's gray colored with these spots, like a robin's egg. Hadley's been training her.

Jamie and I have been working our tails off, I think Hadley is hurt, but he won't admit it. He gets so grumpy, then he gets mad if there's one little spot on the bridles. I had to clean them twice.

Jamie dropped a bucket of water on Vanguard's hooves, and didn't hurt him, but Hadley boxed Jamie's ears for being clumsy. I think Jamie will be deaf in one ear for a while. Maybe forever.

I'm curious. How do you know what Hadley's hat smells like?

One last thing, a riddle.

Library. Red. Spider.

Oh dear, I hope Hadley doesn't hit you—he shouldn't! Poor Jamie, it was an accident!

The only thing I can think of for your riddle is that time when we were in the library with the old Battleaxe governess and Tristin put a spider on her shoulder and she fainted. Then when she woke up you threw a red pillow at me, missing of course, and hit her right in the face with it. You and Tristin got the belt! Am I right?

Moonsilver, what a beautiful name. I wish Da would let us girls ride the horses. They are so beautiful.

Marie and Bella were arguing, get this, over who wears green better. I stayed out of it. Even though it clearly is Marie. Bella is blue for certain, not green.

Tristin is always by Da's side, learning the business. He struts around here like he's important, like he's the boss now. Wilkins face gets all screwy, like he's jealous of Tristin.

Haven't seen Ma much. I would love to tell her all about what you're doing. But I guess that would be the wrong thing to do.

I have a riddle for you.

Cinnamon. Kitchen. Cookies.

As for Hadley's hat, I was merely guessing it smelled just like your boots.

Answer to your riddle: *Radcliffe.*
(Just like you, the Battleaxe will never forget my name or Tristin's.)

Ground rules for this riddle game because you forgot:
– Three clues only.
– It can be a person, place, object, or event.
– It has to be something from *Château Saignoral.*
– No cheating with 'blue' 'green' 'Marie' as your clues, unless you want me to guess 'pointless argument.'

By the way, your note about Ma—I wish you could tell her too. Maybe someday.

And your guess about Hadley's hat was accurate.
Which is annoying.

But not as annoying as you winning at riddles.
(Barely.)

The starlings came back. Normally we make noise to get rid of them, they are an annoying species. I suggested we should take more drastic measures, so Hadley and I are killing them with throwing knives.

You probably didn't know Hadley has been teaching me how to throw knives.

Well, now you know.

With so many apples in the orchard, I started keeping an apple in my pocket and giving it as a treat for Vanguard. Problem now is he nudges me every time I come to him, wanting an apple.

Hadley says if I feed him too many apples it'll make him sick.

Hadley also yelled at me because I wasn't cutting up the apples for him, I guess the horses can choke on a whole apple.

Blue. Scowl. Gloves.

Shades!

Why are you killing birds? That's so cruel.

They're just little things—you shouldn't be hurting them or any other animal. They didn't do anything to you.

Throwing knives is dangerous. I don't like it. Neither would Ma.

Everyone knows—even The One Tree—you can't feed whole apples to horses.

Gabrielle tried to tell me what to wear to our next tea social. She said, "Your Ma would want you to wear this," and it made me furious.

She's not my Ma.

I didn't say anything. I don't want to get into trouble.

Ma stays in her room. She and Da shout at each other constantly.

Bella says they fight because Ma doesn't love Da anymore.

I don't understand.

Answer to your riddle: Wilkins.

Apples. Smashed. Disaster.

Ugh. You had to bring that up.

Who keeps an antique bowl for apples in a house with five clumsy children?

I scrubbed the floor *twice*. And it didn't even need scrubbing.

I guess the answer is: *The Broken Apple Bowl.*

Ma and Da should've named me Broke.

Sorry—*Brokecliffe.*

Starlings are terrible! Hadley says they invade other birds' nests, take over, and ruin food supplies. We have to get rid of them—they're pests. And no one needs to worry.

(Except maybe for the birds.)

I wish I knew why Ma and Da are fighting.

It's probably because of me—not because they don't love each other.

Gabrielle should mind her own business.

Too bad we don't have a spider to put on *her* shoulder.

The sunrise was golden this morning.

Wilkins stomped through the garden and tripped on a tree root—made me laugh. I wish he'd planted his face in the dirt.

Hadley let me ride Moonsilver. She's a gentle horse—not slow, not fast. Not like Vanguard. He can gallop like the wind. Even Shadow can't keep up.

I saw a fox in the orchard. It looked at me like *it* owned the place... then vanished.

Puddle. Splash. Wet.

Rad, we went to a cotillion last week—it was magical!

They hired a wizard—there were dancing lights and showers of sparks. He had a colorful bird that talked! And he made ice!

The ballroom was so grand, with chandeliers and musicians playing all night. I had three names on my dance card. Three!

And I danced with three different boys, and one of them said my dress was the prettiest in the room! It made Bella and Marie mad.

His name was Jace.

Jace! He loved my dress.

I'm trying to convince Da to host one here at the manor.

Bella and Marie are on my side, of course, but Ma says it's too much work. I begged Da to let us host a dance, but he told me there is no advantage to hosting.

I don't know what that means.

It would be so much fun, like our own gala. And I could invite Jace. It was so much fun.

You lose. The riddle was Tristin.

(Several scratched-out lines follow.)

I've got work to do. I don't have time for cotillions.

Surprised the wizard didn't catch the dance floor on fire.

(More scratched-out lines.)

Glad you had fun at your *fancy* cotillion.

It sounds ridiculous. Dancing with three boys?

Jace? He's probably blind. Did he have a walking stick?

I wouldn't know how to dance—what are you supposed to do, twirl around in circles and hope you don't fall on your face?

And hosting one here at the manor?

Sounds like a lot of work just to prance around in itchy clothes under chandeliers all night.

(You said your dresses are itchy.)

But... if it makes you happy, I hope Da lets you do it. You deserve to have something fun—even if it's something as stupid as a cotillion. No way Da is letting a wizard come here, good luck with that.

Hadley made me clean all the bridles again yesterday, and Jamie spilled oats *everywhere*.

He won't be hearing any cotillion music anytime soon with his ears still ringing.

If I *did* go to a cotillion, I'd probably fall asleep in the middle of it.

Boring.

For the seventh day in a row, Radcliffe approached the gazebo with a flicker of hope. The morning sun had barely crested the horizon, and the grass was still damp with dew as he crouched to check beneath the loose floorboard.

Empty.

Rad exhaled through his nose and slammed the board back into place. He dusted his hands on his trousers, then leaned against one of the gazebo's wooden columns, staring out at the quiet garden. He pounded the column with his fist.

Why hasn't she written?

He repeated the cotillion entry in his mind again.

Had he been too harsh? What if she'd taken it to heart? Perhaps she thought he didn't care.

"She knows I didn't mean it," he muttered, kicking a stray pebble across the floorboards. "Not really."

But did she?

Rad made his way back to the stables for the morning routine, but his mind wasn't on bridles or buckets.

Abby had never gone this long without writing. She was always the one encouraging him—teasing him when he was grumpy, lifting his spirits when the work was too much.

Now, her silence worried him.

What if she'd given up on him, like everyone else?

By mid-afternoon, Rad couldn't take it anymore. After finishing his responsibilities, he slipped into the secret passageways. The narrow, dusty corridors had become a second home to him, and he moved through them without thinking about it.

Reaching the peephole overlooking Abby's room, Rad hesitated.

What if she was angry at him? What if she didn't want anything to do with him anymore?

He pressed his eye to the peephole.

Abby was sitting on her bed, her knees drawn up to her chest, her face buried in her arms. Her shoulders trembled. She was crying.

Rad's stomach twisted.

What had he done? Was this his fault?

He pulled away from the peephole, leaning his head against the wall. For a moment, he sat there, guilt weighing on him like a stone. After a short time, he returned to the solace of his room and took a small piece of paper, quill, and ink. He scribbled the note, made his way down the stairs in his stockinged feet, then slipped the note under Abby's door.

Abby,

I'm sorry for what I said about the cotillion. I didn't mean to hurt your feelings. If it was important to you, then it matters to me, too. I miss talking to you. Please write back.

—Your loving brother, Rad.

CHAPTER NINE

∞

I'm Thinking

The morning began like any other. Rad rose before dawn, his body aching from yesterday's work. The stables were quiet, still touched by shadows, and the smell of straw and horse lingered thick in the air.

He brushed Vanguard, filled the feed troughs, and hauled buckets of water—every task done faster than usual, his mind elsewhere.

By the time the first blush of sunlight crested over the eastern vineyards, Rad was already heading toward the gazebo, boots damp, shirt sticking to his back with sweat. He didn't run, but he didn't walk either.

His fingers hovered over the loose floorboard.

Please let it be there.

With a deep breath, he crouched and pried it up.

The journal was there.

Rad blinked once, then twice, as if the sight of it might vanish. His hands trembled as he pulled it free of the canvas cover, the leather still cool.

He didn't open it then—not yet. Not with the rising sun catching the rooftops and the estate waking up. Instead, he tucked the journal under his shirt and made for the stables, where the hayloft waited— quiet, hidden, and safe.

Only once he'd climbed the ladder and settled into the straw did he open the book and find Abby's reply.

He held it with trembling hands and opened it to Abby's response:

Rad,

You were right.

Stupid cotillion.

I went to a dance last week, and these mean boys made fun of me because I was acting like a silly, giggling fool. I tried to ignore them, but they made it worse. They laughed at me, and it... it hurt. So I hid until it was time to go. I was so embarrassed.

I'm sorry for ignoring you.

I didn't know what to say.

You're my best friend, Rad. I promise not to shut you out again.

Your loving sister, Abby.

Rad's relief was short-lived.

He tucked the journal beneath his arm and climbed down from the hayloft, planning to write a quick reply at the small desk near the feed room. There was always ink and paper on hand for stable notes and ledgers.

He hadn't even reached the ladder when Hadley's voice bellowed from below.

"Rad! You better not be up there napping. Get down here!"

Rad winced. "Coming!"

The journal was quickly buried in the straw, hidden until he could return. He spent the next few hours tending to the morning routine—mucking stalls, brushing down Moonsilver, hauling buckets. Only after the midday meal did he slip away and scrawl a hasty reply at the desk—

I'm sorry they treated you like that, Abby. I won't let anyone treat you like that.

Ever.

You didn't deserve it, and you never will.

You're better than all of them. Don't let them get to you.

You have to fight.

—ink still drying as he tucked the journal under his shirt and made for the gazebo.

But when he reached the familiar spot and crouched down to lift the floorboard, it didn't budge.

He tried again, harder this time. Still stuck.

Frowning, he ran his fingers along the edges. The board had been nailed shut—repaired, no doubt, by one of the estate's handymen.

"Shades," he muttered under his breath.

Rad stood, brushing dirt from his knees, and scanned the garden. The gazebo was no longer an option. He would have to find another way.

Later that evening, as Rad sat on his bed flipping through the journal, reminiscing, an idea began to form.

The library.

The thought made his pulse quicken.

He could use the secret passageways to access it without being seen. Abby could leave the journal on a specific shelf, and he could retrieve it through the hidden door.

He smiled to himself, his mind already racing with possibilities. The library wasn't used much now that the children were older, and if he was careful, no one would know.

Slipping into the secret passageways, Rad made his way to the concealed entrance behind the library's bookcase. After ensuring the room was empty, he eased the hidden door open.

Their journal, ordinary in appearance, would blend in among the other worn tomes.

He tucked it behind a dusty, oversized atlas—one he was sure hadn't been moved in years—then disappeared into the passage.

Back in his room, he scribbled a quick note and crept to Abby's door, slipping it underneath.

Abby,

The gazebo won't work anymore. I've hidden the journal in the library—second row from the back, behind the big dusty atlas no one ever touches.

Don't worry about how I'll get it.

I have a way.

Trust me.

—Rad

The next day, he checked t̲̲̲,̲̲̲̲̲̲l. Abby's neat handwriting greeted him when he opened it:

The library?

How are you getting it from there?

Wait, I don't want to know, do I?

Be careful, please.

Rad grinned as he took the journal to his room so he could write to her.

Be careful?

Who, me?

I'm always careful, even when I'm breaking stuff. Mostly. Usually. Sometimes?

Never—that's what Hadley would say.

Now things are back to normal, how about a riddle?

Curtains. Pillow. Scream.

Jamie swears he saw a 'thing' creeping around the back areas near the orchard and farms. Hadley told him this estate was guarded tighter than a frog's arsehole, and no bloody creature was roaming around.

Plus Da's dogs would have found it for sure.

I got to go to the city again to get supplies. We ate these mince meat pies while we drove the wagon home. It was so tasty, I could eat a dozen of them, I'm so hungry all the time.

Can you leave some chocolates for me?

I took a walk in the vineyards, there are so many bunches. I'm sure they will be busy at the harvest.

It is hot today.

Yes, I'm sweaty and smelly.

Answer: Bella.

That night you hid in Bella's room and moaned into the pillow to scare her because she was afraid of ghosts. She knocked the curtain rod off the wall trying to hit you with it.

You screamed louder than she did, so the answer could be YOU.

Da's dogs are useless. One of them barks at clouds.

You always come back from the city talking about food. I'm starting to think you only go to get pies.

Chocolates?

We'll see. Depends on how rude you are in your next entry. No one wants to give sweets to a sweaty stable boy who smells like old boots and Wilkins' slippers.

I'm glad you took a walk.

I wish we could walk together. We did, when you first began working at the stables. I gave you a basket of goodies and some books. That seems like such a long time ago.

New riddle:

Dust. Ink. Whisper.

Let's see how clever you really are.

I will hide the chocolates in the library desk drawer, the one desk with the ink stain from when Tristin got mad.

You'll remember it.

Gabrielle has been telling us girls we need to be more ladylike. That we can't behave like fools, even when we're alone—we have to be proper, like she taught us, and be proper, like Ma.

Blah.

Tristin is flirting with Florence, the attractive servant girl. If Da or Wilkins catches him, he'll be in so much trouble.

There is another cotillion coming up. I'm not going. They will probably make fun of me anyway.

Your birthday is soon, I can't believe you will be thirteen!

I have a gift for you!

I'll sneak it into your room.

(Don't ask me how, trust me.)

Uh, there was nothing in my room for my birthday.

Are you sure you got the right one?

Because I saw Tristin chomping on—not one, not two—but *three* chocolate bars.

Suspicious.

I'll let the evidence speak for itself.

As for your riddle—Dust. Ink. Whisper.—*easy.*

That was the time you spilled ink on your dress during lessons and crawled under the dusty stairs to hide. I brought you a clean dress from your room and we whispered back and forth trying to figure out how to cover it up.

We tried to burn the stained dress in the fireplace but couldn't get the fire started. All we did was make a big mess and get ashes *everywhere.* At least we were sneaky.

Until we got caught. By everyone.

The Battleaxe screamed at us.

Ma laughed at our sooty faces.

Tristin was smug because we couldn't start a fire.

At least I didn't get the belt for helping.

I'm heading to the vineyard again soon. Maybe I'll bring you a grape. Just one.

If you're lucky. You will just love it, trust me.

New riddle: Cracked. Mud. Chicken.

Let's see what *you* remember.

Thanks for the birthday chocolates. I gave one bar to Jamie and one to Hadley. I kept the rest for myself, hidden in my room.

Thirteen.

I'm a teenager.

What a wonderful life—working in the stables, learning to throw knives, and reading books.

Incredible.

The stables are good though. With these long summer days, I've been walking around the estate more—exploring. Did you know there are fifteen farms, two ranches, and two vineyards along the southern edge of the property?

We're basically a little city.

I don't think you should go to the fancy dance if you don't want to.

But I know Ma will probably make you. So if it happens, stand tall. Don't let anyone make fun of you.

(Only *I* get to make fun of your stinky socks. How are the old thunder-feet doing these days?)

Oh, how tragic.

My heroic attempt to honor your birthday was thwarted by the chocolate-chomping Tristin. As for the evidence... well, let's just say chocolate thieves (like yourself) always leave trails—if you know where to look.

I suggest you start investigating, because I left six bars in what was apparently the wrong room.

Also, I'm done with the stinky socks jokes.

My feet are perfect, thank you.

They do not thunder—unless you'd like me to plant a boot in your backside. Then they will thunder.

You're so kind to think of me during your vineyard strolls.

Any idiot knows you can't eat grapes meant for wine.

Looks like I'm back to writing to a tree. And I had such high hopes.

Cracked? Mud? Chicken?

I have no clue. You made this up.

Nothing ever happened with chickens and mud. And what cracked? Did Vanguard kick you in the head?

Ma didn't make me go to the dance.

It was worse.

Gabrielle told me I'm coming of age and that we girls need to start thinking about marriage.

Marriage, Rad.

It's terrifying. I'm not ready for anything like that.

Bella and Marie talk about it constantly, but Da says we won't be married off to just anyone.

Still... I'm nervous I won't get a choice.

Some girls are matched with whoever their parents choose.

What if he's mean?

What if he's like Da?

We're hosting afternoon tea for several noble families soon. It'll be formal, so I get to go dress shopping with Ma. I already have so many dresses—plus the ones Bella and Marie can't wear anymore.

All blue. All green. All mine?

I still think Ma is sad. I'm going to talk to her. I should've done it long ago.

I don't have a riddle. You win.

(Lantern. Cushion. Blanket.)

Lantern. Cushion. Blanket.

I know what that means.

But bad news—we're way too big to fit on that cushion now. Your elbow would end up in my ribs, and I know you'd steal the blanket like you always used to.

Speaking of which—I *know* you still have that ratty old thing stuffed in the back of your armoire. Don't deny it. I bet you still snuggle with it when no one's looking.

Still...

If you ever want to go up there again—just to talk or not talk—I'll find a way. I can be sneaky when I need to be.

I'll be there. Blanket and all.

Not your ratty one.

(But I'm bringing a bigger cushion.)

Not much going on here. The autumn colors are beautiful, and the harvest is going well.

I saw Da out in the vineyards. I wonder if he's planning another gala to sell wine. Probably not.

Hadley's grumpier lately. His arm is hurting more than he'll admit. Every time I try to bring it up, he snaps at me.

Thanks for the extra books in the library.

I read the one on Elves. I wish I could meet one who could make me a magic sword. Hadley said their language is like High Ornst.

The wizard book? Completely unbelievable. But I still want to meet a real one.

If you can, find something on fey creatures. Or anything, really.

My bones hurt and my clothes don't fit. I'm getting taller. My boots are too small.

I'm finally growing, Abby. Maybe I'll be as tall as Tristin. And stronger.

I mean it—if you want to talk in person, in the east tower, I can get up there.

Just give me the signal.

(Ten chocolate bars stacked neatly in my room.)

That is not a signal. That is a bribe. You are a confused little boy.

I'll think about it.

That's a steep price to huddle in a cramped lantern room with my so-called ratty blanket.

And I would love to see you traipse around the manor with a huge cushion.

No less than five vases would meet their end.

I'll think about it.

Next time I go to the Ornst Library, I'll see what I can find for you. It would be wonderful if you could get permission to go yourself, and we could meet there.

(That's a dumb idea.)

I'm sure the guards would report it. Gabrielle definitely would. She ruins everything.

The library is astounding—you would love it. All those books.

You should ask if you can go. Worst thing they can say is no.

Even if you went by yourself, I think you'd enjoy it.

But I wouldn't go into the city alone. Too scary.

I'm glad you're growing. I saw you the other day—you really are getting tall! Almost as tall as Hadley now. Just don't get as mean as him.

I talked to Ma. She cried a lot. I hugged her. Silently, I gave her a hug from you. I'm sorry she hasn't spoken to you in so long.

She asked if I knew how you were doing.

I told her you were fine. I reminded her that your thirteenth birthday had passed.

She cried again. Said she knew. She still won't tell me why she's so sad. But I'm not stupid, Rad.

I see Da with Gabrielle.

But what can we do?

Da is the boss.

Ma and Gabrielle say I have to go to the Winter Cotillion in two months.

We're going shopping for dresses. (Again.)

I don't have any room left in my armoire or closet.

But there's always room for more shoes. That I can handle.

Need to protect those thunder feet for when they connect with your backside.

~~(scratched out words)~~
I think Ma is broken.

Tell Ma not to worry about me. She doesn't need to cry.

I'm fine—I promise. I'm stronger than I used to be. I can handle all of this. She doesn't need to carry it on her shoulders too.

I know she remembered my birthday. Of course she did. She just couldn't say anything. If she had… well, Da would've found out. And you know what that means.

It's not safe for her—not with everything the way it is.

Don't blame her.

Blame me. I'm the one who got kicked out.

I don't want her to be sad because of me. If you talk to her again, just tell her I'm doing well. That I'm learning. That I'm educated. That I'm growing. That she doesn't need to worry.

When I'm sixteen, things will be different.

I'll be out of here, and she won't have to hide anymore.

She can visit me in the city, and we'll have tea and cookies at one of those fancy shops Bella and Marie like.

No rules. No watching over our shoulders.

Just time to catch up on everything we lost.

I miss her.

But I understand. Really, I do.

I saw Gabrielle walking with Da by the vineyard this afternoon.

She was laughing, and Ma was nowhere to be found.

I don't understand how everyone pretends not to see it. I think they don't *want* to see it.

They even held hands for a few moments.

I should've thrown a rock at them. But Da would've beaten me—if he could catch me.

I'm fast. I can run like Vanguard.

Thanks for the books. I'll let you know when I finish them.

Did you know dryads don't wear clothing? They're naked all the time! They charm men and women into becoming their willing slaves.

I will NOT be going into the forest.

Hadley says I'll shoot up one more time—I can't endure it anymore. My feet and body keep growing. Jamie says I'm eating too much—I say I'm starving.

I'm going to need new clothes and boots before winter. I'm sure Wilkins will be upset having to provide me with a whole new "wardrobe," as he calls it.

Let me know if you talk to Ma.

(My final offer is five chocolate bars.)

(Three.)

Ma and I walked through the gardens today. She didn't say much, but I could tell she was happy to have company. I wish I could do more for her, but she won't talk to me about anything of substance. I don't think she wants me to see her this way.

I told her you were doing well, and that she shouldn't worry. I let her know I was giving you books to read.

I didn't mention the journal or the chocolates. It didn't feel like the right time. But I told her your idea—having tea in the city where no one can tell the two of you what to do.

She smiled and said you were smart.

I went through those growing pains. I'm glad I'm done with all of it. Or I think I am.

At least you're not clumsy.

Remember when I kept tripping over myself constantly? You called me "flop-feet" for a week.

The Winter Cotillion is in one month.

I have an ice blue dress—but I don't care.

I'll go, smile when I'm supposed to, and try not to embarrass the family. Bella and Marie aren't going; they're too old for the cotillions. It's for "young ladies" like me.

I won't be by myself. Gabrielle will be there. All the boys will be slobbering over her.

Ugh.

Gabrielle told me I'm supposed to marry someone important, and that the cotillions are an opportunity to "display my grace and elegance." I don't think anyone should tell me who I can and can't marry.

But I'm afraid of what Da would say.

Bella and Marie are competing. They keep talking about who will marry the richest, most handsome man in Ornst.

I don't think I want to get married at all.

Ma and Da yell at each other. They tell lies.

If that's what marriage is, I want no part of it.

I'm sorry, Abby, that you don't have a choice. No one's ever going to tell me who to marry or what to do—when to eat, when to sleep—nothing.

I'm never getting married.

When I'm sixteen, I'll be gone. I'll have my own business taking care of horses, and I'll be the best in Ornst.

I'll miss Vanguard.

And you, of course.

And Ma.

I wish I could talk to her. I know she's sad because of Da, but I think she's also sad because of me—and how Da treated me.

I overheard Da telling Wilkins the ballroom needed to be spotless. Is there another gala? The servants don't know anything, and Wilkins knows better than to let anyone in on Da's plans. I hope there is one. I'll try to sneak some food from the kitchens if I can.

Have fun at the Winter Cotillion. Whatever happens, be yourself. I hope Gabrielle will protect you this time if those mean boys try anything.

I was in the house near Da's study and heard him shouting at Wilkins. I don't know what it was about, but Da was furious. Wilkins was stiff as a post, trying to stay calm—but I could tell he was shaken.

The man's not cruel, but he's loyal to a fault.

Da uses him like a hammer.

I'll take the quiet stables any day.

Why did you have to remind me of that horrible future date? I still can't believe Da will throw you out when you turn sixteen. You're too valuable. And you're his son.

You're his son!

Ma won't let it happen. I just know she won't. When that day comes, she'll stand up for you.

And so will I.

Maybe you're right—that's why she's so sad.

Because she misses you, and Da won't let her do anything about it. Da can be so difficult sometimes.

Ma has to know about Da and Gabrielle. She never says it, but the way she glares at Gabrielle—it's like Gabrielle's a snake hiding in the grass.

I don't blame her. I'd be angry too. But it's worse than that, I think.

Ma has given up. She's... powerless.

And I don't understand why she lets Da do whatever he wants.

Winter Cotillion is next week.

I'm dreading it thoroughly. I'm so nervous I can hardly eat. What if I say the wrong thing? What if I trip? Still... I'll do my best.

Fortunately, Gabrielle's dress is going to be distracting.

And I mean distracting.

If any boys misbehave, they'll be looking at her instead of me.

The cooks are making sugar cookies—the ones you used to stuff your face with.

The ones you threw up into that vase.

I'll leave some for you in the desk drawer.

You know the one.

Those cookies are deadly. I could eat a hundred of them!

Thanks for the treat—and the reminder about that vase. When the maid found it, it must've smelled awful.

(Another sneaky thing I didn't get caught for.)

Keep the chocolates coming if you can spare them. I'm sure someone's noticed the chocolate supply is mysteriously vanishing, so don't get in trouble.

(Blame Tristin if you have to.)

I saw you walking with Ma. It was cold out. You looked so grown up—I almost couldn't tell you and Ma apart.

You're beautiful, Abby.

Not that I haven't realized it before. Just... I never said it.

If you do have to get married, he'll be the luckiest noble in the world. I hope he's a good man.

(If he knows what's good for him.)

I've seen Tristin with Florence more than once. They're definitely going to get caught. And get this—Jamie says he likes Florence. Hadley says the whole thing is ridiculous and bound to come crashing down.

Have fun at the cotillion.

Don't know what else to say.

(Hope Gabrielle and her dress of distraction help you out.)

(That sounds like a wizard's spell.)

You wouldn't believe how magical the cotillion was. The ballroom was breathtaking—golden chandeliers sparkled like stars in the sky, and the walls shimmered with silk tapestries. There were these paper lights that floated around the dancefloor—enchanted by a wizard! The musicians played so beautifully, their melodies sweeping through the room and making every step feel like part of a story.

And Rad, the attention! So many young men asked to be on my dance card that I couldn't keep up. One of them—Quentin Regenbogen—he has red hair and cute freckles. He told me I was more beautiful than Gabrielle. Can you imagine? Gabrielle! I don't know if he was being polite or if he truly meant it, but the way he looked at me... it felt real.

They were all so respectful. They asked my name, talked about books and music, and complimented my dress (it was ice blue with silver embroidery, and Ma said it brought out my eyes). I danced with Robert Ruud twice because he asked so sweetly, and his jokes were so funny I couldn't stop laughing. For one night, Rad, I felt like I was a queen, and the world was mine to command.

I still don't want to get married—not yet—but this gave me hope not all noblemen are stuffy and self-important. Some of them were kind and interesting, and they made me feel... seen.

I can't wait for the Spring Cotillion. Wouldn't it be wonderful if we hosted one here at Château Saignora? Can you imagine how grand it would be?

Your loving sister, Abby.

I'm happy for you.

Truly, I am.

It sounds wonderful—like something out of those books you've been giving me. I can almost picture it: the grand ballroom, the music, the chandeliers. You deserved to feel like a queen for a night.

You ARE more beautiful than Gabrielle.

I wish I could go to a cotillion someday, just to see it. Not to dance—I'm sure I'd trip over my own feet—but to experience something magical. It must be so different from everything I know.

And I'd like to see a WIZARD!

I'm glad you had fun, Abby.

You deserve worthwhile memories.

As for me, well, the stables don't have chandeliers, and the only music I hear is Hadley's grumbling or Jamie whistling offkey. It's not close to a cotillion, but I suppose it's my place in this world.

Still, it makes me happy to know you're enjoying life.

One day you'll convince Da to host a cotillion here. If it happens, I can sneak in and catch a glimpse of you being the queen of the night again.

And get to sneak some better food.

Your brother, Rad.

I don't know why exactly, but I started crying when I read your last entry. You should be here with us.

(We would have to call you Radcliffe.)

You have a promising future, you have to believe it, you must believe Da will let you come back to the family.

I know it has been three years.

You've grown up, I've grown up.

This household is crazy!

Da and Ma fighting, Da and Gabrielle pretending we don't know what they're up to, Tristin spending time with Florence—I saw her go into HIS ROOM.

Bella and Marie can only talk about getting married and finding a match.

(Wilkins is still an arsehole—he smells like bourbon, and Da says nothing.

I miss when we were little, when we used to play and have the governess, the old Battleaxe, before Gabrielle, teach us.

We didn't have a care, did we? We only had to worry about not breaking the rules.

(That didn't work out so well, did it?)

I guess what I'm trying to say is I've noticed you as well.

You are a handsome young man. You're not little anymore.

I know you take after Ma—and that's something to be proud of. Tristin takes after Da, which... well, I'm not sure that's such a good thing.

You are stronger, stronger than I would be if Da put me in the stables. You might not have a lot of freedom right now, but at least you can dream about your life when you reach sixteen.

I feel like my entire life is already decided for me, without a choice. There are times I wish I could run away.

But I'm not brave like you.

The city scares me, even with the guards protecting us. There are suspicious people about, always looking at us like we're a prize.

But I know if you were with me, I wouldn't be scared. You always had a way of making me feel like everything was going to be all right.

The starlings are back—with a vengeance. Little flying devils. They're a nuisance! I know you disapprove of us killing them, but Hadley and I had a throwing contest. You'd laugh if you saw us running around the barn with our knives, trying to hit them.

(Hadley looks like a chicken when he runs.)

I got twenty-one. He got ten. Massive infestation. I beat him two to one!

I'm getting better with knives, and Hadley's started teaching me how to fight with swords.

(I know I should be scared, but I'm not.)

I'm sorry you feel trapped in your crazy family.

Da isn't changing his mind. If he were going to, he would've done it by now.

I've accepted it—it's my fate. When I turn sixteen, I'll be gone. Two and a half years.

I'll make my own way, without Da's help.

You're right, I'm not afraid of the city.

I'd keep you safe. It's not as scary as you think. When Hadley and I run errands, no one bothers us. I think it's because of Hadley. People cross the street when they see him. They must *feel* him too.

The city has so much to offer—I can't wait to explore it for real one day. I see wizard shops—do they really have magical things inside? I wish I could see, but Hadley gets grumpy when I ask to go inside.

For now, I can only go with Hadley and do what he says.

(But at least he lets me sneak a pie or two. Three.)

I feel bad for Jamie. He thinks Florence is the most wonderful girl in the world. But there are so many rumors about her... and I don't think they're just rumors.

Tristin better be careful.

Next time you're at the Ornst Library, bring back five or ten books. I've been reading all of yours and the extras in the house library.

I'm running out of subjects to master—ha-ha.

(Really, I know *so* many useless things.)

I'm surprised one of you doesn't have an errant knife in your arse.

(I would love to see you explain your injuries to Da and Wilkins.)

Twenty-one? Impressive. Though I feel bad for the starlings—what did they ever do to you? Devils! Hardly.

Ma would faint if she knew Hadley was teaching you knife-throwing and how to use a sword.

(She might faint at the idea of you and Hadley having fun together.)

Have you seen Ma lately? She looks... old. I wish she would go to the stables and see you, but she is so afraid—afraid of something.

I know she loves you, she can't show it right now.

You must believe me. Your plan to see her after you're sixteen is perfect.

So you know... for Jamie's sake...Florence was put in her place by Bella and Marie. They confronted her about Tristin, though I'm embarrassed to repeat what I heard during the discussion.

Gabrielle got involved, and Da.

Da told Bella and Marie to mind their own business.

Can you believe it?

Da said not to bother Tristin.

I think it made everyone upset, because Da is letting this continue without any consequences. What do you think would happen if Bella invited a boy to HER room?

Tristin was smug and told us to leave him be.

(Says he a "man" and can do as he pleases.)

I'm getting ready for the Spring Cotillion. I'm glad it's getting warmer out and I can wear a lighter dress. I'm going to ask Ma to come with me. I'll tell you all about it.

I'll write again after the cotillion.

Promise.

You'll probably have nothing else to read.

Your sister always, Abby.

Rad checked the library again. Still nothing.

It had been several days, and Abby was holding onto the journal. He'd seen her recently—she didn't look sick.

He went over the possibilities.

Was she upset with what he'd written? Had Gabrielle found the journal? Was she reading it? Had Wilkins sniffed out the hiding place in her room? Was he holding it for future ransom? Blackmail?

The thoughts spun, one after another, but none of them felt quite right.

No.

Abby would've warned him if something was wrong.

He stared at the empty spot behind the atlas, the quiet shelf that had held their secret.

She must be holding onto it for a reason.

A good one.

At least, that's what he told himself.

Sorry I held onto the journal. I thought I wouldn't have much else to say. I was wrong.

(For the first time ever.)

Ma went with me to the Spring Cotillion, and it was lovely having her instead of Gabrielle—mostly because of the slobbering gentlemen who trip over themselves to sneak a look at Gabrielle.

Our hosts were Lord and Lady Fairmont. They don't have children, and their estate is modest but immaculate. The inside is beautiful, and while the ballroom was small, it felt more intimate than crowded.

No wizard this time—sorry.

My dance card was full again, and I received many compliments.

(I think we've graduated from calling them "boys," if you hadn't noticed.)

Lord Fairmont said I was a beauty. Then he asked the name of my sister—and Ma blushed. I thought she was going to kiss him.

(I would kiss him. He's handsome.)

Lady Fairmont—Celeste—is stunning.

Her skin is flawless, her green eyes bright, and her auburn hair reminded me of Ma. She's graceful in a way I didn't think was possible. I wish they had a son my age. They were warm, kind, not like the self-important families Da associates with.

I know I said I didn't want to get married. But maybe I was wrong about that too. If I ever meet the right gentleman...

Rad, I haven't been kissed.

I suppose we're in the same situation—though you have the excuse of being younger.

I'm just... curious.

You're still my best friend.

You always will be.

Don't forget that.

And no matter what happens—no matter who notices me or how grown-up we get—you will always be the first gentleman I ever trusted to protect me.

You're growing up. We both are. It's all right to be curious about life, about the world. If we weren't curious, we'd be bored.

I read this passage from a book called *Paths of Enlightenment.* It said, *"Curiosity is the first step toward wisdom and the last step away from fear. To wonder is to grow, for the mind that questions will never be caged."*

I will never be caged, Abby.

I will NEVER be caged.

I'll always be curious. I'll always wonder, think, figure things out. That's what keeps me going.

It'll probably be a long while before I kiss a girl.

(Unless I run into Florence—ha-ha.)

I wouldn't know what to do anyway.

I'm glad Ma smiled. I'm glad she had fun. I wish she could talk to me, but I understand why she can't. Because of Da.

Abby... I feel left out.

It's hard, watching you and the others live this life—dresses, dances, books, birthday treats—while I work in the stables like some cast-off piece of *merred.*

I've been riding Vanguard more, though. Hadley says I'm a natural rider. He also says I've got a knack for throwing knives. More swordplay coming along, but his arm's hurting again. He finally admitted it's always sore. We agreed he should rest it.

He tells stories sometimes—about adventuring, the world beyond Ornst. I know most of it's stretched truth, but I love the stories anyway.

(I tell him they're boring, of course.)

I assume there's going to be a Summer Cotillion, too. You'll be seventeen—surrounded by even more noble gentlemen.

Sorry I don't have a gift for your birthday.
You have everything, anyway.

I read your entry twice before writing this because, honestly, I wasn't sure how to respond.

First of all, thank you for the quote—it's lovely, and it suits you. You've always been curious, even as a little boy asking a million questions about everything.

I suppose that's what I admire about you, Rad. You don't accept things as they are. You look deeper. You ask *why*.

I don't think you'll ever be caged—at least, not in your mind. But... you are caged in other ways, aren't you?

You said you feel left out. And sincerely? I can't argue with you.

It's not fair.

None of this is fair.

And as much as I try to keep you connected—through the books, the chocolates, this journal—I know it isn't enough.

I know it doesn't replace what you've lost.

You're not a piece of merred, Rad.

Stop saying it.

If you believe it, others will believe it too. You're more than a boy in the stables. You're smart, you're strong, and you're destined for something greater—I know it. I know it.

As for my birthday... I don't care if you didn't get me a gift.

You're wrong about me having everything.

I don't have you.

I don't have my brother at my side like we used to be.

That's what I miss the most, Rad.

Not dresses.

Not cotillions.

Not chocolates.

You.

I've risked so much to keep this going, to make sure you know you're not forgotten. So don't you dare talk about being left out when I've fought so hard to keep you in my life.

You are in my life.

Always.

You are not being ignored.

If you don't have a gift for my seventeenth birthday, then write me something.

Tell me a story. Tell me one of Hadley's ridiculous tales. Or better yet—tell me your dreams for the future. That's what I want.

You're not forgotten.

Never.

(Please stay away from Florence.)

Rad sat on the edge of his bed, the journal resting in his lap like it might burst into flames.

He opened it.

Read her words again.

Closed it.

Set it on the desk.

Stared at it.

Opened it again.

Her handwriting blurred as tears filled his eyes. Not from pain. Not really. He didn't know what he was feeling.

It was love. And guilt. And gratitude. And shame. And something else he couldn't name.

He wiped at his face with the heel of his palm and stood abruptly, pacing the room like a caged animal.

She meant every word.

She still believes in me.

He spun back toward the desk, hovering over the journal. His hand reached for it, pulled away, reached again.

His throat burned. His chest ached.

"I don't know what to do with this," he muttered, almost laughing.

He looked out the small window near his bed. The stars were faint behind clouds, but the wind rustled the trees like they had the answers.

Rad ran his fingers through his hair and forced himself back to the desk. He pulled out the chair, sat, and stared down at the open journal. The ink was dry, but her voice was alive.

"I have to be honest with her," he whispered. "Always."

His fingers gripped the quill before he even realized it.

Sorry about what I said before. I didn't mean to be rude. It was uncalled for, but... I was being honest about how I felt.

Just because I have feelings doesn't mean I'm right.

And it doesn't mean I'm wrong.

It just means I *feel* something.

We should always be honest. Say what we mean. Mean what we say.

I read somewhere, "Ignorance is bliss."

I don't believe it.

Not knowing what someone's thinking isn't bliss—whether it's terrible or wonderful, I'd rather know.

I miss the way things used to be. Not long ago, we were still *us*. Remember when we gave everyone nicknames?

I still laugh thinking about "Battleaxe" for the governess, and how she'd scowl like she *knew* what we were calling her.

And Wilkins!

We had him convinced for weeks that his boots were cursed after we stuffed lavender sachets in the toes.

He blamed the maids.

(Still feel bad about that.)

(Not really.)

We weren't perfect, but at least we were together.

Do you remember sneaking into the kitchen for cakes? I can still taste them—somehow they were better when stolen.

(I don't know why that is.)

Or when we'd sneak downstairs at night, whispering about the adventures we were going to have? It felt like a tiny rebellion, like we were free—just for a moment.

I wish I'd broken more rules, Abby. I'd take a hundred punishments to have one of those moments again. Like stuffing that muffin in Tristin's face.

I don't even regret it.

I know things are different now. I know you're growing up, and your world is changing.

For the better.

Mine is too.

But I don't want you to think I don't see everything you've done for me.

The journal. The books. The chocolates.

Your *birthday* presents to me.

You're the only person who makes me feel like I haven't disappeared completely.

It means everything.

You mean everything.

You deserve the world, Abby.

And if Da ever lets you host a cotillion, I hope it's the grandest one anyone's ever seen.

I'll find a way to sneak in—muddy boots and all—and I'll dance with you.

(Then I'll have to scrub the ballroom floors as punishment. As if dancing wouldn't be punishment enough.)

And I *can't* promise I won't step on your toes. Just imagine it—me, on your dance card!

Lord Radcliffe, Duke of Chocolate, Protector of the Hay Bales, requests your hand, milady.

I'll try to write you a story. I don't know if I'll be any good at it, but I'll try. It'll be about two siblings—the clever brother and the queenly sister—navigating this crazy, confusing estate and finding a way to stay connected through it all.

I promise you, Abby—

I'll never stop being curious. About the world. About us. I'll keep wondering, dreaming, and fighting to find my way.

Because we'll make it.

Together.

Always.

(And don't worry about Florence. She's way too busy for the likes of me—the noble Duke of Chocolate.)

Rad slipped into the library early in the morning, his lantern casting faint light against the rows of forgotten books. The room was still—silent, except for the soft creak of floorboards beneath his stockinged feet.

He moved to the shelf where Abby usually left the journal, scanning the rows of dusty spines.

It wasn't there.

She still had it in her room.

His stomach sank, but he told himself it didn't mean anything.

Maybe she hadn't had the chance to return it.

She'd been busy—that had to be it.

The carriage had been coming and going for days, carrying Ma, Gabrielle, Bella, and Marie off to the city to shop or socialize. Abby always went with them now.

Not like before, when she would stay behind to read books.

Rad lingered by the shelf, fingers brushing the edge of a worn volume.

She'd be back soon. She hadn't forgotten.

She wouldn't forget.

Right?

Still, the ache of her absence settled into his chest as he turned and left the library.

A week later, the journal appeared on the shelf—right where it always did.

Rad nearly knocked over a stack of books in his haste to grab it.

He flipped it open, scanning the page, heart pounding as Abby's neat handwriting greeted him.

She had responded.

Without another glance at the room, he ducked into the secret passageway and made his way back to his room, the journal clutched tight in his hands.

I'm so sorry I haven't written in so long.

Life has been... hectic.

Ma, Gabrielle, Bella, and Marie keep dragging me into the city. I've lost count of how many dress shops we've visited. The seamstresses poke at us like we're mannequins. I don't even have room for more dresses, but apparently I must have a new one for every occasion.

Afternoon tea is exhausting. The tables are piled with every kind of treat you can imagine—cakes, tiny sandwiches, biscuits—but the gossip!

Oh, Rad, it's endless.

Who's courting whom.

Who fell out of favor.

Who wore the wrong color to the wrong party.

Bella and Marie thrive on it.

I... don't. I'm not sure I ever will.

But I do want to tell you something. Something real.

There's someone.

Robert Ruud.

He's kind. Polite. Charming in a way that doesn't feel fake.

He danced with me at the last cotillion and—Rad—he told me I was the most beautiful girl in the room.

I think I might kiss him at the Summer Cotillion.

I know that probably sounds silly, but... it's something I've never done.

And he's—well—he's perfect.

Perfect for me.

Enough about me.

Your birthday is coming up—fourteen! I can't believe it!

I have something special planned for you. Something unique.

I hope you'll like it.

And I promise—I won't disappear again.

Rad sat cross-legged on the floor of his room, the journal open in his lap. Evening shadows stretched long across the walls as he read and reread Abby's latest entry—and the ones before it.

He glanced at the wall and chuckled.

The smudge was still there.

Almost bath time.

The journal had grown thick, nearly filled from cover to cover. They'd have to begin volume two soon. Three years of entries, scrawled in two distinct hands, formed a living chronicle of their lives.

Rad marveled at it—not just the words they'd written, but how far he'd come.

Once, he'd struggled to write anything beyond observations and curiosities.

Now, his words carried weight.

Thoughts. Ideas. Feelings.

A record of the boy he was, and the young man he was becoming.

Abby's latest message left him full of emotions he couldn't quite untangle.

Pride swelled in his chest—pride for her.

She was carving out a place in Ornst society, dazzling at cotillions, finding joy in compliments and conversations.

But there was something else, too. A sharper feeling. A pang of loss.

A kiss?

Rad smirked despite himself, imagining the look on Robert Ruud's freckled face if Rad ever confronted him.

Abby was growing up—dancing at balls, drawing admirers, making choices all her own.

And he was happy for her. Truly.

But the gap between them was growing, and Rad could feel it with every line she wrote.

Still, she hadn't forgotten him. Not once in all these years. That was what mattered. One day, when he turned sixteen, he could visit her—wherever she might be.

So long as it wasn't *Château Saignoral.*

He doubted he'd ever be welcome here again.

He ran his fingers down the worn spine of the journal, thinking of all the secrets it held. All the laughter. All the grief.

All the love.

She said she had a birthday gift for him. Something unique. That promise alone was enough to keep him grounded.

Rad reached for a quill, staring at the blank page.

How could he put everything he felt into words? He wasn't sure. But he'd try. He always tried—for her.

Fourteen.

Three years gone in the blink of an eye.

Before he dipped the quill in ink, Rad turned back to the inside cover.

I'm Thinking

(About how much better this journal would be if I were corresponding with something of greater intelligence—like a tree!)

He stared at it for a moment, then scratched through the title with slow, careful strokes.

He set down the quill for a beat, fingertips brushing the leather spine as if steadying something fragile. Then he leaned forward, and in deliberate, even letters, wrote:

The Journal of Rad and Abby
(Volume One)

Volume One.

Because there would be more.

CHAPTER TEN

∞

Rosamund

Like it or not, this marked his fourth year as a servant. At fourteen, Rad's birthday celebration was modest, shared only with Hadley and Jamie in the stables once their work was done. Midmorning, they prepared a stall for the impromptu festivity—setting up a table and chairs and enjoying summer ale Hadley had swiped from the kitchen.

Without permission, of course.

Stolen ale tasted better.

As Rad sipped the pilfered warm drink, he contemplated his severed ties with his family. He, a von Schule by name, was invisible except for trading weekly journal entries with Abby. Despite this, he was resolute in retaining the name, using it as a form of defiance against Xavier. It also lingered in the back of his mind that the von Schule name carried potential future benefits beyond these walls.

People outside of *Château Saignoral* wouldn't know he had been cast aside, unwanted.

Abby was seventeen now, blossoming into a beautiful young woman. She still attended the cotillions—though these next few would likely be her last. Soon she'd be swept fully into Bella and Marie's world: afternoon teas, evening parties, and the endless whirl of Ornst's noble society. Rad wasn't sure if she wanted that, or if she was simply being carried along by expectation. Either way, it felt like she was drifting farther from him, their lives pulled in different directions by the quiet gravity of growing up.

Rad figured it wouldn't be long before Bella and Marie were married off to men from other noble houses. That was how it worked—noble daughters traded like cards to seal alliances and sweeten trade deals. Da would call it tradition, but Rad knew better—it was an investment. These weren't family decisions; they were strategic moves, another way for Xavier von Schule to extend his influence and tighten his grip on Ornst.

The girls still frequented the city with Ma, drifting from one tea session to the next with noble ladies who gossiped like bards and nibbled dainty cookies that—mysteriously—never added a single ounce to their delicate figures.

Rad supposed he should be glad they got to spend time with Ma.

He was.

Sort of.

But the whole thing sounded ridiculous to him. Endless chatter, fragile cups, polite laughter over pointless rumors. It felt like a complete waste of time—unless the cookies were stolen. Then maybe it would be worth it.

Tristin had thrown himself into Xavier's business affairs, which freed up Xavier to spend more time with Gabrielle—both at home and on their frequent countryside excursions. The arrangement wasn't exactly mysterious.

Perplexing, maybe, if you pretended not to see it for what it was.

Rad didn't.

He saw it clearly.

Ma and Xavier still maintained their staged civility, exchanging pleasantries in front of others like seasoned actors. But there was no warmth left, no flicker of affection.

As for Gabrielle… Rad couldn't help but wonder how long it would be before she turned up pregnant.

It seemed inevitable.

Like everything else in this house.

Wilkins, ever the polished steward, remained a fixture of the manor—meticulous, aloof, and perpetually sipping bourbon without fear of reprimand. Gone were the biting insults and veiled threats of Rad's childhood.

Wilkins rarely spoke to Rad unless issuing orders, and even then, his voice carried the bored detachment of someone addressing a piece of furniture. Yet on occasion—when there was an important task—he would call on Rad. Not because he liked him, but because he knew Rad would do it right. Still, Wilkins never acknowledged this, never offered praise or trust—only silence, or worse, pointed indifference.

If Wilkins noticed the subtle fractures forming within the household, he gave no sign. His eyes remained fixed on appearances—on discipline, order, and Xavier's approval.

Rad had capitalized on the hidden passageways within the house to gather countless secrets, noting them in his growing diary. It had become a habit—an obsession.

Every overheard conversation, every fleeting moment of insight, every subtle crack in the perfect façade of *Château Saignoral* was recorded. The diary was his personal archive, a silent witness to everything he had seen and heard. It rivaled the journal he shared with Abby, but unlike their playful exchanges, the diary was far more dangerous.

He knew far more about his siblings than they'd ever guess. Tristin, now a strapping, confident young man, maintained a polished, commanding presence in public. But Rad had seen the contrast—quiet moments behind closed doors, where Tristin's swagger gave way to a softer, more indulgent man. Florence visited often, her expression bright and eager. Whatever passed between them, it was clear Tristin was different in private.

Bella and Marie's endless chatter about society, fashion, and eligible suitors filled the air whenever they were together. Their dreams of marrying into affluent families from Ornst or neighboring duchies struck Rad as shallow—but maybe that was unfair. They were doing what was expected of them, embracing the future laid out by Da with all the grace they could muster.

Rad felt sorry for them.

Sometimes.

They were trapped too—just in a different kind of cage. He would be cast out, forced to build a life of his own, while they were being shaped to serve another man's legacy, possibly one more beastly and controlling than the one they already lived under.

They might never be free, not really.

At least he had the hope of freedom. They had obedience dressed in silk opaque enough to hide the abuse.

Through the peepholes in the master bedroom, Rad had witnessed the slow unraveling of Ma and Xavier's marriage. Their rare conversations were stiff—polite on the surface, but brittle underneath—circling always back to Xavier's quiet threats. He had made a promise: Ma and her bastard son could stay, so long as she accepted his affair with Gabrielle without protest.

They still yelled, sometimes. Rad told himself that was better than silence. At least they were speaking.

At least Xavier hadn't hit her again.

As far as he could tell.

The secrets Rad uncovered rarely shocked him anymore. They simply filled in the outlines of a household teetering on the edge of its own illusions.

And yet, the passageways weren't just a tool for spying—they were an escape. In those dark, narrow corridors, Rad lived beyond the reach of judgment and expectation. They were his sanctuary. A place to think. To observe. To plan.

More than anything, they reminded him: knowledge was power, and curiosity—his greatest strength.

Curiosity is the first step toward wisdom and the last step away from fear. To wonder is to grow, for the mind that questions will never be caged.

Rad had no illusions about his standing in the household. The best he could hope for was to reach sixteen and earn his freedom without incident.

He didn't need perfection. Not anymore. But when he had a family of his own, it would be different. No secrets. No walking on glass. No pretending everything was fine when it wasn't.

There would be truth—even the ugly kind.

He would fight for that, because he'd lived too long without it. He'd lived too long with terrible lies. And he wasn't naïve.

Not anymore.

The world didn't reward kindness. It rewarded cunning, patience, and the will to act when no one else dared.

He could lie. He could steal.

But never to the ones he loved.

Never to them.

And he had proof that goodness still existed in the ruins of this house.

The journal.

He and Abby had built something real in its pages.

Honest.

Brave.

Unforgiving—but always true.

It was proof that not all von Schule blood was tainted. That not every heir of this broken place was lost to illusions of power and privilege.

Abby was good. He was trying to be. And Ma… Ma was a victim of it all.

Of Da's cruelty. Of Gabrielle's quiet ambition.

Of one mistake that turned her into a ghost of herself.

She had protected him once. Paid the price.

And now she, too, survived in silence.

So did he.

But not forever.

Life in the stables was relentless, but not unbearable.

Hadley had kept his promise—Rad was now a capable horseman, a skilled knife-thrower, and stronger than he'd ever been.

Yet as he sat on the edge of his seat, rubbing his calloused hands, a quiet question gnawed at him:

Was this it?

Would he become a horse-master in Ornst, known only to the stables and the animals he cared for?

A life of meager earnings, routine work, and quiet obscurity?

He shoved the thought aside. He didn't care. He couldn't afford to care.

What mattered was freedom—his freedom.

To go where he wanted, do as he pleased, and live without anyone owning his time or commanding his life.

That was enough.

For now.

"You're about as tall as Tristin," Hadley said.

The gruff voice startled Rad out of his thoughts.

"Not as broad," Rad replied, glancing down at his lean frame. "He's getting better food."

"Lad, time's been kind to you," Hadley muttered. "Don't squander it. You used to be a skinny ten-year-old with soft hands and porcelain skin."

"Squander? I could probably catch Vanguard I'm so fast. I can wrestle Jamie to the ground in seconds. You too, old man."

"Last time we wrestled," Hadley said with a rare grin, "I thrashed you good—with one bad arm. Think again before you start bragging about your prowess when you aren't wearing the crown. When you put this old horse-master on the ground, you can brag. Until then, shut it."

"Who here killed twice as many starlings? Who wears *that* crown?"

"Aye, you can throw with accuracy and power. Starlings are no match for you. But your swordplay's still for shit."

"Shitty teacher. I need a better instructor," Rad shot back. "Old man."

"A swift kick in the arse is what you need."

Rad laughed. "I'd like to see you try. Old and slow."

"I may be old and slow," Hadley grumbled, "but I can still plant you flat on your back. Don't get smug 'cause you killed a few helpless birds. I've got a few shitty sword tricks left to teach."

"Let's face it," Rad said, smirking. "You can't even lift your left arm anymore. It's dead weight. You're useless. Old, slow, and broken. I bet a wooden dummy would put up more of a fight. Or Jamie, maybe."

"Not me, no way," Jamie laughed, raising his hands. "Leave me out of this. I'm no match for Rad or your grumpy sword tricks."

Hadley grunted. "Right arm works fine, thank you very much. Left's just sore, is all. Needs rest."

He rolled his shoulder in defiance, but the wince betrayed him. He cracked his swollen knuckles, flexing his fingers like he meant business.

"Seeing it's your birthday," Hadley said, "I've devised a bit of mischief for us."

"You're not going to bore us with your ridiculous stories, are you? Is that my gift? Or is the gift *not* boring us with your ridiculous stories?"

Hadley made a half-hearted swipe to cuff Rad's ear, but Rad deflected it with ease. Jamie burst out laughing as Hadley muttered curses under his breath.

Rad took a long, satisfied sip of warm ale.

Stolen ale tasted so much better.

"You're old and slow, Hadley. Old and slow. So… are you taking me to the Ornst Library?" Rad asked, narrowing his eyes. "Is that my birthday surprise?"

Hadley hissed in displeasure. "Boy, you're at it again—annoying old Hadley. Always with your nose in a book. Not to my liking."

"No Ornst Library?" Rad asked, feigning offense.

"No," Hadley grunted. "You can do that on your own time. Wasting daylight on nonsense."

"What's wrong with reading?" Rad tilted his head, glancing between Jamie and Hadley. "So what if I always have my nose in a book?"

Hadley leaned forward, lacing his gnarled fingers together.

"There are better things to stick your nose into, lad."

Jamie went red.

Rad's grin widened, his own face coloring. "Shades," he muttered.

"Aye, you lads. So young and dumb," Hadley chuckled. "Young and dumb."

Jamie looked like he might melt in his chair. "Rad… what were you reading the other day?"

Rad went with it. "A treatise on strategy—*The Art of Subtle Warfare*. Talks about flanking maneuvers, disrupting supply chains, outwitting an opponent without spilling blood."

Hadley raised a skeptical brow. "A what? What in bloody hell is a *treatise*?"

"Like a book, but shorter," Rad said breezily. "I'll refer to them as *books* for you two uninformed ruffians."

"And what exactly are you planning to do with this knowledge?" Hadley asked. "Lead an army of stable boys into battle with pitchforks?"

Rad ignored the jab. "Ignorance isn't an excuse, Hadley. The more you know, the better prepared you are for anything. Like trade—did you know Ornst's economy depends on exports because of its location? It's a gateway to the west, south of the mountains. With the port, goods flow in and out by ship."

Hadley grunted. "Where'd you learn that, then? One of your books?"

"Several," Rad replied. "Haddensack's landlocked, except for the icy north. They rely on Ornst and Biggs as proxies for sea trade."

Hadley blinked. "Well, I'll be."

Rad wasn't done. "Did you know the elves used to trade enchanted weapons with humans before the age of the Mages? That's why their smithing techniques are so prized. Oh, and dwarves—"

"All right, all right," Hadley interrupted, raising a hand. "I get it—you're a bloody genius now. And yes, I do know about the dwarves and their expertise forging weapons."

There was a glint in Hadley's eye—just enough to make Rad wonder.

"Show off," Hadley muttered, cocking his hand for a slap not delivered.

"I'm not showing off," Rad said, crossing his arms. "It's… why wouldn't you want to know how the world works? People act like you're born with knowledge, but you're not. You have to learn it. Reading is training for my mind." He tapped a finger to his temple. "Same as we train with knives. No different."

Hadley looked at him the way he might study a blade—gauging its edge, testing its balance. After a moment, he gave a grunt of approval.

"Fair enough," he said. "But if you're going to fill that head of yours with all this wisdom, make sure it doesn't explode. And don't forget—life's not all books and fairy tales. Sometimes it's just about surviving the day. Making sure you're still breathing when the sun goes down."

He paused, scratched his chin, then added, "Read that in a book."

Rad grinned. "I've survived so far."

Hadley gripped his ale and shifted in his seat. A flicker of pain crossed his face as he set the mug down and rubbed his left shoulder, wincing when he hit a tender spot.

Rad took another sip, watching him. The truth of Hadley's condition was written in the stiffness of his movements. The shoulder wasn't healing—it was getting worse. Over the past few weeks, Rad had noticed the growing reliance on his right hand, even for simple tasks. Mounting a horse had become a chore. Training had slowed. No matter how often Hadley claimed rest would fix it, Rad knew better.

"So," Rad said, leaning back in his chair with a smirk, "back to my birthday. What's this mysterious gift you've got for me?"

A mischievous grin spread across Hadley's face. "I got permission from your Da to take you into the city today for some fun—if you're up for a little excursion with old Hadley."

Rad shot to his feet, fists raised in triumph. "Yes! Finally! I've only ever gone for errands—this'll be my first real trip. About time!"

Hadley chuckled. "Settle down, you fool. We've a few things to do first."

Jamie remained silent, his expression hesitant. A polite smile lingered on his lips, shadowed by an internal conflict he clearly hadn't resolved.

Hadley raised an eyebrow. "Spit it out, Jamie. You're among friends. No offense taken if you'd rather stay behind. Ornst's taverns aren't to everyone's liking."

"Tavern, yes!" Rad exclaimed, then caught Jamie's scowl and sat back down, sobering a bit.

Jamie ran a hand through his dark hair. "I do want to go," he said quietly. "But I already made plans. I can't back out now. Florence would never forgive me." He glanced down. "I forgot it was your birthday."

Hadley muttered a string of unintelligible grumbles before clearing his throat. "Lad, listen to me. Florence isn't going to give you what you're looking for. You'd be better off coming to Ornst with us. That city's full of opportunity for a young man like you. Believe me—you're wasting your time with that girl."

Jamie shook his head. "I like her, Hadley. Even when she's moody. And she likes me too. Maybe—just maybe—there's a future for us. I have to start thinking about that. A family. I'm a stable hand, but she likes me anyway."

Rad let out a short laugh and shook his head. "She likes everybody, Jamie. She likes the dogs. You're probably the only one she hasn't thrown herself at."

Hadley stepped in before the jokes could cut any deeper. "She's going to string you along, lad. You'll come to understand. Don't waste your youth chasing empty promises. Come with us instead. You'll have a fine time—I promise. Been saving up for this day, so it won't cost you a thing but your time."

"Come with us," Rad echoed, this time more earnestly. He glanced sideways at Hadley. "What exactly are we doing?"

Jamie's polite smile faded, a flush creeping into his cheeks. "Don't talk about her like that," he snapped. "She's not some girl who toys with people. She's kind and sweet, and you're swallowing gossip just because she's pretty and friendly. People always spread rumors about girls like her. I don't know why you believe them."

He shoved his chair back and stormed out of the stables, each step echoing his frustration.

"Bringing the dogs into it?" Hadley said, grinning as he shook his head. "That was cold. Boxing your ears is finally working."

Rad shook his head and said, "I don't care what anyone thinks. I'll say what I want, to whoever I want. Florence? She's like the rumors say—a whore. Jumps on every man in this house who's willing. Every man *but* Jamie."

Hadley tapped his mug with a gnarled finger, his face alight with laughter. "She's not a whore, lad. Whores get paid."

They both burst out laughing, the sound echoing off the stable walls as they clutched their sides.

"To Jamie!" Hadley said, raising his ale in mock tribute. "That poor lad needs to get a clue."

"To Florence!" Rad added with a grin. "She needs one too."

They drained their stolen summer ales in long, steady gulps and slammed their empty mugs on the table. Hadley's hit first, earning him a crooked, defeated grin from Rad.

"You ready for an adventure?" Hadley asked, wiping foam from his mustache with the back of his hand.

Rad caught the glimmer in Hadley's eye, one he knew well—the promise of excitement. "What do we have planned? Tell me!"

"It's a birthday surprise," Hadley said. "Go change out of your work gear. Put on something plain—common. Nothing that makes you look like a spoiled fancy boy begging for a beating. No shiny black shoes, no top hats, and leave those ridiculous scarves you like so much in the drawer. We're not running into anyone who cares for high society today."

Rad chuckled, shaking his head. "Spoiled fancy boy? You don't have to worry about it. I outgrew my old wardrobe ages ago. Tossed all that nonsense in the trash. Ended up with Tristin's hand-me-downs—plain stuff, but it fits me better." He slid off the chair, straightened up, and started toward the stable door. "I'll see you at the front gate. I assume we're walking, unless, we can take Vanguard and Shadow…"

"No borrowing horses today. Leggin' it. Wasn't part of the deal. Was hard getting this much approved, so stop yappin' about how we're going to get there."

Rad opened his mouth to argue, then shut it. If it had taken Hadley effort to pull this off, complaining about the details was being ungrateful. He turned toward the stairs, the old resentment toward Xavier bubbling at the edges of his thoughts—but he pushed it aside.

For today, at least.

Why spoil his birthday?

Ascending the stairs to his room, Rad entered his sanctuary—unchanged over four years. The bare walls, simple furnishings, and empty closet reflected his no-frills existence. The space held no warmth save for the secret it concealed: the hidden passageway he had carefully guarded.

As he unbuttoned his shirt to change, his eyes landed on a small box resting on his bed. It was wrapped in an elegant lavender silk scarf, tied with a delicate pink bow. Embroidered on the edge were the initials *AvS*—Abigail von Schule. The softness and care of the wrapping stood in sharp contrast to the plain, rugged simplicity of his room.

A single note was attached.

Happy Birthday—A

He smiled in anticipation—in the journal she said his gift was going to be unique. The simple message, penned in Abigail's elegant hand, brought a bittersweet pang to Rad's chest.

Memories of past birthdays surfaced—each one marked by chocolates, a precious indulgence for a boy now accustomed to meager scraps. He reflected on their shared journal, his lifeline, cherished like a family heirloom. He grabbed the beautifully wrapped package.

The gift had weight to it.

Bursting with eagerness, Rad pulled away the scarf, revealing a polished wooden box beneath. He lifted the lid, and he gasped seeing the contents. Chocolate truffles sat nestled among arranged stacks of coins: fourteen coppers, fourteen silvers, fourteen gold, and to his astonishment, fourteen platinum.

The glint of the platinum coins made his heart race.

Platinum was rare because of their worth compared to gold.

While he couldn't fathom how Abby had procured such a fortune, he understood the gift's significance. Each coin marked a year of his life, spanning all the denominations. It was thoughtful, extravagant, and bewildering all at once.

He popped a chocolate truffle into his mouth, savoring its richness, while his thoughts raced.

How had she managed this?

Silver and copper were accessible to the von Schule children, but gold and platinum?

Those were treasures too valuable to misplace unnoticed. He would have to ask her how she came by those, then a thought occurred to him, why was he questioning a gift?

She hadn't questioned him about how he got into the library. Perhaps a simple thank you would suffice. It reminded him, he needed to write a short story for her.

An idea popped in his head—perhaps he could write about this birthday adventure with Hadley.

Yes, that was the perfect idea!

Rad slipped a few coins into his pocket and hid the rest, stashing the box and scarf behind the closet's hidden door. The concealed space housed all his most precious possessions: his diary, notes and sketches from his secret observations, trinkets left behind by guests, and the puzzle sheets bearing the ominous words *Leskaré Never Sleeps*.

His eyes lingered on the notes about the puzzle. Its arrangement teased at something just out of reach. How long had he spent trying to decipher it? Would he ever unlock what lay hidden behind the door?

Rad ran his fingers over the edges of the puzzle papers, imagining the treasures—or dangers—awaiting on the other side.

Hadley was at the front gate, his weathered hands resting on his belt where his cherished dagger, *Darter*, was sheathed. Concealed throwing knives adorned his person, ready for use should trouble arise.

Rad mirrored him in this regard, his own hidden knives a constant companion now, no longer against Hadley's rules.

Hadley looked presentable for once—his trousers were free of patches, his shirt clean and tucked in, and both hair and beard had been combed into a semblance of order. But the battered straw hat remained, as stubborn and worn as the man beneath it.

Together, they worked to open the gate when the guard ignored them, Rad pausing to study the estate's fortified defenses. The newly constructed guard towers loomed over the grounds, stark reminders of Xavier's desire for control.

Or growing paranoia.

More guards patrolled the estate than ever before—professional soldiers and hired fighters alike. The ladies, when venturing into Ornst for their social engagements, traveled with clusters of armed escorts instead of only a few guards. The unease these precautions conveyed wasn't lost on Rad.

What had changed?

Or what change was about to unfold?

Stepping through the gate, Rad was struck by an unexpected sensation of freedom, as though the estate couldn't confine him. The avenue stretched before them, and soon they managed to hitch a ride downtown with a passing delivery service.

Rad marveled at the cityscape as they approached. The buildings greeted him, each adorned with intricate carvings, bright banners, and signs beckoning customers inside. The streets bustled with life, filled with voices carrying snippets of conversation, laughter, and the occasional heated exchange.

"Where are we going?" Rad asked as they disembarked from their ride.

Hadley gestured toward a lively street further ahead. "To a fine establishment called The Sweet Hatchet. It's a tavern I used to frequent years ago, long before I started working for your Da. Might be some familiar faces still knockin' about there, if I'm lucky."

Rad's face lit up at the prospect. A real tavern, alive with music, stories, and strong ale—it was the kind of adventure he'd only dreamed of and read about in books.

He wondered, what tales would he hear today? He imagined a table
of warriors, Elves, and Dwarves poring over maps, sipping ales and
planning their next assault on ancient ruins.

Hadley motioned down the bustling avenue, grinning. "Birthdays
are meant to be memorable. Trust old Hadley on this—The Sweet
Hatchet will take care of you."

"I didn't realize I was in such dire need of care," Rad muttered.

"You're fourteen." Hadley studied him a second longer than usual,
a flicker of curiosity in his gaze. "Every lad your age needs a proper
introduction to manhood. The Sweet Hatchet's got games to test your
skill and luck, ladies to please you if you fancy their company, and
strong drink to knock you flat on your arse."

Rad chuckled but kept his pace steady beside Hadley. "Well,
Wilkins won't let us linger all night enjoying the company of ladies and
guzzling ale. Besides, we've got work tomorrow."

"Let's survive today first, and we'll worry about tomorrow when it
arrives," Hadley said with a grunt. "Now stop gawking at the city like
you've never seen it before and get your arse moving! Old and slow,
eh? We'll see about that."

Rad quickened his pace, keeping stride with Hadley as they
approached the heart of the bustling city, the promise of The Sweet
Hatchet drawing them closer.

The Sweet Hatchet was an unassuming tavern, a stout rectangular
structure with three floors above ground and likely a cellar beneath. Its
plain wooden exterior showed years of wear, but the lively hum of
voices and laughter spilling out onto the street promised energy and life
within.

Rad's keen eyes scanned the building as they approached.

Stairs clung to one side, winding upward to balconies on the
second and third floors, and the tavern stood so close to the
neighboring structure leaping between rooftops was plausible.

He filed away the observation, a habit born of survival and caution.

"What are you studying, lad?" a curious Hadley asked.

"Ways to get in and out of the building," Rad replied, not breaking stride. "Can't help it. Habit, I guess."

"You'll live longer thinking like that." Hadley clapped him on the shoulder with his good hand.

They stopped at the entrance, and Hadley turned to Rad, his grin fading.

"Now, listen here. You're allowed one drink for your birthday. One. Don't think about asking me for a second, or I'll box your ears so hard you won't hear for a week. Understand?"

Rad smirked, his defiance playful. "You've only got one working arm, and you're too slow. Hollow threat. I'll drink as much as I want."

"Don't test me, lad." Hadley's gruffness was softened by a faint grin, but his next words were firm. "While we're here, you don't mention who we work for. Best not to give anyone any ideas about where we live or who pays us. Got it?"

Rad wilted under Hadley's stern gaze and relented, nodding. "Understood. I'll keep my mouth shut. Though I'll admit, this place is more interesting already—and that's before my one generous drink. You're a real miser, Hadley. You'd think working for von Schule would be more rewarding."

Hadley chortled at the jab, unoffended, and his grin widened for reasons Rad couldn't quite place. He clapped Rad's shoulder again, a gesture between affection and warning, and gave it a firm shake before motioning toward the door.

"Let's go in and see what sort of trouble we can avoid."

They stepped into The Sweet Hatchet, brushing past two burly men stationed at the entrance. Their scarred faces and hulking frames gave the impression of danger, but Rad assessed their intimidating aura was more for show than substance.

Inside, the first floor opened into a lively, albeit modest, tavern space.

To the right stretched a long, well-worn bar where drinks of every conceivable concoction were being poured. The air was rich with the tang of spilled ale and the faint sweetness of liqueurs.

About half of the barstools were occupied, the patrons nursing drinks or conversing in hushed tones.

Around the room were scattered tables, some small and intimate
for two, others built for larger groups, all connected by narrow
pathways for the servers to navigate.

A few tables hosted early-day drinkers, but most sat empty because
of the hour. Rad's attention shifted to the two women weaving through
the room, their presence impossible to ignore. They wore short, tight-
fitting dresses that accentuated their figures, the vibrant fabric hugging
their bodies as they moved.

The first woman caught his eye with her striking, athletic build. She
was petite but carried herself with quiet confidence. Blonde hair framed
an undeniably sweet-looking face, and her ears sparkled with an array of
small hoop earrings. Her gray eyes held a mysterious sparkle, giving her
an air both approachable and intriguing.

The second woman was taller, her dark hair cascading in waves
down her back. Her eyes, deep and dark, held secrets worth
discovering.

She moved with a captivating grace, her curvy figure drawing the
gaze of every patron in the room, including Rad's. He found himself
staring longer than he should, mesmerized by her beauty.

She was unlike anyone he had ever seen, a vision leaving him
speechless. Long ago he thought Gabrielle was the most beautiful
woman he had ever seen. He was wrong, dead wrong.

A voice clamored from behind, "Hadley! You old fool! It *is* you!"

Rad tore his gaze away from the enchanting woman and saw an
older woman approaching them.

She was wispy-thin and fragile, with brown hair streaked with gray.
Her youthful blue eyes contrasted with the rest of her age-worn
features. Adorned with an assortment of colorful glass jewelry, she
made an effort to appear more opulent than her modest adornments
suggested. Her blue glass earrings dangled like drops of rain, catching
the light.

"Glenys!"

Rad blinked, startled by Hadley's exuberance. He had never seen
the horse-master this animated. The two embraced, a reunion of old
friends. Hadley, still favoring his left arm, kept it at his side.

The sight stirred an unexpected pang of guilt in Rad for how often he teased Hadley about his injury. Poor bastard couldn't hug a woman who was willing to hug him.

Glenys giggled with joy. "I haven't seen you in years!"

"I don't get out much," Hadley admitted with a wry grin. "Keep to my corner of the world. You know how it goes for a man with my... past endeavors. I hoped you were still here. The place is decent. Intact, surviving. Thriving?"

"Still own half, that hasn't changed," she replied. "Surviving is the word for it. Most of the faces are new, but Ewen and I keep this little hovel going. Enough to live decently, not enough to retire. I'll be here until I drop or until Ewen gets daft enough to buy me out."

"Where's the old dog?"

"He's not in till the evening shift—we alternate these days. If you're here later, you can catch him. Otherwise, I'll leave a note saying you stopped by."

Her sharp gaze flicked to Rad, studying him up and down. "Well... are you going to introduce me to your boy? Your *son*?"

Hadley cackled with half delight, half amusement.

"He's far too pretty to be sired by the likes of me. This is Rad. He works with me in the stables. A good lad. It's his birthday today, so I brought him to The Sweet Hatchet for a proper introduction to the world."

Glenys's expression softened.

"Welcome, Rad. Any friend of Hadley's is welcome here. Let's get you two gentlemen seated at a decent table, and I'll send the girls over. You won't be disappointed, I promise."

Hadley waved her off with his hand.

"Not for me. You get old enough, and certain parts stop working—the ones you enjoy the most. I'll stick to my drink today. Let the lad have his pick of the ladies. On me. It's his birthday."

Glenys chuckled. "Very well—"

"Her."

Rad cut her off, pointing at the dark-haired woman in the red dress. Her curves defied reason, and he couldn't tell if she was wrapped in thin silk or painted in color. Either way, he didn't care—she was mesmerizing.

Glenys arched a brow.

"The man knows what he likes. Rosamund is a striking beauty. You're certain? I could bring the other girls over to meet you first. Plenty to choose from."

"She's what I want."

"Rosamund," Glenys called, a subtle motion summoning her as well.

The woman sauntered over to them with a smile promising mischief. Each sway of her hips commanded the room. Eyes followed her.

"Take Rad upstairs. It's his birthday," Glenys instructed.

"Which one of you is Rad?" Her voice was as alluring as her presence.

Rad straightened. "I'm Rad."

"Happy birthday!" Rosamund said as she took his hand.

She leaned in and kissed his cheek, her lips soft and round, leaving a faint tingle on his skin. With her warm, delicate hand still clasping his, she led him toward the staircase.

Rad felt a strange, unfamiliar excitement rising within him. Her hands, free of calluses or blemishes, were too soft. Up close, her skin appeared flawless, with a velvety texture that glowed in the light.

A subtle, alluring fragrance surrounded her, faint but intoxicating. He couldn't recall ever being this close to a woman so captivating. His attention went to the delicate gold anklet around her right ankle—the only piece of jewelry she wore.

Unsure of what to say, he followed as she guided him upstairs. On the landing, he glanced back at Hadley. Seated at a table below, the old man appeared relaxed, engrossed in a coin exchange with Glenys.

"Are you left-handed?" Rad asked as they ascended the staircase.

"I am. How did you know?"

"Your anklet is on your right. Makes it easier to clasp with your dominant hand, I'd think."

Rosamund giggled—a light, genuine sound. "You're observant. I never thought about it, but you're probably right." She tilted her head with a playful smile. "Now it's my turn. Righty or lefty?"

"Both," Rad replied. "My hands are equally dexterous. Ambidextrous it's called."

She laughed, a touch of challenge in her eyes. "We'll see about that."

As they reached the second floor, there was a lively atmosphere of games and merriment coming from the areas. A crowd of patrons played cards, rolled dice, worked puzzles, and tossed darts at circular targets with numbers.

The darts drew his attention—compared to throwing knives, it was laughably easy. His confidence swelled for a moment, but Rosamund tugged his hand, urging him up another flight of stairs, and he let the games fade from view.

"I'm not… experienced," he admitted as they reached the top of the staircase.

"It doesn't matter," she said without missing a beat. "You'll figure it out. All men do, one way or another."

The third floor was quieter, lined with hallways and doors, some adorned with red ribbons signaling they were occupied. Muffled sounds drifted from behind the doors—sounds Rad recognized from Tristin's escapades with Florence.

His confidence wavered and his steps faltered, unfamiliar nerves creeping in.

Rosamund kept hold of his hand and glanced back with a reassuring smile.

"This way."

She led him to her door, tied a ribbon around the handle, and guided him inside before securing the door with two clicks.

Her room was modest but carried an air of quiet charm. A comfortable bed dominated the space, flanked by a basin for washing and a chamber pot. Two well-worn chairs and a small table sat near one wall. The room was adorned with numerous pillar candles, their wax dripped, though none were lit. The simplicity of the furnishings was offset by the warm, inviting atmosphere.

Rosamund crossed to the window, positioning the inner shutters to dim the natural light. Moving with effortless grace, she began lighting the candles one by one. The flickering flames cast a soft glow, making her movements appear more fluid and enchanting.

Rad's gaze darted around the room, taking in every detail, before settling on her again.

"What do you want me to do?" he asked, his voice uncertain.

"Nothing for now. Just watch me," she instructed, her tone both soft and commanding. "Eyes on me. Stop studying the room like you're looking for an escape route. Eyes on me. Follow every move, every curve of my body. You like my curves, don't you?"

Rad obeyed and focused on her as she lit the remaining candles. Their golden light bathed the room, deepening the shadows and highlighting her figure in ways that made her more captivating.

She slipped off her soft leather shoes and placed them on a nearby chair. With a single, fluid motion, she removed her dress. It fell to the floor like a discarded veil, revealing the fullness of her beauty.

What the dress had concealed, the candlelight now accentuated— her flawless, fair skin and softly defined curves.

She was breathtaking, her confidence as striking as her appearance.

Rosamund moved toward him, her smile inviting and unhurried. Standing before him, she rested her hands on his shoulders and began to massage them with her thumbs.

"Let me help you out of those clothes," Rosamund said, her voice as soft and inviting as her smile.

Before she could begin, Rad raised a hand.

"I'll do it if you don't mind," he said quickly, his thoughts racing.

Her brows lifted and her tone shifted to one of mild concern.

"Are you certain? Is something wrong?"

Rad locked eyes with her smoky gaze, steeling himself to be as honest as he dared.

"I have throwing knives hidden," he admitted. "I don't want you to accidentally cut yourself. Don't worry—I'm not going to hurt you."

Rosamund tilted her head, her lips curving into an intriguing smile. She took a cautious step back, cocking her hip in a way both reassuring and undeniably alluring.

"Go ahead," she said, giving him the space he needed.

Rad's movements were controlled.

He started with his boots, doing his best not to appear hurried.

One by one, he removed his garments, folding them on a chair as he went.

When he placed his knives and their dual sheaths on the table, his skin felt warm and flushed.

Rosamund's smile deepened as her playful eyes roved over him.

"Someone is eager," she teased.

The nervousness gripping him melted away, replaced by a surge of excitement.

"I don't know what I'm doing," he confessed, his voice steady.

Rosamund stepped closer, her movements fluid and graceful.

"After today," she said, her voice rich with promise, "you'll have plenty of experience. I guarantee you'll be different after this. Shall we?"

Rad nodded as she leaned in, her lips meeting his in a warm and inviting kiss, igniting a fire he hadn't realized was there.

His first kiss was from the most beautiful woman he had ever seen.

When she pulled away, her gaze held his, full of playful confidence.

"The world can have you tomorrow," she purred. "Right now, you're mine. All mine."

This experience was *not* going into the shared journal.

As Rosamund had quietly assured him, he did indeed feel changed.

Descending the stairs to the second floor, Rad let his thoughts drift away from the enchanting woman he had just been with. He had never been this… distracted.

Ahead, the room buzzed with activity.

Games of chance and skill were in full swing—cards being dealt, dice clattering against tables. He felt an itch to try his hand at dart throwing but stopped himself.

Hadley's voice echoed in his mind, as clear as if the old man stood beside him.

Don't show off.

He had drilled it into Rad during their years of practice together. The skill was a secret—one Hadley insisted they keep buried.

No one was to know.

No one was to see.

Only Jamie, Abby, and Hadley knew.

No one else.

In one corner, a young man, about Tristin's age, was hunched over a table, focused on a half-formed image taking shape on the surface. Curiosity piqued, Rad wandered closer.

The man was solving puzzles with startling ease—his hands moved in swift, fluid motions, rearranging pieces as if the solutions came to him without effort.

Some involved forming seamless images, others required aligning colored squares into precise patterns. It was intricate work, yet he moved through it like it was second nature, reminding Rad of the puzzle door back at the manor house.

"You're good at those," Rad remarked, stepping closer to the table.

He glanced up, startled but not annoyed by Rad's interruption. The young man was taller than himself and sturdily built. Sandy blond hair fell across his forehead, framing sharp blue eyes that assessed Rad as much as they had studied the puzzles. His hands bore the marks of a laborer—rough skin, dry patches, and a scattering of small cuts, each one speaking of hard, honest work.

"Hard to find challenging puzzles these days," the young man said, his tone casual. "These are too easy. I could do them blindfolded."

Rad chuckled. "This is an odd place for puzzles—whores upstairs, drinks downstairs, gambling over there, and puzzles for kids waiting on their Da."

The young man laughed, deep and unrestrained—a laugh belonging to someone who didn't care what others thought.

"My Da isn't upstairs, trust me. Puzzles used to be a thing when I was a kid, back when The Sweet Hatchet had more… prestige. The nobles loved solving puzzles—it was all the rage. Not so much anymore. I hang out here to kill time before work. Glenys and Ewan don't mind as long as I keep out of trouble and buy a drink now and then. Plus, I figure practicing puzzles is like training with a sword—just for the mind."

Like reading books.

"Sounds logical. What kind of work do you do?" Rad asked.

The man paused, his hands still moving the puzzle pieces as he considered the question. He completed the puzzle with ease, showing a small image of a fox, then reset it.

"I run errands. Nothing fancy. Small jobs keep me busy. I've been all over Ornst and know every street in every district. Probably every shortcut, too."

"Important work, fetching things," Rad teased. "I imagine solving puzzles helps you stay sharp. Errands can get tricky, particularly for intelligent types like you. You're quite the expert at sliding puzzles. Think you can manage the ones that actually require thinking?"

Rad picked up another puzzle frame and placed it in front of the young man with a challenging grin.

This one was a three-by-three sliding puzzle, eight tiles with one space unoccupied.

The man grabbed it eagerly, sliding the pieces without thinking. In mere seconds, he revealed a faded picture of a horse.

"This one? A million times. You can't rearrange it to make it harder."

"What about a five-by-five? Twenty-four tiles?"

"It would take longer, sure," he admitted, his eyes bright with excitement. "But it's doable. You have a five-by-five? I would love to solve a five-by-five."

Rad patted his sides. "Not with me today."

The young man rolled his eyes. "Oh, sure. Perhaps it's down your pants? Go ahead, check. Not like there's anything else down there worth noting."

Rad grinned, unfazed. "Not in my pants today, sadly. Left it back at my estate, sitting right there on the dining room table, next to the crown jewels."

The young man chuckled. "Too bad. Now you've got me curious—what's this puzzle about?"

"I've got a five-by-five I've been working on. Memorized the starting position of every tile, and I know where each one is supposed to end up. Problem is, no matter how I try, I can't get the tiles to line up. It's maddening. Silly, really. I'm embarrassed talking about it. Puzzles." Rad sighed. "It's impossible—unless you're smarter than everyone thinks."

The young man raised a brow at the challenge, ignoring the jab at his intelligence.

"Bring it here, and I'll solve it. It might take a little time, though. Like ten minutes for a smart person like me."

"I can't bring it here," Rad admitted. "It's not mine. It belongs to the nobleman I work for. It's one of *their* puzzles. I'd love to sort it out before anyone in the manor does—be the first to crack it."

The young man gave him a sideways glance. "What family do you work for?"

Rad mirrored the glance. "Didn't say. Who do you run errands for?"

"Didn't say," he answered.

Rad crossed his arms. "I see we have an understanding. So, can you solve a five-by-five or not? This conversation's getting stale, and I've got things to do."

The boy shrugged and said, "I'd need to see the actual puzzle."

"Can you grab some parchment or cloth? A charcoal stick or chalk? I'll show you the starting order. You can solve it and note the moves for me."

The boy rubbed his chin. "A lot of work. I don't have time right now. Just take me to the puzzle—"

"Here's the starting order."

Rad flipped over the horse puzzle's wooden frame and etched a five-by-five grid onto the back using the tip of one of his throwing knives. His quick hand moved precisely as he scratched numbers into the squares.

"All you need to do is figure out the steps to solve it and write them down. Doesn't have to be today—deliver the solution to my place of work, and I'll reward you for the effort."

The young man mulled it over, his eyes flicking between the puzzle and Rad, wrestling with the notion.

Rad thought of the coins stashed away in his room—gold and platinum were far too generous for such a simple task. A copper was appropriate for the job, but not enough to entice this busy young man.

"A silver?" Rad offered. "I'll give you one silver if you can solve the puzzle."

The boy's eyebrows shot up in astonishment. "A whole silver? You're too poor to have silver. If you're lying, I'll beat it out of you."

"I've got silver where I live," Rad assured him. "Believe me, I can pay. So, will you do it?"

"Are you joking? A silver to solve a kid's puzzle?"

"One silver," Rad repeated.

The boy's expression darkened. "If you welch on me, I know a few thugs who'd be happy to break your fingers after I mess up your pretty face."

Rad didn't flinch, his expression calm. Hadley had trained him well to keep his composure under pressure.

"Do we have a deal or not?"

The boy held his gaze for a moment before nodding. "Fine. Where do I deliver the answer?"

"The von Schule estate."

The boy's eyes narrowed. "I know where it is. Delivered there a few times. Guards are arseholes. You work there?"

"In the stables," Rad said. "I take care of horses. Name's Rad. Now that we're doing business, I should know who you are."

"Faucet Chilcott. Call me Chilcott."

They shook hands. Chilcott's grip was unyielding, his strength surprising.

Rad continued, "Address your note to Hadley, the horse-master. Write on one side that saddles are available for purchase and you need a one-silver deposit. On the back, put the sequence for solving the puzzle. Got it?"

"Sounds easy enough." Chilcott snatched the horse puzzle and stuffed it beneath his shirt. "I've got to get to work. My boss has no patience for excuses if I'm late."

Rad's eyes flicked to the square sheath on Chilcott's hip.

"That's an interesting sword."

"It's not a sword," Chilcott replied. "It's a razor. Sometimes I have to cut things off in my line of work. A razor works best."

"You need an oversized razor to do your job?"

"You're asking too many questions." Chilcott's tone grew curt. "I have to go."

"Finish the puzzle and I'll pay you the silver I owe."

Chilcott didn't reply.

He turned and scurried down the stairs to the first floor, vanishing into the crowd below.

After Chilcott left, Rad returned to the first floor. He expected Hadley to ask about his time with Rosamund, but the old horse-master said nothing as Rad settled into his seat.

Instead, Hadley signaled the bartender for another round, including a drink for Rad.

"Thank you for the birthday gift," Rad said, glancing at the dark, viscous liquor in Hadley's glass.

The drink looked potent, thick, and distinctly unappealing.

Hadley fidgeted with his drink and replied, "It pains me to say this, but you've earned it. Don't think this is out of the kindness of my heart. I always have my reasons. There's something in it for me too."

"It was fine," Rad said, "if you're wondering about the quality of her company."

Hadley scoffed.

"I'm not some gossiping wench, you dolt. Keep your whoring stories to yourself. And let this be a warning—if you run your mouth too much about your conquests, your friends, your family, or your talents, it'll come back to bite you in the arse—or worse. Now, let's get to the real reason we're here. I'm getting older..."

"No shit," Rad interrupted.

Hadley nodded and took a needed breath.

"As you've noted, repeatedly," Hadley continued, unbothered. "My left arm's gone to rot. Can barely lift it now. Before long, I won't be able to do anything with it. I can survive well enough with my right, but there are things I can't do one-handed."

"Like get on a horse. A horse-master who can't ride is useless."

"Aye." Hadley grimaced. "If your father discovers I'm not as useful as I once was, he might cut me loose. Terminate my employment, or worse, stick me in the kitchen with those prissy pricks. I need your help, Rad. I need you to take on more of the work with the horses— quietly. I'll handle the tasks I can still manage."

Rad leaned back in his chair, crossing his arms. "What's in it for me?"

"Rosamund, for starters. Every year on your birthday, I'll get permission to bring you here. And, depending on how things go, we might manage a few other visits to The Sweet Hatchet too."

Rad's expression flattened. "I could have Florence for free if I wanted. Why bother with Rosamund?"

Hadley ignored him. "One more thing. After this drink, we're going to see Thratmam."

"Thratmam?"

"A squirrely old dwarf I've known for years. He's a damn fine weaponsmith, knows his way around a forge better than anyone I've ever met. He made a dagger for you, like my *Darter*. It's waiting for you—if you want it. You know the price."

Calling this unexpected would be an understatement.

Rad had long coveted a dagger like *Darter* ever since he first laid eyes on it.

Hadley wasn't the type to joke about weapons—though he exaggerated stories and issued playful threats, he treated training and armaments with the utmost seriousness.

Thrilled by the prospect, Rad fought to contain his excitement. One of Hadley's most repeated lessons was to keep emotions in check—steady as a rock, immune to provocations or tells.

"You're speechless. Too excited, eh?"

Rad nodded, feigning reluctance. "Thank you. I'll help you with the horses. But if you welch on this, I'll make sure neither of those arms work."

Hadley knocked the table with his fist, grinning broadly.

"That's my lad! You've been paying attention. And 'welch,' huh? Never heard you say it before. Where'd you pick it up?"

Before Rad could answer, their drinks arrived, interrupting the conversation.

Hadley nudged Rad's glass toward him with authority.

"Down it. One gulp. Don't waste time sipping it. Get it done like a good lad who knows how to drink Stagwater."

Rad obeyed but instantly regretted it.

The fierce drink had a faint, bitter taste, like stale pecans, and it burned as it went down.

He gagged, coughing in fits, his throat searing.

Desperate for relief, he grabbed Hadley's untouched ale and drained it in a series of long, gasping gulps. He slammed the mug down on the table, face red from the ordeal but wearing a triumphant grin.

"That was mine," Hadley grumbled, irritated and not amused. "You owe me a copper. One drink, I said. One."

Rad belched, pounding his chest with a fist.

"We're even. The ale's payment for making me drink that hellish shit. Poison doesn't count as a proper drink."

Hadley chuckled, shaking his head.

"*Proper drink*, what the hell do you know anyway? Babes drink Stagwater where I come from."

Rad tapped his fingers on the table, his gaze steady.

"So, tell me, where's this dwarf? Let's go."

"Patience."

Hadley leaned back, slowly savoring his liquor.

"He's not far from here. Let me finish my drinks, and after I'll take you. Where's my copper, though? Cough it up!"

Chapter Eleven

∞

The Treasure Chest

Approaching *Château Saignoral,* Rad's mind was uncharacteristically scattered, drifting to thoughts of Rosamund. Her warmth lingered in his memory, not just the physicality of their encounter but the way her presence had enveloped him.

The softness of her skin, the kindness in her smoky eyes, and the confidence with which she had guided him through an experience both new and transformative, left an impression refusing to fade.

Rosamund had treated him not as a boy fumbling his way into adulthood but as a man worthy of her time and care. That acknowledgment alone had shifted feelings deep within him.

Rad was not one to get distracted; years of servitude had honed his focus. Yet, as he passed through the gates of the estate, he found himself replaying her laughter, the brush of her lips on his cheek, and the way she'd told him, *the world can have you tomorrow. Right now, you're mine, all mine.*

For those fleeting moments, he had been seen—understood.

Not as a von Schule servant, not as the bastard boy pushed to the fringes of his family, but as himself.

Rad.

As he sensed an unusual event unfolding at the estate, his thoughts continued to wander.

Guards were stationed in greater numbers than usual, their presence unnerving. New faces dotted the grounds, their unfamiliarity casting an air of tension.

Hadley and Rad passed through the gates without incident, though their arrival was scrutinized as if they were strangers. The subtle shift in atmosphere clawed at Rad's instincts.

One of the household servants confirmed his suspicions, whispering an important man had come to see Xavier von Schule, accompanied by a small army of guards and a wizard.

The mention of a wizard immediately captured Rad's attention. Wizards seldom ventured far from their towers or the magnificent courts where they served. Their presence was often a sign of significance, whether diplomatic or dangerous.

Rad couldn't help but wonder if this visitor was one of the 'foreigners' Xavier often conducted business with—the enigmatic figures who haunted whispered rumors yet left no trace of their dealings behind.

Their day was officially finished, according to Hadley, so Rad headed toward his room. He moved with purpose through the hushed manor, his mind still pulled in two directions: the day's peculiar events and the memory of Rosamund. He couldn't decide which occupied him more.

Once inside the manor, he followed his usual routine, removing his boots and carrying them upstairs to avoid the sharp echoes that would betray his movement.

The eerie manor house was quiet, silence pressing on his ears and amplifying every creak of the floorboards.

Rad placed his boots in the closet and stood for a moment, contemplating his next move.

There were several hours until supper. On any other evening, he would have welcomed the reprieve, perhaps scribbled in his journal or wrote to Abby or revisited the cryptic puzzle that had long consumed his curiosity.

But tonight, the pull of the secret passage was too strong to resist. He needed to know what was happening. If this visitor was truly one of Xavier's foreign partners, he might finally uncover clues about the source of his stepfather's power and wealth—a mystery that had loomed over his life for as long as he could remember.

All the books he had read didn't give him any insight into Xavier's dealings.

He put on his soft leather shoes to muffle his steps and slid into the secret passage hidden behind the panel in his room. The familiar coolness of the passage walls greeted him as he navigated the narrow corridors. He moved quickly, but with care, his destination clear: Xavier's study. If this visitor was as important as the whispers suggested, that's where they would be.

Rad's thoughts shifted as he moved. Rosamund had told him he would be different after their time together.

She had been right.

He felt older somehow, more aware of the vastness of the world beyond the estate. The experience had been a gift, a reminder life could offer unexpected moments of beauty and connection—even for someone like him, caught in the tangled web of the von Schule household.

But now, the weight of his circumstances pressed down once more. Whatever Xavier was plotting with this mysterious visitor, Rad intended to find out.

The world could have him tomorrow.

Tonight, he would have the truth.

"As always, I appreciate your discretion, Xavier," the man said, his voice measured and laden with authority. "This matter cannot be discussed with anyone—including those you trust most."

"I understood that from your enigmatic correspondence," Xavier replied, his tone guarded as well. "I have fortified my estate at your urging and without question. I listen to my old friends and business associates, and I heed their advice."

Rad observed the scene from his hidden vantage point, his heart steady as he committed every detail to memory.

The man, whose name he didn't yet know, had a face that would be etched into Rad's mind forever.

A deep, jagged scar ran across his forehead as though someone had tried to cleave his skull with an axe. His features, lined with age, betrayed an air of weariness, but there was no mistaking the power he carried in his presence.

Older than Xavier, he bore the marks of indulgence: a thick, corpulent frame straining the limits of his tailored white shirt. Strained buttons clung to their holes, while a loose silk vest, red and gold, hung from his shoulders like an afterthought. Its inability to fasten over his girth spoke to his decadence.

Despite the lavish attire—the gold-stitched trousers, polished black boots, and a belt clasped with a shining golden buckle—one element was oddly out of place: the aged wooden chest he cradled in his arm.

Its surface was cracked with wear, the iron bands dull and weathered. It was locked with a sturdy clasp, though the mechanism was basic. The way the man handled the box hinted it held more than mere valuables.

Rad felt a flicker of confidence—he could pick the lock in moments.

His curiosity burned. What could be so important to warrant such secrecy and protection?

The man gave the treasure chest a firm pat.

"No doubt you're wondering what the excitement is about."

Xavier responded with slow nod. "We can get to that soon enough. My valet should be here any moment. Please, make yourself comfortable."

Wilkins.

As if Rad's thoughts had summoned the vile man, a sharp knock came at the door. True to form, Wilkins entered after the customary single heartbeat of waiting time, his movements precise as always.

"*Monsur* Killigrew," Wilkins said as he bowed, "your belongings have been delivered to one of the suites reserved for our most honored guests." He stepped further into the room, bowing a second time. "Your guards are settled in the barracks alongside your wizard companion. If there is anything you require, please inform me, and I will see to it immediately."

"Certainly," the indifferent Killigrew replied. "I shall require a bottle of *De'Artois* bourbon. Do you know of it?"

Wilkins' face lit up, though his attempt to mask his eagerness was only partially successful.

"Yes, of course, sir. It is the finest spirit ever crafted. I have only had the privilege of tasting it once, and the experience was unforgettable. You have excellent taste, *Monsur* Killigrew."

The flattery slid off Killigrew.

"I'll take the bottle in my room after dinner. It helps me sleep."

Wilkins began to respond with his usual effusive enthusiasm, but Xavier interrupted by raising a hand, his practiced smile sharp enough to cut through the exchange.

"Dear Perran, you're welcome to join me after dinner for drinks. We'll enjoy a pipe, like the old days, alongside your favorite bourbon. We're as cultured here in Ornst as you are in Faustron. I might have a druid blend tucked away… for occasions such as this."

Rad's ears perked up.

Perran Killigrew.

He repeated the name in his mind several times, committing it to memory. Killigrew hailed from the Duchy of Faustron—a region so vast and resourceful it could rival the kingdom of Haddensack. The one thing that struck Rad about Faustron was their use of a Judiciar—a man with absolute power over every living subject in the duchy.

He was the judge, jury, and executioner.

Rad thought Killigrew's imposing presence and apparent wealth aligned with the duchy's reputation for ambition and opulence. There was a moment of unnatural silence, and Rad noted it with interest. The sneaky Wilkins lingered near the door, his posture stiff with concealed hope.

Killigrew's expression shifted as he weighed Xavier's invitation. Wilkins, ever the opportunist, yearned for a gracious nod from Killigrew—one that might extend an invitation for him to join their after-dinner indulgence.

It was a longshot, but Rad had seen Wilkins occasionally worm his way into a snifter or two with an unsuspecting guest.

Not this time.

Killigrew's glance brushed past Wilkins as if the man were no more than a speck of lint on his otherwise immaculate silk vest.

He turned back to Xavier with a faint smile, ignoring the valet.

"Perhaps tomorrow night," Killigrew said, stretching his flabby arms in an exaggerated display of fatigue.

He forced an unconvincing yawn.

"This journey has been long and taxing, and I need one evening to myself. Thank you for the offer, Xavier, but tomorrow night we shall indulge and share tales of old. We're not as young as we used to be, and tonight, I need my bourbon and my rest."

"Indeed," Xavier replied, inclining his head. "And you shall have both while you are under my roof."

Killigrew nodded in acknowledgment before his gaze snapped to Wilkins. With a pointed finger he said, "Why does your manservant linger? Off with you!"

"Wilkins," Xavier commanded, his voice firm, "see to it *Monsur* Killigrew's bourbon is prepared and delivered to his room without delay. You are dismissed."

Wilkins gave a stiff bow and turned on his heel, retreating through the door.

As the door closed, Xavier turned his attention back to Killigrew, his tone softening.

"Your note about this treasure was cryptic," he said as he moved toward the middle of the well-appointed room. A substantial, ornately carved desk dominated the floor, flanked by cushioned wingback chairs and a polished oak table suitable for maps or documents.

The sitting area, adorned with exotic rugs and leather chairs, exuded luxury, while a modest library lined one wall, its shelves filled with volumes both decorative and practical.

Jutting from the far side were more shelves forming a 'U' shape.

Rad thought it a poor design and a waste of space.

The study could've had far more room if not for those oddly placed shelves.

Xavier crossed to the door, locking it with a soft click, ensuring their privacy.

"Please, Perran, sit and put your burden down. We are secure here. You are among trusted friends. No harm will come to us in this household."

Killigrew hesitated, his grip tightening on the aged chest in his lap.

Reluctantly, he moved to one of the wingback chairs and settled into it with a groan, but he kept the box clutched, his fingers curling possessively around its edges.

The chest was the size of a plump housecat, yet Killigrew held it as though it contained the world's greatest secrets. Its weathered wood and tarnished iron bands hinted at a long history, though its true purpose remained a mystery.

Rad's attention was fixed on the chest.

What was inside it? Gold? Jewels? Documents?

Or something far more valuable?

His curiosity burned, spurred on by Xavier's cryptic language.

Why would Xavier call treasure a burden? Rad wondered.

His eyes darted back to Killigrew, noting the way the man's hold on the treasure chest was as much out of anxiety as it was out of determination.

Whatever lay within, it was more than mere wealth.

"I must keep knowledge of this relic's existence secret. This find will make me richer beyond my wildest dreams," Killigrew said, his voice hushed but brimming with greed.

Xavier's sharp gaze flicked to the worn chest.

His tone, measured but edged with concern, cut through the room's stillness.

"You have me intrigued, Perran. But I'm also deeply concerned about why you've brought it to me—to Ornst. If Leskaré were to learn I'm harboring valuables of such magnitude, they might come for it. You've not only endangered me but my entire family, my livelihood, my name."

Killigrew waved a dismissive hand and made a sharp *psssst* noise, shaking his head.

"No one knows of its existence. No one knows I've brought it here, nor what lies within this chest. I alone have seen it. Old friend, I would never knowingly bring harm to your house. You know that. You're the only one I trust with this matter, and I trust you'll do right by me. Besides, Leskaré does not concern me. I know well enough of your dealings with them to be certain you have those details under control."

Xavier leaned forward, his expression steeled.

"Leskaré aside, tell me, what is it you've hidden inside the chest?"

Killigrew's fingers tightened possessively on the box, his tone reverent.

"An artifact of the ancient past. A relic with value beyond reckoning. To the right buyer, it could fetch millions of gold crowns. And I intend to collect. But, as you understand, in this business, finding the perfect buyer is no simple task. It could take years, perhaps decades.

I may not live to see the coin. This isn't the kind of treasure one flaunts at public auction."

Xavier's eyes narrowed as he processed the implications.

"Is that why you're traveling with a wizard?"

Killigrew nodded, leaning back.

"Wizards are... useful. This one, in particular, has no allegiance to the Wizards of Arcana. He operates independently, a freelancer if you will. I've no fear of ties to the Tower."

"You're certain?"

"Positive," Killigrew replied with confidence. "I've vetted him thoroughly."

Xavier raised his hands, his expression easing for a moment.

"I don't employ a wizard here for precisely that reason. Their loyalties are unpredictable, often skewed toward their own enigmatic goals or the Tower's interests. It's difficult, nearly impossible, to find a wizard untainted by the Wizards of Arcana. If you've succeeded in securing one, then I commend you. It's no small feat."

Rad, concealed in the secret passage, absorbed every word.

The weight of their conversation only deepened his curiosity.

The artifact must have been extraordinary—but what could be worth such risks, such secrecy? And why would it necessitate the presence of a rogue wizard? The questions churned in his mind as he struggled to piece together the implications of what he'd overheard.

"Thank you for your praise. Any other wizard would undoubtedly report matters back to the Tower. Imagine the catastrophe." Killigrew's voice was steady, but there was a flicker of unease behind his words. "I'm fortunate to have secured a wizard who cares solely about gold and serving my interests."

"Lucky you," Xavier replied, his tone mocking.

Killigrew tapped the top of the chest with his thick, ringed fingers, each *clink* echoing in the room's heavy silence.

"This must never fall into the hands of the Wizards of Arcana. Ever. This is why I chose you. You run your household wisely, without entangling yourself with their ilk."

"I see," Xavier said, inclining his head. "You're convinced this treasure is worth millions?"

Killigrew leaned back in his chair, his expression turning smug.

"Millions," he repeated, savoring the word.

Xavier's curiosity sharpened, his gaze lingering on the chest.

"You've captured my attention, Perran. What relic could command such a staggering value?"

"This," Killigrew said, tapping the chest again as if the object within would announce itself.

From his hidden vantage point, Rad's eyes remained fixed on the battered chest. Its weathered exterior, with splintered wood and tarnished iron bands, belied the fortune it supposedly contained.

He tried to imagine what could fit inside something so modest in size yet hold such immense value. Gems or fine jewelry came to mind, but those were insufficient to explain such astronomical worth.

Magic.

It had to be magical.

Perhaps a tool of immense power—a ring imbued with ancient spells, a talisman, or a weapon.

A long dagger was plausible given the chest's dimensions.

His thoughts churned as he considered why Killigrew would go to such lengths to shield it from the Wizards of Arcana.

The name of the organization evoked images of scholarly authority and a vast network of influence. Rad had read tales of the Wizards of Arcana's insatiable curiosity, their tendency to pry into all things arcane, and their unyielding allegiance to the Tower.

To them, knowledge was paramount, and their reach was far and deep.

Whatever Killigrew sought to conceal, it had to be significant enough to provoke their interest—and their intervention.

"I can accommodate you," Xavier said after a moment of reflection, breaking Rad's thoughts. "But you understand my fee will reflect the magnitude of this endeavor. Substantial, Perran."

Killigrew smirked. "Naturally. You can take a commission from the sale when the time comes, or I can offer a generous flat fee for safekeeping—your choice. As I mentioned, it could be years, decades, before I find the right buyer."

Xavier's eyes flicked once more to the chest, the gears of his mind turning.

"Years, you say. And in the meantime, the responsibility—and the risk—falls to me."

"Precisely," Killigrew said, leaning forward. "But peril has always paid well—for those bold enough to court it. And you've never been one to flinch, old friend."

The tension in the room hung heavy, and Rad felt it as if he were sitting between them. The mystery of the chest intrigued him, but so did the implications of Xavier agreeing to hold such an object.

Whatever it was, Rad was certain it would bring trouble—and he suspected it was trouble of a kind he'd never seen before.

Xavier tapped his fingers together, each movement deliberate, as if orchestrating the rhythm of their negotiation.

His smile was as thin as his patience.

"A relic of such significance as you describe will require not only a commission on its eventual sale but also a monthly fee. Security of this magnitude demands resources—guards, specialists, discretion. If I cannot employ enough men or secure the necessary measures, this priceless treasure could be lost or stolen. Surely, you agree such precautions are worth the investment, particularly if the Wizards of Arcana must remain unaware."

Killigrew's expression darkened, his lips pulling taut as he cradled the chest protectively.

"You're bold, Xavier. Bold to suggest I pay both. There are plenty of people—plenty—who would be honored to keep this item safe for me. They wouldn't dare attempt to gouge me as you are. Insulting, for an old friend." He paused, leveling a scowl at Xavier. "No, my dear friend, it will be one or the other. A commission after the sale or a one-time fee. You do not get both."

Xavier steepled his fingers, gesturing vaguely toward the u-shaped bookcase of his ornate study.

"You're forgetting who I am. I can *guarantee* the safety of your item, Perran. I have a vault no wizard can penetrate—unbreakable, enchanted with spells older than Ornst itself. The only way in is through me. Upon my death, the knowledge will pass to my son Tristin, and no one else. I offer security—a wizard-proof vault ensuring your relic will remain untouched and undisturbed."

Vault?

Rad's curiosity flared, his attention fixating on the u-shaped bookcase. That's what the empty area was—a vault, hidden in plain view. From his concealed vantage, he strained for any clue to its secrets.

Did it pivot, revealing a hidden passage?

Or perhaps there was a more intricate mechanism?

Whatever it concealed, it must hold more than the promise of safety for Killigrew's chest.

What treasures might Xavier already keep locked within?

Gold? Gems? Magical artifacts?

Killigrew barked a short laugh, his fingers drumming once more on the worn chest. "A *guarantee?* Moments ago, you implied the risk of losing it due to insufficient resources, and now you claim its safety is assured without question. Which is it, Xavier? If your security is as impenetrable as you say, then it shouldn't cost you so dearly. My offer stands—one or the other."

Xavier's lips pressed into a thin line, his face unreadable.

"My dear Perran," he purred, "for an artifact of the ancient world, one must take extraordinary measures. This is not some common trinket you've stumbled upon. Proper protection demands more than your standard guard. *Château Saignoral* will require fortifications, patrols, redundancies. You would sleep far easier knowing I've taken every precaution, wouldn't you?"

His voice dropped an octave, persuasive yet firm.

"A modest, minimal, monthly stipend will ensure the necessary security, and a commission upon the sale will allow me to share in your eventual success. Neither burden would weigh heavily on a man of your considerable means."

Killigrew leaned back, his fingers tightening around the chest.

"Bah! It *cannot* be both! I told you!"

Xavier let the room fall into silence for a moment, the tension coiling between them. He stroked his chin in a show of deliberation.

"We're at an impasse. But I understand the strain of travel, my friend. You're tired, and exhaustion clouds judgment. Perhaps a restful night, paired with Ornst's finest bourbon, will help you see reason."

He straightened, his tone light but steady.

"Dinner will be served shortly, and I assure you, my chefs will present a meal befitting a man of your stature. Enjoy a comfortable bed and your drink of choice, and we shall resume this conversation tomorrow, refreshed and with clearer minds."

Killigrew's laugh was gravelly and humorless.

"Xavier, you presume too much. You think to dismiss me like one of your underlings?"

His eyes narrowed, the weight of his indignation settling in the room.

Xavier stepped forward, his presence imposing.

"I am done—for today. Persist in haggling, and I may increase my price. You know no one is better suited to this task than I. No one."

He punctuated the final words with an air of finality.

"Consider that while you rest."

Killigrew snorted dismissively, waving a ringed hand.

"Psssst. Idle threats, Xavier. I'll humor your hospitality for now."

He shifted the chest on his lap, clutching it protectively.

Xavier pointed to the treasure chest, his voice strong and unyielding.

"We are done for now. I will secure your treasure in my vault until we can resume our civilized discussion tomorrow. However, before I place it there, you must show me what it is. Not negotiable."

Rad's heart sank as he adjusted his position in the cramped hidden passage.

From his angle, he couldn't see the chest's contents.

His pulse quickened, a silent plea running through his mind—*move out of the way!*

Killigrew's hesitation was unmistakable. His plump fingers lingered on the key for a moment before he inserted it into the lock. The chest creaked open with a reluctant *click*.

He lifted the lid high enough for Xavier to see inside, holding it open for no more than a handful of seconds before snapping it shut with an audible *clack*.

The key turned once more, securing the lock with a decisive *snick*.

"Satisfied?" Killigrew asked as though the word cost him.

Xavier's expression was inscrutable, but his voice betrayed a note of intrigue.

"An artifact? Are you certain? What exactly is it?"

"It belonged to one of the Yholl brothers. That's all you need to know, and all I intend to tell you."

For a moment, Xavier's face remained a mask, unreadable as he processed this revelation. He nodded.

"Now I understand the peril you've placed upon me. The price will not get cheaper, I assure you. And let me make something else abundantly clear—there are no others who can hold this relic and keep it safe as I can."

Killigrew raised a skeptical eyebrow, but Xavier pressed on and asked, "Do you know the history of this estate? How I came to acquire it all those years ago?"

Killigrew shrugged, shifting his considerable weight.

"I know you took it from Leskaré. What was it called—Souterrain Hall? This was their base of operations, or so I heard."

"Indeed," Xavier said, his voice taking on a proud edge. "I won Souterrain Hall from Leskaré with no tricks, no deception. With it came immunity, *trust*, and business opportunities. I helped solve a significant problem for them, and in return, I became one of their most reliable partners. The Leskaré may thrive on chaos, but they depend on me to bring order to their operations. My influence ensures they stay semi-organized, and my profits from their endeavors are unmatched."

Killigrew squinted, a trace of confusion breaking through his guarded demeanor.

"And why is this relevant? What does this have to do with your exorbitant fee?"

Xavier leaned forward, his voice dropping to a near-whisper, each word laced with gravity.

"Leverage, old friend. With my connections, Leskaré will not touch anything within these walls. No other custodian you might consider could offer you… immunity. To anyone else, your relic would be a target. With me, it is untouchable. Think hard on it before tomorrow's negotiations."

Killigrew rose from his chair with a grunt, his reluctance plain.

"Your point is understood. I'll think about it once I've rested. And, Xavier, your veiled threat is noted. Amusing, but not subtle."

Xavier allowed himself a faint smile and motioned toward the chest.

"I will secure it while you rest. You have nothing to fear from me. Even if I knew what it was, I could make no use of it. My concern is solely for its safety."

Unlocking the door to the study, Xavier extended his hands.

"Now, give it here."

Killigrew hesitated for only a moment before relinquishing the chest.

Xavier took it with both hands but staggered under its unexpected weight.

"Why is it so heavy?" he asked, shifting the chest to one arm.

"Lead," Killigrew answered with a glimmer of pride. "Thin sheets, lining the inside. My wizard's idea—to block magical detection. The poor condition of the chest itself was my contribution. A disguise to discourage unwanted interest."

Xavier grunted under the weight and shifted the chest against his hip.

With his free hand, he grabbed a small bell and rang it sharply.

Moments later, a hurried knock preceded Wilkins's entrance.

"*Monsur* Killigrew," Xavier began, "you will dine with us this evening before retiring. Afterward, Wilkins will see to your satisfaction and accommodations. Whatever you require—refreshments, bourbon, anything—will be provided. Wilkins?"

The valet snapped his boots together with precision.

"Certainly. This way, sir."

Killigrew turned to Xavier with a pointed finger.

"I expect my bourbon promptly, Xavier. Do not delay."

Xavier smirked. "You'll have it. Rest well, Perran. Tomorrow, we'll settle this matter properly."

As Killigrew followed Wilkins out of the study, Rad's mind raced. A relic of the Yholl brothers, two of nine Mages who decimated the world with their magic.

Though he had read several books on the matter, what had happened wasn't clear. What he did know was the Mages wielded godlike magic—spells capable of reshaping reality.

They also created magic books, *Librums*, which could do wondrous things.

Each *Librum* had a unique purpose.

He searched his memory, recalling what he could of their history.

The Mages dominated the world, then there was a war between the two brothers, and with the *Librums,* there was mass destruction.

They were ultimately overthrown by their followers and enemies alike, despite their godlike abilities.

One brother was beheaded, the other, legends said, was crushed by a mountain falling from the sky.

Rad didn't believe that—*a mountain?*

What fascinated Rad was the *Librums.*

His love of books piqued his interest, and he often wondered, what these magic books were and what could they do? He was confident, no certain, somewhere lost in the Ornst Library was knowledge of these tomes.

One day he would find it.

Perhaps with knowledge and study he would find a way to locate them.

Rad knew a *Librum* wasn't in the chest, otherwise Xavier would have made mention of a book. The same would go for a weapon or ring, so it had to be something extremely odd.

But what it was, he couldn't figure.

Rad held his breath as he watched Xavier, his thoughts racing. A hidden vault. He hadn't known such a thing existed within *Château Saignoral,* and now he was about to witness Xavier unlocking it.

His mind buzzed with questions.

What could be inside?

He pictured heaps of gold coins, glimmering jewels, or rare magical artifacts, but he tempered his imagination.

This was Xavier, after all—calculating, meticulous, and secretive.

Whatever lay within was valuable, but not the overflowing treasures of legend.

Killigrew had departed, leaving Xavier alone in the study. He approached the bookcase and selected a black book embossed with gold lettering, pulling it outward with a soft *click.*

The entire bookcase shifted, revealing a concealed door inlaid with gold runes arranged in a five-by-five grid.

Rad's pulse quickened at the sight.

The arrangement suggested a magical lock—one requiring an incalculable number of combinations to bypass.

His sharp eyes tracked Xavier's movements as he began pressing the runes in a specific sequence.

Rad committed each touch to memory: first an 'L' pattern, then a 'Z' formation, totaling twenty-two points.

The sequence was elegant, easy to recall once known, but impossible to guess without prior knowledge.

A metallic groan echoed through the room as the door swung open.

Xavier propped it ajar with a wooden block and disappeared inside, out of Rad's sight.

Rad leaned closer to the peephole, his heart thundering.

This was his first glimpse of the secret vault, and he didn't want to miss a detail. His earlier fantasies of overflowing riches gave way to the reality of Xavier's personality.

Instead of a chaotic hoard of wealth, the vault contained orderly rows of pine wood crates, their secured tops nailed down and labeled with placards detailing their contents.

The scene spoke of precision and purpose rather than unchecked greed.

Xavier reappeared moments later, the treasure chest left inside the vault. He removed the wooden block, letting the door swing shut with a satisfying *thud*. A scraping sound followed as the magical lock reset itself, the gold runes glowing faintly before fading into stillness.

Rad withdrew, letting his thoughts settle.

The discovery of the vault was a revelation.

What else had Xavier hidden away?

Could there be other secrets within *Château Saignoral*, other concealed spaces waiting to be found?

He had to admit—Xavier's strategy made sense. If the estate had once been a Leskaré stronghold, it was logical to assume they had built it with secrecy in mind.

Back in the study, Xavier poured himself a measure of bourbon, swirling the amber liquid before downing it in one swift motion. He was lost in thought, no doubt contemplating the negotiations with Killigrew.

Rad closed the peephole's slider and retreated into the secret passageways.

His curiosity about the relic and Xavier's dealings had grown, but he knew better than to be impulsive. The vault's contents were an enigma; one he would need time and patience to understand.

Back in his quarters, Rad pulled on his boots, savoring the quiet focus the act afforded him.

His gaze landed on his new dagger, sleek and deadly.

He had named it *Darter* in honor of Hadley, though he chose to keep the name private.

The dagger was a weapon, not a trophy.

Personalizing it with an etched name might be a tradition, but Rad saw the potential risks.

A named weapon could betray its owner. If lost or stolen, it could be traced back. Worse, it could be used as evidence in a frame-up.

Evidence didn't care about intent—it carried weight regardless of how it was found.

Rad tucked *Darter* into his sheath, feeling its reassuring weight at his side.

He made his way to the stables, the cool evening air brushing against his face.

Tonight, he would train.

Not only with *Darter*, but with the discipline and focus required for the life he was carving out for himself.

He was no longer Xavier's son in any meaningful way.

He was a von Schule by name, but every day that passed, he felt himself stepping further into his own identity.

With Rosamund's warmth still lingering in his thoughts and *Darter* in his hand, there was a promise of a future for him.

He wasn't ready to leave this place just yet.

But when the time came, he'd leave on his terms.

And he'd leave with more than his freedom.

CHAPTER TWELVE

∞

The Black Storm

Abby, thank you for the birthday gift. It was completely unexpected—and appreciated. The gesture was symbolic, clever, and very *you*. You've always had a sharp mind and a kind heart.

Hadley took me into the city for my birthday—to a place called The Sweet Hatchet.

We had a drink—Stagwater—(awful stuff—I don't know how people stand it) and played puzzle games. Not what I expected, honestly. I've probably read too many books because the place wasn't nearly as mysterious or exciting as I imagined.

Lively, yes. But mostly loud and kind of boring.

A visitor arrived at *Château Saignoral* with a wizard and guards. Must've been someone important. We took care of their horses—fine animals. The visitor handed Hadley a gold crown for his trouble. Jamie and I didn't see a single copper.

I've been thinking about asking for permission to visit the Ornst Library. It's time. I want to go properly—not just for errands or in passing.

If I could, I'd invite you to join me. I know it's impossible, but the offer still stands. I thought you should know—you're always on my mind.

The Summer Cotillion is coming up, isn't it? Best of luck with your long-awaited kiss from what's-his-face.

(*Robert. I didn't forget.*)

I'm so glad you liked the gift. I put a lot of thought into it—I wanted it to be meaningful, something you'd truly appreciate. I'm happy it made you smile.

Hadley sounds like he went all out for your birthday! The Sweet Hatchet? What a name! I can't imagine what it must've been like, though the drink sounds dreadful—Stagwater? I suppose not all books prepare us for how things actually are. Still, I'm glad you got to go—it's important to get out and see the world, even if it doesn't quite match our imaginations. At least you don't have a half-dozen guards swarming you every time you leave the house.

As for the Ornst Library—you absolutely *should go!* It's the perfect place for you. I'd love to come with you, of course, but we both know how impossible that would be. Still, I'll imagine us there, wandering the stacks, getting lost in all those stories. Maybe one day we'll find a way.

The Summer Cotillion came and went. And... no, I didn't get kissed. Robert wasn't there! Gabrielle said he was probably sick, but I was still disappointed. I know, silly of me. My dance card was full, and I did enjoy myself—I danced with a few kind young gentlemen—but it wasn't the same. I suppose I built it up too much in my mind, and when it didn't happen, I felt a bit broken up inside.

I'm looking forward to the cooler days of autumn. The heat's been unbearable. I've been pestering Da about the idea of hosting an Autumn Cotillion. He hasn't said yes... but he hasn't said no, either. With some convincing from Gabrielle and Ma, maybe—just maybe—it'll happen.

Take care, Rad. And try not to spend all your time with your nose in a book—though I suppose asking that is like asking me not to think about shoes or cotillions!

Your loving sister,

Abby.

Weeks had passed since the mysterious relic had been brought to the estate. Perran Killigrew's visit had spanned seven long days. During his stay, he had not only depleted

Xavier's prized stock of bourbon but also departed with a collection of complimentary bottles set aside for such indulgent contingencies.

Rad assumed the negotiations had gone in Xavier's favor; the chest containing the relic remained secure in the secret vault.

On this day, the atmosphere at the estate felt heavier—especially near Hadley. A storm cloud of gloom hung over him, darkening his usual gruff demeanor further.

The perceptive Rad, sensitive to his mentor's moods, chose to steer clear. Instead, he busied himself with exercising the horses, dedicating more time to the task than usual. It gave him a convenient excuse to avoid Hadley's dour presence.

Hadley had retreated to his shed, seeking solitude and leaving the bulk of the stable duties to Rad. Rad took up the slack without complaint, cooling down the horses after their workouts. Jamie had been a willing helper, lightening the load as they worked in near silence.

"I'm meeting Florence tonight out by the orchards," Jamie blurted out, breaking the quiet as he arranged the brushes in a cabinet. His excitement was unmistakable. "We're having an evening picnic. I hope there's a beautiful sunset we can watch together."

Rad considered Jamie's words but remained measured in his response. Normally, he would have leapt at the chance to needle him with cutting remarks about Florence's well-known habits or her frequent visits to men's chambers.

But today, Hadley's somber mood weighed on him, muting his usual inclination to tease.

"Good for you," Rad said with genuine warmth, brushing down Shadow with smooth, slow strokes. "I hope you and Florence have a wonderful evening together. Enjoy."

"Thanks," Jamie said, sounding surprised at the lack of mockery. "Do you think I should bring her a gift? Girls like presents, don't they?"

Rad hesitated, the smirk forming. Jamie's earnestness was almost endearing.

"Not my field of expertise," he admitted. "You'd be better off asking someone who actually knows about relationships. You can ask one of the older servants who's been around."

"Do you think your brother would give me advice? Tristin likes me."

"Not the best idea," Rad said, shaking his head. "If you want actual advice, ask someone who won't steer you wrong. I would suggest another woman, like the governess. Gabrielle would probably love to help. She's nice enough, and she might know what Florence likes."

Jamie's eyes brightened. "True. I like that idea. Gabrielle…"

Rad interrupted, setting the brush down and stepping back from the horse.

"I need to talk to Hadley before it gets too late. Finish up with Shadow, put her in her stall, and take off for your picnic. Find Gabrielle if you need to. Good luck with Florence. Remind her of the truth—you've treated her well. Let her see your kindness."

Jamie beamed, startled by Rad's uncharacteristic encouragement. "Thanks. I will."

Rad nodded, offering a faint smile before turning toward Hadley's shed.

Apart from Jamie's intense preoccupation with Florence, he proved to be a reliable friend. He had a knack for staying silent about the happenings in this place. Rad considered Hadley had employed dire threats to ensure Jamie's discretion—death being the most likely one or shoving a body part up another body part.

While Jamie's enthusiasm might have been infectious on another day, Rad's thoughts were elsewhere.

He was intent on finding out what was going on with Hadley.

The door to the shed stood partially ajar, and as Rad approached, he employed his boot to nudge it open.

Inside, Hadley sat in his chair, his head hung as if defeated. His unkempt hair and beard appeared more disheveled than usual. A sense of misery emanated from him.

Rad knocked and said, "Jamie's headed off to see Florence. He won't figure out what's happening until she on top of him grinding away."

Hadley didn't say anything, he only stared at the floor.

"I've been practicing with *Darter*. I can put it exactly where I want at ten paces. It's a master crafted weapon."

Hadley nodded and said, "Aye, I've noticed your skill. You have natural talent with blades, I expect the same with swords when we get back to training with those. Both hands?"

"Both hands," he replied. "Ambidextrous."

There was a palpable pause.

When Hadley didn't grumble about his fancy word choice, Rad asked, "You feeling all right? Are you sick? Hurt?"

Hadley stared at the ground and dragged his fingers through his beard. He scratched underneath his chin.

"It's my right. It's starting to feel like my left. I can barely move my left, it's like it's frozen. If my right goes lad, I won't be long for this world. Your Da will get rid of me for sure, as I won't be able to wipe my arse. Without the use of my arms, outside this estate, I'd be dead in a matter of days. A cripple is useless in Ornst."

"Perhaps we can fix your arms. Can we go to a healer? They have potions and magic. I got coin for my birthday, in fact it's a tidy sum."

"Isn't going to help. These aren't wounds or cuts, this is my old body breaking down because of my own neglect."

He rolled his shoulder, the discomfort evident on his face.

"I need to rest my right. Been using it too much to compensate for my left."

Rad considered Hadley's words and figured they needed to do something drastic, turn the logic around.

"Let's think about this. Resting is what you did with your left, and it got worse. I think you need to do the opposite; work your shoulders harder than ever. Exercise these parts until it hurts like bloody hell, and they start working like they're supposed to. Don't rest them, force them to work. Fight your aging body. You have to fight!"

"It hurts lad to lift my arm. I don't tolerate pain like I used to and I'm tired. I'm an old man Rad, and my days are numbered. I'm getting older by the minute to be truthful. I knew this day would come when self-neglect would catch up with me. So much damage from the past with unknown consequences for the future."

Rad scoffed and gripped Hadley's shoulder. He was giving in to old age and quitting before trying.

"You can't give up. You need to last two more years. When I'm sixteen, I'm getting kicked out of here. We can leave at the same time.

We can work for your friend at The Sweet Hatchet or find a tradesman who can use us, or better yet, open our own stables. Visit Rosamund a couple times a day, spend our money on whores and that shitty Stagwater liquor you like. Don't give up on me, don't give up on yourself."

A smile blossomed on Hadley's face.

"Aye, sounds glorious, retire whoring and drinking Stagwater. You really think you can get my arms back to normal?"

"We can exercise your arms and shoulders after work. We'll have to experiment, see what movements work. If it hurts too bad, we'll try something else. But we got to get your arms moving again so you can work with the horses, so you can throw with both hands. So we can train more; I was getting better with a sword and I need your training to improve."

"Rad, I'm useless."

Rad stood in the doorway, absorbing Hadley's words. The sight of his mentor—a pillar of rough wisdom and grizzled strength—reduced to this despondent state was like a blow to the gut. The idea of Hadley, the man who had taught him everything he knew about survival, becoming incapacitated and useless was almost too much to consider.

"You're not useless," Rad said, stepping across the threshold. "You're just… tired. Rest up and we'll exercise your arms hard in the evenings. Let me handle the heavy lifting for a while. Between me and Jamie, the stables will run fine."

Hadley chortled, though it sounded more like a groan.

"Jamie is at his limit, and you… You're good, lad, but you're not me. Not yet. It will be hard for you two…"

"Then teach me," Rad countered, crossing his arms. "Teach me everything I need to know about the stables so I can make sure this place doesn't fall apart. You said yourself I'm a quick study. You need to let go of the reins and let Jamie and I prove to you we can do it."

At last, Hadley lifted his head, his eyes heavy with a mix of weariness and gratitude.

"I've been teaching you, lad. More than you realize. You've got the makings of a man who can handle himself anywhere, not only in the stables. But some things can't be taught. You think Xavier keeps me around because I know my way around horses? He keeps me because he knows I'll do the dirty work. Even crippled, I've got value as long as my reputation holds."

Rad swallowed hard, remembering Xavier and Ma's conversation about Hadley. "Reputation doesn't throw hay bales or exercise horses. But it can give you an instant advantage when you need it. You're more than a horse-master."

Hadley let out a humorless laugh. "Am I now? That's the nicest thing anyone's said to me in years."

"I mean it," Rad insisted, stepping closer. "But if you won't help yourself, then let me help you. Stop trying to prove you're still twenty years old. Let me and Jamie take care of things for a while so you can get your arms going again."

Hadley rubbed his temples, the weight of his condition etched into the lines of his face. "You're a good lad, Rad. Too good for this place. Too good for me."

Rad hesitated.

He found the words and asked the question he'd been carrying for years. "Why do you teach me these things?"

Hadley didn't speak at first.

When he did, his voice was matter-of-fact.

"Because I'm tired of seeing boys die stupid."

Rad didn't know how to respond—not right away. The silence stretched, heavy with understanding.

Hadley sighed, a long, deflating exhalation. "All right, lad. For now, you'll take the reins. But if this gets too much… if I can't pull myself out of this… you've got to promise me something."

"What?"

"If I lose the use of both arms, you've got to help me go out on my own terms. A man like me doesn't die in bed, pissing himself like an invalid."

Rad's stomach churned at the request. "You're not dying anytime soon, Hadley. Let's fix the problem before we start planning the end. We will find a way to fix your arms."

Hadley nodded, his lips pulling into the faintest ghost of a smile.

"Aye. But don't forget what I said, lad. Sometimes a promise is the only thing a man has left."

Seeing Hadley so subdued was... unsettling. It stripped away the tough, unyielding image Rad had grown accustomed to—the man of sharp words and sharper threats, who wielded violence like a shield.

In this moment, Hadley wasn't the invincible figure Rad admired and mocked as a friend. He was human, vulnerable, carrying fears like anyone else. It stirred a deeper sense of loyalty and a desire to help, to prove Hadley didn't have to face this alone.

"We'll start tomorrow," Rad said with quiet resolve.

Hadley didn't reply, instead he motioned toward the figure standing in the doorway.

It was Tristin.

His dress was casual, his bleached white shirt unbuttoned to reveal his now hairy chest. His square shoulders filled the frame of the door, giving him an imposing presence. He wore black trousers and practical leather boots, the attire of a man ready for business rather than leisure.

Flanking him were two mercenaries who had accompanied him from the manor house.

Without waiting for an invitation, the three men stepped inside, filling the cramped space of Hadley's shed.

"I need Shadow ready to ride this evening," Tristin announced without preamble. "We'll need two suitable mounts for my guards as well."

The two mercenaries stood like sentinels, armed with knives, longswords, and small crossbows. Their rugged appearances told the story of their lives: rough beards, scarred faces, and leather armor bearing the emblem of the von Schule family—a black half-moon intertwined with a green 'VS.' Their silent, watchful stance contrasted with Tristin's restless movements.

Something significant was happening tonight.

Hadley nodded in acknowledgment.

"They'll be ready. What time are you heading out?"

"Around sundown," Tristin replied.

Hadley motioned weakly with his right arm. The movement was slight, but noticeable to Rad, who knew Hadley's condition all too well.

"They'll be tied up outside before sundown and ready for you. When you bring them back, give them to Rad or Jamie. I'll be asleep. One of them will be here all night waiting for you."

Rad didn't say anything. Jamie would be in the orchards fumbling with Florence, Hadley would soon be asleep with a belly full of liquor and arms that couldn't work like they should, and he himself would be left in his room with nothing to do.

"I'll get them ready," Rad offered.

"I already said that, lad! Are you deaf?" Hadley's voice was sharp and cutting. "No need to go over what's already been settled. I said they'd be ready, and they'll be ready!"

Rad waited for a mocking laugh from Tristin, but it never came. Instead, his half-brother remained focused, his demeanor tense, as if burdened by the weight of the evening's purpose.

Beads of sweat glistened on Tristin's forehead, betraying a mix of nervousness and determination.

Hadley pointed toward the door, his patience wearing thin.

"Go on, Tristin. Take your two bunny rabbits back to the manor. My shed's getting stuffy from their woman parts."

The mercenaries bristled at the insult, their eyes flashing with anger, and one of them took a step forward.

"I don't believe half the stories they tell about you, Hadley the Pillager," the mercenary sneered. "You're a broken old man. Impossible you murdered an entire village."

Hadley's gaze darkened, his voice guttural and dangerous.

"Lad, I can kill you in ways you've never thought possible. Scram before I embarrass you in front of Master Tristin and this young lad. You so much as touch your hilt, and I'll shove it right up your woman parts."

Tristin held up a hand, halting the mercenary. "Enough. Make sure the horses are ready."

"I've said that already! Don't you learn either?" Hadley's irritation boiled over. "The horses will be ready! Why are we still talking about this? Get out of my shed! Go on now!"

Tristin didn't respond. With a nod, he turned and strode out, the mercenaries following behind. Their heavy boots thudded against the ground.

Hadley exhaled and slumped into his chair.

"I know I don't have to tell you what to do," he muttered, flexing his right arm with a wince. "It's all for show. Got to stay mean as a hell hound if I'm going to survive. I didn't—"

"Don't explain," Rad interrupted. "Three horses. Ready at sundown. Done."

Hadley groaned, leaning back in his chair. "Run along before those mercenaries come back to take my head off. Don't want you to see old Hadley losing his head to those delicate ladies."

Rad hesitated at the door.

"You didn't murder an entire village, did you?"

Hadley met Rad's eyes, his expression grave.

There was no denial, no disgust, only a weariness aging him further.

"There are things you don't need to know about old Hadley. I was a terrible man once, full of violence, hate, and murder. Cold-blooded murder. Those days are gone. We'll talk about it another time—when we leave this place to find our fortunes, I'll come clean. I was a bad man, lad, the worst sort you can come across. Now go. Get the horses ready."

Rad didn't press further.

He ran to the stables, hoping to find Jamie and enlist his help. But Jamie was long gone, no doubt already meeting Florence. It didn't matter. Rad would get three horses ready for Tristin and his mercenaries—and he'd prepare one for himself.

Rad pushed the horse hard, determined to exit the estate through one of the rear gates. He urged Vanguard, his trusted dark bay stallion, to press on as they cleared the confines of *Château Saignoral*.

His goal was clear: circle the estate's perimeter and approach the front gates, positioning himself to trail Tristin and the two mercenaries unnoticed.

Curiosity got the best of him.

The von Schule family's collaboration with Leskaré and their ventures with the foreigners were shrouded in mystery, and Rad was eager to peel back the layers.

By shadowing Tristin, he hoped to uncover the inner workings of their schemes, knowledge he could one day use to bring Xavier von Schule to his knees. He guessed Tristin was meeting someone important, perhaps a representative of Leskaré.

With his sixteenth birthday approaching in two years, Rad felt the pressure of time; he needed every advantage to secure his future. This was an opportunity he couldn't afford to squander.

As he completed his circuit and reached the front gates, Rad settled into a comfortable rhythm, ensuring he could follow the group without losing track of them.

Tristin and the mercenaries weren't in a hurry, making it easier to anticipate their path. Rad's primary challenge was navigating the city's crowded streets while remaining inconspicuous.

He wasn't worried about being spotted—years of sneaking through the estate and its hidden passages had made him an expert at blending into the background.

Vanguard's steady gait beneath him was reassuring, and Rad felt an almost uncanny connection with the stallion, as if their thoughts were synchronized.

Dressed in black—shirt, boots, and pants—Rad was a shadow in the dimming light.

Darter rested at his hip, and his eight hidden knives were snug in their sheaths.

Despite feeling well-equipped, he couldn't help but wish for a sword. One day, he thought, a sword would be his.

Another reason for him to get Hadley healthy.

When Tristin entered Ornst's industrial district, Rad wasn't surprised. The air here carried the acrid tang of molten metal, a constant reminder of the blacksmiths, armorers, and weaponsmiths who plied their trade.

Fletchers lined the streets as well, their shops brimming with master crafted arrows. This district was not far from where Hadley's friend, Thratmam, had his forge.

The Sweet Hatchet was only a few blocks away, marking the border between Ornst's gritty industrial area and its rougher tavern quarter.

For a fleeting moment, Rad's thoughts drifted.

He wondered if Rosamund would remember him when he returned for his next birthday. The memory of her lingered like a distant warmth, a contrast to the cold ambitions driving him forward.

He pushed the thought aside, focusing once again on the three horses ahead.

The faint glow of street lanterns and occasional light spilling from windows illuminated the dark surroundings. The bustling streets were alive with activity—carts trundling by, horses clopping over cobblestones, and people weaving through the chaos—providing Rad with ample cover to remain unnoticed by Tristin or his mercenaries.

Up ahead stood their destination: a warehouse.

It was a modest and functional structure, built for practicality, not beauty. Its lower half consisted of sturdy fieldstone walls rising eight feet high, their rough surface fitted together with precise mortar.

Above the stone, wooden planks framed evenly spaced windows, designed to let daylight flood in during working hours. The building's utilitarian charm was matched by its sheer size, looming above the neighboring shops and flats.

Rad's sharp eyes assessed the layout.

Entry points were limited—there were two man-sized doors and a set of industrial-sized barn doors. The barn doors were fortified with heavy steel chains and multiple locks, their purpose clear: to deter the most determined thieves.

While Rad was confident in his ability to pick locks, the sheer number and size of these obstacles posed a daunting challenge. It would take time, too much time, with too many eyes watching.

He also noted the reliable Ornst patrols, the paid militia who moved through the streets with regularity, were absent tonight.

Reining in Vanguard near a neighboring building, Rad guided the stallion into the shadows. He stayed within earshot of Tristin, careful not to make any sound to betray his presence.

The noise of the city formed a consistent background hum—the soft murmur of conversation, the metallic clang of tools striking iron, the hiss of bellows fueling forges, and the rhythmic clatter of hooves on uneven streets. Wagon wheels groaned as they passed over the cobblestones, each creak audible in the still night.

Rad tuned his senses, focusing on his brother.

"You two stay out here," Tristin ordered, his tone firm. "The representative will be here shortly. His name is Duwy. He's supposed to be alone. If he isn't alone, turn them away—with force, if necessary. The Ornst militia has been paid to stay away from this area for the evening. If it comes to violence, dispose of the bodies quickly and quietly."

Rad's grip on Vanguard's reins tightened.

The calm exterior Tristin had worn at the manor had shifted into a colder, more calculating disposition. His words weren't idle—they carried the weight of a man used to issuing life-and-death commands.

Rad remained motionless, his heart pounding as he absorbed the significance of the conversation. This wasn't just another business meeting. This was... dangerous.

The guards confirmed their orders with curt nods.

Tristin produced a key and unlocked the standard-sized door, slipping inside without delay. The two mercenaries took up their posts near the entrance, their broad shoulders and well-worn weapons forming an impenetrable barrier.

There was no chance of sneaking past them undetected.

From the street, Rad would learn nothing of the meeting or the mysterious Duwy. The only way to gain any useful information was to get inside.

After tethering Vanguard to a sturdy post in the alley, Rad slipped into the darkness, moving along the warehouse's outer wall without making a sound.

He stuck close to the rough stone, his body brushing against its cold surface as he crept towards the corner. Peeking around the edge, he assessed the mercenaries again.

Their stance was confident, their watchful eyes scanning the area.

Rad frowned.

Getting through the front door was impossible without alerting them.

He hesitated, weighing his options.

Should he linger in the shadows and wait for Duwy's arrival, hoping for a distraction to allow him to slip by? Or was it better to search for another way in?

His gut told him waiting wouldn't suffice. Time was slipping away, and the more he delayed, the greater the risk of missing the meeting.

His gaze shifted to the warehouse itself, analyzing its structure. These buildings were designed to keep intruders out, yet no construction was flawless.

Somewhere, hidden amidst its fortified walls or tucked beneath its eaves, there had to be a weakness—a forgotten unlocked door, a loose board, or a poorly secured window.

Determined, Rad decided to circle the building, his eyes sharp for any detail that might reveal a way inside.

"Good evening, my name is Duwy. I have a meeting with Tristin von Schule. Is he here?"

The man was the picture of ordinariness, and it was unsettling.

In the chaotic streets of Ornst, this figure would be the last to draw notice.

He had the nondescript air of a man who made blending in an art. His short, neatly combed black hair disappeared beneath a modest gray hat with a narrow brim, and a well-groomed black goatee contrasted with his pale complexion, hinting he didn't spend much time outdoors.

His attire further reinforced his unremarkable disguise. A simple white shirt was tucked into black pants, the latter sporting an odd, crisp yellow pinstripe running down the sides. Over the shirt, he wore a light brown coat, the kind made from sturdy, no-frills fabric, and a leather belt secured a short sword sheathed at his hip.

He also had a leather satchel for carrying documents or messages.

His calf-high leather boots, fitted with straps, suggested both comfort and practicality.

Those caught Rad's attention.

The boots puzzled him.

Though unassuming at first glance, they weren't a common style seen in Ornst. The craftsmanship, the fit, and the polished but understated finish marked them as being distinct.

They didn't align with the local styles or the rest of Duwy's outfit.

Rad's instincts told him while the man's clothes were an attempt to pass as a local, the boots betrayed an origin far from the city.

Duwy, it appeared, wasn't from here—the question was, where was he from?

"Leave the steel here," one of the mercenaries said, stepping forward and holding out his hand. "You can collect it when you're finished."

"Of course."

While Duwy fumbled with his weapon belt, Rad slipped into the shadows of the alley, his movements fluid and purposeful. He kept to the edges, scanning for potential entry points into the warehouse.

The obvious options were the windows, but they were high up, latched from the inside, and breaking the glass would create a racket, drawing unwanted attention.

It wasn't a risk he could afford.

Rounding the corner to the rear of the warehouse, Rad found a staging area for wagons. Loading docks lined the back, built to make unloading easier—their raised platforms dark and deserted.

The sparse lanterns cast weak pools of light, leaving generous pockets of shadow where Rad felt most at ease.

Moving in a crouch, his steps silent on the compacted dirt, he prowled like a creature born to the dark.

Against the back wall, he spotted a promising stack of damaged crates and abandoned pallets. They were scattered but created a crude pathway upward.

It was the best chance he had to reach one of the windows.

He hoped—prayed—one might be open.

Testing the bottom crate with his foot, he determined its stability. Satisfied it wouldn't collapse under him, he began to climb, methodical and quiet.

Each movement was measured, his weight shifting as he worked his way upward. As he reached the midpoint, his eyes saw a faint, dusty boot print atop one of the crates. It was subtle, almost invisible, but Rad's sharp eyes and heightened awareness picked it out immediately.

Someone had been here before him.

Recently.

He paused, heart thudding.

The imprint, though faded, was unmistakable, and it sent a ripple of unease through him.

Who had taken this same path, and why?

His mind raced with possibilities, each darker than the last.

Pushing down the dread rising in his chest, Rad resumed his climb, slower now, more cautious. As he neared the top of the stack, he steeled himself, his instincts prickling. When he finally reached the window, it became glaringly obvious—someone was already here.

At the apex of his climb, Rad reached an eight-panel window. The bottom left and right panes were broken, creating enough of an imperfection to make the window appear closed from the ground.

With care, he pushed it up, the sash groaning softly in protest.

Sliding under the raised frame, Rad dropped into the shadows inside, leaving the window open to ensure his exit remained uncomplicated.

The interior of the warehouse unfurled before him in muted light.

To his right, a cluster of lanterns illuminated the space where Tristin was likely conducting his meeting. Their glow cast long, flickering shadows, turning the columns and stacked goods into looming specters.

To his left, Rad spied a workshop designed for wagon repairs and the processing of crates and pallets. The organized chaos of the warehouse stretched around him—orderly bays filled with pallets and crates, each labeled with a ledger hanging from hooks.

The structure itself was a grid of precision and purpose. Thick wooden columns stood at twenty-five-foot intervals, their bases anchored in the compacted dirt floor, rising to meet the slightly pitched roof above.

Rad noted the warehouse's scale: seventy-five feet wide and one hundred twenty-five feet deep, a cavernous space packed with possibilities. Each column bore bold numbers and letters to guide workers, ensuring the meticulous placement of inventory.

Directly below his perch, the floor was bare, save for a thin layer of dust hinting at frequent activity.

Rad tightened his grip on the wooden wall, his fingertips pressing into the rough surface as he scanned his immediate surroundings.

With strong arms and hands, he lowered himself to the narrow, four-inch ledge of the fieldstone foundation. His balance held steady, his breathing slow and even. With a controlled hop and a mid-air spin to orient himself, Rad landed on the warehouse floor without a sound.

He remained crouched, knees bent and muscles coiled like a spring, listening for any indication his arrival had been detected.

The warehouse buzzed faintly with distant sounds: muffled voices from Tristin's direction, the rustle of fabric, the occasional clink of metal against wood.

A rat scurried across the floor near his feet, disappearing behind a crate.

Rad exhaled, letting his held breath escape in a slow, quiet sigh.

His lungs expanded as he drew in a steadying breath, his mind sharp and focused. His heart maintained its rhythmic calm; steady, confident.

Yet, the mystery of what was unfolding in this space, combined with the memory of the dusty footprint on the crates, heightened his wariness.

He crouched and began to move, his steps soft and cautious.

The tension in the air was palpable, a mix of secrecy and anticipation.

Ahead, Tristin and Duwy were beginning their conversation.

As he snuck along the floor, another rat scampered away.

"Your insistence on meeting in person has irritated my father," Tristin said, his voice carrying down the length of the warehouse.

Rad was stunned by how intimidating Tristin sounded; there was an authority in his tone not heard before.

"It is how we do business where I come from. In person," Duwy replied, his tone cool and measured. "Besides, letters can be intercepted and read by unscrupulous individuals. I'm honored the esteemed Xavier von Schule has sent his only son to negotiate on his behalf. Now let's get down to business. I'm authorized to negotiate an agreement with you tonight. I have the contracts with me, and I have an offer Xavier von Schule won't be able to refuse."

A pang of loss struck Rad, sharp and unexpected.

The outside world had erased his connection to the von Schule name.

Forcing the pit in his stomach aside, he crept along the dusty floor, his keen eyes catching a print in the dirt. He followed it, his ears tuned to the conversation.

Tristin's voice rang out, clear and firm.

"We will continue to refuse your offer, and our position will not waver. You have wasted your time coming here, wasted my time. Only by the grace of my father are you allowed to be here."

There was a muffled laugh.

"You are fully aware of my affiliation?" Duwy asked. "Did your father explain what we do? Who we are?"

"Yes, completely," Tristin answered. "You are no different than Leskaré."

"We are often compared to them, yes," Duwy admitted, his tone taking on an edge. "But Leskaré doesn't have the extensive network of operatives that we do. We work in all corners of Eldor—north, south, east, and west. Leskaré is regional, with close ties to Ornst and Haddensack. They are complacent and lazy. We are not."

"Your information is outdated," Tristin said. "Leskaré has expanded beyond Haddensack. They have operations in Biggs and Pehrone. And from what we hear, your resources are stretched too thin by having such an extensive reach. I'll reiterate: we will not entertain working with you. Our agreement, for now, is exclusively with Leskaré. We don't need more inventory or another partner."

"You call this inventory?" Duwy scoffed, gesturing broadly. "This warehouse is empty. Working with us, this place would overflow with goods and profit."

"We have dozens of structures throughout Ornst, Haddensack, Biggs—you name it, Xavier von Schule has a presence. We have sellers and buyers everywhere. We already make a tidy profit. In fact, we cleared out this warehouse the other day."

"This is precisely why we want to partner with you," Duwy countered, his voice rising with intensity. "We can take advantage of your established network in conjunction with our extensive presence for mutual benefit. Imagine this: we store our goods here, cataloged by your system, and sold by our agents. You earn a hefty commission on each sale. Everyone wins. The money is there, the only limit is your imagination. Think of the profit."

Tristin didn't miss a beat.

"You're not thinking like a businessman. Not everyone wins. Increased inventory means we must expand our footprint. That means hiring more men, which drives expenses up to intolerable levels. In addition, we'd have to invest in property to handle the influx of your goods. Our plans are not for expansive type growth. Any additional outlay of capital is nonsensical. We are in a strong position partnering with Leskaré."

The tension in the warehouse was palpable, hanging thick in the air as Tristin and Duwy clashed over profit, power, and risk.

Rad took in the exchange, his sharp mind piecing together the implications, and he found himself unexpectedly admiring Tristin.

His half-brother's poise and resolve stood out—the way he skillfully countered Duwy's arguments, deflected his pressure, and stuck to Xavier's instructions.

There was a measured intensity in Tristin's tone, a calm authority reminding Rad of Hadley on his best days, when the old horse-master's unflinching confidence made you believe he could face down the world with one bad arm and win.

For a fleeting moment, Rad felt a pang of regret.

He could have been part of this world, learning the family business and honing the economic and negotiating skills Tristin wielded so effectively.

Despite being a bastard, he was still half-related to these people, bound by blood.

Had things been different, perhaps he could have stood where Tristin stood, representing their shared name and wielding the von Schule influence.

I'm honored Xavier von Schule sent his youngest son to negotiate with us...

The regret was bitter, but it didn't last long.

It couldn't.

The memories of Xavier's cruelty to Ma flared hot and raw, quickly dousing any wistful notions.

He remembered the harsh words, the indifference, the cruel blow—still stinging in his memory as if it had struck his own cheek.

No, Xavier had ensured he would never in fact be part of the family. He had severed ties long ago, treating him like an outsider and casting him down to the stables.

Steeling his resolve, Rad let the bitterness fuel his determination.

He would see the day when Xavier von Schule regretted underestimating him, regretted kicking him out. One day, he vowed, he would prove himself—not as a von Schule but as a man far greater.

Let them have their negotiations and their network of power.

He would carve his own path, one that would make Xavier take notice.

Rad remained on the far side of the warehouse, crouched behind the pallets and well-hidden, his ears attuned to every word exchanged between Tristin and Duwy a hundred feet away.

His focus was razor-sharp, his position perfect for listening.

He was preparing to shift to a better vantage point when a faint, acrid tang in the air stopped him mid-move.

Weak vinegar.

Salt.

The smell clung like sweat after a hard day's labor.

He wasn't alone.

Over the pallets, his gaze caught the faintest movement.

Two figures were crouched, hidden as he was, their forms near invisible in the dim light. Dressed in all black, they blended into the shadows. The only detail standing out was their boots.

Rad's stomach tightened as he recognized the design—those strapped leather boots like Duwy's, a marker binding them to the man Tristin was negotiating with.

Knives glimmered, cruel and wicked blades meant for puncturing hearts, lungs, or gouging out eyes.

These weren't tools for defense; they were weapons of murder.

Neither assassin carried a sword, but the way they moved, the masterful control of their bodies, screamed lethal intent.

Their proximity struck like a thunderbolt—just ten feet away.

Too close.

Another rat scampered by.

Deeper in the shadows, Rad saw a calico cat, tail flicking in the air. It studied him for a breath, then padded after the rat.

The two assassins weren't bothered by the soft noises of rats and cats nearby.

They were focused.

One of them exhaled, quiet and steady, but audible to Rad's sharp ears. He could hear the faintest shuffle as a hand adjusted its grip on a blade.

The other was unnervingly still.

A pang of fear surged through Rad, his heart hammering in his chest, but he forced himself to regulate his breathing, steadying the tremble in his hands.

Calm.

Control.

Focus.

The words echoed like Hadley's voice in his mind.

Yet, there was no panic.

A serenity washed over him, quiet and steady, as if the world had slowed to a crawl.

He relaxed further, reviewing various scenarios in his mind. The advantage he had was simple—they didn't know he was behind them, poised to strike.

It was a prime spot to do lethal damage, and he wasn't about to squander it.

Rad's thoughts raced.

These assassins weren't only lingering here.

They were advancing with purpose toward Tristin.

There was no hesitation in their movements—this was their plan.

To kill him.

Or kidnap him for ransom.

The mercenaries stationed outside wouldn't have a chance to react in time.

It was up to him.

The thought of the von Schule heir bleeding out on the warehouse floor churned in his gut.

But so did the knowledge he had never been in a real fight, not one that mattered.

He might freeze, might fumble.

A flash of self-doubt surfaced, but he crushed it down.

Stop overthinking, lad, Hadley's voice came again, clear as day. *Make your plan and do it.*

He studied their positions, taking in their posture, the gleam of their knives, the angles they would move next.

There was no time to wait.

He remembered what Hadley had drilled into him.

Be aggressive.

Put the man down once.

Don't waste resources.

Land the blow.

End it.

Confirm the kill.

Two foes, two blows.

Rad's fingers curled around the hilt of *Darter*, the smooth leather grip grounding him. He tested its weight, letting its comforting heft settle his nerves. This wasn't about skill or training—it was about resolve.

There was no room for error.

His body tingled with the sharp awareness death was near, for himself or for them.

He calmed himself and took measured breaths, centering his mind.

He would land a swift strike from the shadows before they realized he was there.

One decisive move to shatter their plan and preserve Tristin's life.

His fingers tightened on *Darter*.

"I thought all businesses were looking for growth," Duwy argued, his voice carrying a sharp edge. "That's how they make more money! Growth equals profits! Don't you see?"

"Businesses make more money by gaining efficiencies," Tristin countered, his tone unwavering. "By leveraging their position in the marketplace and being loyal to their business partners. I appreciate you came all this way to talk with me in person. Our answer is the same: no. I will tell my father our meeting was cordial, and I will ensure he knows you would have treated us fairly as potential business partners. I'm not closing the door on a future relationship, so you may take that back to your superiors. For now, we deal only with Leskaré."

"Let me make one additional point before you dismiss me," Duwy replied with an edge to his words.

Rad's attention shifted as he caught movement in the shadows.

The assassins began to creep along the edge of the bay, their steps silent as they melted into the darkness.

Their target was clear.

They were positioning to flank Tristin, to catch him off guard and strike before his guards could react from outside.

Their movements were methodical, professional.

They signaled to each other with sharp, silent gestures—hands darting through the air in a language Rad didn't understand.

One slid ahead, his shadow merging with the gloom, while the other followed a few paces behind.

The assassins were ten feet away, their wicked blades glinting in the dim light.

The realization hit Rad like a bucket of cold water.

They don't know I'm here.

Rad gripped *Darter* and slid it free from its sheath without a sound. The knife felt perfect in his hand, the weight familiar, like an extension of himself.

His mind snapped into focus, clearing away hesitation.

This was about survival, about stopping these men before they killed Tristin.

His muscles coiled as he prepared to strike.

No overthinking. Make the plan. Do it.

In his mind, Hadley's weathered face mouthed, *Show off.*

With an elegant crow hop, Rad hurled *Darter* with precision honed through endless practice.

The stout blade streaked through the air, reaching its mark in a heartbeat. It struck true, burying itself into the base of the crouching assassin's skull. The man crumpled forward, collapsing to the ground with a muffled thump.

The sound, though slight, was enough to alert the second assassin.

He spun, his body already coiled to react, but Rad was faster.

Two knives followed in swift succession—one whistling through the air to lodge in the man's eye, the other sticking in his hand as he reflexively raised it to block the onslaught.

The assassin let out a choked gasp, his weapon falling from his grip and clattering on the ground as he tumbled lifeless to the floor.

Rad sank deeper into his crouch, his breath steady despite the adrenaline pumping through his veins.

He counted to himself, each beat of his heart a reminder of what he had done.

Two heartbeats. Three. Five. Ten.

Neither man stirred.

They were dead.

Dead by his hand.

A rat sprinted across his feet and slipped underneath a crate, followed by the hunting calico cat.

Rad stayed frozen, absorbing the gravity of the moment.

The warehouse around him was too quiet, still like a mirrored lake.

His fingers tightened on the hilt of his throwing knife, though no further threat appeared.

"What is that clatter? What are you playing at?" Duwy's echoing voice was laced with suspicion. "Is someone here with us?"

Tristin's response was measured, calm, and convincing. "No one is in here. It's the alley cats chasing vermin and knocking over tools in the shop. The lazy workers always leave crumbs lying around. I assure you, no one else is in here."

Rad remained motionless, his gaze flickering to the growing pools of blood beneath the fallen assassins. The coppery tang of it filled the air, mingling with the lingering scent of sawdust and sweat.

A soothing breath steadied him as he eased closer to the bodies. Careful not to make a sound, he crouched beside the first assassin and reclaimed *Darter*.

The blade resisted before sliding free with a faint, squelching sound.

The throwing knives came next.

One was clean, but the other...

The assassin's lifeless eye clung grotesquely to the blade.

Rad fought the spike of nausea, forced his hand steady, and wiped the weapons clean on the assassin's black clothing.

The dislodged eyeball plopped into the shadows as he tossed it aside.

His chest tightened, the adrenaline that had carried him through the kills now ebbing. A jittery fatigue threatened to take hold, but he fought it off.

Breathe, he told himself. *Just breathe.*

"You were saying?" Tristin's voice cut through the warehouse's silence.

"One more point," Duwy said, though his tone faltered, uncertain. "Ah, well, yes. It is beneficial we keep our options open for the future. I appreciate your willingness to keep us in mind. My superiors will appreciate it too."

Rad stayed motionless, his hand tightening around *Darter.*

Duwy's stalling, he realized. *Waiting for reinforcements that will never come.*

The thought offered grim satisfaction, but the blood still leaking from the assassins unnerved him.

His gaze clung to the way it shimmered in the faint light, an undeniable reminder of what he'd done.

"If you have nothing else to say, this concludes our meeting. You may leave," Tristin said, his tone unyielding.

From the direction of the front office, Rad heard the faint scrape of chairs being pushed back.

"Tell your father our paths will cross again," Duwy said, his voice regaining composure. "Perhaps we will find mutual satisfaction in the future?"

"We look forward to it. Best wishes to you. On your way out, please instruct my guards to come inside."

"Of course," Duwy replied, his footsteps retreating toward the door.

Rad stared down at the lifeless bodies sprawled before him, their blood pooling in the dirt.

What could he do with them?

He couldn't leave them in plain sight; by morning, they'd be swarmed by rats, their deaths discovered.

But moving them wasn't easy.

The assassins were slighter than the mercenaries outside, yet their dead weight would still slow him down.

He clenched his fists.

If only Hadley were here. Hadley would know exactly what to do.

A deep breath filled Rad's lungs, but the metallic tang of blood clung to the back of his throat, refusing to be ignored.

His eyes darted around the warehouse.

There had to be a way to conceal them, even if it was temporary.

The sharp slam of the front door cut through his thoughts. Rad froze, his pulse steady but his muscles tensed. The metallic scrape of a heavy bar sliding into place followed, trapping him inside.

The unmistakable sound of heavy booted steps echoed through the warehouse.

"Check the back of the warehouse," Tristin's voice rang out. "I heard noises during the meeting. Probably our cats chasing rats. A vagrant may have snuck in and is sleeping here at night. If you find anyone back there, kill them."

Rad's stomach tightened as he heard the deadly hiss of swords being unsheathed.

"Split up," one of the mercenaries barked.

The dead bodies couldn't stay here, exposed.

Rad dropped to a crouch and grabbed the farthest assassin by the arms, dragging the corpse toward the second one. The modest scraping noise sent dread coiling in his gut, but he moved as quickly and quietly as he could manage.

Blood smeared across the floor, a telltale sign he couldn't erase, but it was the best he could do.

He scanned the area, spotting a nearby wooden pallet. It was heavy, but it was his best option.

Gritting his teeth, he hefted it upright, angling it to shield the bodies and himself from view. It wouldn't fool a careful eye, but the darkness might be enough to work in his favor.

"Who's there?" a voice called out, sharp and menacing. "Come out! Save yourself some trouble! We know you're here!"

Rad pressed his back against the pile of crates behind him, forcing his breaths to remain quiet and measured.

The footsteps drew closer, muffled by the dirt floor.

His grip tightened on the pallet.

His heartbeat remained steady—but his mind raced for a solution.

Across the way, the calico alley cat perched on a barrel.

Its tail swished back and forth, and its head tilted as it watched Rad with an unnervingly intelligent gaze.

It didn't hiss or run.

Instead, it sat there, studying him as though it were trying to decide if he was friend or foe.

Rad's hand crept to the ground beside him, fingers brushing over a discarded bolt. He gripped it and aimed.

The cat didn't flinch as he threw, the metal bolt spinning through the air to its destination.

It struck the barrel with a sharp clang.

The cat bolted with a screech, leaping off the barrel and dashing across the mercenaries' path, its claws scrabbling on the dirt floor.

"Bloody cats," muttered one of the mercenaries, halting mid-step.

His lantern swung in his grip, its light jittering.

"Tristin, must've been the cats. Smells like they've been at the rats again."

A breeze swept in from the far side of the warehouse, stirring dust.

The precarious flame of the mercenary's lantern flickered.

"One of the windows is open back here," said the second mercenary, his voice farther off now. "Glass is broken."

"It didn't sound like broken glass," Tristin called out from the front of the warehouse, irritation evident in his voice. "Get a ladder and latch the window. We'll deal with the broken panes later. Do you see anyone?"

"No one, just the cat," the first mercenary replied. "If there was anyone in here, they're long gone through the window. They heard you and fled."

Rad held his breath as the mercenary walked right by his hiding spot. The man set his lantern on a barrel nearby, the light casting long, flickering shadows across the pallets.

Rad's fingers itched to grab *Darter*, but he stayed still, crouched near the pallet, counting the seconds.

The mercenary disappeared into the back where the workshop was, his boots crunching in the packed dirt.

Moments later, the faint sound of wood dragging on stone reached Rad's ears.

The man reappeared, now hefting a ladder. He grabbed the lantern and vanished again toward the window.

Rad heard the ladder scrape against the wall, followed by a faint creak as someone climbed it.

The slam of the window startled him, but he stayed motionless.

A latch squeaked shut, followed by the scrape of the ladder being dragged down.

"It's locked," the mercenary called.

The second voice replied, closer now, "Tristin, nothing's back here. If someone was here, they're long gone."

"Must've been the cats and rats," Tristin said from a distance. "Get back here so we can lock up and go home."

Rad let out his held breath, his body still tense but his mind sharpening.

The danger wasn't over yet.

He had to do decide what to do with the bodies.

Across the way, at the edge of his vision, a rat scurried past, dragging an eyeball behind it, with a calico cat stalking close on its heels.

CHAPTER THIRTEEN

∞

The Razor and The Ghost

Rad waited a full five minutes after the last footsteps faded before emerging from his hiding spot. He eased the shield-like pallet down with care, mindful of every sound in the quiet stillness.

Moving in the darkness, he guided himself by touch, his fingers brushing against the rough surfaces of crates as he crept forward.

Pale moonlight filtered through the windows above, casting faint silvery beams that illuminated the rows of pallets, crates, and barrels.

Urgency pressed at him.

The bodies had to be dealt with, but how?

His mind raced as he envisioned Duwy discovering his missing men and jumping to conclusions. If the bodies remained, suspicion would for certain fall on Tristin or Xavier.

Relocating them might confuse the timeline or location of their deaths, but it wouldn't change the outcome; Duwy would still think it was von Schule's doing.

Unless…

Rad froze in thought, weighing his options.

Disposing of the bodies would erase the evidence and prevent any retaliation. But how could he make two grown men disappear without a trace?

He had no idea… not even how to start.

Lacking the means or knowledge, he abandoned the thought and resolved to leave the bodies where they lay.

Whatever repercussions followed, he would deal with them later.

He moved toward the rear of the warehouse, his steps light and deliberate. A sturdy wooden door barred from the inside came into view. Its thick iron handle gleamed in the moonlight.

Rad examined it before lifting the heavy bar and setting it aside. The muffled scrape of wood on metal sounded loud to his ears, but no one was nearby to hear.

He slipped outside into the open air, letting the door settle with a muffled *thud.*

The night was cool and still, the faint hum of the city in the distance.

Rad's eyes darted to the right, where a haphazard stack of crates and pallets cast jagged shadows in the moonlight.

On his left, the loading docks stretched out, ghostly and silent

He was about to make his move when the sharp clop of hooves on cobblestone froze him in place.

Rad ducked, pressing himself against the stack of crates.

His heart rate remained steady as he recalled Hadley's advice: *Don't panic. Think.*

The approaching rider slowed as the sound of hooves softened. Rad remained still, eyes scanning the faint shadows.

Duwy.

The man sat rigid on his horse, his intense eyes scanning the warehouse and its surroundings, searching for any sign of his companions. From his elevated position, he scrutinized every shadow, every misplaced object, his intent unmistakable.

Rad remained motionless, pressed against the rough crates, willing himself into invisibility.

The flicker of lantern light brushed close to his hiding spot as Duwy's horse clopped nearer.

The man whistled; the probing sound echoed in the quiet night.

He paused, waiting, but when no answer came, he turned his mount around.

With a final, lingering glance at the warehouse, Duwy urged his horse forward and disappeared into the dark.

Rad let out a slow, measured breath, staying frozen until the last sound of hooves faded.

He darted back to where Vanguard was tethered. The stallion greeted him with a soft nicker, sensing Rad's tension, and nudged him affectionately.

He mounted, resisting the overwhelming urge to ride hard back to the estate—a reckless gallop would draw attention he couldn't afford.

As he guided Vanguard along the quiet avenues, the rush of emotions refused to subside.

The act of killing those men didn't disturb him in the way he thought it might. They were assassins, sneaking through the shadows to murder or abduct his half-brother.

Their deaths were justified—necessary.

What lingered in his mind wasn't guilt, but the unfamiliar surge of power and confidence it brought.

Darter's precision had been startling.

The way the blade had buried itself into the first assassin's skull played over in his mind, a vivid memory of speed and accuracy.

The second kill had been just as swift, though not as clean—one knife had missed its mark because of the assassin's futile attempt to deflect it.

Yet Hadley's voice echoed in his thoughts: *You don't have to kill a man twice.*

The adrenaline ebbed as he rode, leaving a dull weariness in its wake. His hands ached from gripping *Darter* and the reins, though he hadn't realized it until now.

Tristin, the mercenaries, and Duwy were nowhere in sight.

The streets stretched before him, quiet but watchful. The city was indifferent to the blood Rad had spilled minutes ago, but he knew better.

Somewhere, Duwy would be piecing things together, and Rad doubted the man would let it rest.

The Sweet Hatchet came into view, alive with energy.

Laughter, clinking mugs, and lively chatter spilled into the street, drawing him in.

Rad felt the pull of the place, a world removed from the troubles of *Château Saignoral* and the weight of his thoughts.

His fingers brushed over the few copper coins in his pocket—not much, barely enough for a single drink.

Tracking down Rosamund would be a luxury he couldn't afford tonight, assuming she was still around.

The idea of spending another evening in her company was enticing, but practicality won over desire.

A quick ale, nothing more, he told himself.

He tethered Vanguard outside among a throng of other horses, the rhythmic stamp of hooves and soft whinnies blending with the tavern's noise.

He was already in trouble for taking Vanguard and leaving the estate without permission. Reckoning would come later—the punishment would be worth it.

He saved Tristin, yet he couldn't tell anyone, including Abby.

He pushed open the door and stepped into the warm chaos.

Inside, The Sweet Hatchet was a hive of activity. Every table was packed, drinks flowed in steady streams, and the air buzzed with the murmur of deals, jokes, and flirtations. Servers weaved through the crowd, balancing trays of ale and wine, while the women of the house worked their charm, searching for willing patrons to escort upstairs into candlelit rooms.

Rad edged his way through the bustling crowd, managing to snag an ale from the bar with one of his precious coppers.

And then, he saw her.

Rosamund.

Her dark, smoldering gaze locked onto his, and the clamor of the tavern melted away, leaving only the intoxicating pull of her presence.

A cascade of midnight-black hair framed her face, glossy and silken, catching the dim light like liquid shadow. Her crimson dress caressed her every curve, hugging her body with unnatural grace, as if it had been sculpted to fit her alone.

With each step she took, the fabric shimmered and swayed, following her movements like an obedient lover.

Her beauty was magnetic, her elegance effortless, and to Rad, she was the most stunning thing in the world—a vision that made the bustling room around her fade into insignificance.

She smiled.

"Rad!"

"Rosamund," he said, his voice steadier than he felt. "Pleasure to see you. I'm here for a quick drink. I wish I had more time."

Her smile deepened, a spark of amusement lighting her eyes.

"I'm here all night if you change your mind. Perhaps another time?"

"Another time," he echoed with a faint, regretful grin. "See you later."

She lingered for a moment, her expression inviting, before turning away.

Rad couldn't help but watch as she sauntered back into the crowd, her curves swaying with effortless grace. His thoughts clung to her—her warmth, her softness, the way she saw him as if no one else existed.

Another time.

"Your friend has been asking about you," came a voice from the side, spoiling his daydream.

Rad turned to see Glenys, the co-owner of The Sweet Hatchet, making her way toward him. Her wispy frame was adorned with her usual assortment of colorful glass jewelry, the pieces catching the dim light.

"I don't have any friends," Rad said, a hint of suspicion in his tone. "You must be mistaken."

"Well," Glenys replied, her blue eyes gleaming, "he keeps asking if I've seen you. He's in the game room if you want to talk with him."

"I don't know who you're talking about."

"Faucet Chilcott," Glenys said with a knowing smirk. "Puzzle Boy."

Rad blinked, surprised.

Faucet Chilcott.

"He's not a friend," Rad muttered, though curiosity flickered in his mind.

Why would Faucet be asking about him?

The instructions had been clear: deliver the solution to the sliding square puzzle at the von Schule estate. Was he one of those people who were both incredibly smart and profoundly stupid at the same time?

"Thanks. I'll see what he wants."

Rad maneuvered through the lively crowd, weaving past servers and patrons. He reached the staircase and jogged up, his drink balanced in his hand.

Not a single drop spilled.

The raucous noise of the common room below dulled to a moderate hum on the second floor. Here, the atmosphere was different—focused and intense.

Numerous games were underway.

Gamblers crowded around tables, betting on cards and dice rolls.

At another station, darts thudded into a target with precision.

The sight of the darts called to him, an ache to test his skill and leave onlookers amazed.

Yet, Hadley's gruff voice echoed in his mind.

Don't show off. Don't let them see what you can do.

Rad turned his attention to the puzzle table, where Faucet Chilcott sat.

The stocky young man, broader and sturdier than Rad, shot to his feet the moment their eyes met. The odd-shaped blade at Faucet's hip swayed with his sudden motion.

"There you are! I thought I'd never catch you. Don't get out much, do you?"

"I instructed you to take the solution to the von Schule estate."

"I did! Like you asked," Faucet replied, his voice rising with frustration. "But they turned me away. Some *secuse* told me Hadley doesn't deal with townsfolk or unapproved leatherworkers. I tried to explain, but the piece of shit wouldn't listen and wouldn't deliver the note either. If I ever see him in town, I swear, I'm going to punch the arsehole right in the face."

Rad smirked. *Secuse.* High Ornst for 'jerk.' "Wilkins—he's the valet. I've wanted to do the same for years."

"So, I solved your five-by-five puzzle. Now, where's my coin?"

Rad pulled a silver coin from his boot, the emergency stash he always kept hidden. He handed it over, accepting the piece of paper Chilcott produced in return.

Rad's eyes scanned the page, confusion flickering across his face as he noted the convoluted sequence of arrows and numbers.

"What is this?" he asked, shaking the parchment at Chilcott.

"The sequence I used to solve it," Chilcott replied with a self-assured grin. "What you asked for."

Rad pointed to the arrows, his brow furrowing further.

"What does this gibberish mean?"

Chilcott let out a heavy sigh.

"It means you'll need to move some squares out of order to get them two spaces apart. The arrows show you how to make room and line them up. Here, let me show you. It'll take ten minutes, tops."

They replicated a five-by-five grid, leaving one square empty as in the original puzzle. Chilcott began rearranging the pieces, demonstrating a method to move two misplaced tiles into the correct order by creating space between them.

Recognition dawned.

The deceptive process was simple, the kind of solution that was obvious once revealed.

"For the bottom two rows," Chilcott explained, "you need to stack sixteen and twenty-one on top of each other first. Then seventeen and twenty-two. You keep pairing them, row by row."

Following Chilcott's instructions, Rad moved the pieces himself. Sure enough, the solution unfolded as promised, and within ten minutes, the puzzle was solved.

A quiet confidence settled over Rad—he now understood how to unlock the puzzle-locked door beneath the manor house.

Rad leaned back.

"So, in essence, I paid you a silver to teach me something this basic?"

"No," Chilcott corrected. "You paid me to solve the puzzle and give you the sequence—that was the contract. Teaching you was free. Unless your magic, money-spitting boots are hiding more silver you want to part with."

Rad's lips twitched in annoyance, but he couldn't suppress a grin.

"I do have one more silver in my boot. But to earn it, you'll have to help me with a task far more serious."

Chilcott scoffed, waving a dismissive hand. "Serious? What *serious* matter could a skinny runt like you possibly have?"

Rad met his gaze, tone flat. "Serious enough. Do you want to earn another silver or not?"

Chilcott stood up, towering a bit over Rad, his muscular frame lending an imposing air. Despite being the same height, Chilcott was solid—strong as a bull.

"I've got time," Chilcott said, his tone cautious but intrigued. "What's the job?"

"Come with me. You'll see."

Chilcott folded his arms, his face draped with skepticism.

"I'm not stupid. You don't walk blind into a job with some skinny runt you just met. What's the job?"

Rad leaned in close, lowering his voice to a whisper. "I need help moving two dead bodies."

Chilcott's eyes narrowed and he smacked Rad with a backhand to his shoulder.

"*Conerre.*" His tone was mocking, sharp. "Skinny *merred* like you couldn't strangle a kitten, let alone kill anyone."

"It's not bullshit, and keep your voice down," Rad hissed. "I had to kill them."

Chilcott arched an eyebrow, lowering his voice enough to match Rad's. "Skinny *merred* like you couldn't strangle a *sleeping* kitten."

Rad stood straighter, his face hardening. "Forget it. I'll find someone else."

"Hold up," Chilcott said, raising a hand, though the grin on his face lingered. "You're lying. There are no dead bodies."

Rad stepped back, crossing his arms. "One silver if you help me move them. Those are my terms."

"If you actually killed two people, I'll move them for free."

Rad tilted his head, studying him for a moment.

"Deal."

They shook hands, Chilcott gripping tighter than necessary.

"Lead on, skinny *merred*," Chilcott said, a hint of amusement still in his voice.

Outside, Rad swung up onto Vanguard's back and nudged the horse into a walk, heading toward the warehouse.

Chilcott shuffled along beside him, his boots scuffing the cobblestones in protest at the pace.

Rad could already imagine the mix of anger and disbelief that would soon explode from him—once Chilcott realized he wasn't lying about the bodies and he'd agreed to move them for free. The thought made him smirk.

"You're quite the criminal," Chilcott said, already huffing a little. "Two dead people and a stolen horse. What's next? Going to sell stolen goods? Join Leskaré?"

"Dead people, true. Stolen horse, false. This is Vanguard. He's from the stable where I work. I take care of him every day. I borrowed him for the evening."

"Borrowed, stolen—same crime, different word. Hey, slow down, I'm not a bloody racehorse."

"Fat *merred* like you needs exercise. Keep up. You can't borrow any of my skinny."

"This fat *merred* is going to kick your scrawny arse if you don't shut your bloody trap. I'll have to move three dead bodies."

"For free?" Rad shot back. "You wouldn't get close to me. You'd be dead before you opened your stupid mouth."

"You are so full of shit."

They wound their way through the warehouse district, Rad guiding them along a twisting route of alleys and side streets. He took four right turns in quick succession, keeping an eye out for anyone who might be trailing them.

The hour was growing late, and the streets were quieting, the chatter of taverns and the occasional clatter of hooves the only sounds breaking the stillness.

Chilcott trudged on, his breath audible but steady.

Rad had to admit he was impressed—despite all the bluster, Chilcott hadn't once complained about the winding detour. He followed without hesitation, the odd-shaped blade at his side swaying with each determined step.

They arrived and stopped in a shadowed alley near the warehouse. Rad tied Vanguard to a post, patting the horse's neck as he glanced around for any lingering eyes.

Chilcott leaned against a wall, wiping his sweaty forehead.

"For a skinny *merred*, you're smart," he muttered. "Four right turns... like a professional bastard. Why do I get the feeling I'm about to be moving dead bodies for free?"

"Because you are."

Chilcott shook his head, his breath still catching up to him. "I don't know why I'm doing this for free. Dead bodies? Job's worth at least a gold."

"Deal's a deal," Rad shot back. "Free, not a gold crown, not a silver."

Chilcott muttered, half to himself, "Next time, I'm charging upfront. Two silvers, minimum, for this kind of mess, at least two."

"You're absolutely brilliant," Rad said with a smirk. "Negotiating against yourself. This job's free. You can count the extra silvers you didn't earn while you work."

"Magnificent," Chilcott echoed with a dry laugh. "Helping a killer move bodies. For free. Bloody brilliant."

They moved through the shadows, Chilcott content to let Rad lead the way. The warehouse loomed ahead, its silent bulk intimidating in the faint moonlight. Rad took them on a cautious circuit around the building, eyes scanning for any signs of life. Finding none, they returned to the rear door.

Chilcott eyed the door skeptically. "Those doors are barred from the inside, you idiot," he hissed through his teeth, trying to keep his voice down. "We'll need to go through a window. Those crates over there can get us to a window."

Rad didn't answer.

Instead, he grasped the handle, gave Chilcott a smug glance, and pushed the door open with a satisfying creak.

He stepped inside without hesitation, leaving Chilcott to gape after him.

The scene was the same as Rad had left it.

The bodies lay side by side in their pooled blood, now dark and thick. The moon cast pale streaks through the windows, giving the place an otherworldly glow. The air was heavy with the metallic stench of blood, mingled with the earthy tang of rat droppings.

At the sound of their entry, the rats scattered, their claws skittering over the floor as they melted into the shadows.

"Shit," Chilcott muttered, staring at the bodies, his normal boisterous voice subdued.

"Have you moved bodies before?" Rad asked, his tone too calm for Chilcott's liking.

"You killed them?"

Chilcott's gaze flicked from the bodies to Rad, his expression a mixture of disbelief and grudging admiration.

"No choice. It was me or them," Rad replied, not explaining further as he crouched beside the corpses.

Chilcott stepped closer, careful to avoid the blood.

"They aren't guards. They aren't mercenaries."

He paused as a thought occurred to him.

"Shit. They better not be Leskaré."

"Definitely not Leskaré," Rad stated. "We're wasting time."

Chilcott grumbled as he assessed the warehouse.

"I hope you got paid for this," he muttered. "Because I'm not."

Rad ignored him, his attention focused on the task ahead.

The clouds shifted, blotting out the moonlight, and the already dim warehouse sank into deeper darkness.

The rats were emboldened by the change, their scratching and squeaking growing louder.

Chilcott flinched at a sudden noise, peering into the gloom.

"No alley cat this time," Rad murmured, more to himself than Chilcott. "Must've caught a rat and moved on."

"Lucky cat," Chilcott muttered. "Wish I could say the same."

"Stop complaining."

"Find a lantern," Chilcott said, his tone curt as he scanned the area. "There's a shop in the back. I'll see what else we can use. Do you know who owns this warehouse?"

"Xavier von Schule," Rad replied, focusing on the task.

Chilcott stiffened and shot him a glance—sharp, questioning.

"Your boss?"

"You're asking too many questions. Shut it and get to work."

"Get the lantern, skinny *merred*," Chilcott said, unease creeping into his voice.

Rad located a lantern tucked on a dusty shelf, lighting it with steady hands. He adjusted the shield until the glow dimmed to a faint but usable light.

By the time he returned, Chilcott had assembled a wheelbarrow, several burlap sacks, a wooden box, and a toolbox, all laid out like a morbid toolkit.

He stood over the bodies with an appraising eye.

"Strip them," Chilcott instructed, his tone all business. "Anything valuable goes in this box. Use their clothes to mop up the blood. There is sawdust in the back to absorb the rest. Sack everything up—clothes, boots, the lot. We'll load the bodies into the barrow and dump them somewhere quiet. They won't be found for a couple of days, hopefully. Got a solid alibi?"

"No one saw me and they aren't from Ornst," Rad said, crouching near the nearest body. "Don't need an alibi."

"How do you know they're not from here?"

"Look at their boots," Rad replied, gesturing at the distinctive footwear. "I've never seen anything like them before."

Chilcott's face was filled with skepticism.

"Skinny *merred* knows his fashion too? You sure you're not some fancy boy slumming it in the stables?"

Rad didn't rise to the bait, he merely nodded in silent agreement.

He wasn't about to tell Chilcott about Duwy or the setup to capture Tristin. The less Chilcott knew, the safer they both would be.

They worked in a grim silence, the task consuming their focus.

As Rad stripped the bodies, he gathered their scant belongings into the wooden box. A few coins, a pair of wicked knives, and an empty locket were all they carried.

Cleaning the blood from the floor proved more challenging—the stubborn liquid had thickened, clinging to the compacted dirt.

They scrubbed in a rush, scattering sawdust across the mess, but only managed to leave behind blotchy smears of crimson.

Chilcott paused, frowning as he inspected one of the bodies.

"Shit. This worries me."

Rad head jerked up. "What?"

"Both of them have the same tattoo on their shoulders." Chilcott pulled the shoulder toward Rad, revealing the ink. "It's not only a mark. It's a brand. They're someone's property. Someone's going to come looking for them. Shit."

Rad leaned closer, squinting at the symbols.

Two designs were inked into the skin in stark black. The first resembled a 'P,' but with an extra circular flourish to the right. The second was a backward, curved 'E.'

The meaning was lost on Rad—they weren't symbols he had seen before.

He searched the reaches of his memory and all the books he had read—nothing came to mind.

"What now?" Rad asked.

"This is going to get gruesome," Chilcott said grimly, unsheathing the oversized razor strapped to his hip. The stout handle gleamed with an edge sharp enough to part bone.

"You're the expert," Rad muttered, stepping back.

Chilcott didn't waste time.

With a practiced flick of his wrist, he sliced cleanly through the tattooed skin, severing the marks from both corpses. He tossed the bloodied scraps of flesh into the darkness, letting the rats take care of them.

Setting his feet, he raised the razor and brought it down with precision, severing one head in a clean, merciless stroke.

Blood pooled anew, thick and dark.

He turned to the second body and repeated the motion—two strokes, two heads.

Rad's stomach tightened as Chilcott grabbed the burlap sack, scooping up the severed heads like trophies.

The sight was horrifying, yet Chilcott moved with calm efficiency, as if this were another chore to complete.

"We're going to split up," Chilcott said as he handed Rad the sack of heads.

Rad took it.

The weight hit harder than he expected, dragging at his arm—a grim weight, heavier than it should've been.

"You take care of the heads and the clothing. I'll ditch the bodies. Here." Chilcott fished into the box of valuables and pulled out a small pile of coins. "We split fifty-fifty. I'll get rid of everything else. Deal?"

"Deal."

Rad studied the coins before pocketing his share, but the weight in his hand didn't ease the weight in his chest.

"Is this what you do for your employer?" Rad asked.

"Only once. Usually, I take a few fingers from people who don't pay what they owe. My razor's is perfect for that."

Chilcott tapped the oversized blade at his side with satisfaction.

"I can tell." Rad smirked. "I should call you 'Razor Boy' instead of 'Puzzle Boy.'"

Chilcott chuckled. "It does have a certain ring to it. I like it. Call me 'Razor.' Sounds deadlier."

"Faucet 'Razor' Chilcott. Terrifying," Rad said, deadpan, "but only to blind cripples. Or kittens. Sorry, *sleeping* kittens."

Chilcott burst out laughing, shaking his head.

"After this, I never want to see your skinny arse again. Got it? You don't know me, I don't know you, and if we run into each other a couple of years down the road, we'll grab a drink and laugh about this mess."

"What about The Sweet Hatchet?" Rad asked, quirking an eyebrow.

"Not going back there. Not after this." Chilcott body stiffened, his grin fading. "You keep your head down, keep your mouth shut, and this whole thing will blow over. Got it?"

"Got it." Rad nodded, noting the subtle shift in the air between them.

They moved with efficiency, loading the headless bodies into the wheelbarrow and covering them with burlap sacks.

Rad stuffed the bloody sack inside another and tied it off with hemp, its awkward weight tugging against his fingers as he hefted it. The uneven shapes felt wrong, almost alive, but he shook the thought aside and carried it to the door.

Outside, the air was still and damp.

No footsteps, no voices, only the faint buzz of the city in the distance.

Rad set the sacks down and scouted the perimeter with slow, careful steps, his breathing steady as he melted into the shadows.

The side avenue was clear.

Satisfied, he returned to find Chilcott waiting with a guarded expression.

"Gotta say," Chilcott murmured, pointing at the door, "you've got a knack for vanishing. I think I'll call you Mister Ghost."

Rad gave a small shrug. "Just Ghost. Drop the Mister."

Chilcott smirked. "Fine, Ghost. I *won't* see you later."

"And I *won't* see you, Razor."

The two shook hands, a silent acknowledgment of the bleak business they had concluded.

Razor hefted the long wheelbarrow, now camouflaged with debris, trash, and shards of wood, and pushed it through the open door.

Without a backward glance, he disappeared into the shadows, leaving Rad alone with his burdens.

Rad waited five minutes, counting each heartbeat as he reviewed the consequences waiting for him back at the estate.

Taking Vanguard without permission would for certain earn him a harsh punishment—perhaps lashes, perhaps worse.

As for the events of the night, those would stay his secret.

They had to.

The sacks were awkward and unwieldy as he attached them to Vanguard's saddle. Even with Vanguard bearing the weight, the uneven load jostled with every trot, throwing off the balance.

He focused on the task ahead: first, burning the clothing.

The estate had dedicated bonfire pits for disposing of branches and other debris. It would be the simplest way to erase the evidence.

The heads were a different matter. They would need to be buried. He wasn't sure he could manage it tonight, not with how late it had become. The best he could do was stash them in the stables until he could dig a proper hole.

The streets were empty now, the city quieter.

The muffled clop of Vanguard's hooves against the cobblestones was the only sound as Rad navigated the winding avenues.

The darkness pressed in, deep and still. It was later than he'd realized, and the emptiness of the roads only heightened his awareness of his own exhaustion.

He slouched forward in the saddle, the events of the day catching up with him. It wasn't only the physical strain—the work, the chase, and the weight of the sacks—it was deeper. A weariness settled in his bones and wrapped around his thoughts.

He was tired in a way that sleep wouldn't fix, but he couldn't stop yet.

There was still too much to do.

His mind drifted, unbidden, to the men he had killed.

The memory of the first assassin falling without a sound under *Darter's* strike.

The second crumpling after the throwing knives found their marks.

He tried to sort through his emotions but found little clarity. He wasn't upset. He wasn't angry or sad. He simply felt... hollow.

Shouldn't it have been more?

Shouldn't he feel something?

Rad told himself their deaths were justified. They had been there to kill Tristin—or worse, to take him hostage.

Yet doubt remained.

Who were they?

Did they deserve what happened?

Could their lives have been spared?

The questions were distressing, but there were no answers—only the silence of the night and the soft creak of leather from Vanguard's saddle.

The truth weighed on him.

He wasn't innocent anymore.

He was part of the harsh, brutal world Xavier von Schule had forged.

By killing those men, he had stepped onto a path he wasn't sure he could ever leave. Perhaps this was what Xavier had always wanted—for Rad to be shaped by violence and necessity, to do terrible things.

And now Xavier's wish had come true.

The stables were as quiet as anticipated when Rad rode in on Vanguard.

A faint glow from a lantern flickered behind the curtain of Hadley's shed, but the rest of the area was steeped in darkness—just as Rad preferred.

The sack containing the heads was a deep, sticky red, much like the bag holding the blood-soaked clothes and boots.

He dismounted, leading Vanguard inside and leaving the sacks on a heap of straw.

After stripping off the saddle, he carried it to its proper storage place. The weight felt heavier than it should, though he knew it was his fatigue and guilt making the task harder.

Tomorrow, he'd have to inspect the saddle and gear, wiping away any traces of blood.

As he returned to Vanguard, the dim glow of a lantern approached, accompanied by the rich scent of pipe tobacco.

Hadley's weathered face emerged from the shadows, the soft light casting flickering highlights on his lined features. He nibbled on the stem of his lit pipe, smoke curling from the bowl as he drew closer.

"Horse thieves get harsh punishment," Hadley said, his voice carrying a hard edge. "Stable boys who abandon their duties get harsher punishment from the horse-master. You better have a damned good explanation."

"I only borrowed Vanguard," Rad replied in a rush of words. "I didn't steal him."

"Borrowed?" Hadley raised an eyebrow, taking a healthy pull on his pipe before blowing a perfect smoke ring into the cool night air. "Visiting Rosamund, were you?"

Rad hesitated.

He had always been honest with Hadley.

When he made mistakes with the horses or shirked his chores, he owned up to it. If he was late, he gave no excuses. He thought about lying but dismissed it—Hadley would see right through him.

"I ended up at The Sweet Hatchet," he admitted, "but I didn't visit Rosamund."

Hadley's sharp eyes narrowed as he chomped harder on his pipe.

"Boy, you lie to whores and the Ornst militia. You don't lie to Hadley. Come clean. *Now.*"

"I'm not lying," Rad said, his voice steady despite the tension between them.

Hadley leaned closer, his face stern.

"This isn't acceptable, Rad. Taking Vanguard off the estate without permission is a major offense. You've always been straight with me, and I've always been straight with you. You don't break our trust."

Rad scoffed, frustration bubbling to the surface.

"Straight with me? You lie all the time, Hadley! Your threats, your shady past—you're not exactly the shining example of honesty!"

Hadley's expression softened for a moment as if conceding the point.

The toughness returned.

"It doesn't change what I expect from you. Now, tell me the truth, or I'll have no choice but to turn you over to Xavier. If he finds out what you did, there won't be anything I can do to protect you."

Rad was trapped.

If he stayed silent, he would face brutal consequences—whipping, being cast out into the streets, or worse.

But confessing meant trusting someone else with what he had done.

Chilcott might know the outcome of the night's events, but not the full truth. The incriminating evidence in the sacks needed to be dealt with right away.

Delay meant discovery, and discovery meant disaster.

Hadley would work it out soon enough, and the fallout would be worse if he tried to cover it up.

He realized there was only one option.

Trusting Hadley was his only choice.

"I'll tell you," Rad said. "But you need to listen to everything before you decide what to do."

Rad met Hadley's gaze, forcing himself to speak despite the knot tightening in his chest.

"I followed Tristin, thinking I could learn more about Xavier's business," he began, his voice steady, though his insides tightened. "He had a meeting with a man named Duwy, from some group like Leskaré. There were two assassins hiding in the warehouse, waiting to kill him or take him hostage. I killed them so they wouldn't harm Tristin."

Hadley's sharp eyes bore into him, searching for cracks in his words.

The silence stretched, heavy and expectant, as Hadley bit down on the stem of his pipe.

With a long inhale, he let the embers glow bright. The exhaled smoke swirled in the dim light, and he coughed once before spitting on the stable floor.

"You've dropped a load of *merred* on me, lad," Hadley said. "Let's get Vanguard taken care of. You're going to tell me everything—every detail, no half-truths, no holding back. If what you say is true, details could be the difference between waking up tomorrow or not waking at all."

Rad nodded, swallowing hard as he turned back to Vanguard.

The horse shifted, as though sensing his unease. The horse nudged him, as if encouraging him to trust the horse-master.

Rad wasn't afraid Hadley would betray him—it wasn't Hadley's way. If anything, the man was too direct, too rooted in his own sense of loyalty to do something so underhanded.

But trust came with a price.

This confession would only deepen the debt he owed Hadley, one he couldn't begin to repay.

What unsettled him wasn't whether Hadley would help—it was how Hadley might use this knowledge down the road. He was handing Hadley a blade, sharp and ready, to wield however he chose.

Hadley stayed quiet, his pipe glowing in the dim light as Rad began tending to Vanguard.

He brushed the horse down with steady, methodical strokes, letting the familiar rhythm calm his nerves.

The truth he'd spoken moments ago had shifted the balance between them, and Rad could feel it, like an invisible weight pressing down on his shoulders.

Vanguard nudged him, a reminder of simpler tasks and simpler times, before tonight's revelations had tied him closer to Hadley than ever.

"I don't have an apple," Rad muttered to Vanguard, patting him lovingly before he departed.

"You're playing a dangerous game, lad," Hadley said as Rad returned. His tone was measured, thoughtful. "You're trusting me with this, and you don't know what I'll do with it."

Rad met Hadley's eyes without flinching.

"I know you won't betray me."

Hadley nodded, the faint glow of his pipe illuminating the hard lines of his face.

"No, I won't betray you, lad. But let me tell you something about trust—it's never free. Comes with strings, always has, always will. You remember that. Trusting others is like a debt, and one way or another, you'll pay the cost."

Rad's jaw tightening and he felt the panic welling.

"I didn't have a choice. I had to... Tristin... he would be dead."

"Aye, you didn't have a choice," Hadley agreed, his pipe stem shifting between his teeth as he took another puff. "You didn't."

They stood among the withered remnants of the orchard, a stretch of land abandoned and forgotten, left to fade while the others flourished. Their gnarled branches clawed at the night sky, the bark mottled with patches of decay. The ground was littered with blackened, dead twigs, the air sour with the scent of abandonment.

It was a fitting place for the unpleasant task ahead.

They buried the heads at opposite ends of the orchard, digging deep enough to ensure they would never be found.

The weight of the soil pressing down on the burlap sacks felt heavier than it should have, as though the earth itself protested the act.

They soaked the clothing in oil and lit with the flame of Hadley's pipe, reducing it to smoldering ash. They tilled the remains into the soil, the last remnants of acrid smoke curling upward into the darkness.

By the time they finished, it was well past midnight.

Rad was utterly drained, his arms trembling from the digging, his calloused hands cracked and bleeding from the effort. He followed Hadley back to the stables in silence, each step dragging as though the earth sought to claim him too.

Once inside, they worked in weary tandem to clean up.

Rad scrubbed at the bloodstains on his clothes with cold water, while Hadley cleaned the tools they'd used. The atmosphere between them was heavy, laden with unspoken thoughts.

Rad could feel it—Hadley was holding back, weighing his words before they came. Rad broke the silence, his voice determined.

"Just as you demanded the truth from me, I want the same courtesy. What do you know? What are you holding back? Is it something about Tristin? The meeting? The two men? What?"

Hadley leaned against a wood column, chomping his pipe between his teeth, the ember casting fleeting shadows across his face. After a moment, he nodded.

"Aye, lad, you deserve to hear it. Those two men—those marks your friend cut off their shoulders—those were the symbols of the Black Storm."

Rad froze.

The words hit him like a physical blow.

The Black Storm.

Assassins.

Thieves.

Cutthroats.

He had read stories about them. The name was whispered in hushed tones, spoken with the kind of reverence reserved for death itself. They were like Leskaré but darker and crueler.

"I've heard of them," Rad said, his voice cautious. "Like Leskaré."

Hadley shook his head, his expression intense.

"Worse than Leskaré. Leskaré's got rules, twisted as they may be. The Black Storm? They're fanatics—killers who relish the act itself. You want someone dead, you hire the Black Storm. And if you don't pay, they'll kill you too. This lot? They don't forget, and they don't forgive."

Rad swallowed hard, his throat dry. "Do you think they'll come looking for those two?"

Hadley's gaze darkened, and his voice lowered to a growl. "Aye. They don't leave their own unavenged. And if they find out who killed those men, they won't stop until you're dead."

The words settled over Rad like a dark veil, suffocating and inescapable.

"Your Da must've crossed them," Hadley continued. "Could be he rejected an offer. Perhaps they wanted to disrupt his business, or those men were there to send a message. Either way, tonight wasn't only a simple meeting. It was a warning—or a declaration of war. And now you're in the middle of it."

Rad reeled, replaying the events of the night, trying to make sense of them.

"Duwy," he said. "Do you think he'll come back?"

Hadley nodded. "Aye. Duwy will be sniffing around, looking for answers. The things you did tonight? They'll hold for now, as long as your friend keeps his mouth shut. And me? You don't need to worry about me, lad. I know how to keep a secret."

He paused.

"But remember, the smartest move you can make now is to pretend this never happened. Put it out of your mind—for now, at least. Let's see how this plays out before we say another word about it. There is some safety behind the walls of *Château Saignoral.*"

The stable fell into silence again.

Rad nodded, his exhaustion evident as he asked, "What's my punishment for taking Vanguard?"

Hadley's pipe flared in the darkness as he let out a puff of smoke.

"I already punished you, lad. You dug your own grave tonight, literally and figuratively. Let it be a lesson on what a damned fool thing it was, taking Vanguard to visit Rosamund. I hope she was worth it."

Rad felt the sting of Hadley's grip as the man grabbed his hands, inspecting the torn callouses from the night's labor.

"These wounds are the cost of your stupidity. Now, get washed up and into bed. Your shift starts in a few hours, and I expect you bright-eyed and working like this night never happened. If anyone asks, the only thing you know is the sky is blue and your snot is green. Got it? And if your father or Tristin so much as mention the Black Storm or the meeting, you're to act dumber than you already are. Understand?"

"Yes."

"Now go." Hadley gave him a firm pat on the shoulder, softer than his usual roughness, but still enough to prod him forward. "Get some rest, lad."

Rad trudged out of the stables, his legs reluctant and heavy with the weight of the night. Moonlight illuminated his path, guiding him toward the manor house. His thoughts lingered on the evening's events, particularly the loose end he'd left in Chilcott.

A cold thought crept in, unsettling but persistent—perhaps he should silence Chilcott permanently to ensure the secret was safe.

Yet his gut told him otherwise.

Razor was someone he could trust, at least for now.

He needed to rely on instinct and heed Hadley's advice: forget this night ever happened.

The guards at the manor's back door waved him through without question.

Inside, Rad slipped off his boots, carrying them under his arm as he made his way toward the staircase. The stillness of the manor was broken by the soft creak of floorboards as Wilkins emerged from the shadows, his face twisted in irritation.

Dressed in bedclothes and a long house jacket, his posture rigid, his presence too timely to be coincidence.

"You'll get the whip for this one," Wilkins said, his voice chilled.

Rad raised his hand, displaying his blistered palms and torn callouses.

"Hadley already punished me. Took Vanguard for a ride. Made me dig my own grave, scared the shit out of me."

"Not enough," Wilkins sneered, his beady eyes narrowing. "I'm going straight to your father about this."

Rad stiffened.

Wilkins wasn't above blackmail, and Rad knew better than to assume the man's threats were idle.

"What do you want?"

Wilkins' lips pursed as he considered the price.

"Two bottles of your Da's *De'Artois* bourbon. Poured into plain containers, of course, so no one will suspect a thing. Deliver them to me, and I'll forget about your little joyride tonight."

The request was a trap.

Rad could see it in the valet's eyes.

Either Wilkins would catch him in the act or find a way to pin the theft on him later.

But rejecting the deal would mean facing Xavier's wrath—a punishment far worse than Hadley's scolding. At least with Wilkins, there was a slim chance of control.

"Fine," Rad said, his voice tight. "Put the empty containers in my room. Once it's done, we're even."

"Deal," Wilkins replied, his grin widening as he gripped Rad's hand in a handshake.

The squeeze was intense, sending a jolt of pain through Rad's tender callouses.

Rad fought the urge to recoil, meeting Wilkins' smug gaze with a calm stare.

Without another word, he ascended the staircase to his room.

His body screamed for rest, and he collapsed onto his bed, knowing full well morning would arrive far too soon.

CHAPTER FOURTEEN

∞

Lanny Zeh

Sorry I haven't written in a while. I won't make any excuses, it has been harder to sit down and write these days. I've been meaning to get to the Ornst Library, but haven't asked for permission from Da.

I still owe you a story for your birthday, so here goes. It's about a boy who finds a magic puzzle, solves it, and unleashes... well, you'll see!

I enjoyed your story, you have a wonderful imagination. You should write books, or that's something you could do after you leave here. The puzzle door was interesting and how it finally unlocked to reveal another puzzle, which led to the treasure guarded by the Wilkins-dragon.

That was so funny, and tricking the Wilkins-dragon with poisoned bourbon was brilliant.

Autumn Cotillion is going to be held at the Ruud estate, so I'll definitely get to see Robert this time.

I'm hopeful for a first kiss—I keep obsessing over it!

I'm terrible, aren't I?

But I can't stop thinking about it, replaying how it might go in my mind.

I've already chosen a dress for the occasion. It's more daring than anything I've worn before—a hint of boldness—but still modest compared to Gabrielle's gowns.

Bella and Marie think it's perfect, and Gabrielle approved without a single comment, which is a small miracle.

It makes me feel... grown up, I suppose.

Oh, and there's news for the spring.

Ma, Tristin, the girls, and I will be going on a trip to Haddensack to represent the family at court. It doesn't happen that often.

It's supposed to be a great honor, though Gabrielle is acting like it's the grandest thing ever. She keeps talking about how important it is to make connections and leave a 'favorable' impression.

I'll admit, I'm excited.

It's a chance to see Haddensack and its famous Falconspire Castle, but I'll miss you, Rad. I'll find a gift for you while I'm there—something from there to show you I'm always thinking of you.

For now, all I can think about is the cotillion and how Robert might react when he sees me in my new dress.

Wish me luck!

A month had passed since the warehouse incident, and in that time, Rad had remained silent about what had transpired, sharing the details only with Hadley during brief, cautious conversations.

Processing the whirlwind of emotions and implications of the night had required patience and restraint. He had saved Tristin—of that, he was certain. But the weight of it still clung to him.

There would be no recognition.

No thanks.

Life at the von Schule estate had resumed its usual rhythm, as though nothing had happened at all.

Hadley, as irascible as ever, showed encouraging signs of physical recovery.

The tailored exercises they'd developed together—throwing knives, swinging swords, and testing his shoulders with controlled repetition—were proving effective.

His left shoulder, though still stiff, had gained a surprising amount of flexibility, and his right had almost returned to its full range of motion.

The positive shift in Hadley's mood was noticeable.

Cooler weather brought crisp autumn mornings, and the sprawling estate was painted in vibrant hues of orange, red, and gold. The most bountiful grape harvest in decades had ripened on the vine, and Xavier von Schule would surely find a way to profit—likely with another counterfeit gala to deceive Ornst's highborn fools.

Rad's days were consumed with the stables, training, and an unexpected task—procuring Xavier's prized *De'Artois* bourbon for Wilkins.

The valet continued to threaten him over the Vanguard incident but had yet to act, making it clear his true desire was the bourbon.

Wilkins was unaware Rad had already found a solution.

Hidden at the back of the wine cellar, buried under twenty cases of stacked bottles, was a misplaced case of *De'Artois* bourbon.

By taking two bottles from the case, Rad ensured they wouldn't be missed for years—perhaps a decade.

With the bottles transferred into plain, nondescript containers used for syrups, he was ready to fulfill Wilkins' demands.

But Rad suspected treachery.

Wilkins was not one to let an opportunity for leverage slip through his grasp.

The planned meeting in the carriage house felt like a trap.

So Rad decided to flip the arrangement.

At the appointed time, instead of meeting Wilkins, Rad placed the disguised bourbon bottles in the valet's room. Alongside them, he hid the empty bourbon bottles, their distinctive labels intact.

If someone were to discover them, the evidence would implicate Wilkins rather than himself. It was a calculated risk, but Rad wasn't too concerned.

If Wilkins was smart—and Rad doubted it—he'd dispose of the empty bottles without protest and stick to their agreement.

If not, the fool would expose himself.

Either way, Rad would walk away unscathed.

That night, the household remained hushed.

No knocks at his door.

No confrontations.

No accusations.

Rad rested on his bed, staring at the dark ceiling, half-expecting the door to burst open.

But no one came.

By morning, he concluded the matter had been resolved, at least for now.

Yet, the exchange left a lingering bitterness.

The whole affair was another reminder of Wilkins' pettiness and Xavier's influence over his life. Someday, Rad vowed, he would reverse the situation on Wilkins. When the moment came, the valet would regret every slight, every threat, every insult.

And when the day arrived, Rad would savor it.

For now, he let the matter lie, sinking back into the life he was building, day by day.

With so much happening around him, Rad had forgotten about the puzzle he'd left unsolved.

It took him ten minutes to unscramble the wooden tiles into their correct places. When the message revealed itself, the words sent a shiver down his spine: *Leskaré never sleeps.*

The mechanism clicked, and the sound echoed faintly in the confined space. This place, once a stronghold for Leskaré, held yet another layer of mystery.

Souterrain Hall.

Rad felt a surge of excitement and trepidation.

Behind the heavy door lay treasure that could change his life.

He stood at the basement's edge, calculating his position: about thirty feet from the manor's exterior walls.

This area, he figured, must still remain hidden, as he didn't recall a visible entrance from the exterior.

Whatever was beyond the door, whether another passageway or room, he was about to uncover it.

Rad's heart raced as he gripped the handle, turning it and pulling the door open.

His lantern cast flickering light into the void beyond, revealing a dark passageway stretching into points unknown.

His pulse quickened.

It wasn't only the thrill of discovery but the weight of stepping into a part of the estate's hidden past.

He slid one of his throwing knives between the metal door and its frame, ensuring it couldn't lock behind him. He had no intention of getting trapped, like a forgotten relic of this place.

The air smelled stale, damp, and metallic—rusty.

His boots crunched on debris as he moved forward, and when he lowered his lantern, he saw fragments of smashed wood on the floor—puzzle tiles, like the ones he'd just solved, but shattered and discarded from the other side of the door.

To his left, a shape caught his eye.

He swung the lantern toward the wall and froze.

A body.

Or what was left of one.

The corpse was old, nothing more than bones and tattered remnants of clothing, the flesh long devoured—likely by rats.

A set of black leather armor sat to the side, untouched.

It shouldn't be pristine.

Leather should have cracked, dried out, or rotted over time, but this armor defied decay. It was deep black, an inky darkness that absorbed the lantern's glow.

Beside the bones, a row of rusted daggers had been laid out with strange precision, as if in tribute.

The scene was unsettling—like the remains of a man still guarding the place, even in death.

Rad swallowed hard and stepped closer, careful not to disturb the pile of bones as he inspected the armor.

Was it enchanted?

Cursed?

He didn't dare touch it—not yet.

He extended the lantern ahead, its light cutting into the shadows, and stepped over the bones.

The tunnel stretched forward, its walls the same rough-cut fieldstone, until it ended in a jagged heap of rubble.

A collapse?

The ceiling was solid—no signs of a cave-in from above. Could it have been filled in from the other side?

Rad hesitated, thoughts racing.

Should he try to dig through?

There could be a passage beyond—a secret, a clue, anything.

But the stone was tightly packed and ancient, untouched for decades. And if his instincts were right, he was near the outer edge of the manor.

Silence pressed in around him, broken only by the distant drip of water deeper in the passage.

He stood still, weighing his options.

The tunnel had secrets.

He could feel it in his gut.

But time was running short.

Reluctantly, Rad turned back.

He'd return another day, better prepared.

As he approached the skeleton once more, a flicker of silver caught his eye—something he'd missed before.

Embedded in the smooth stone wall was a faint lattice of silver wires, their pattern forming runes arranged in a four-by-four grid.

His pulse quickened.

A magical lock.

Just like the one guarding Xavier's vault.

Heart pounding harder now, Rad stepped closer.

With nothing to lose, he raised a hand and traced the familiar pattern—*L*, then *Z*—the initials carved into his memory.

The silver lines pulsed with light.

A soft *click* echoed through the passage.

A thrill surged through Rad as the stone wall shifted, swinging inward with a weighty groan to reveal a hidden chamber.

Treasure? Gold? Jewels?

Enough to fund his escape with Hadley and never look back?

He lifted the lantern and stepped inside.

The chamber wasn't filled with riches—it was empty.

Cold.

Forgotten.

Roughly ten feet by ten, the vault was lined with old brick and crisscrossed with silver wire, like a grid meant to hold something in—or out.

Empty wooden shelves lined the left, center, and right walls, their contents long removed.

Faint impressions in the dirt floor marked where heavy chests had once stood, now long gone.

In the center of the room stood a single wooden table. On it sat a stoppered green glass vial, a dried inkwell and quill, and a sheet of aged parchment held in place by a small dagger.

Rad hesitated at the edge of the table, a sudden weight pressing on his chest. He set the lantern down with care, his fingers brushing the hilt of the dagger that pinned the parchment in place.

The crest on the hilt was unmistakable—Xavier's insignia.

His pulse kicked up.

Then he saw the name. Torn at the corner, the parchment still bore a clear, bold heading: *Lanny Zeh.*

Rad's stomach twisted. Beneath it, written in Xavier's precise, arrogant hand, was a message. He read.

> Lanny Zeh
>
> Well, well.
>
> If it isn't the infamous LZ—skulking through my manor like a rat. Imagine my delight upon uncovering your little secret. The tunnel is sealed now. You'll find no escape. I destroyed the magical lock you so meticulously installed. Ingenious, yes—but not ingenious enough.
>
> Your hidden wealth is gone. I claimed it, just as I claimed Souterrain Hall from Leskaré.
>
> You lose, LZ. Every piece you thought was yours now belongs to me.

The vial on the table holds your only mercy. You
won't last long down here. When thirst and madness
grip you, you'll welcome the poison.

No one will find you. No one will hear your screams.
No one will come. You'll rot in the dark.

And your name will vanish with you—like the
coward you are.

As for your child—when Justine births your little
bastard, I may kill it out of spite.

    — XvS

Rad read the letter again, each line settling into him like stones.
The truth was undeniable.

He was the child Xavier referenced, and Lanny Zeh—this
mysterious figure—was his true father.

A wave of anger, confusion, and stark realization crashed over him.
This manor hadn't only been Xavier's prize; it had once belonged to
Zeh, who had used its secret passages for his clandestine dealings. Rad
figured Zeh was the voyeur stationed above the master bedroom...

Rad shuddered.

Xavier had discovered his rival's hidden sanctuary here in the cellar,
stolen everything of value, and left Zeh to die a slow, agonizing death.

The meaning of the initials 'LZ' on the vault mechanisms became
clear—Lanny Zeh.

Had his real father designed these intricate puzzles himself?

Rad pondered the possibility as his fingers brushed over the faint
glow of the runes. It was unlikely, given the skill and magical
knowledge required to create such mechanisms.

Yet, the evidence pointed to Zeh's intimate involvement. Perhaps
he wasn't merely a cunning man but someone with arcane talent or the
resources to commission such enchantments.

The puzzles, the hidden chambers, the exactness of it all—it spoke
of a mind far beyond the ordinary.

Rad's thoughts swirled.

What if his real father had possessed some hidden power, a secret
talent for magic or engineering?

It wasn't beyond belief.

Zeh had been smart enough to use these passageways undetected, outmaneuver Xavier, and hide his wealth.

But Xavier's note painted him as a rival caught and crushed—his final gambit undone by betrayal or arrogance.

Perhaps both.

It was clear to Rad that Xavier hadn't solved the puzzle and gone through from the outside, otherwise these secret passageways wouldn't be a secret.

Every puzzle Rad had encountered in this place was like a bridge to the past, a connection to the man he'd never known. It was strange, thinking of the meticulous care required to build these things, only for them to become part of a tomb.

He wondered, what other puzzles remained in *Souterrain Hall*?

Had he found them all?

Rad's thoughts wandered, taking him down a path from which there was no return.

He couldn't confront Xavier head on—he would have to tread carefully.

Perhaps Hadley could help him untangle the threads of this revelation.

He was certain his mother, Justine, held answers, but broaching the subject would be perilous.

He couldn't admit to finding his father's remains in a sealed tunnel. Too much would unravel if he dug too deep. This was where his father had died. And yet, the air still felt heavy with secrets, as if the place were whispering.

Rad folded the letter and tucked it into his light jacket. The truth might be more dangerous than he ever imagined, but it was his truth now.

He left the vault as he had found it, ensuring it remained untouched.

The heavy stone door swung back into place with a soft finality, and he waited to see if it would lock. A muted click confirmed it was sealed again.

For a moment, Rad stood in silence, his eyes drawn back to the skeletal remains of his father sprawled against the stone wall.

It would take time to gather the bones and make arrangements for a proper burial.

The thought brought an ache to his chest.

Perhaps his mother would want to be there, to pay her respects and bid farewell to the man she once loved.

The idea his father had died here, alone and trapped, unable to say goodbye, bothered Rad. Today had begun with promise, his determination focused on unlocking the puzzle door and uncovering hidden treasure.

Instead, he'd unearthed a piece of his own history—a puzzle far more personal, and one with no clear solution.

As the minutes passed, he began to gather the bones, arranging them with care into a neat pile. Each piece was like a fragment of a story he didn't quite understand.

The leather armor resting beside the remains caught his attention once more. Its condition defied time; the supple material felt almost new, light and flexible. However, the rats had done their damage elsewhere, gnawing through the boots, gloves, and a purse.

The breastplate, pauldrons, vambraces, gauntlets, cuisse, and greaves were intact.

Rad figured it would take at least two trips to transport the armor and the bones to his room.

As he sifted through the debris, a glint of gold caught his eye. Scattered coins were hidden among the rubble.

Rad gathered them one by one, his thoughts drifting to the small stash of coins Abby had given him. Together, they might be enough to support him when he turned sixteen and left the estate.

The small collection of gold was like a lifeline, but it also made the future dauntingly real.

Inside the breastplate, there was a folded piece of parchment wedged against the inner lining. It was cracked and withered, the passage of time having left it fragile yet intact.

Rad held his breath as he reached for it.

Could this be a message from his father? An explanation of why he was here? Was a note for his mother, a final missive undelivered?

With delicate fingers, he unfolded the brittle note, mindful of its fragile edges. The faint scent of decay clung to the paper, and the ink, once smeared, had dried into dark stains.

His heart sank as he read the three words written there:

REST IN AUDITORIUM

LZ

The initials below it were unmistakable: *LZ*—Lanny Zeh.

The 'LZ' was underlined twice.

What did it mean?

The handwriting, while shaky, was like Rad's.

Rad frowned, the cryptic message sparking more questions than answers.

Did it mean to lay his father's bones to rest in the abandoned auditorium on this level of the basement?

Or was there something else in the auditorium—a hidden clue, another piece of the story waiting to be discovered?

He folded the parchment again, tucking it safely into his jacket. One thing was certain—he would find out.

A cool autumn breeze whispered through the open stable doors, rustling the scattered straw and carrying with it the faint scent of turning leaves. Outside, the trees shed their vibrant foliage in steady intervals, the wind plucking the stubborn ones clinging to branches.

Hadley had dismissed both Rad and Jamie for the day, though Rad lingered, broom in hand, his movements aimless. He swept the same patch of straw twice, watching from the corner of his eye as Jamie sauntered off, humming to himself.

When Jamie was no longer visible, Rad slid the broom into its holder and made his way over to Hadley.

The horse-master leaned against the wall, rolling his shoulders in slow, deliberate motions—a new habit speaking volumes about how much his condition had improved.

His trademark gruffness was offset by a vitality that had been absent for years. His mood, perched between irritation and scorn, was lighter, touched by… enthusiasm.

Rad cleared his throat. "I need to ask you some questions."

Hadley raised an eyebrow, chewing on the stem of his unlit pipe.

"Well, lad, I didn't think you were hanging about to admire my pretty face." He gave a grunt and scratched his back against the stall. "If you were, I'd say your taste needs serious fixing."

Rad gave a tight, impatient smile. "Have you heard the name 'Lanny Zeh'?"

Hadley's expression flickered with surprise, and he answered after a moment, "Not in some time. Your Da and him were business partners a while back—long before my time here. Had a falling out, though. Zeh up and disappears into thin air. Never heard from again. This was right before you were born. How old are you? Fourteen? Has it been that long? Fourteen years?"

Rad nodded, his throat tightening. "What can you tell me about him?"

Hadley let out a long sigh, trying to gather thoughts.

"Let's head to my shed. My memory's hazy but sitting on my arse might help shake a few things loose. Or a stiff drink."

"Did you know him, or know of him? There's a difference."

"Of him. Only talked to him once about horses. He knew who I was and didn't trouble me. My bad reputation has its perks."

"Hadley the Pillager?"

The older man's face darkened, and his voice turned sharp.

"Don't call me that. You've not earned the right to know who I was, and you'd do well not to dig where you don't belong. I've done terrible things, lad. Bad things. Things I'll be paying for till the day they put me in the ground. The moniker is a reminder of my shame, not something to toss about like a jest."

Rad nodded. "Understood."

It surprised him to find the small shed tidy, a stark contrast to its usual chaotic state.

Hadley gestured for Rad to sit at the worn wooden table. The surfaces gleamed in the lantern light, and the bed—not much more than a nest of rumpled blankets—was made, the pillow fluffed as though awaiting a guest.

Rad's gaze lingered on the life-sized carved wooden owl perched in a new spot on the shelf.

"Your arms must be working better," Rad said, breaking the silence as he sat down. "This place isn't a pigsty anymore. How are they holding up?"

Hadley rolled both shoulders again, the movements fluid, almost triumphant.

"Better. Not perfect, mind you, but better than they've been in years. Your training helped more than I thought it would."

Rad leaned forward. "What about Zeh? What do you know?"

Hadley narrowed his eyes. "Why are you asking about him? How'd you come by his name?"

To answer truthfully would reveal the existence of the secret passageways, something Rad wasn't willing to do. Instead, he would skirt the truth, offering enough detail to satisfy Hadley's curiosity.

"I found a note in the cellar written by my Da, addressed to Zeh. It mentioned the manor house and my Ma. It didn't make much sense to me."

Hadley leaned back, his brows knitting in thought.

"Zeh was Leskaré. One of their top men—their Chief Scout. He and your father were close business partners once, friends, from what I recall. This was twenty years ago? This manor house you're so fond of poking around? It belonged to Zeh. He used it as a hub for Leskaré, part of their operations I think. But Zeh lost it to your father in a wager. Card game, I think. Ownership passed to Xavier von Schule, and they moved in from another, smaller estate. Even after that, they kept up their business relationship."

Hadley paused, letting the words hang in the air like a sharp blade.

"Mind you, you didn't hear any of this from me. Your father's dealings with Leskaré? They're nothing but whispers."

Rad scoffed.

"I already knew that from Tristin's meeting with Duwy. It's not only occasional dealings; it's a full-fledged business arrangement. My Da and Tristin run goods for Leskaré. They've got warehouses, operations across Eldor—it's all connected."

"Aye," Hadley muttered, rubbing his chin. "Makes sense. Leskaré steals what they can, and they need fencers. Your father's a master at appearing respectable—just enough to stay clean. What I can't figure is what caused Zeh and your Da to part ways. I heard whispers about Zeh and your Ma. There were times he was seen around the manor or on the property—and not with anyone's knowledge."

Hadley's voice dipped, rough with implication.

"Might not be true. Could be gossip. But it makes the most sense, don't it? Nothing like a woman to drive a wedge between two men. No one knows what happened. No goodbyes, nothing. I suspect some ill fate befell him. Thing is, when men like Zeh meet their end, bodies have a way of turning up."

It reminded Rad of the two Black Storm operatives Razor had disposed of. He wondered how thorough Razor had been. Had the bodies been concealed well enough to avoid detection?

The thought pricked at his mind, intertwining with Hadley's words as Rad processed the information.

Was this starting to make sense?

He wasn't sure.

Zeh and Xavier had been business partners, then Ma came between them. The truth was laid bare: he was the bastard son of Justine von Schule and Lanny Zeh.

Xavier had trapped Zeh, left him to die, and murdered him in a way, leaving no trace.

The realization sparked ire in his chest.

"What was Zeh like? Do you remember anything?" Rad asked, his voice steady but laced with curiosity.

Hadley furrowed his brow, thinking.

"Not directly. I only remember what people said about him. Savvy businessman—by Leskaré standards, meaning a master thief. Had a reputation with swords and with women, though I reckon you're not chasing down his courting advice. If you want real answers, you'll have to find someone who knew him well. Rad, you're overly interested in Zeh. All this from a note you found? There's more to this, isn't there?"

Rad hesitated, considering how much to say. "The note led me to another message. It said, 'rest in auditorium,' signed with his initials—'LZ.' The auditorium is down in the basement, isn't it? But it's abandoned, not in use. Could be there's more down there, something to explain all of this."

Hadley nodded, puffing his pipe. "Aye, it's where Leskaré held their meetings back when this stronghold belonged to them. You can go down there. It isn't forbidden, but it's nothing fancy either. What are you hoping to find? And what is Zeh to you? Spit it out. Old Hadley knows when you're holding back."

Rad swallowed hard, his reluctance bubbling up like a dam about to burst. Yet, he trusted Hadley. The Pillager might have been a self-proclaimed lout, admitting to a lifetime of bad deeds, but he could be relied upon.

Rad had no one else to confide in, and he couldn't tell Abby.

"Zeh is my father, not Xavier von Schule. The letter I found confirms it. Zeh was having an affair with Ma. It's why Xavier turned on him—it's why Zeh disappeared."

Hadley leaned back in his chair, letting out a whistle as he rubbed his jaw.

"Well now, that would explain why you're down here with the servants instead of prancing around like the master's heir. Explains why your Da is taking his pleasures with the governess while your Ma says nothing about it."

He chuckled, his weathered face creasing with amusement.

"So, you're a bastard, eh? A proper bastard."

Rad tensed as Hadley slapped his knee and burst into laughter.

"Bastard!" Hadley repeated, his voice booming in the small shed. "Bastard!"

Hadley's mirth felt like a sharp jab, but it was free of malice, as if he were proclaiming a title rather than an insult.

Still, Rad's face flushed with the weight of the word, even though it was the undeniable truth.

Rad took a deep breath, steadying himself. Hadley's laughter wasn't cruel—it was Hadley being Hadley.

"I am a bastard," Rad said, his voice firm, though the words were heavier than he expected. "And it's no wonder I never fit in with this family. I want to know about him, Hadley. Anything! He's my father!"

Hadley nodded, his expression softening as the weight of Rad's emotions became clear.

"Aye, it does. But I'll say this—you'd best tread carefully. Curiosity's a sharp blade, lad, and you might find it cuts both ways. Asking about Zeh, specifically to your mother or anyone tied to Xavier, could stir up trouble you're not ready for."

He tapped his pipe against the edge of the table, the hollow sound punctuating his words.

"You ever hear the saying, 'no good deed goes unpunished?' Well, bringing Zeh back into the family's thoughts might not be the good deed you think it is. It could conjure demons you don't want to wrestle with. Be cautious. For now, it's enough to know the truth."

Rad hesitated, absorbing Hadley's warning.

"I promise I'll be careful."

Hadley's gaze lingered on him, as if searching for any cracks in the young man's resolve. He gestured toward the manor house with the stem of his pipe.

"Should we go see what's in the auditorium?"

Rad blinked in surprise. "You want to come with me?"

"I've always liked a proper treasure hunt," Hadley replied with glint in his eye. His smile was… inviting, then he glanced at the wooden owl. "Who knows? I think Zeh left us gold, stashed away in the auditorium. If we find any coin, we split it. Fifty-fifty. My curiosity needs to be satisfied."

Rad arched an eyebrow. "Coin, fifty-fifty. Anything else is mine. And by the way, I think you mean 'sated,' not 'satisfied.'"

"Those books are going to annoy me until the end of my days," Hadley muttered. He chuckled and swung his arm toward Rad in mock indignation.

Rad caught it in a swift, fluid motion, twisting Hadley's wrist downward and forcing him to back off.

"You're learning," Hadley said, a mixture of pride and irritation in his voice as he winced. "Damn shoulder. Soon, though. Soon it'll be back to normal, and you know what that means?"

"You'll still be too slow," Rad answered.

"You need an arse kicking."

"Old and slow," Rad said, shaking his head, "old and slow."

"Aye, lad, better than young and stupid. Let's see what treasure Zeh left behind."

Hadley leaned in conspiratorially, glanced around his shed looking for eavesdroppers. "Probably an empty bottle of bourbon."

It reminded Rad of the bourbon bottle stashed above the master bedroom. He shuddered, not wanting to believe it was left behind by his father. But just because he didn't want to believe it wouldn't change the truth. Most likely, it was his father's.

A grin broke across Hadley's face, and for a moment, his usual gruff demeanor gave way to fatherly warmth.

"Bastard," he added with a laugh, the word landing like a term of endearment instead of an insult.

Rad couldn't help but grin back.

"Let's go see," Rad said. "Make sure your *satisfied.*"

The auditorium was cavernous and still, its silence amplifying the faint creaks of the wooden floorboards beneath their steps.

Rad couldn't shake the unease creeping over him.

The chandeliers overhead hung like ominous shadows, unlit and coated with a fine layer of dust. Oak-paneled walls lined the room, their pale finish offset by decorative moldings of the same wood. Twelve rows of broad, empty seats spanned the space, their fabric cushions long gone. At the center of the raised stage stood a speaker's stand, flanked on either side by long tables covered in undisturbed layers of dust. The chairs surrounding them had vanished over time.

They worked in tandem, placing lanterns at strategic points around the room, their faint glow too weak to illuminate the high corners of the space.

Each step kicked up small puffs of dust, the stale air thick with the scent of neglect.

Hadley believed they might uncover a hidden passageway in the walls or a concealed compartment beneath the stage.

They combed through every inch of the room, their search yielding little more than dust and frustration.

After an hour, they had found nothing of note, though Rad couldn't help but feel the oppressive weight of history hanging in the air.

This room had been the primary meeting place for Leskaré and it sent a rare chill down his spine. He tried to picture the infamous thieves' gatherings here—their whispered plans, their underhanded deals. His knowledge of the organization was limited, but he knew enough to see the connections.

Xavier von Schule, his stepfather, had to be more than tangentially involved. The goods Leskaré stole had to be moved and sold, often far from Ornst, and Xavier's dealings with the so-called foreigners made more sense. He was a fence, orchestrating the movement of stolen wares across an expansive network of warehouses.

Rad stepped up onto the stage, drawn to the solitary podium at its center. It loomed as a symbol of authority, of a master thief presiding over the chaos of Ornst's criminal underbelly.

He moved to the front stand, resting his hands on its edge. For a fleeting moment, he felt a strange rush of power.

Could this be his future? Would he follow in his real father's footsteps and join the notorious organization of thieves?

It would be an avenue towards disrupting Xavier's livelihood.

He imagined the power he would wield if he was in charge of Leskaré—certainly enough power to cut off Xavier at the knees.

The question of his future lingered as he ran his fingers along the edges of the podium.

It shifted slightly under his grip.

Curious, he shook it gently, and the faint sound of an object rattling within caught his attention.

"Hadley," he called, his voice tight with excitement. "I think I found something."

"What is it?" Hadley asked from the back of the room, his lantern bobbing as he made his way over with eager steps.

Rad crouched to inspect the base of the podium. One of its panels had been nailed shut, but faint scratches in the wood suggested it had been opened before.

Etched in one corner of the panel was a delicate 'LZ.'

Lanny Zeh.

"It's him," Rad murmured, more to himself than to Hadley.

He pulled a hidden throwing knife from his sheath and wedged it under the panel.

With steady hands, he pried it loose, the nails groaning in protest. The board came free, revealing a black container made of light metal.

Silvery runes shimmered, forming an intricate design across its surface.

The container was lengthier than he expected—about four feet—and its craftsmanship was meticulous. This was the third time he'd encountered locks like this in the house, each bound with the same magic. His fingers traced an 'L' and a 'Z' across the runes.

That's why the 'LZ' was underlined *twice* in the note.

A soft *snick* confirmed the mechanism had released.

Rad lifted the lid, his grip firm and steady.

Inside, gray fabric lined the container, its edges frayed with age.

Resting in the center was a sword.

The hilt was wrapped in black leather, its grip smooth and sturdy. The pommel was spiked, a practical design for a weapon meant to intimidate. The blade was housed in a sheath of the same inky leather as the armor he'd found hidden in the secret passageways next to the remains of his father.

He inspected the container, hoping to find a note or clue, but the interior was empty save for the weapon.

With a mixture of awe and disappointment, he closed the lid and turned, only to find Hadley standing at the base of the stage, his expression unreadable.

"What did you find, lad?" Hadley asked.

"A sword," Rad answered.

Hadley smiled. "Go on, pull it free. Be mindful of the edge."

Rad cradled the sword and scabbard with both hands, marveling at its craftsmanship.

It was longer than a short sword but not as unwieldy as a longsword, sitting at a comfortable in-between length.

He drew it fully from its sheath, and the inky black blade shimmered under the lantern's glow. Faint silver runes lined both sides, visible only when held at a precise angle

The runes were alive, shifting as they caught the light. The blade's edges were lethally sharp, and its balance made it feel almost weightless in his hands.

A soft hum emanated from it, faint yet distinct, like a vibration attuned to his touch.

"It's warm," Rad whispered, his voice carrying a mix of wonder and unease.

Hadley raised an eyebrow and held out his hand.

"Let me see."

Rad passed the weapon over, noting how the warmth lingered on his palms.

Hadley gripped the hilt and swung the blade.

The motion was smooth despite his lingering injury.

He stabbed at the air, testing the sword's precision and balance, but his shoulder faltered, and the blade dipped.

Hadley exhaled and recovered, sliding the sword back into its sheath before handing it back to Rad.

"A great find," Hadley said, his tone unreadable. "No one's sniffing around for it—too much time's passed. Only Zeh knew it was hidden here, and I doubt he left a treasure map behind for anyone else. Best hide it where no one'll think to check. You have a spot?"

Rad nodded.

"I know a couple of places. Should I give it a name?"

Hadley's eyes flicked to the blade.

"Aye. A sword like this deserves one. Those runes might already hold its name. We'd need a wizard to read them, though, and it'll cost more than a few coins."

Rad studied the weapon, its aura pulling at him. "I'll come up with a name in the meantime. Something fitting for a blade of this quality."

Hadley smirked faintly. "Best make it a worthy one. Swords have a way of living up to their names."

Rad paused, weighing his next words.

"How are we going to split this fifty-fifty?"

Hadley grinned.

"You said coins, lad. Everything else is yours. Deal's a deal."

Rad considered the small pouch of seventeen gold crowns he'd found near Zeh's bones. Sharing them was fair, and it would buy Hadley's trust. "I found gold crowns with the note. We'll split them. Eight crowns and five silvers for each of us."

Hadley's smirk widened, his expression mischievous.

"How about you give me ten gold, and I keep my mouth shut about all this? Otherwise, eight, and I'll mention to Wilkins about you sneaking into the basement and snooping about."

Rad glared at him but couldn't hide the hint of a smile.

"Ten it is. Your silence comes cheaper than I thought it would."

Hadley's grin faded, his hands trembling as he sat down. His eyes misted over, and he stared at the blade as tears came.

"Aye," he murmured, his voice raw. "It does these days. In my terrible past... I... I would have murdered you for that sword."

Rad froze, startled by the admission.

Hadley turned his face aside, unable to meet Rad's eyes.

He wiped the tears away.

"Back then, I'd have slit your throat without a second thought. But now... now I understand."

He shook his head, rubbing a hand over his face. His shoulders slumped as he fought back additional tears.

"Time changes a man, lad. Changes what he values. Don't you forget that."

Rad tightened his grip on the sword, feeling the weight of Hadley's words as much as the blade in his hands.

He concealed the empty case back into the podium—a magic box was as unexplainable as the sword. Clutching the fine blade to his chest, he resolved to find its name—and its purpose—another day.

That evening, Rad found himself drawn to the hiding place of the sword.

He visited it often, unable to resist the quiet awe it inspired in him. The sleek blade, its softly glowing runes, and the inky black armor alongside it felt like pieces of a grander story—fragments of a past now belonging to him.

They were his—his father's legacy, finally united—and they filled him with a mix of pride and apprehension.

One day, he told himself, he'd summon the courage to ask Ma about Lanny Zeh. The truth about his father was so close, yet so far away.

Waiting for his sixteenth birthday, less than two years from now, felt like an eternity. He would leave the von Schule estate, charting his own course. Until that day, he resolved to heed Hadley's advice: keep quiet about Zeh, the sword, and the armor—and everything else.

After he left the estate, though, he would get the answers he needed from Ma.

The idea of reaching out to Leskaré crossed his mind more than once. He was certain they knew more about Zeh—perhaps about the armor and blade.

But the risks were too numerous.

Zeh's status within Leskaré, dead or not, was a dangerous unknown. Was he still revered as a legend, or had he become a cautionary tale of failure and betrayal?

The wrong question to the wrong person could raise suspicions.

What if Leskaré started asking about the items Rad had hidden?

His imagination spiraled.

What if someone came looking for the sword and armor?

What if their discovery brought the storm of Leskaré's wrath or Xavier's punishment down upon him?

For now, silence was his shield.

He would guard the sword and armor as fiercely as they would guard him.

Chapter Fifteen

∞

An Eye for an Eye

Abby, I love you, and you are my sister, my best friend. I don't know how to say this, so I think it's best I dive into this mess and pray you don't hate me for it. I'm going to tell you the truth... my truth.

While exploring the cellar, I found a secret passageway. At first, it felt like one of those old adventure tales from my books—dark corridors, hidden places—but this wasn't just some forgotten passage.

Inside, I found... remains.

Human remains.

A man who died before I was born.

I know what you're thinking. It could have been anyone. Some stranger who got lost or trapped.

But it wasn't.

Abby, he's my father.

There was a note with him, buried under years of dust, confirming it. This man—this poor soul—was in love with Ma. They were together while she was with Xavier.

It was an affair, Abby.

A secret.

He died down there, trapped in a collapse, and no one ever found him.

I'm still trying to figure things out.

It's like the ground beneath me has shifted, and I'm standing on air, waiting to plunge into the depths.

You're my half-sister.

But I don't care about it, not one bit. You'll always be my sister, my family, my Abby.

That won't ever change.

I'm begging you to keep this between us. No one else knows this—only me, you, Ma... and Xavier. I don't think Tristin or the others have the slightest idea.

Please don't say anything to Ma or Xavier. I know you might feel like you should, but I don't want to cause more pain for Ma, and Xavier... well, he's not my Da.

I've stopped calling him that, at least in my heart.

He's Xavier. And it's fine.

I've wanted to tell you for weeks now, but I was too scared of what you'd think, of how you might judge me after you knew. But you're the only person I trust with this. If anyone can hold this secret, it's you.

I don't know what this changes, but I know it doesn't change us. You're still Abby, the sister who makes me feel like I belong, even when the world says otherwise.

Your brother, always, Rad.

The tolling bells shattered the stillness of the night, their desperate clang interrupting Rad's deep slumber. He jolted awake, the hour making him sluggish. For a moment, his mind lagged as well, heavy with the fog of sleep.

The world around him began to take shape.

The tolling wasn't ordinary—it carried urgency, panic.

He scrambled to his feet, pulling on his boots, and grabbed his work gloves out of habit.

From his third-story window, an ominous flickering orange light danced against the backdrop of darkness.

Fire.

He didn't bother gazing out the window, it couldn't be anything else.

Rad shot out of his room into the dim corridor. The manor stirred with movement; servants in varying states of disarray darted in all directions, their faces pale with terror.

His half-sisters emerged from their rooms, swaddled in thick white robes, their young faces stricken with fear.

"Stay in your rooms!" he barked, his words more a plea than a command.

He bolted down the stairs, feet barely registering the path beneath him.

When he reached the estate's grounds, his heart clenched at the sight.

The stables were ablaze, the hungry flames licking at the night sky, a cruel mockery of the stars above being blocked out by thick smoke.

Shadows of people, guards and servants roused from their beds, crisscrossed the firelit chaos. Barefoot and disheveled, they carried buckets and scrambled to form a fire brigade.

Rad threw himself into the fray, muscles straining as he passed buckets from troughs, wells, and barrels—any source of water they could find.

The acrid stench of burning wood filled his lungs, stinging his eyes.

Horses screamed, a sound that pierced through the cacophony and lodged deep in his chest. Some thrashed wildly, trying to escape the inferno, while others stood frozen in terror.

He scanned the crowd desperately for Hadley but didn't see him.

Please, let him be safe. Please. And the horses. Let them be safe.

Despite their frantic efforts, the fire was relentless. The flames were too well-developed, the stables too rich with fuel. After an hour of fighting, the battle was over. Half the stables were lost, a smoldering, skeletal husk of what they once were.

Through the thick, lingering haze, Hadley finally emerged with Jamie. The two men directed the surviving horses to safer ground, their faces grim and ash-streaked.

Hadley pulled down the cloth covering his mouth, his voice raw.

"Just terrible. Bloody hell. We lost five horses, including Vanguard. I know he was your favorite. I'm sorry, Rad. We did what we could."

The news hit Rad like a blow to the gut.

He couldn't respond right away, the shock left him without words.

Vanguard.

The best horse in the stables.

His favorite.

His friend.

Gone.

Who was he going to share apples with?

"How did it start?" Rad asked, his voice rough from effort. "We're careful about the lanterns. Always."

Hadley shook his head, a mixture of anger and sorrow in his eyes.

"Don't know. I was dead asleep until I heard the horses. Screaming, lad. Woke to see the far end already on fire. But here's the thing—someone nailed everything shut. Every door. Had to grab a prybar to break them open. Who does that? Traps horses? It's evil. If I find the bastard…" His voice broke, his fists clenching. "I'll kill him."

Rad nodded numbly.

The thought chilled him, not only because of the cruelty, but because this situation felt… off. The nails weren't to kill the horses— they were to ensure the fire couldn't be stopped, to ensure the residents of *Château Saignoral* were occupied fighting the blaze.

He removed his ash-stained gloves and stuffed them in his pocket.

"I'm going to the house. I'll be back in a bit."

Hadley started to reply, but Rad didn't wait.

He darted away, ignoring Wilkins' barked orders as he slipped past.

His focus was on the manor house, now an unsettling hub of activity. Guards patrolled the grounds, swords drawn, inspecting every shadow.

Other guards were leading the dogs on leashes, searching.

Lanterns swung in the breeze, casting flickering pools of light as they searched the perimeter.

The back door was ajar.

Inside, he could see his family gathered, their distress unmistakable from the threshold.

Bella and Marie were huddled together, sobbing. Their pale faces were streaked with tears, their voices broken by cries of anguish.

Xavier sat slumped in a chair, his hands covering his face as Gabrielle knelt beside him, her hand rubbing slow, comforting circles on his back, though her own face was red and streaked with tears.

Against the wall, Tristin stood rigid, his face buried in his hands.

Rad pushed into the room.

"Tristin. What happened?"

Tristin's shoulders trembled as he sniffled, his voice choked.

"They… they were having tea in the breakfast nook. Ma… and Abigail."

The words hit Rad like ice water, a cold panic flooding his veins. Rare were the moments when fear overtook him, but now it surged.

Without another word, he turned and bolted toward the kitchen, his legs moving faster than his thoughts.

The scene in the breakfast nook stopped him dead.

Bodies lay crumpled on the floor, surrounded by a pool of darkened blood.

Ma and Abby.

Their white robes were soaked through, turned crimson, then black with the sheer volume of it.

Their throats had been savagely slashed at a depth they were nearly decapitated.

Rad's breath caught, his chest tightening to the point of pain.

His mother.

Abby.

The two people he cared for most in the world were gone, taken in a moment of brutal violence.

He staggered back, his mind struggling to comprehend what his eyes were seeing.

The joy he'd once clung to shattered like glass, leaving nothing but raw, aching emptiness.

Servants moved around the room, their faces pale and their movements careful as they tended to the horrible task of cleaning.

Some gathered blood-soaked cloths, while others worked to cover the lifeless forms with sheets.

The muted sounds of their efforts contrasted with the deafening chaos in Rad's mind.

He stepped deeper into the room, his movements slow, his breaths shallow. The metallic tang of blood filled the air, sharp and nauseating, as his boots stuck to the floor with each step.

He skirted the edges of the scene, unwilling to disturb the workers or draw their attention, but his eyes remained fixed on the two bodies.

Ma and Abby.

So much blood.

He had never seen so much blood in his life—not in dreams, not in nightmares.

It pooled on the floor and clung to the broken porcelain of the tea set, a mocking reminder of the innocence shattered in this room.

His gaze shifted, catching words scrawled across the table where they had once sat.

He drew closer, his heart hammering in his chest until it hurt.

The words were crude, written with haunting malice in their blood.

an eye for an eye we are even

Beneath the words, stamped unmistakably, was the emblem of the Black Storm.

The same mark had branded the shoulders of the men he had killed in the warehouse.

Rad's legs buckled, and he sank into a chair at the edge of the table, his hands clutching the wood as though it might anchor him against the tidal wave of emotion crashing over him.

His throat constricted, his chest heaving with the effort to breathe.

The meaning of the note was clear, its message cutting sharper than any blade.

This was his fault.

The Black Storm had retaliated, their vengeance swift and merciless.

In exchange for the two lives he had taken, they had stolen away the two people he loved most in the world.

The realization crushed him.

He had killed those men to protect Tristin, to save a life, never grasping what it would cost. In choosing to save Tristin, he had signed the death warrants of Ma and Abby.

His vision blurred with a burst of tears and anguish, and his body trembled as guilt, anger, and sorrow tore through him.

His stomach lurched and twisted with nausea, the acidic burn rising into his throat. He doubled over, retching onto the bloodied floor.

Again and again he convulsed until there was nothing left.

Only the hollow ache of his gut and the unbearable agony in his chest remained.

Rad slumped against the table, his breathing ragged, his hands trembling as he stared at the cruel message.

The room spun around him, the world he once knew unraveling thread by thread.

Rad awoke in his bed, unsure of how he had been brought there. The sour stench of vomit lingered in the room, unmistakably his own. His stomach ached as if it had been pummeled, and his limbs were leaden with exhaustion.

The events of the night came rushing back to him, crashing over him with unrelenting force.

Ma and Abby were gone.

Their deaths were an inescapable truth, their absence a void that gouged his chest.

Their loss was suffocating.

And at the center of it all lay an ugly truth: their deaths were his fault.

The Black Storm's vengeance was clear. Their retribution stemmed from him killing the two assassins in the warehouse.

The note was unmistakable.

They had sought payback, and in their twisted justice, they had taken the two people he cherished most.

How had they pieced it together?

The question burned in his mind, a relentless torment.

Had Chilcott been caught and forced to talk, enduring unimaginable torture until he revealed the truth?

Or had Duwy stumbled across the evidence, discovering the bodies Rad and Razor had disposed of?

His thoughts spiraled, but the simplest answer began to rise above the chaos.

Duwy must have *assumed.*

The Black Storm would have drawn the obvious conclusion: Tristin von Schule had ordered the assassins' deaths to protect his own life.

The nefarious group, in retaliation, had targeted two souls from the family because they didn't know the exact truth.

It was inevitable, Xavier and Tristin would question the note's meaning. But how could they ever learn the truth unless Rad told them?

He swore he never would.

He wouldn't utter a word, including under threat or pain of death.

Letting them know would only deepen his anguish and burden their lives with truths too heavy to bear.

Tears brimmed in his eyes, blurring his vision.

Then they fell.

Hot, unrelenting, silent.

He let himself weep, his chest trembling with the force of his grief.

He had saved Tristin's life.

But two lives taken to protect one had claimed two more.

An eye for an eye.

Later, Rad joined the dreadful task of clearing the carcasses and debris from the burned stables. Plans for a new structure were already in motion.

Hadley, ever practical, remarked the fire presented an opportunity to build better. The new stables would have larger stalls and aisles, and improved ventilation through the roof—a more efficient design while retaining the charm of the old building.

Despite the encouraging plans, the weight of what had been lost hung heavily in the air.

Rad worked without resting, his muscles aching from lifting charred beams and shoveling ash into wheelbarrows. Sweat soaked his clothes, and his arms trembled from the effort.

As the morning stretched into afternoon, he realized he hadn't eaten all day.

A wave of dizziness swept over him, forcing him to sit on a patch of grass.

Hadley settled beside him, easing down with a groan. His weathered face was somber, shadowed by the events of the last day.

"Nasty business, this," Hadley remarked, staring at the remains of the burnt stable. "I'm sorry you lost your Ma and Abigail. They didn't deserve it. No one does."

Rad tried to hold back the tears that pricked his eyes, but the dam broke.

He wept, his face buried in his hands, the sobs raw and unrestrained.

"It was the Black Storm," he whispered through his fingers. "Revenge for the assassins at the warehouse." He lowered his voice. "*I killed them.*"

Hadley's brows knit tightly. "How do you know?"

Rad's voice cracked as he explained, "The note they left… it said, 'An eye for an eye. We are even.' It had their emblem, like the tattoos on the men I killed in the warehouse. They came because they thought Tristin ordered their deaths. I'm sure of it."

Hadley leaned closer, his tone steady.

"Rad, listen to me. Listen good. This is the last time you ever speak of that night. Hear me? Never again. Not to me, not to anyone. The story goes to your grave, mine as well."

Rad nodded, his tears slowing but his chest still heaving.

"Nothing will come of it but trouble—and regret," Hadley continued, his voice firm. "It didn't happen. You know nothing. You will *say* nothing."

"What if Xavier talks to the Black Storm and finds out?" Rad asked, his voice trembling.

Hadley was silent for a long moment, chewing on the thought.

"He won't get a word out of them. The Black Storm doesn't admit to their failures, and they won't admit they sent assassins after him or Tristin. This fire, the note—it's a warning. They've got their revenge. It ends here. Don't dwell on it. Worry about what you can control—your mouth. Mine's shut. And we better hope Razor keeps his shut, too."

"Chilcott will keep quiet," Rad said, his voice more certain than he felt.

Hadley gave a grunt that sounded halfway between agreement and protest.

"I trust your judgment. Now let's get back to work. Nothing fixes a heavy heart better than labor so hard it leaves you too tired to think. The sooner we finish clearing this mess, the sooner we start rebuilding. For now, the carriage house will do for the horses. Routine stays the same—they still need care."

Hadley pulled an apple from his coat pocket and drew a knife. With impressive skill, he peeled the fruit, the skin falling in a single, continuous curling ribbon.

He sliced it into neat pieces, cut out the core, and flicked it aside with a deft motion before biting into the crisp flesh.

Rad's stomach growled loud enough to hear.

Hadley chewed with maddening nonchalance, evidently in no mood to share.

Rad sighed. "I need to eat something. I'll be back to help."

Hadley nodded, his eyes already drifting back to the ruined stable. "Don't take too long. Work's not going to finish itself."

Rad pushed himself to his feet and trudged toward the manor, leaving Hadley alone with his thoughts and the ruins of what once was their stables.

The *Château Saignoral* cemetery lay nestled within a grove of ancient oaks on the estate grounds, not far beyond the outermost buildings. Their gnarled branches reached skyward like twisted fingers, a stark contrast against the somber gray sky.

A cold wind stirred, rustling the last of the autumn leaves and carrying the faint scent of damp earth.

Rad stood with the others, head bowed, listening to the priest of Unara's melodic voice as he recited the final rites.

The small gathering was quiet except for the occasional sniffle or rustle of fabric in the breeze.

Gabrielle, draped in a black veil, clutched Xavier's arm, her face pale and drawn. She had been weeping since they arrived.

Xavier, in his dark mourning attire, stood stoic, though his grief was evident in his furrowed brow and the way his lips pressed into a thin line. His eyes, however, burned with anger.

Yet beneath that fury, a flicker of uncertainty lingered—a question unspoken, a calculation unfinished.

Rad kept his gaze on the polished caskets. Ma and Abby—side by side, as they should've been in life, now joined only in death. The sight sent a fresh wave of pain washing over him.

He wanted to cry, but he couldn't bring himself to do so.

Instead, his emotions churned beneath the surface like a storm held back by sheer will.

To his right, Hadley and Jamie were motionless, their hats in their hands. Jamie's expression was one of earnest sorrow, while Hadley's was inscrutable, though Rad could see the tension in the horse-master's jaw. Florence lingered behind Jamie, clutching a small bouquet of white flowers in her trembling hands.

Wilkins lingered at the edge of the gathering, somber but adrift. His gaze wandered often to Xavier, as if unsure whether to mourn or await a command.

Habit kept him alert, even here—watching, waiting, half-hoping for some task to excuse him from the weight of grief he didn't quite know how to carry.

Rad shifted, feeling invisible stares on his back.

He couldn't shake the sensation Xavier's grief-stricken anger was directed at him. The note from the Black Storm flashed in his mind, its damning words and emblem etched into his memory.

Did Xavier suspect him?

Could Xavier sense his secret?

Gabrielle's voice broke through his thoughts as she stepped forward, placing a single rose on each coffin. Her hand lingered on the wood, trembling.

"We'll miss you both," she whispered.

Rad went rigid.

The weight of his guilt pressed down on him as he pleaded for forgiveness—from Ma, from Abby, from himself. He should have been stronger, smarter, faster.

He should have found a way to stop this from happening.

The priest of Unara concluded the ceremony with a final prayer, and as tradition, he placed a lone copper coin on each coffin to signify the cost of life.

The small group began to disperse.

Xavier lingered for a moment, staring down into the graves.

His gaze swept over the gathered faces, not lingering on any one figure, but searching—as if answers might be buried among them.

Then, without a word, he turned and walked away. His strides were rigid, carrying not just grief, but questions no prayer could settle.

Servants lowered the caskets and shoveled dirt into the open graves.

Rad stood there, unable to walk away.

Hadley placed a steadying hand on Rad's shoulder.

"Come on, lad," he spoke. "Let's leave them to their peace."

Rad nodded, following Hadley and Jamie away from the graves.

As they went toward the manor house, he glanced over his shoulder one last time.

Two fresh mounds of earth now marked the final resting place of Ma and Abby, along with gray granite headstones.

He vowed to ensure their deaths wouldn't be in vain.

The air in *Château Saignoral* was heavy, saturated with the muted hum of conversation and the clink of glasses. Nobles in dark silks and fine brocades moved like somber specters through the halls, their voices hushed but carrying enough to sting Rad's ears.

He lingered at the edge of the crowd, shoulders hunched, his servant's tunic marking him as out of place among the sea of black finery.

His eyes darted to the staircase, calculating his escape route.

Xavier moved among the gathering with mechanical grace, a snifter of *De'Artois* bourbon in hand, offering careful pours to a handful of his most esteemed guests.

His gestures were smooth and practiced, the image of a man who grieved not by retreating, but by asserting the wealth and strength still in his grasp.

At a curt nod from Xavier, Wilkins slipped away toward the cellars, summoned not for mourning, but to fetch more of the rarest bottles.

Even now, *Château Saignoral* would not be seen wanting.

Rad ducked his head, pressing past a knot of gossiping nobles.

Lord Fairmont's voice rose above the murmur of the gathering.

"Such a terrible sickness," Fairmont said, his voice thick with forced sorrow. "To take Lady Justine and young Miss Abigail so suddenly... they were the highlight of the Spring Cotillion I held at my estate. I can't believe they're gone."

"Sickness?" another voice scoffed—a woman's voice, sharp and skeptical. "The Black Storm's name is whispered everywhere. Rumors of treachery. Xavier von Schule has many enemies."

Rad froze mid-step.

Beyond the tangle of nobles, he caught sight of Xavier again, near the hearth, greeting a pair of titled guests with the same brittle courtesy he had shown the others.

His smiles were curt, thin as knife-blades. His grief, if it existed at all, was hidden behind the same polish that clothed his estate and servants.

"He buries them and doesn't shed a tear," the woman added near the wine table, lifting her cup as if in toast. "Whatever else they say of Xavier von Schule, they should say he is made of stone."

Someone nearby chuckled under their breath.

"I think stone would be offended to be compared to Xavier."

Rad shoved past them, the words cutting deeper than he cared to admit.

He froze again as a young man approached, shoulders squared, his face flushed with grief or rage—or both.

It was Robert Ruud.

Rad's throat tightened. He remembered Abby's shy confession, her bright hope of a kiss she never got. Robert's eyes were bloodshot, jaw rigid, his hands tugging at his fine waistcoat.

"I loved her too," Rad whispered as he passed, his voice catching like a splinter in his throat.

He didn't wait for an answer.

He jogged upstairs, fleeing the press of silk and sorrow before it smothered him completely.

His words hung behind him, sharp and weightless, unheard or unanswered—it didn't matter.

Rad found his way to the hidden door with ease, his movements automatic. The grooves of the wood were familiar under his fingertips as he pressed the latch and stepped into the cool, dark passageway. The smell of damp wood and dust greeted him, bringing back memories of hours spent exploring these forgotten halls.

He went as fast as he dared, lantern in hand, his pulse quickening despite himself. The journal had been on his mind since the fire, but he hadn't dared to retrieve it.

What if Abby had read his confession?

What if she had hated him for it?

Or what if…

The thought of her leaving him a final response—her words, her handwriting—made his chest tighten.

Not excitement.

Dread.

The library was quiet, the faint noise of the wake reduced to a murmur through the thick walls.

Rad approached the journal's hiding place with trembling hands, crouching to pull it from its secure spot behind the atlas.

There it was.

His breath caught as he cradled it in his hands.

For a moment, he couldn't move.

He stared at the leather cover, his mind swirling with possibilities.

The lantern light flickered, casting his shadow long across the room.

With a shuddering breath, he tucked the journal under his arm and left the library, retreating to his room through the passageways.

Back in his room, Rad plopped on the bed, the journal resting on his lap. He ran his fingers over its familiar cover, hesitant.

Finally, he opened it, flipping to the last page.

There was nothing.

No response from Abby.

His chest tightened, a sharp ache spreading through him as he stared at the blank page.

The weight of Abby's absence hit him all over again, and his vision blurred.

"I'm sorry," he whispered, his voice cracking in the silence.

He rose and carried the journal to his desk, sitting down to write.

The words came slowly at first, halting and jagged, before spilling out in a torrent.

Abby,

I don't know if this will help or tear me apart more, but I need to write to you. You always listened—even when I couldn't speak the words out loud—and writing will feel like I'm still talking to you.

I found secret passageways in the house, Abby.

They wind through every room, every wall

They let me see things I shouldn't have. I spied on the family—on Ma, Da, everyone. I know things no one else knows. Sometimes I think I should have kept my curiosity in check, but I couldn't.

You know me.

I had to know.

And now I know too much.

I think I'm in love with a woman, Rosamund. She sells her body to men, and I don't care. She's kind, and she listens, and she doesn't judge me for what I am. I love her because she doesn't expect anything from me. I love her because she showed me how to be a man without making me feel awkward.

Tristin.

I saved him from death, Abby. He doesn't know it was me, and it's for the best. I had to kill two men to save him. They were Black Storm, and their blood is on my hands.

Killing them... it wasn't easy. Not the fighting, but the after. The memory of it. I see their faces when I close my eyes, and I smell the blood. I can still hear the squelch of the eyeball I pried off my throwing knife. Hadley says it'll pass, but I don't know if it will.

And you. You, Abby. I feel responsible for your death.

The Black Storm got their revenge.

They came for Ma, for you.

I wasn't there to protect you.

If I'd been stronger, faster, smarter... you'd still be alive.

Ma would still be alive.

I miss you so much it feels like my chest is caving in. The journal was ours, our secret, and now it's just mine.

And I hate it.

I hate I'm writing to a ghost instead of you.

But I don't want to stop.

I can't stop.

You were my anchor, Abby, and without you, I feel like I'm drifting into nothing.

I'll keep writing to you. I don't know if it'll help, but I'll do it anyway. It's the only way I know how to hold on to you.

Always your brother, Rad.

Rad closed the journal, his hands trembling as he wiped at his eyes. He crossed the room to the secret door in the closet, where his father's sword and armor lay. Tenderly, he placed the journal alongside them, his fingers lingering on the worn leather cover.

He closed the panel shut, sealing the journal—and his confession—away.

"I love you, Abby," he whispered to the empty room.

Later that night, long after the last guest had departed and the last light had been snuffed in the guest halls, Rad crept through the secret corridors of *Château Saignoral.*

He carried nothing with him—no journal, no keepsake—only the gnawing ache that refused to let him sleep.

A pinpoint of light shone from the peephole to Xavier's study. Rad pressed himself into the wall, easing closer without a sound. His heart hammered against his ribs, but he made no move to retreat.

Inside, the fire burned low, throwing long, weary shadows across the room.

Xavier sat alone in a high-backed chair, a snifter of bourbon resting loosely in one hand, a half-smoked pipe dangling forgotten from the other.

His mourning coat was gone, replaced by a burgundy smoking jacket, the velvet worn thin at the cuffs from his constant tugs.

On the side table, three empty bottles of *De'Artois* bourbon lay toppled among a scattering of pipe ash.

Rad waited, hardly breathing, searching for a sign—a break in the mask.

He wanted to see Xavier rage.

Weep.

Curse the gods.

Anything to prove he was still flesh and blood.

But Xavier only lifted the glass again, swirling the last mouthful of bourbon with absent, mechanical care.

And then, into the hollow quiet, he spoke—a voice so low and tired that Rad nearly missed it.

"Goodbye," Xavier said.

No names.

No prayers.

No mourning.

Just a single word, heavy as the grave, fading into the smoke.

Rad stood frozen, heart aching, the truth settling cold and sharp in his gut.

Xavier would not scream or weep or fall to pieces. He would drown his grief in bourbon and velvet, in rituals of power and possession, and call it survival.

Rad turned away, jaw tight, and slipped back into secret passageways. As he walked, the final judgment formed cold and certain in his mind:

I thought you were a man who did devilish things. But now I see you for what you are—a man who belongs in the Seven Hells with the rest of your kind.

He did not look back.

A month had passed, yet Rad's guilt lingered, a smothering weight he couldn't shed. It clung to him like a heavy cloak, relentless and unyielding.

In his struggle, Hadley became his sole confidant.

Though gruff and often dismissive, the old horse-master never betrayed his trust.

Whenever Rad expressed his guilt, Hadley would grumble, "Keep it to yourself, lad. No one needs to know."

Despite the curt responses, it was a relief to have someone to confide in.

There was no one else Rad could turn to.

After his day's work, Rad threw himself into training. Using wooden swords, he honed his skills with Hadley's guidance, sometimes sparring with a reluctant Jamie.

Each session sharpened his movements and boosted his confidence.

His ambition was to wield *Vanguard*, the black sword he had named in honor of his favorite horse lost in the fire. The blade, with its subtle hum and intricate runes, made him feel stealthy and lethal—like a predator lying in wait.

Armed with the sword and his father's black armor, Rad envisioned himself as unstoppable, a shadow in the night.

No longer prey, but a predator.

The new stable's frame had risen over the weeks, its walls stretching toward completion. With luck and effort, it would be finished in another month.

Winter's chill crept into the days, but Ornst's southern position and coastal winds spared it from the heavy snowfall that blanketed the northern lands like Haddensack, the towering mountains to the northwest, and the sprawling territories northeast and beyond.

Rad was finishing his work for the day when a house servant appeared at the carriage house, looking for Hadley. The servant's demeanor was odd—a nervous energy that prickled at Rad's senses. He directed the servant to Hadley but lingered nearby, watching the exchange with growing unease.

Hadley wiped his gnarled hands on a towel as he approached Rad, his expression grim.

"Your Da wants to see me," he rasped.

Rad's jaw tightened. "He's not my Da."

"Xavier," Hadley corrected. "He wants to see me in his study." He paused, glancing toward the manor house. "I've only been summoned there once before, and it didn't end clean. Whatever this is, it won't end clean either. This is bad, worse than bad."

Rad felt the blood leaving his head.

Hadley leaned in, his voice firm and urgent.

"Listen to me. Go to your room, lock the door, and don't open it for anyone but me. Understand? Anyone else comes knocking, you don't let them in. You tell them you'll only see Hadley. Got it?"

Rad hesitated for only a moment before nodding.

"Go!" Hadley barked, shooing him off with a wave of his hand.

Rad scurried across the expanse of yellowed grass toward the manor's deck, his movements quick.

The late afternoon sun cast long shadows across the estate, and the guards grunted as he passed them.

Once inside, he slipped off his boots, the familiar act muffling his steps as he crossed the great room. He ascended the grand staircase, the plush carpet muffling the sounds of his quickened pace and made his way to the third floor.

In his room, he locked the door as Hadley had instructed, taking a moment to glance around. He arranged his bed as fast as he could, rumpling the sheets and plumping the pillow to make it appear as though he was sleeping.

Discarding his boots, he slipped on a pair of soft-soled slippers and entered the secret passageway, his heart pounding in his chest.

The hidden corridor was narrow and cold, the air heavy with the scent of stone and old wood.

Rad traveled as fast as he could to the peephole overlooking Xavier's study. He slid the metal shield to the side and peered through, adjusting his breathing as he settled into his hiding spot.

Xavier was seated at his desk, focusing on a leather-bound ledger. The faint scratch of his quill as he made notations was barely audible, but it resonated in the quiet space.

Rad's gaze wandered to the ornate vault on the far, U-shaped wall—the one housing untold riches and, more intriguingly, the chest from Perran Killigrew.

He imagined the mysterious magic item inside, its power calling to him. The thought of stealing it flitted through his mind, filling him with a surge of daring, but he quickly dismissed it.

The consequences of its absence would be catastrophic...

A soft knock broke the silence, and Rad stiffened.

"Come in," Xavier said, his voice measured.

Hadley entered, his hat held in both hands across his midsection. The hair he had left was a stringy, tangled mess, framing his unkempt beard and mustache. The bald spot on the top of his head was pale, covered with age spots.

The grizzled horse-master was a sharp contrast to Xavier's polished demeanor.

"You sent for me?" Hadley's tone was cautious.

"Yes, please sit down and make yourself comfortable," Xavier replied, gesturing toward the chairs in front of his desk.

Hadley hesitated, his eyes narrowing, before lowering himself into one of the leather armchairs. He shifted awkwardly, his gnarled hands gripping the armrests as if the chair might bite him.

"Not used to furnishings like this," he muttered, his voice rough. "What do you want, Xavier? The more time you keep me here, the less time I can spend with your precious horses."

Xavier didn't respond at first.

He adjusted the cuffs of his crisp white blouse, his movements precise.

Rising from his chair, he walked to the serving table near the wall, taking his time to retrieve a cut crystal decanter of bourbon and two glasses.

Xavier placed an empty glass in front of Hadley with a purposeful clank, the other he set on the corner of his desk where he chose to stand.

His piercing gaze settled on Hadley, the tension in the room building.

Xavier hefted the crystal decanter, studying the amber liquid within.

"*De'Artois*," he said. "The finest bourbon I've ever come across."

Hadley shifted in his chair, placing a rough, calloused hand over the empty glass in front of him.

"If I develop a taste for *De'Artois*, it'll ruin me. Thank you for the offer, but no."

His voice was blunt, almost dismissive.

"Spit it out. What do you have to say?" Hadley asked.

With a steady hand, he poured himself a generous portion of the amber liquid, the glass clinking against glass. Xavier lifted the glass to his nose and sniffed it before taking a sip and sitting down.

He savored the drink, his sharp eyes fixed on Hadley as he leaned back in his chair.

"You've been working closely with Radcliffe for quite some time now," he began, his tone measured. "Your reports indicate he's a diligent worker."

Hadley's brow furrowed, and he crossed his arms over his chest.

"Aye, he's a good and hardworking lad. Trust him with any one of your horses. He's bright too, despite what you think of him."

"Don't tell me what I think."

"Don't patronize me," Hadley shot back, leaning forward. "I know you hate him for what he is. I know you promised Justine you'd keep him here until he turns sixteen. Is that what this is about? You want to get rid of him now Justine's passed?"

Rad's breath caught in his throat as he listened from the hidden passage. Hadley's boldness startled him; few dared to speak to Xavier in such a way, and fewer still lived to recount the exchange.

Xavier drained the rest of his glass in one smooth motion and set it down with a decisive clink.

His gaze hardened and he said, "You're alive because of my graciousness? This is a friendly reminder."

"Graciousness?" Hadley's voice carried a sharp edge, and his eyes narrowed. "You mean the privilege of working my fingers to the bone for nothing? Of serving you until the day I keel over? It's not grace, Xavier. It's slavery."

"Nonetheless," Xavier replied, his voice cold, "you are alive because of me. Don't forget."

Hadley leaned back, his expression darkening.

"And you're alive because you haven't pushed me too far. These other servants might quake in their boots and kiss your feet, contrite and meek, but not me. If it ever comes to it, I wouldn't hesitate to strangle you in your sleep. You know what I'm capable of."

He paused, his voice dropping to a near growl.

"Another murder won't make the gods notice me more than they already do. My place in the Seven Hells is long reserved. Nothin' going to change that."

A heavy silence hung in the room, broken only by the faint clink of crystal as Xavier poured himself another drink. He studied Hadley for a moment before extending the decanter toward him again.

"Move your hand," Xavier ordered, his voice insistent.

"I told you," Hadley replied, his hand remaining over the glass. "I don't want to taste that stuff."

"This isn't about taste," Xavier said, his tone softening. "This is a peace offering. Move your hand. I know what you've done, Hadley. It's why I saved you from the gallows, why I brought you here. Your talents for murder and mayhem are unmatched. I haven't had to call upon your talents—yet. But I'd rather not tempt fate. Move your hand."

Hadley hesitated, his eyes locked with Xavier's in a tense standoff.

A moment later and with a gruff sigh, he shifted his hand away.

Xavier poured a measure of bourbon, the amber liquid swirling in the glass.

Hadley picked up the glass and downed it in a single gulp, slamming it back on the desk with finality. He pushed it out of reach.

"One's enough," he said, his voice like gravel. "Now stop dancing around it, Xavier. What is this about?"

"Two items to discuss," Xavier began, his voice restrained. "First, this business with the Black Storm murdering Justine and Abigail. Over the past month, I've searched for answers and found none. Not even Leskaré could help me if I so dared to involve them. You were a scoundrel once, just like them. Tell me what you think."

Hadley's expression remained impassive, though his eyes glinted with an understanding honed by years of surviving the darker corners of life.

"Why would the Black Storm bother killing two women?" he asked. "What do they gain from it? Makes no sense to me."

"They left a note *written in their blood*," Xavier said, his words sharp. "'An eye for an eye. We are even.' What does it mean?"

Hadley frowned, his lips pursing as he weighed the implications.

"A life for a life," he said. "They must think you took two of their own."

Xavier drained half his glass in one gulp, setting it down with a dull thud before sinking back into his chair.

"I don't engage in that sort of act," he stated. "I don't kill directly, nor would I condone it unless necessary. Angering the Black Storm serves no purpose. I entertained business dealings with them months ago, but it didn't make sense to sacrifice my relationship with Leskaré. Tristin met with them, declined their offer, and sent them away. He did mention the man, Duwy, was... off during the entire exchange."

Hadley rubbed his jaw, the scratch of his calloused fingers against his stubbled cheek breaking the silence.

"This may sound morbid," he said with caution in his voice, "but being 'even' with the Black Storm isn't the worst thing. Whatever they think happened is done. Justine and Abigail can't be brought back, same as whoever they think you killed or had killed. You could spend months—shades, years—chasing answers and find nothing. Start poking around too much, and the Black Storm might take offense, or worse, Leskaré will wonder why you're talking to them. Better to leave it be, don't you think? You owe them nothing, and they owe you nothing."

Xavier's jaw tightened as he absorbed Hadley's words.

"Senseless," he muttered. His hand clenched into a fist, pounding the desk with sudden ferocity. "I had my differences with Justine, but she didn't deserve death. And Abigail... she was innocent!"

He struck the desk again, his voice rising with grief.

"Innocent!"

"I'm sorry for your loss," Hadley said, his solemn tone free of his usual gruffness. "Truly, I am. But nothing will bring them back. If you learn the why of it, it won't change the what. The knowledge will only drive you mad."

Xavier's hand trembled as he poured another bourbon, lifted the glass, and downed it, slamming it back onto the desk in a storm of anger and despair.

"What if I commanded you to find out who did this and bring them to justice?" Xavier asked.

Hadley took his hat from the desk and stood, his movements stiff.

Reaching for the decanter, he poured Xavier's glass to the brim and his own half full.

He lifted his glass, meeting Xavier's gaze with steady resolve.

"I'll drink to health and prosperity," Hadley said. "Not to death and destruction. If you send me out there to chase this, I won't return. I'd be as dead as Justine and Abigail."

He took a small sip of bourbon, setting the glass down with care.

"I still have time left to serve you as horse-master. You have the finest horses and stables in all of Ornst. Let me keep doing what I do best."

Xavier stared at him, his expression unreadable.

Hadley, unflinching, returned his gaze, the weight of the moment settling between them.

Xavier nodded and took another long swig of bourbon, the amber liquid vanishing from his glass.

Hadley drank his glass empty, set it down, the faint clink of crystal breaking the silence.

"This *De'Artois* stuff ain't half bad," he said, his gruff voice tinged with reluctant approval.

He sat down.

Xavier managed a weak chuckle, a sound muted by exhaustion and grief.

"What's the second thing you wanted to discuss?" Hadley asked, leaning back in the chair.

"Radcliffe," Xavier said, his tone darkening. "I was considering turning him out on the street because Justine has passed."

He paused, swirling the dregs of bourbon left in the decanter.

"Clearly, it won't be happening. I will honor the promise I made to Justine—on one condition. You ensure he stays in line."

Hadley crossed his arms, his face unreadable.

"Aye," he said after a moment. "I'll keep my thumb on him at all times. The lad's a quick learner. I'll teach him what I can, make sure he's ready to survive when you cast him out. With your permission, though, he needs to learn swordplay. Ornst is a harsh place. If you want him to make it when he's on his own, he'll need to train."

Xavier considered, his face tight with conflicting emotions. At last, he gave a reluctant nod.

"Fine. But write this in blood, Hadley, when he turns sixteen, he will be cast out. There will be no hesitation, no leniency. He will leave this estate, and he will not return. If he does, I will see him buried next to his mother and sister."

His voice cracked, though he quickly steadied it.

"When I send him away, I'll make it clear to him."

Hadley let out a heavy breath, grabbed his hat, and motioned toward the bourbon decanter.

"Thanks for the drink," he said. Without another word, Hadley departed, the door shutting behind him with a quiet but firm thud.

Xavier drained the last of his glass and leaned forward, pressing his hands against his face.

His shoulders sagged under the weight of unspoken grief.

From his vantage point behind the spyhole, Rad could just make out the trembling of Xavier's hands.

He wasn't sure, but as he slipped away from the hidden passage, he thought he saw Xavier wipe away tears.

If they were tears, Rad wasn't sure who they were for.

Chapter Sixteen

∞

The Relic

Sore from a day of hard labor with the horses and relentless training with Hadley, Rad sat on his bed, mulling over his life. The approaching reality of being cast out by the von Schule family was on his mind all the time.

In a year and a half, he would be 'set free' from their service—not because of merit, but because his stepfather wanted him gone. He remained only because of his Ma's wish and Hadley's efforts to hold Xavier to the promise.

The thought of being discarded like a useless piece of *merred* twisted his insides.

He thumbed through the shared journal, rereading Abby's entries and his replies. The memories and her words soothed him, giving him a reprieve from the day's toil.

Though he was tired, sleep wouldn't come.

Rad slipped into his closet and entered the secret passageways, his sanctuary of shadows. Navigating the narrow, hidden halls in silence, he made his way to the study's spyhole, eager to glimpse anything that might lift the weight of his thoughts.

What he saw froze him in place.

Xavier wasn't alone.

Sitting across from him, scar and all, was Perran Killigrew.

Rad's breath caught as he strained to hear their conversation.

"Nasty business," Killigrew said, leaning back in his chair. "I can't fathom why the Black Storm would leave a note if you didn't provoke them. And, frankly, I don't see why you're asking me. I'd rather stay clear of affairs not concerning the relic."

"I thought perhaps your unique perspective might offer some insight," Xavier replied, his voice measured.

He placed the old chest from the secret vault on the desk.

"But we'll speak no more of it. Your note was cryptic, and your arrival was unannounced. I assume you've found a buyer?"

Killigrew opened the chest, and his gaze lingered on the contents before he closed the lid and set it back on the desk.

"I have a buyer," he confirmed. "An odd sort, but no friend to the Wizards of Arcana. That much is certain. And not someone to trifle with. When he arrives, we will allow him to handle the relic as he deems fit. He is a wizard of exceptional skill and must be respected."

Xavier's expression darkened, though he gave a slight nod.

"Understood. He shall have whatever he needs. Now, let us discuss something more pleasant—my payment. Is it arranged?"

Killigrew reached into his coat and produced a piece of parchment, sliding it across the desk.

"The sum should meet your expectations. The wizard will bring his voucher with him, and your funds will be available once mine are in hand."

Xavier snapped the parchment with his fingers, scanning it.

A smile crept across his face.

"More than I anticipated. I can't help but wonder if I should have haggled harder."

Killigrew smirked.

"You delivered on your end. And what are a few gold crowns between friends? Besides, if I'd entrusted the chest to anyone else, the contents would surely be lost. A few buyers were... less than pleased when they couldn't locate it."

"I'm glad my reputation remains intact."

Xavier paused, his expression concerned.

"Though I can't help but worry about the unscrupulous people you must have dealt with over this relic. The world is full of shady characters, after all."

The laugh bellowing from Killigrew reverberated in the study.

"Oh Xavier, that is precious, just precious!"

Xavier wasn't amused.

"Two of my loved ones were murdered. And it coincides with you discovering a buyer for the relic, and you tell me other buyers tried to locate it. How do I know this isn't anger directed at me?"

"You're imagining things Xavier, this is borderline paranoia. My relic, and your housing of it, had nothing to do with those murders. I'm sorry for your loss."

With a solemn nod, Xavier let the matter drop.

Killigrew drummed his fingers as his eyes wandered to the treasure chest, then to the decanter on the desk.

"Speaking of reputations, I recall yours includes fine bourbon." He winked. "Shall we toast with *De'Artois*? A celebration feels only fitting."

Xavier chuckled. "I'll set aside a case to take with you. And yes, we will celebrate."

"Splendid."

Pouring two glasses, Xavier lifted his in a toast.

Their crystal rims clinked softly; the sound delicate yet sharp.

"To profitable ventures and well-placed trust," Xavier said.

Killigrew swirled his glass of bourbon. "And to the rare satisfaction of a deal concluded without complications," he replied, his voice carrying a faint note of relief.

They drank, the silence between them promising future schemes.

"I have a surprise for you," Xavier said, setting his empty glass aside. "Let's visit my cellar. I've saved a rare indulgence for the occasion. Trust me—you won't be disappointed. Are you familiar with Sonner wines?"

Killigrew's eyes lit up. "Of course. The finest vintners in Eldor. Rumor has it you've managed to hoard a few of their rarest bottles."

"Not a rumor. A reality. I have three words for you: *Maitrasse Cru Bonnage.*"

"The Eclipse Wine? You're joking. You have a bottle?"

"Or two. Or three. Or four." Xavier winked, his tone teasing.

Laughter filled the room, warm and laced with the undercurrent of their shared secrets.

Xavier took the chest and approached the bookcase.

Blocking Killigrew's view, he traced the runes with smooth, exact patterns to unlock the hidden vault.

Once the chest was secured, he closed the bookcase and motioned toward the door.

"A man of your taste will appreciate my cellar," Xavier said.

Killigrew rose, adjusting his coat.

"Why wasn't I shown this treasure trove on my first visit?"

"There was no need to divulge all of my secrets."

Their laughter continued as Xavier grasped the door handle, pulling it open.

"After you," he said.

As Xavier and Killigrew's voices faded down the hall, Rad remained rooted, eyes locked on the now-empty study.

The chest was gone—but its presence lingered, heavy in his thoughts.

A powerful wizard would soon claim it, and this might be his only chance to glimpse what lay inside.

His curiosity clawed at him.

What relic had been hidden in that box? What secret worth so much effort and secrecy?

Rad's heart raced as a plan formed in his mind.

Quietly, he retraced his steps through the secret passageways and back to his room.

He removed his shoes, leaving him in his stockinged feet.

It was silent as he descended the grand staircase.

The manor was hushed, the few remaining guards preoccupied with their rounds outside.

There would be no second chance.

Once inside the study, he moved with purpose, his steps quick. The faint odor of bourbon lingered, as did the strong cologne of Killigrew.

The bookcase loomed before him, a sentinel guarding its secrets.

Taking a deep breath, he pulled open the disguised door with ease by grasping the black book.

In front of him was the magical lock, the runes dull and cold. With his finger, he traced the familiar letters, *L* and *Z*.

Lanny Zeh.

His true father.

A faint glow pulsed in response, followed by the soft snick of the lock disengaging.

The hidden door swung open, revealing the vault's treasures.

Rad hesitated only for a moment before stepping inside.

The sight greeting him stole his breath.

The chamber was a shrine to wealth and influence, more than he'd ever imagined his stepfather possessed.

Crates of pine wood slats lined the walls, each labeled and brimming with coins. The gold and platinum stacks were bound in paper sleeves, their gleaming edges not dulled by time or handling.

His eyes found a small pinewood crate marked *#232: 5,000 platinum coins.*

In a separate area, there were other crates—*#55: 5,000 gold coins.*

The enormity of the numbers left him reeling.

Xavier had a dragon's hoard in this vault.

Each area was paired with a ledger, a careful record of the riches in the stacks. On the shelves above, more crates sat stacked, their labels denoting vast quantities of wealth.

Scattered across the floor were chests bound with thick iron clasps, each too heavy for him to carry alone. Toward the back of the room, armor and weapons stood on proud displays. A gleaming suit of plate mail caught the lantern light, its surface etched with intricate runes Rad couldn't decipher, but he did recognize the outline of a bird—a falcon.

Nearby, swords, daggers, and spears rested in pristine racks.

Two massive bureaus, each with eight drawers, flanked the rear wall. The drawers' labels hinted at their contents: gold rings, gemstones, necklaces, bracelets, earrings.

The fortune within those drawers alone could buy a kingdom.

At the center of the room, on a small table, rested the object of his obsession: the chest.

The sight of it sent an unnatural shiver down his spine.

The secrets within were at his fingertips.

Rad stepped forward, his pulse hammering in his ears, and laid his hand on the chest's lid.

With deft movements, he unlocked the chest's simple mechanism and lifted the lid, his heart pounding with anticipation.

This was it—his chance to glimpse a treasure of immense power, a relic from the ancient world, steeped in magic and mystery.

For a fleeting moment, thoughts of theft flitted through his mind, but he dismissed them quickly. There was no conceivable way to make off with such an object unnoticed.

If anything, the wizard would catch him—find him.

Still, the allure of seeing it was enough to ignite his curiosity.

What lay within, however, was not at all what he expected.

A skeletal hand, grotesquely preserved, rested atop the chest's plush red velvet lining. Its shriveled, leathery skin clung to the bone, as though time itself had chosen not to finish its work.

Rad stared, unnerved.

In death, bones separated, and flesh decayed—this defied nature's order.

Magic.

It had to be magic.

But why would anyone go to such lengths to preserve a hand?

Why was this relic so coveted it warranted secrecy, wealth, and danger?

Compelled by an almost irrational curiosity, Rad reached out and placed a finger on it.

The moment his skin made contact, a searing bolt of pain lanced through his body.

It was as if lightning had struck him, setting every nerve alight in a blaze of unbearable agony.

He gasped, his breath caught in his throat, as his muscles locked and his limbs refused to obey.

His mind screamed at him to pull back, but his body betrayed him.

The pain surged again, more intense than before, and a sharp, humiliating warmth spread across the front of his trousers.

Rad's vision blurred.

Desperation clawed at him as he summoned every ounce of willpower to break free.

With a final, wrenching effort, he tore his finger away.

The connection severed, and he stumbled back, his chest heaving. The aftershock rippled through him, and he doubled over, his stomach tumbling.

His trembling hands fumbled as he slammed the chest shut and re-engaged the lock.

The nausea hit like a storm.

Clutching his midsection, he stumbled away from the vault. He managed to seal the bookcase, the mechanism clicking into place with cold finality.

His legs wobbled as he exited the study, his heart racing.

The house remained silent; no one had noticed his trespass.

But relief was fleeting.

The pain lingered in his muscles, a cruel reminder of whatever malevolent force he had disturbed.

Panic swirled with sickness.

Rad's stomach roiled, and he swallowed hard to keep its contents down. He veered toward the nearest exit, navigating through the manor with single-minded determination to get outside.

The grand room and lounge blurred as he passed through, the walls collapsing around him as his vision faltered.

The cool air beyond the deck promised relief.

The moment his stockinged feet touched the grass, his body betrayed him.

He retched as a wave of nausea gripped him, collapsing to his knees as the contents of his stomach sprayed onto the ground.

He didn't have time to brace himself before he fell forward, his vision dimming.

The acrid taste of bile burned his throat, but it was the overwhelming exhaustion that pulled him under.

As the world spun around him, Rad's strength ebbed.

He slumped into the grass, unable to escape the reek of vomit.

Darkness swallowed him whole.

When Rad regained consciousness, the sharp stench of vomit was absent. Someone had cleaned him up.

He lay in his small clothes, a cool cloth resting on his forehead. For a fleeting moment, hunger came, but it gave way to a fresh wave of nausea.

His stomach churned with discomfort, and though it was empty, offered nothing to expel.

Jamie's voice broke through the haze.

"I'll tell Hadley you're awake," he said, giving Rad's shoulder a light pat before departing.

Rad's bones were throbbing with pain and his muscles aching as if he had endured a brutal beating.

His belly felt as if it had been tied in tight, unforgiving knots.

The room spun and wavered, and he shut his eyes, hoping to find relief in the darkness. But shutting his eyes brought no relief—faint gray wisps still danced behind his lids, drifting like smoke.

He clenched his fists, determined to fight off the sickness, willing it to leave.

Time passed, and as he reopened his eyes, the ghostly shapes faded.

Summoning what little strength he had, Rad managed to sit up in bed. Every movement took monumental effort. The cool cloth on his forehead slipped, and he caught it before it fell. He stared at it, as if it might offer answers to the strange event.

Heavy boots thundered up the stairs, each step reverberating in his ears.

He winced in pain, raising his hands to shield his hearing from the unbearable noise.

The door creaked open, and Hadley stepped into the room, his concern etched across his weathered face. His heavy presence was followed moments later by Jamie, who was lingering in the doorway.

Hadley said, his tone stern, "I told you to stay at the stables. Go on, back to work. I'll be there later to help you finish up. Go on! Now!"

Jamie hesitated, then obeyed, retreating with a reluctant glance.

Hadley shut the door behind him and dragged a chair over from Rad's desk. Its polished wood and fine upholstery clashed with the ragged man who now sat upon it, his grizzled features heavy with fatigue.

Rad's voice was hoarse as he croaked, "What… what happened to me?"

Hadley's usual gruffness softened. "We found you out on the grass, thought you were dead." His voice carried a tremor as he added, "You were pale… drained, like the life had been sucked right out of you."

He paused, his eyes distant as if dredging up a memory best left buried.

He shivered, breaking the moment.

"I've seen something like this, a long time ago. Don't think it's connected to your situation, though—it can't be."

Rad's stomach twisted tighter at Hadley's words, but he said nothing, waiting for an explanation.

Hadley leaned forward, elbows on his knees.

"Glad you're awake. You've been out for two days, drifting in and out of consciousness. Kept mumbling to your Ma and Abby."

His voice lowered.

"Was like you thought they were right there, talking to you."

Rad's mind was foggy, like he was navigating through a thick, impenetrable mist.

The last clear memory was of the desiccated hand.

The cursed thing.

"I don't remember anything," he muttered, his voice hoarse and unfamiliar to his own ears.

"Trauma works that way," Hadley replied, his normal gruff absent. "Takes time for the mind to piece things back together. You think you can eat?"

Rad's stomach convulsed in response, and his body bucked in a dry heave. He fought to keep control, gripping the blanket in his fists, eyes staring straight ahead.

"Guess not," Hadley remarked with a grimace of his own.

Gathering his willpower, Rad forced himself upright against the bedframe. The room swayed around him, but he held his ground.

"You said you've seen this before? How?"

Hadley rubbed at the scruffy beard on his chin, his gaze distant as if staring into another time.

"Let's see how best I can explain it. There was this lad I knew, got himself tangled up with undead creatures. They sucked the life out of him, turned him into one of their own after he died. Creepy, unnatural business. When we found you, it reminded me of him—like your soul had been ripped clean out of you."

He paused, a shadow passing over his features.

"But it can't be true. Can it? How could you encounter an undead creature here on the manor grounds, in broad daylight? Makes no bloody sense."

Rad's insides clenched with dread.

The hand.

Could it be?

Undead?

What did this mean?

Undead were creatures that guarded tombs and devoured entire villages.

He shook his head, forcing out the only answer he could muster. "I don't remember anything."

Hadley leaned in, giving Rad's hair a playful ruffle. "You're still feverish, but no worse for wear if you ask me. You're breathing, it's something if you ask me."

Rad met Hadley's gaze, searching for reassurance. "Thanks for caring for me. I suppose you're the reason I'm still alive."

Hadley snorted, sitting back in his chair.

"Don't go thanking me too much. You've got Killigrew to thank as well. Xavier's got some important business going on with him, and he didn't want you mucking about during it. I told him if you died, I'd haunt him till his last days. So, Killigrew brought in a healer. You owe them both."

"A healer?"

"Aye, saved your sorry hide," Hadley said, crossing his arms as he pressed back into the chair until it creaked.

Rad's eyes were bright. "Like with potions and spells?"

"Aye," Hadley answered. "Cost more than a few silvers."

Rad rubbed his face with his hands. "What's going on? I mean here, at the estate?"

Hadley cocked his head.

"A wizard's coming tomorrow to do business with Xavier and Killigrew. Can't imagine what it's about, but I'd wager it has to do with whatever Killigrew came with long ago. He's like a bloody magpie, hoarding shiny things that ought to stay lost."

Rad nodded, his thoughts spiraling.

The hand.

The chest.

The relic.

Everything was converging, and none of it made sense.

"When will the wizard be here?" Rad asked.

"Tomorrow," Hadley replied. "The place is locked down tighter than a virgin's chastity belt. Guards everywhere, and not even a rat's getting past them."

Rad wished the defenses would have been tighter the night Ma and Abby were murdered. Perhaps it had been, but the Black Storm was proficient at what they do.

He pressed his hand to his aching stomach, suppressing another wave of nausea.

"I think I can eat. I should try, doesn't matter if I throw it up. Might help me recover."

Hadley's critical eyes surveyed him before giving a curt nod.

"I'll fetch bread and strong tea. Get as much rest as you can while you can. Or old Hadley will kick your arse properly."

As Hadley left the room, Rad lay back on the bed and stared at the ceiling.

His mind was filled with questions he couldn't answer. Yes, rest was necessary.

But not just to recover.

Tomorrow, he would spy on the transaction.

He needed to see the wizard uncover the secrets surrounding the hand.

He hoped to understand why it had almost killed him.

Château Saignoral was on lockdown when the wizard arrived. Guards patrolled with extra vigilance, their presence doubling at key points throughout the grounds.

What intrigued Rad most, however, was the wizard had come alone.

No entourage, no guards—a single man whose air of authority and confidence suggested he needed no such protections.

The wizard was nothing like Rad had imagined.

Tall, graceful, striking, and handsome, he exuded an aura of refinement and mystery. His tailored brown garments gleamed with embellishments of gold buckles, buttons, and fine chains, catching the light as he moved.

A fur-lined brown cloak draped over his broad shoulders, its edges swaying with each step.

Rad's eyes lingered on his boots, polished to a high sheen. Their sleek, northwest design resembled those worn by the Black Storm assassins, yet they bore not a single scuff or mark. Pristine and gleaming, they were almost untouched by the world—an oddity Rad found unsettling.

Stories of wizards teleporting vast distances flooded his mind, and he wondered if this man, whose name was Brak, had used such magic to arrive.

Hidden in his secret vantage point, Rad settled in, his breathing steady.

Xavier and Killigrew sat at their usual places, sipping *De'Artois* bourbon like they sold ancient relics every week.

Brak stood near the desk, his long fingers lifting the chest's lid.

He began his intense examination, his expression composed but focused.

He scrutinized the hand from every angle, taking in every small detail.

The wizard stood tall, thinking, while his hand stroked his well-trimmed goatee.

"Brak, please join us for a drink," Killigrew offered with a congenial smile, lifting his glass. "*De'Artois* bourbon—a finer drink has never graced a table."

Brak glanced toward them, his deep, resonant voice carrying with ease through the room. "I am familiar with the label. Later, perhaps."

His tone was polite, but it carried an unmistakable edge of dismissal.

He turned his attention to the chest's contents once again.

"It will take me ten minutes to examine this relic with my spells. I would appreciate solitude and space to work uninterrupted."

Xavier swirled his bourbon, tilting the glass toward the chest as his brow furrowed in suspicion. "And we're supposed to trust you won't grab it and vanish? Teleport away, leaving us empty-handed?"

Brak's lips curved into knowing smile.

"An intriguing notion, but know this, I am no thief. Not Leskaré, not Black Storm, not the ilk you do business with. Transporting this relic by magical means would be… unwise. Its nature is delicate, and the risk of exposure far outweighs convenience. I require time to confirm its authenticity. If it is what I believe, I will pay Killigrew the agreed sum and leave by more conventional means—on foot. If it is not, then I will depart empty-handed, and the false relic will remain yours to find another buyer."

Killigrew exchanged a glance with Xavier before nodding. "That is acceptable to me."

Xavier drained the last of his bourbon and set the glass down with a sharp clink. "Agreed. You shall have this room for as long as you need."

Brak's piercing, discerning gaze swept over them, his patience wearing thin. "Leave me to my work, gentlemen. I require only this *empty* study and ten uninterrupted minutes."

He flashed four fingers and his thumb twice in their direction.

"Go enjoy another drink in the charming lounge I passed. I will summon you when I am ready to discuss my findings."

Xavier rose, his expression unreadable, and motioned for Killigrew to follow. Together, they left the study, the door closing with a *thud* behind them.

The room fell into silence, save for the rustling of Brak's cloak as he moved to the door. There he locked it, then put his fingers together and cracked them.

Above, Rad's heart raced.

Whatever this relic was, it had drawn the attention of influential men—and now a wizard whose very presence suggested he was used to commanding forces beyond comprehension.

Rad leaned closer to the peephole, unable to look away.

He had to see what Brak would uncover.

Rad held his breath, his body as still as stone.

He had never seen a wizard cast a genuine spell before. The so-called magic at the gala had been nothing more than a parlor trick to dazzle the wealthy attendees—a pale imitation of true wizardry.

Now, hidden in his secret vantage point, Rad prepared himself for a different display of magic.

Would there be crackling lightning, eerie lights, or the unearthly sounds he had read about?

Rad's mind wandered to a story he had read months ago about a wizard on a battlefield, standing defiant against an entire army. He recalled the vivid image of the wizard weaving spells with one hand while holding a staff in the other, fire erupting from his fingertips to engulf ranks of charging soldiers.

When their archers let loose a volley of arrows, a shimmering barrier of force surrounding his body protected him from harm.

At the height of the chaos, the wizard summoned a spectral blade that danced through the enemy's flanks, turning the tide of battle with sheer magical brilliance.

Rad marveled at the idea of such power—how one person could reshape the fate of hundreds with a flick of their wrist.

Brak moved with purpose now that he was alone.

From his satchel, he produced a small wooden bowl, a dark, gnarled stick, and a handful of long, pale teeth gleaming in the lamplight.

Rad frowned, his curiosity piqued.

What kind of magic required such strange items?

The wizard placed the stick into the bowl and muttered a single phrase.

The wood ignited, producing a smokeless flame burning a deep, unnatural blue.

The teeth were arranged with care, standing upright like small ivory towers over the bowl. They formed a pyramid-like structure, the tips aligned at the top.

As the flame intensified, a thick, sickly-sweet incense wafted into the air, curling upward in delicate spirals.

Rad's nose wrinkled when the cloying scent got to him, but he didn't dare make a sound.

Brak's hands moved in intricate patterns through the smoke, his long fingers weaving invisible threads in the air. His voice was rhythmic, muttering phrases Rad couldn't understand.

The wizard's words carried weight, resonating with an eerie power humming in the stillness of the study.

With each gesture, faint glowing runes materialized in the air, hovering before fading into nothingness.

The ritual continued for ten tense minutes, each second stretching interminably.

Rad's pulse quickened as the smoke thickened, swirling and shifting as though alive.

Without warning, the flame extinguished, the incense dissipated, and the teeth vanished—consumed.

There was no flash, no bang—just an abrupt and absolute silence, as if the air had swallowed the remnants of the ritual.

Brak turned his attention to the skeletal hand inside the chest. His movements were careful, reverent, as his gloved hand lifted it with care to study it from every angle in the presence of the lingering magic.

The desiccated skin absorbed the room's light, making the hand appear darker, more menacing.

Brak's smiled, then it faltered.

He stilled, glancing sharply to his left, then to his right, brow furrowed in suspicion.

He turned slowly in place, casting a long, searching look behind him.

For a breathless moment, Rad feared he had been seen.

But after a pause, Brak lowered his head, dismissing whatever prickle of doubt had stirred him.

Then Brak smiled—a slow, triumphant grin spreading across his face like the rising sun.

The sight wrenched Rad's stomach, the memory of his own encounter with the relic flooding back like bile.

The smile sent an unnatural chill down his spine.

Just as Brak's eyes lifted again, sweeping upward, Rad closed the shutter and pressed his back to the wall, willing himself to vanish into the plaster.

Rad lay on his bed, his eyes fixed on the ceiling as his thoughts tumbled restlessly. The wizard had departed with the chest, leaving behind a redeemable note for Killigrew to exchange for his payment. Not long after, Killigrew had also gone, leaving the estate quieter than it had been in weeks.

Rad's mind kept returning to the spell Brak had performed earlier. Though the ritual had appeared straightforward, he couldn't recall all the words or the intricate hand gestures.

Frustration came, but exhaustion was stronger, pulling him toward sleep like a heavy anchor.

He shut his eyes, hoping rest would come soon.

It needed to.

He was worn thin, and lack of proper sleep would only make him weaker.

Staying awake was a small comfort—he was spared the recurring nightmares of Ma and Abby—dark visions that clung to him like a shadow.

Rad stirred, unsure if he was awake or still dreaming. He found himself descending the stairs from his third-floor room, his feet floating as if guided by an unseen force.

The house was cloaked in darkness, the kind found only in the dead of night.

His surroundings were illuminated, bathed in a surreal gray haze blurring the edges of reality. The mist wasn't cold, nor warm—it was like nothingness, a void mirroring his own body's temperature.

The sensation alone sent unease crawling up his spine.

By the time he reached the first floor, a distant voice broke through the silence.

"Radcliffe..."

The sound of his name, spoken in his Ma's voice, was unmistakable yet off—higher, thinner, tinged with an eerie echo.

He moved toward the voice without thinking, his steps quickening, his breathing shallow.

The air around him held the same strange, neutral temperature, but his skin prickled with unease.

The voice called again, and he followed it outside, astonished to find the night unchanged from the eerie atmosphere within the manor.

Fog blanketed the grounds, thick and swirling, but it lacked the weight and dampness he associated with mist. It wasn't moist, carried no scent, and left no dew where it passed.

It was more illusion than tangible.

It wrapped him in an unnatural shroud.

"Find me, Radcliffe..."

The voice urged him onward.

His legs moved of their own accord, drawing him across the estate grounds. He barely registered where he was heading until he reached the cemetery.

The hallowed ground was before him, its headstones rising like ghostly sentinels in the haze.

Wispy figures hovered near the graves, their outlines shifting like smoke caught in an invisible breeze.

They bore human shapes but lacked substance, their forms flickering and transparent, as though struggling to remain anchored to the world.

Rad froze, his breath catching in his throat.

The chorus of voices grew louder, overlapping in a cacophony of whispers pressing against his ears.

"Come closer..."

"Join us..."

"Stay with us..."

The ghostly shapes beckoned him, their gestures slow and fleeting, their pale hands reaching out toward him through the swirling fog.

Rad's pulse quickened, a cold sweat breaking across his skin despite the ambient temperature's uncanny stillness.

He tried to take a step forward but found his legs rooted to the ground.

Was this a dream?

A vision?

Or something worse?

Rad's eyes darted across the cemetery, trying to make sense of the otherworldly scene.

"Ma?" he called out, his voice trembling.

The specters didn't answer, but the chorus of whispers surged again, insistent and hypnotic.

"Come join us..."

Rad clenched his fists, his body trembling. Fear coursed through him, raw and unrelenting.

What was happening?

Why was he here?

And why couldn't he wake up from this nightmare?

"Yes, join us."

The voice cut through the thick, unnatural fog, tinged with a tinny, hollow quality that sent shivers down Rad's spine.

The apparition before him bore the likeness of his Ma, yet it was wrong.

Her features were faint, blurred at the edges, and her movements lagged, as though caught in another time. The sound of her voice, familiar yet unnervingly high-pitched, made his chest tighten.

"You were supposed to join us," she continued, floating closer, her translucent form swaying in the still air. "I have so much to tell you."

Rad's throat was dry.

His voice came out as a whisper, uncertain.

"How did this happen?"

"Existence was taken from your existence," she said, her voice ringing with an eerie finality. "You should be with us. Your life is ours. You belong with the dead. Do you not feel it?"

Rad took a step back, shaking his head in confusion.

"I don't understand."

"You will understand when you join us. I have so much to tell you. Come closer. Join us. There is no pain."

Another voice broke through, softer but carrying the same unnatural resonance.

"Join us, Rad. There is no pain, only joy."

Rad's breath hitched as he turned his gaze to another figure emerging from the mist.

It was Abby.

Her familiar outline shimmered as she drifted forward, her young face twisted into an uncanny semblance of its former self.

The cemetery was coming alive—or rather, filling with the ghostly dead.

Shapes began to emerge from the fog, forming human-like outlines.

Some figures rose higher, spectral forms suspended midair, while others inched toward Rad as though carried by an invisible current. The swirling mist at their feet began to dissipate, revealing dozens of ghostly apparitions behind Ma and Abby.

"Yes, join us."

The voices harmonized into a chilling chorus, high-pitched, childlike, insistent. The words repeated in waves, their intensity growing with every utterance.

Rad's pulse raced.

He backed away, careful not to trip on the uneven ground.

"What do you have to tell me?" he called out, his voice trembling.

"Join the dead, and I will tell you," Ma said. "I will tell you everything. I will tell you about your father. But you must join us."

"Yes, join us! Join us!"

The chorus swelled, echoing in his ears.

"I don't want to be dead!"

The apparitions surged forward.

Ma and Abby remained still, their ghostly forms fading into the background as the mass of hostile spirits rushed at Rad.

Their translucent arms reached for him, claws of swirling mist stretching out to claim him.

"It's a dream!" Rad shouted, squeezing his eyes shut and willing himself to wake up.

The ghosts dissipated in an instant, their spectral forms vanishing like smoke in the wind.

Rad gasped as the frigid air hit him.

His body was trembling, and steam billowed from his lips with every breath.

He opened his eyes to find himself standing in the cemetery, the graves of his Ma and Abby beside him.

The earth was cold beneath his bare feet, the damp soil squelching between his toes. He examined his hands, pale and trembling, then looked back at the gravestones, his heart pounding.

What had just happened?

Rad didn't wait to find answers.

Turning on his heel, he sprinted toward the manor house, his breath coming in ragged gasps.

He didn't dare look back, his mind replaying the ghostly chorus.

Join us.

They were ghosts, weren't they?

The peculiar visions clung to Rad's mind like an unwelcome fog, refusing to disperse. Every detail was sharp and vivid—leaving his room, walking to the cemetery, seeing Ma and Abby, and the ghostly figures urging him to join them.

Yet, there was an odd inconsistency: he hadn't felt the cold until he'd woken up.

The realization worried him as he approached the manor house, slowing his frantic pace to a cautious walk.

What was happening to him?

His thoughts circled back to the decrepit hand he had touched in Xavier's vault.

The ghostly voices had claimed his life was taken from him.

Did the hand's unnatural magic do this?

He was certain touching it should have killed him.

Yet, here he was, alive but shaken to his core.

Rad scrubbed his boots against the grass, knocking off as much dirt as he could before the guards' curious looks hurried him inside.

The air was thicker, warmer, but not comforting.

It was as if the weight of the evening's events had followed him indoors.

The staircase loomed ahead like a mountain.

Each step was an effort, his legs leaden, his normally boundless energy utterly spent.

By the time he reached the sanctuary of his room, he was too tired to think, let alone analyze the surreal encounter. He only had the strength to clean his feet with a towel before sliding into bed.

The familiar softness of the mattress embraced him.

He pulled the covers to his chin, seeking refuge in their warmth.

As his head hit the pillow, a wave of exhaustion washed over him, deeper and heavier than any he'd felt before.

His eyelids fluttered shut, and within moments, sleep claimed him.

But sleep offered no escape—the whispers of the graveyard lingered.

The ghostly dreams didn't return, much to Rad's relief. He credited their absence to his recovering health. As his strength, appetite, and energy rebounded, he began to feel like himself again.

Work was still exhausting, more so with the added strain of tending to the horses while the new stables took shape.

Yet, physical fatigue was a welcome distraction from the lingering questions swirling in his mind.

In casual conversations with Hadley, Rad began to probe for additional insights about the undead, trying to make sense of his encounter without letting on too much.

To his surprise, Hadley had an impressive depth of knowledge on the subject beyond the meager amounts he had read in books.

"Undead aren't all the same," Hadley said one evening as they leaned against the paddock rails. "Zombies—your basic walking corpses, all rotting flesh and shambling hunger. Ghouls—faster, nastier bastards made by necromancers to do their dirty work. Blightghouls? Poisonous ghouls. They like to station them near something important—pair them with ghouls for twice the fun. Then you've got wights—life-sucking horrors. Used to be human, until something dark hollowed them out and brought them back. They don't just kill you. They take your life bit by bit…"

Hadley paused, taking a long draw from his pipe, the embers glowing faintly in the dusk.

"Wights drain the life out of you. Not all at once—slow, like they're peeling it away."

He exhaled smoke that curled into the evening air.

"Vampires. Most powerful undead I've ever…" He hesitated, jaw tightening, "…heard of. Creatures of darkness. Cursed. Not dead, not alive. They drink blood to keep going, and if they get their teeth into you—well, you don't die. You stop being *you*. Become their servant. Body's yours, soul isn't."

Rad's stomach tightened as he listened, his mind leaping to the preserved hand in the chest.

Could it have belonged to a wight? Or worse, a vampire?

The thought clung to him, its claws deep in his imagination.

Hadley must have noticed Rad's furrowed brow because he added, "Not that you'd come across one of those things often. They're rare. Cursed items? More common. Most curses don't stick unless the magic is strong."

Rad nodded absently, turning the information over in his mind.

Was the hand cursed? Was it imbued with the dark power of a wight or vampire?

The notion was plausible, but as his health improved and no lingering effects emerged, he found himself less preoccupied with the incident.

Still, the experience left an impression—one he couldn't shake.

What troubled him more was the memory of his mother's words.

I have so much to tell you.

Her ghostly promise stirred his curiosity.

She meant to reveal the truth about his father—Lanny Zeh.

But she didn't know he had perished in the collapsed tunnel beneath the manor.

Would she be... upset?

He also wondered, what secrets had Lanny Zeh taken to the grave?

Rad imagined his mother knew these secrets.

If he could only speak with her again, perhaps he could piece together the puzzle of his lineage and learn the truth of what had transpired.

Yet, the thought of the other ghosts filled him with unease.

Unlike his Ma and Abby, the other apparitions had felt invasive, as if their outstretched hands sought to pull him into their world against his will.

If I ever return to the gray realm, Rad vowed to himself, *I'll stay far away from the others. I'll focus on Ma and Abby. They're the only ones I can trust.*

But how could he venture back to the land of the dead on purpose?

That was the question.

Rad had no answers, only the faint hope a path would present itself, a way to unravel the secrets of the veil between life and death.

Until that time, the weight of his unanswered questions would remain.

- 352 -

Chapter Seventeen

∞

The Treatise

Abby, somehow, I entered the world of the dead through my nightmares. I can't explain it, but it must be from when I touched the decrepit hand.

It cursed me, made me sick.

A sickness that is deep inside me, and I don't know how to cure it.

The realm of the dead wasn't anything like what I read in any book.

The air, it wasn't warm or cold, it was like being in nothing.

I could move without much effort, I felt like I was floating.

I heard Ma's voice calling out, she told me she would tell me everything about my real father.

But the other dead wanted me to join them—they weren't friendly, so I fled.

I haven't been able to go back.

In fact, I don't know how to get back.

I need to find out what is happening to me and why and how I was drawn into the realm of the dead. I need to get back there so I can talk to Ma, and you. You were there, but you didn't say much.

You were... sad.

I'm going to the Ornst Library to get answers, to learn more about the undead and the realm of the dead.

I hope I can go back to talk to you and Ma.

I miss you so much.

Love, Rad.

Rad secured permission to visit the Ornst Library, renowned for its vast and prestigious collection of written matter. He reasoned dedicating a few hours to perusing its shelves could deepen his understanding of the undead.

With the help of librarians to guide him to the right tomes and his own proficiency in reading, it would be inevitable he uncovered useful information.

Still, he couldn't help but admit he'd rather spend his day at The Sweet Hatchet with Rosamund.

The thought of explaining to her that he had been at the library instead of visiting her didn't sit well. She'd laugh in fact, perhaps teasing him for choosing dusty pages over her company.

As expected, Hadley scoffed at the idea.

"No bloody library for me," he had grumbled.

Rad set off alone on his day off, leaving the grand estate early in the morning and hitching a ride with a kindly merchant heading into town.

When the Ornst Library came into view, it took Rad's breath away.

Spanning an entire city block, the towering structure was the grandest building in Ornst. Eight stories tall and crowned by five majestic towers piercing the heavens, its thick stone façade was adorned with soaring arches, intricate carvings, and stoic gargoyles watching over the city like silent sentries.

High above the main entrance, chiseled into the stone in bold, weathered letters, he could just make out the library's oldest motto:

KNOWLEDGE IS THE FLAME THAT DEFIES THE DARK

The library grounds were as magnificent as the building itself. Four manicured parks surrounded it, filled with ancient shade trees, carefully trimmed hedges, and winding gravel paths. Stone benches bore the names of forgotten scholars. Small stone book boxes stood at intervals along the edges, filled with weathered volumes free for the taking—a quiet reminder that knowledge was for all, not hoarded for the few.

Though meant to be a haven for scholars and students, the parks often played host to beggars and wanderers, who were quietly chased off by the Ornst militia each morning. Today, the grounds were peaceful and inviting, a rare pocket of tranquility against the bustling city beyond.

Rad's boots echoed sharply on the cobblestones as he crossed through the wide plaza toward the grand archways. Near the entrance, scholars clustered at stone seating areas, some scribbling furiously into journals, others deep in animated discussions about politics, history, or theories of magic.

In one corner of a park, several tables had been set up for games like chess and checkers, drawing small, murmuring crowds who moved pieces with careful deliberation.

The sight stirred a memory of Faucet Chilcott, the acquaintance who had once helped him dispose of bodies. A cold shiver ran down his spine as the thought turned to the Black Storm and their cruel revenge. Ma and Abby. The pang of loss resurfaced, sharp and unforgiving.

Over the main doors, another ancient phrase caught Rad's eye, carved into the keystone arch:

THE MIND THAT WANDERS BUILDS NEW ROADS

Rad hesitated a moment before stepping forward, feeling the weight of it all—the history, the voices, the millions of pages housed beyond those heavy oak doors.

He wasn't sure if he belonged here.

But he was here now.

And the library, like the city itself, would not turn him away.

He stepped through the heavy oak doors, surprised to find they weren't locked during the day.

Casual guards lingered nearby, more for show than real defense—an unspoken reminder to behave rather than a true wall against trouble.

Rad couldn't imagine criminals bothering with this place.

What fool would risk prison over a pile of books?

It wasn't like you could fence them for coin on a street corner.

Besides, here in Ornst, anyone could take books freely, so long as they promised to return them.

It was an old tradition—one built on trust, not fear—and Rad found himself admiring it more than he expected.

In a world where so much was hoarded or stolen, it was strange—and strangely comforting—to see something precious simply offered.

Inside, the library stretched without end.

Tables and chairs were scattered across the vast stone floor, occupied by scholars hunched over thick tomes and brittle scrolls.

Floor-to-ceiling shelves groaned under the weight of countless books, parchment rolls, and loose-bound papers. Shorter shelves formed winding labyrinths of aisles, each leading to what felt like a thousand more.

Rad paused, turning a slow circle to take it all in.

At the distant corners of the floor, he noticed thick archways leading into the base of each tower—vault entrances, no doubt, where the rarest works were sealed away behind heavier doors.

The towers even had banners hanging beside them, stitched with faded mottoes in curling script:

Preserve the Past, Protect the Future

The Fool Forgets; the Wise Remember

Knowledge is a Burden Best Carried Together

He turned back to the main floor, counting rows instinctively.

Two hundred bookcases in this section alone.

If the layout held true across the building, that meant nearly eight hundred cases per floor—each crammed with at least five hundred volumes.

His mental calculation left him staggered:

Four hundred thousand books per floor.

Eight floors.

More than three million written works.

The number made his head spin.

How could so many books even exist?

Maybe some were duplicates. Maybe a few were barely legible scraps tucked away for preservation's sake.

It didn't ease his growing anxiety.

One book an hour. Over a thousand years.

He would never reach the end.

He needed help. Not a guide—a dozen guides, clawing over each other to be the best.

Rad smiled faintly to himself.

A contest. That would do it.

It came together in a flash.

He thought back—reluctantly—to one of Xavier's schemes: the infamous wine gala, a masterpiece of manipulation.

It had been careful work—a fake vintage created with just the right blend of old barrels, dusted labels, and carefully seeded rumors.

At the gala, Xavier had staged a perfect scene—a few planted guests loudly doubting the wine's authenticity, the dramatic protest of Xavier's own men, the tearful insistence that the wine was real, preserved from a lost age.

The tension had been unbearable.

The guests had wanted—*needed*—to believe.

And when Xavier "reluctantly" allowed the wine to be sampled under strict conditions, rapture swept the room.

It was all false.

Every cask, every whispered claim.

But by the end of the night, Xavier's vaults were heavy with noble gold, and no one wanted to question the dream they'd bought into.

Rad ground his teeth lightly at the memory.

He hated giving the man credit.

But clever was clever.

Maybe it was time he used his brain to get what he needed.

Rad wandered through the aisles, weaving his way toward the center of the floor. The librarians were easy to spot in their uniforms: the men wore sturdy green pants, white shirts, and green vests loaded with pockets; the women wore simple knee-length green dresses, their hair pulled back with matching green ribbons.

The men's hair was cut short. Their faces were cleanshaven. Orderly, efficient—like everything else here.

Rad circled the central librarian station, moving slow, scanning the attendants for the oldest among them.

A plump woman caught his eye.

Her silver hair was cropped too short to tie back like the others. A faded scar curved along her neck, nearly lost in the folds of her skin. Her knuckles were swollen—whether from years of work or the weight of time, Rad couldn't tell. But she moved with ease, sorting books without pause.

Steady hands. Sharp mind.

Good.

He stepped closer.

"Excuse me," Rad said, schooling his voice into polite urgency. "I need assistance."

"Over there," she said, not lifting her gaze from her task. "Get in line. They'll help you when it's your turn."

Rad didn't move.

"I'd prefer if you helped me. You're smarter than the rest."

Her lips twitched—more irritation than amusement.

"Flattery won't get you anywhere," she muttered, still working without pause. "Get in line like everyone else. Or better yet, flatter those ahead of you so you can cut."

"It'll only take a moment," Rad pressed, keeping his tone polite but firm. "And I'm sure you'll have the answer."

At that, she froze mid-task, dropping the book with a heavy thump onto the station.

She looked up, annoyance sharpening her features.

"Get in line, or I'll call the guards. Last warning."

Rad said nothing.

Instead, he snapped a silver coin onto the book she had just handled.

The sharp clink cut through the hum of the library like a blade.

The woman's eyes narrowed at the sound.

"You must be either impatient or rich," she said, still not touching the coin.

Her eyes locked onto his, steady and unamused.

"Which is it?"

"Impatient," Rad answered. "Impatient because I have a job to do. I'm not rich, but the man who employs me is. I work for Xavier von Schule."

The mention of the von Schule name made her pause. Her expression shifted, the irritation fading into something closer to curiosity.

"Go on," she said.

"He sent me here on an important errand. My name's Rad. He told me to find the smartest person here and give them a coin if they helped me. Go on—take it."

Ragna plucked the coin from the book with nonchalance, tucking it into her apron.

"My name's Ragna," she said. "The von Schule family is well-known for their patronage of this library. In fact, a few of the artworks here were donated from your employer's collection."

She gave him a measuring look.

"Your coin has bought you a few moments of my time. What does Xavier von Schule require?"

"There's going to be a contest," Rad said, leaning in slightly, lowering his voice to a conspiratorial whisper. "It's for the most knowledgeable scholars. Five platinum coins to the winner."

Ragna's eyebrows lifted sharply.

"A tidy sum," she said. "And what's the subject of this contest?"

Rad took a measured breath, schooling his features into the proper seriousness.

"He's curious about wights, vampires, night creatures," Rad said. "He wants a written work about all known undead—their classifications, and anything else worth knowing."

"Ah, an intriguing topic," Ragna said. "A treatise?"

Rad tilted his head, feigning confusion.

"Sorry. I'm not sure what that is."

"It's a formal, written discussion about a subject," Ragna explained, her tone reminiscent of a lecture.

Rad nodded quickly, playing along.

"That would work. What he wants is a comprehensive list of undead creatures, a discussion about their nature, and relevant details— where they live, their origins, any stories about them."

He hesitated a fraction, as if worried he'd said too much.

"Do you think scholars would be interested?"

Ragna smiled faintly, as if she knew something he didn't.

"For five platinum coins? Oh, yes. There are scholars who'd leap at such a prize. I'd wager a few are already lurking in the stacks. Maybe we could get Merrow Keff—he's an expert in all things."

She leaned in slightly, voice lowered to a whisper.

"But if word of this gets out," she warned, "you'll have hundreds clamoring to participate. A hundred treatises on the undead would be an unfathomable task to evaluate. Even Xavier von Schule would struggle."

Rad nodded, grave.

"He doesn't want quantity over quality," he said. "Quite the opposite. Only the best scholars should be involved—like this Merrow Keff you mentioned."

Ragna eyed him, testing. "Do you have a contract? Rules?" she asked, arching a sharp eyebrow.

"Not with me, unfortunately," Rad replied. "I was sent to gauge interest and find someone on the library staff to help organize the contest."

He shifted slightly closer, dropping his voice, making the offer conspiratory.

"If you assist me, I'll give you another silver later today for your trouble. And when the winner is determined—one gold."

He held her gaze, steady and certain, as if this deal was already written.

Ragna chuckled, her silver hair gleaming in the library's soft light.

"What if I want to enter the contest myself and win the platinums?" she teased, watching him closely.

"Do you know much about the undead?" Rad asked, keeping his tone even.

"Of course not!" she said, waving it off. "But for five platinums, I'd give it a go."

Rad sighed, letting just enough frustration show. "This is exactly what I was told to avoid. Mister von Schule only wants the brightest scholars working on this."

He leaned in slightly, lowering his voice into something more personal.

"If you want to earn your gold, ensure only the best are involved. Do you know anyone qualified? Could you assemble them discreetly?"

Ragna tapped her chin thoughtfully, her sharp eyes still reading him.

"I have a few in mind," she said after a moment. "Ten or twelve, maybe. There are groups of scholars who meet here regularly for debates and discussions. Keeping it within those circles would limit the noise. Otherwise"—she chuckled again—"you're right. Hundreds might swarm."

Rad nodded, considering her suggestion.

"What if the contest was for the best treaty—"

"Treatise," Ragna corrected, one eyebrow arching.

"Treatise. Right. Thanks."

He gave a faint, sheepish smile that was mostly show.

"What if two groups competed against each other? Would that keep things cleaner?"

Ragna's face tightened, skepticism sharpening her features.

"They might not like splitting the reward," she said. "Scholars are proud. They won't want to share the credit—or the winnings."

Rad tapped the counter, the sound sharp against the quiet hum of the library.

"What if I convince Mister von Schule to sweeten the prize?"

His voice dropped to a persuasive whisper.

"Five platinums for the winning group, plus two gold for every participant, even if they lose. Everyone walks away with something."

Ragna studied him a long moment—more curious than wary now.

"You're either a very good errand boy," she said, lips twitching, "or a very bad liar."

She didn't sound angry.

If anything, there was a faint glimmer of amusement behind her sharp gaze. This street-smart boy with too much confidence and too much nerve… well, he wasn't the worst thing to happen to her today.

And after all, she had nothing to lose by helping him.

A little intrigue.

A little silver.

Maybe even a little fun.

Ragna agreed with a nod.

"You'll need to back this up with a proper contract, or nothing will happen."

Rad leaned in slightly, his tone earnest but controlled.

"You misunderstand part of this. If I mess this up, I'll be punished—severely. I can't go back to the estate with bad news. I need to ensure at least two treaties—"

"Treatises," Ragna corrected again, her amusement plain.

"—are submitted," Rad continued smoothly, as if he hadn't made a mistake. "For five platinums and around twelve gold. Sound about right? I'll convince him it's worth adding extra prizes for individual participation."

"Thirteen gold," Ragna said, arching an eyebrow. "You're forgetting me."

Her sharp gaze pinned him like a needle to cloth.

"What else must I do for this gold piece you promised?" Her tone was cool, but not unfriendly. "What's the catch?"

"No catch," Rad said quickly. "Your job is to select the groups competing and make sure no one else finds out. They'll need to swear secrecy. If word of this contest leaks to the masses—or back to Xavier von Schule himself—the contest will be called off. No gold. No platinum. Nothing."

He held her gaze evenly.

"Make it clear this is for a man of High Ornst blood—discretion is paramount. Quality is expected."

Ragna tapped a finger against her crossed arms.

"What's the timeframe?" she asked.

Rad hesitated. "I... hadn't thought about it. How long would they need to write a treatise? What's fair?"

Ragna tilted her head, considering.

"Scholars could take months if you let them. They love chasing details—and agonize over conclusions. If you want results, limit the time. No more than two weeks, or you'll end up with half-finished books instead of what you asked for."

"Two weeks it is," Rad agreed before any other doubts could surface.

Ragna gave a short nod, the closest she'd come to approval yet.

"I'll need contracts before I approach anyone," she said.

Rad flashed an eager smile.

"I'll see to it. I'll be back with the contracts this afternoon."

He paused, glancing around the towering shelves with open curiosity.

"But first… I'd like to explore the library a bit. I've never been here before. Say—" His eyes brightened with a flash of real boyish interest. "Is there a section on runes?"

"Ancient runes? Magic runes? Dwarven runes? Elvish runes? Blood Runes?" Ragna asked, each suggestion punctuated by a tilt of her head. "Can you be more specific?"

"All of them, I guess," Rad admitted, realizing too late that he hadn't thought his request through.

"They're in different sections," she said, rocking on her heels as she awaited clarification.

"I'll start with magic runes," Rad decided, his fingers brushing the folded parchment in his pocket—the one where he had sketched the strange runes etched onto the blade of *Vanguard*. He still hadn't cracked their meaning.

Maybe today he'd start.

"Up two levels," Ragna instructed. "Find the seven-hundred series subsection. One of the curators can assist you. Some of those books are fragile and require care."

She leaned in, her voice dropping to a confidential murmur.

"If you have another silver," she said, "the curator might speed things up for you. Aldric is his name."

"Understood. Upstairs it is."

Rad gave her a grateful nod.

"I'll be right here when you return with the contracts," she added, shelving another thick volume onto her portable cart.

"Thanks. You're very kind—and incredibly helpful."

Rad headed toward the grand staircases, resisting the temptation to bolt to the top and work his way down like a boy on a dare. Instead, he kept his pace measured, purposeful.

As he ascended the wide marble steps, he passed a series of engraved plaques set into the stone walls—ancient mottos of the library.

One caught his eye, carved deep into a slab of dark granite:

KNOWLEDGE IS NOT GIVEN FREELY.

IT MUST BE SOUGHT, EARNED, AND ENDURED.

Rad touched the words lightly as he passed, the stone cool under his fingers.

The second floor was busier than the one below. Rows of overstuffed shelves loomed in every direction, and nearly every table was crowded with scholars, patrons, and students hunched over open texts.

The air buzzed with quiet industry—low whispers, the scratch of quills, the soft thud of books being set down.

Workers bustled among the aisles, offering directions, retrieving volumes, or assisting visitors.

Rad scanned the room with a practiced eye—and spotted one of the curators straight ahead, near a tall pillar marked "700."

The man exuded the aura of a keeper of secrets, his gaunt frame and weathered face shaped by decades of service in the halls of knowledge. His brown eyes held a quiet intensity, and a faint tobacco stain on his cracked lips reminded Rad of Hadley.

The man's trembling hand slid a book into place with practiced care, a bead of sweat trailing down his temple.

Rad fingered the silver coin in his pocket before approaching.

"Excuse me, sir, are you Aldric? I need help deciphering a sheet of runes my master gave me." He placed the coin on the table with a sharp click. "Perhaps this will buy a little of your expertise? Enough for a potent smoke or a strong drink after work?"

The curator licked his lips, glancing at Rad. "Who sent you?" he asked.

"My master is Xavier von Schule," Rad replied.

The man's eyes widened. "No, who *here* sent you to me?"

"Ragna," Rad answered.

The curator extended his hand, curling his fingers to beckon.

Rad handed over the folded parchment and the silver coin, which disappeared into the man's pocket. Aldric strolled to a nearby bookcase, choosing a short table to spread the parchment.

He muttered softly as his fingers moved over the symbols, his brow furrowed in concentration. From time to time, he hummed under his breath, his head bobbing back and forth like a bard searching for the right tune.

"Are there books that might help?" Rad asked.

"I can decipher this for you," the curator said, his expert eye fixed on the symbols. "The runes on the left are magical representations. From top to bottom, they read: Stealth. Speed. Angelic power, or perhaps godly power. Precision."

He tapped the right side of the parchment.

"These here are written in an old elvish dialect. It reads, 'Stalker.' Like a predator stalking its prey."

Aldric paused, his finger resting lightly on the parchment.

"This dialect... it is ancient. Whatever bore these marks is very old, and Elven by origin."

He glanced at Rad, his voice lowering. "Do you know what it is?"

Rad shook his head. "My master sent me to figure it out. I think... it might be a weapon."

Aldric nodded slowly. "Ah. Then it could be from before the Age of Expansion. Perhaps even forged during the Bloodletting."

Rad knew the names. He had read about the wars and the shattered kingdoms that followed, and he felt the urge to say so—to prove he was no fool in such matters.

But he caught himself, forcing a simple nod instead.

Don't show off.

Aldric, pleased to have an attentive audience, went on without prompting.

"It was a brutal time. Elves and men both tore the world apart, and the magic of that age... it had teeth. If your master's weapon bears these runes, it was born of blood and ambition."

The curator's eyes gleamed.

"I wish I could see the runes carved in the steel itself," he said wistfully. "The parchment is good, but the work of old hands—that is where the true story lies."

He handed the parchment back to Rad, who mouthed the runes to himself: stealth, speed, angelic power, precision. *Stalker.*

A fitting name for his blade.

"Do you have more silver for other riddles?" the curator asked, his tone a mix of amusement and hunger.

"Not today," Rad replied with a faint smile. "But if I come across anything else, I'll find you." He extended his hand. "Name's Rad, by the way."

"Aldric Thorne," the curator replied, inclining his head with surprising formality. "At your service—anytime."

Rad shook the curator's hand and pivoted on his heels, moving briskly toward the staircase.

As he climbed the remaining five floors, his thoughts shifted to the counterfeit contracts he needed to craft. Replicating his stepfather's signature wouldn't pose much of a challenge; he had the skill for such precise forgery. He had the required materials on hand and access to Xavier's wax seal, which would lend the documents an air of legitimacy.

The key was to keep emphasizing discretion, ensuring Ragna and the scholars involved understood the importance of secrecy.

Reaching the eighth floor, Rad came to the entrance of the towers. The corner towers were cordoned off, their upper floors hidden from view.

The central tower, however, stood open, revealing a grand spiral staircase that twisted upward.

People climbed the stairs with books in hand, and a few carried viewing instruments Rad recognized as tools for surveying distant sights.

He joined the ascent, careful to stay unobtrusive, weaving between the scholars' purposeful strides.

As he neared the spire's apex, a line of people formed along the staircase, vanishing around a bend and out of sight.

Carved into the stone above the final landing was an inscription:

ONLY FROM THE HEIGHTS CAN ONE SEE THE TRUE SHAPE OF THE WORLD

Rad tilted his head, considering the words. He supposed it made sense—the higher you climbed, the more you saw.

Still, a part of him wondered if it had a deeper meaning.

At the base of the final stretch, a library staff member stood waiting.

Her green dress was rumpled, and wispy blonde hair framed her youthful face. She had a slender frame and a harried look, the marks of constant demands.

Rad stepped closer, curiosity quickening his pace. "Where does this go?" he asked.

She raised an eyebrow, her tone bordering on incredulous.

"You walked all the way up here and didn't know why?"

Her response grated on him. "It's a simple question. Do you know or don't you?"

With a roll of her eyes, she relented.

"Of course I know. It's my job! It leads to the observation deck. Fifteen people at a time, five minutes each."

Rad's gaze swept over the line.

Estimating the number of people he couldn't see, he said, "So, a twenty-five-minute wait from here? It better be worth it."

She blinked, caught off guard by his statement. "How did you figure it out?"

"Math," he replied with annoyance. "I counted the people, divided by fifteen, then multiplied by five. Seventy-five divided by fifteen is five; five times five is twenty-five."

The staffer frowned, clearly running the numbers in her head.

"You know this library holds over three million books, right?" Rad asked.

"There aren't that many!" she retorted, crossing her arms. "Can't be!"

"I have a proposition. If I prove the number's real—three million—you take me up for a five-minute view, alone. If I can't convince you, I'll never bother you again."

She laughed at him. "I can't lose. You can't convince me; I could lie to you."

"But you won't. You strike me as honest."

He pointed upward.

"Tell me—how many stories does this place have with shelves?"

"Easy. Eight."

"How many bookcases on a floor?" Rad asked.

"I don't know," she answered.

"I do. I counted. Eight hundred. How many books in each case?"

Her eyes narrowed and her head cocked to the side.

"You are a strange boy."

"Five hundred. Each floor has four hundred thousand books."

She blushed for unknown reasons. "I'm not good at math."

"What's eight times five?" Rad asked.

"Forty. Easy. Even I know that."

"What's a hundred times a hundred?"

"That's easy too. Ten thousand. You add the two zeros."

"What's forty times ten thousand?"

She paused a moment to work it through.

"Well, you add a zero and times by four. So four hundred thousand? Right? Four hundred thousand?"

"And what's four times eight?"

"Thirty-two. So it's thirty-two hundred thousand?"

"Correct! Yes, three million two hundred thousand books."

She was stunned into silence.

"You're right! How did you make the math so easy?" she asked.

Rad smiled. "Here's an easy way to break down numbers. What's three times ninety-eight?"

She stared at a spot in the air, frowning. After a moment, she gave up.

"I'd need paper."

"Round it up to a hundred, multiply, then subtract the small piece you added." Rad shrugged. "Three times a hundred is three hundred. Subtract six. Two hundred ninety-four."

She blushed. "You make it sound so easy. It isn't easy!"

"Try one," Rad said, grinning. "What's three times ninety-five?"

She thought it through carefully.

"Three hundred... minus fifteen... two eighty-five?"

"Yes! See?"

He lowered his voice and leaned in, as if sharing a secret.

"It's useful in my line of work."

"Are you a money lender?"

Rad laughed. "No! I take care of horses."

"How is math useful for taking care of horses? You're being silly!"

"You'd be surprised. So, my private tour? I think I earned it."

She inclined her head. "Those in line ahead of you might not like it."

"Not my problem. A deal's a deal—and you're honest. Name's Rad, by the way."

"My name is Karin. Nice to meet you." She paused. "I think."

Karin unhooked a rope barrier and cordoned off the stairs behind Rad.

She motioned for him to follow—and for the others to stay put.

They climbed the stairs, murmuring apologies as they slipped past the others.

At the top of the line, Karin whispered to the man regulating the entrance.

The attendant let the patrons through the exterior door, then cordoned off the top level and called them back to the library.

Once the fifteen visitors had cleared out, Rad was granted access to the deck.

On a whim, he grabbed Karin's hand and pulled her outside with him.

She pulled her hand back.

"Your hands are rough. I should get back to work."

"Suit yourself."

The deck formed a square, offering an unobstructed view of the sprawling city. The towering central spire stretched upward, disappearing into the heavens. It was the same spire he could spot from his room at *Château Saignoral.*

A gust of wind tore at him, whipping his shirt against his ribs. He reckoned many hats had been snatched away up here, lost to the heights.

As Karin walked away in her rumpled green dress, he watched her briefly.

Too skinny for his liking, he thought.

He preferred women with more curves—like Rosamund, whom he cherished.

Turning back to the railing, he leaned into the sturdy stone and let the vastness of Ornst fill his senses.

The city was immense, layered, alive.

In the distance, he picked out *Château Saignoral*—his home. The land it covered rivaled entire districts of the city. *Château Saignoral* could have been its own district.

Its own town.

His gaze shifted.

There—the Sweet Hatchet's crooked roofline.

He thought of Rosamund, wondering about her well-being—wondering if he truly loved her.

Farther out, he spotted the old warehouse where he had confronted the Black Storm assassins.

A pang of dread clutched him.

Whatever choices he had made, someone he loved would have been lost.

Saving Tristin had only led to the deaths of Ma and Abby.

Time slipped by unnoticed as he drank in the city sprawled below. The sensation of height coursed through him, awakening something restless and fierce.

Regardless of what Hadley thought—he needed this.

He needed this view.

He needed this library.

"Time's up."

Rad turned toward the commanding voice, pivoting smoothly on his heel, carried by the energy of the moment.

Without hesitation, he moved toward the worker, who waved him efficiently toward the exit.

The worker guided him from the platform as the next group of ten visitors climbed behind him, their hushed murmurs blending with the faint whistle of the wind.

Rad took the stairs down at a brisk pace, the way ahead clear.

The sounds of the city rose as he moved lower, and he glanced back once at the view fading behind him.

Near the bottom, Karin stood by the railing, her blonde hair catching the light.

Rad exchanged a quick smile with her, one she returned with a subtle nod before turning back to her duties.

Rad lingered in the library another hour, wandering its maze-like halls. Each turn became a chance to memorize the building's layout. He noted the clear signage marking every entrance and exit, impressed by the foresight of the architects.

Emergency ladders along the outer walls caught his attention.

Designed for escape, perhaps—but Rad saw something else.

A way out was almost always a way in.

His steps slowed as he pondered the nature of what the library might conceal beyond its endless rows of books. Surely, in a place so vast and so carefully tended, something of real value lay hidden within its walls.

He passed a scattering of faded paintings—fruit bowls, dusty scholars, the usual clutter meant to dress up old stone—but his mind raced ahead.

Relics might be tucked away.

Scrolls penned by forgotten wizards.

Trinkets so ordinary no one guessed their worth.

Even magical works, their danger buried beneath dust and neglect.

A thought struck him—Aldric Thorne.

Rad grinned to himself.

A man like that could be steered, if handled right.

A little silver here, a little curiosity there.

Perhaps it wasn't just books waiting to be discovered.

Perhaps there were treasures.

As he made his way toward the exit, his gaze caught on an inscription carved high along the archway:

THAT WHICH IS BURIED IS OFTEN BURIED FOR GOOD REASON

Rad tilted his head, studying the words.

A faint thrill stirred in him anyway.

He smiled and slipped out into the city.

The heavy oak doors swung closed behind him with a soft thud. The cool breeze of late afternoon brushed against his face, carrying the scents of stone, parchment, and distant hearthfires.

His path back to the estate stretched ahead, the cobblestones glinting in the fading light. As he walked, his mind turned not to the streets ahead, but to the halls he had just left behind.

He thought of Aldric Thorne—odd, brilliant, eager to share what he knew for the price of a little silver.

It wouldn't be hard to slip back in, to ask for a few books on magical runes—to start something.

The idea quickened his steps.

He wouldn't waste the chance.

Abby had given him that love once—quietly, secretly—passing books when no one was looking.

The books hadn't just filled him with knowledge; they had filled him with joy.

And knowledge wasn't just comfort.

It was power.

And now he had three keys to the library's vaults: Ragna, Aldric, Karin.

The weight of the plan settled back onto his shoulders as he neared the road leading home.

There was still work to do—the contest to set, the scholars to manage.

But the light inside his soul burned a little brighter now.

He would come back—not only for himself, but for Abby.

While scheming and lost in thought, Rad wandered down the avenue toward *Château Saignoral.* A curious sign caught his eye—five concentric rings that glowed faintly, even in daylight.

The Fifth Ring
Magister Pellimor Thatch
Wizardry for Daily Use — Established RH400

The same year I was born, Rad noted.

The shop was tucked between a cobbler and an herbalist on a quiet side lane—neither dangerous nor particularly safe. The sort of place Hadley might describe as "keep your senses sharp, but don't panic if someone says hello."

The shop's windows were darkly tinted, but not opaque. Now and then, a faint glow flickered inside—green or violet, Rad couldn't be sure.

Just outside the red door stood a placard:

No Charms Tested Without Payment.
No Refunds.
No Second Chances.

Below that, a list of common services:

- ❖ Block of Ice – 5 Gold
- ❖ Permanent Lights – Starting at 50 Gold
- ❖ Earth Molding – By Quotation Only
- ❖ Mending – 15 Gold per item
- ❖ Arcane Locking – Starting at 150 Gold
- ❖ Arcane Warding – 100 Gold per ward

Inquire inside about additional magical services.

Rad stepped up and opened the door. At once, a grating squawk blurted like a startled bird, followed by a booming voice:

"Welcome to The Fifth Ring—your destination for magical and arcane solutions!"

The door shut behind him.

The shop was smaller than it appeared from the outside. To his left stood neat rows of shelves, racks, and crates. Straight ahead, a door marked *Wizards Only* bore a painted eye that looked disturbingly lifelike, tracking his movement. To his right, behind a cluttered counter, sat a stooped man in plum-colored robes, hunched over a ledger.

Each item bore a white placard:

A barrel of long rods: *Everflame Torch – 250 Gold (Magical flame that never goes out. No heat.)*

Neatly folded cloaks: *Waterproof Traveler's Cloak – 400 Gold (Keeps wearer bone dry—even underwater!)*

A stack of round tins: *Wakeful Mints – 40 Gold per pack (Mild enchanted candies to aid alertness.)*

Rad stepped closer to a glass case of jewelry. Brooches, rings, amulets, and bracelets sat beneath the glass, each labeled with enchantments—protection, clarity, resistance...

"Is there something specific you're after?" the man behind the counter rasped, his voice like parchment being crumpled. "Or are you just another curious lad I'll have to chase out?"

Rad turned. The man was older but sharp-eyed, small and stooped, with shaggy white brows and three pairs of spectacles dangling from cords around his neck.

"I was curious," Rad admitted. "I saw a green light—or maybe purple—through the window."

The wizard flicked his finger. A glowing disc zipped from his hand, circled the room, then returned to his palm. "Like that?"

Rad nodded. "Yes. That's what I saw. My name's Radcliffe von Schule."

The wizard lifted one pair of spectacles to his face and squinted. "Magister Pellimor Thatch," he said, puffing his chest. He stepped out from behind the counter and gave Rad a closer look. "Von Schule, is it? I worked on *Château Saignoral* once—permanent lights in the cellar. Do the sconces flicker when it rains?"

"Not that I know of."

"Water-triggered enchantments are fickle."

"Noted," Rad said as he crossed his arms.

He peered at Rad again. "You don't favor your father."

"I take after my mother, Justine. My brother Tristin looks more like Da—except lighter hair."

"Ah. And what brings you here, Master Radcliffe? Perhaps a flickerstone for reading? Anti-stink crystals for your boots? You look like a working lad."

Rad's insides dipped, remembering teasing Abby about her stinky socks. He wished she was alive so he could tease her—or gift her these crystals as a jest. "How long do the crystals last?"

Pellimor shrugged. "Depends how stinky your boots are."

"Normal?"

"Then a few months. After that, they stop working. Over-saturated." He waved a hand. "What about the flickerstone? Handy for reading under the covers at night."

"I have plenty of places to read with normal light. I do like to write though."

"Then you, my lad, might appreciate one of my finest creations." Pellimor's eyes gleamed. "Behold—the Scribing Heuristic Apparatus for Repetitive Penmanship & Ink Engagement. Writes endlessly. Never runs dry. Never fails. I've got one right here. Careful—the ink's permanent. And I mean permanent."

He flourished a wooden quill from his pocket. His fingers were stained black.

Rad examined it, careful not to touch the tip. He drew a straight line on a parchment placard. The ink flowed smooth and dark.

"If it's permanent, you should sell it to tattoo artists," Rad said.

Pellimor froze. Then his eyes widened. "A Dermaglyphic Imprinter of Eternal Enchantment! Guaranteed to last longer than regret! Brilliant! My D.I.E.E. line—pronounced *dye*—will be a sensation!"

Rad grinned. "How much for the Scribing quill?"

"I call it SHARPIE for short. Normally one hundred gold. For you—ninety."

Rad handed it back. "I can't afford that."

"You're a von Schule. Put it on your father's account."

Rad shook his head. Going around town and racking up debt in Xavier's name would have dire consequences. "Not without his permission. Thank you, though. It's an interesting shop."

Pellimor's shoulders sagged. "Very well," he said, sliding the quill back into his ink-stained pocket. "Good day to you."

Rad turned to leave. As he opened the door, Pellimor called after him.

"Von Schule—I can't let you leave empty-handed."

Rad turned in time to catch a small tin tossed his way.

"Wakeful Mints," Pellimor said. "If you need to stay up all night, take one. Only one. Instructions are on the back."

Rad flipped the tin.

Do not exceed one mint per day.

"What happens if I take two?"

"The magical effect is exponential," Pellimor said with a sly grin.

"Math," Rad muttered. "Exponential..."

"Yes. One mint—twelve hours of wakefulness. Two—twenty-four. Three—forty-eight."

"Four would be ninety-six hours."

"Exactly!" Pellimor said, delighted to find a fellow mathematician. "Six would keep you up for two weeks."

Rad shook the tin. "Let me guess, only six in here?"

"That's all anyone needs," Pellimor said.

"Thanks. I'll put them to good use."

"Farewell, von Schule. Until we meet again."

Rad turned down the lane, grinning as he pocketed the tin.

I wonder how many I can sneak into Wilkins' bourbon.

Two weeks had passed.

Rad stood near the librarian's desk, his posture composed. Hands clasped behind his back, he maintained an air of calm, though restlessness simmered beneath his collected exterior.

The treatises were complete at last—bound, sealed, and awaiting his stepfather's review.

Ragna, having taken her final payment for organizing the contest, accepted an additional silver from Rad as assurance for her silence.

The gleam of coin had promised her discretion, but Rad's sharp instincts told him she might still whisper about the unusual contest if pressed.

Rad didn't mind.

Ragna had proven to be a great resource for navigating the complexities of the Ornst Library. He had joked once that she should run the place, and her answer had been a single upraised eyebrow.

Before him on the desk lay two sealed packages, thick with pages, their substantial weight promising a wealth of information.

He had a week to study them, decide on the winning entry, and announce the prize.

Yet Rad had no intention of letting either document slip from his grasp.

Both were critical to his secret pursuits.

The treatises held the potential answers to questions that had plagued him since the harrowing moment in the vault. He yearned to understand the sickness that had nearly claimed him—and, more importantly, to uncover a way back to the realm of the dead.

The voices of his Ma and Abby haunted his thoughts, their cryptic words filling him with both dread and determination.

If the scholars had uncovered even a fragment of truth, it might be enough to lead him toward understanding the mysterious force that now governed his life.

For a moment, he ran a finger across the edge of one package, the coarse paper crackling faintly under his touch.

A small plate of bread and cheese sat near his elbow, along with a cooling cup of tea he had pilfered from the kitchens.

Stolen tea tasted better.

He had brought the treatises straight to his room, settling in at his desk with supplies enough for a long night's work.

Within these volumes lay not just academic insights, but the threads of his own destiny.

He drew a slow breath, letting the weight of the moment settle over him, then reached for the first package.

The treatises surpassed Rad's expectations in both depth and complexity, though their intricacies proved more challenging to grasp than he had anticipated.

They would require careful study—and time.

One was titled *A Treatise on the Undead: Characteristics and Known Environments*, while the other bore the name *A Treatise on the Undead: A Compendium of Fiends*.

Despite their differing titles, their structures mirrored one another, organized with scholarly precision.

Each treatise began with a title page listing the authors, followed by a preface outlining the scope and intent of the work. The introductions provided succinct summaries, leading into chapters devoted to individual creatures.

These meticulous chapters explored each entity's nature, habits, vulnerabilities, and—perhaps more critical—its connection to the living world.

The concluding sections listed thorough bibliographies—sources, interviews, and evaluations of anecdotal evidence.

To Rad, the distinction between anecdotal and factual information was of little concern. He wasn't a scholar pursuing academic accuracy; he was a young man seeking answers.

Every word might hold a clue to what had happened when he touched the decrepit hand.

Somewhere in these pages, he hoped to uncover the key to understanding the sickness afflicting him—and the haunting connection it had forged between him and the realm of the dead.

As Rad delved into the treatises, he realized they were treasure troves of extraordinary knowledge.

The first treatise was a paragon of order, adhering to a strict and factual approach. It left blanks when information was incomplete or unverifiable, a restraint that only underscored its credibility.

The *Compendium*, by contrast, was less constrained. While it contained fewer hard facts, it overflowed with captivating tales of encounters with the undead, drawing him in with its vivid narratives.

Rad kept returning to those accounts, drawn by the chance they might explain his affliction.

Both treatises explored the origins and mechanics of the undead in remarkable depth, outlining their creation through reanimation, spells, atrocities, curses, and infections.

This strange knowledge felt personal to Rad.

The unknown sickness aligned with either a curse or an infection.

Infection seemed more likely; the rapid onset of his symptoms pointed to sickness invading his body the moment he touched it.

But what did it mean? Could he already be undead—or perhaps only partway there?

The question unsettled him.

The treatises cataloged an extensive array of undead beings: liches, shadow-fiends, skeletons, zombies, ghouls, blightghouls, mummies, wights, umbrals, will-o'-wisps, ghosts, shadows, specters, vestiges, vampires, vampire spawn, dread wolves, and wraiths.

Each entry bristled with details—some terrifying, others strangely poignant.

As he pored over these descriptions, Rad's suspicions turned inward.

Could he have become a ghost?

The idea troubled him as he pieced together the implications.

He lingered over the sections detailing ghosts and their peculiar dual existence in two planes of reality.

It was a revelation.

He had never considered that such planes existed—worlds of the living, the dead, and shadows, coexisting yet distinct.

According to the treatises, ghosts occupied both the Material Plane—where the living resided—and the Ethereal Plane, a ghostly realm of endless twilight.

A ghost could linger for eternity in the Ethereal Plane—unless the curse or unrest binding it to the living world was broken.

Rad mulled over what this could mean for him.

His encounters with the apparitions of Ma and Abby, the beckoning voices, the otherworldly fog—all pointed toward a connection to the Ethereal Plane.

Could it be that the decrepit hand had killed him, but his sheer will to live—or some latent power—had prevented his full transition to death?

Perhaps he had become part ghost, straddling the line between the living and the dead.

The idea was terrifying yet compelling.

If it were true, what did it mean for his future? Would the Ethereal Plane continue to call him, pulling him closer to its grasp?

Or could he find a way to sever the connection—and reclaim his life as it once was?

The treatises offered possibilities—startling, dangerous ones.

Some spells, when invoked, allowed purposeful travel to the ethereal realm.

Certain gateways naturally bridged the material and Ethereal Planes—unique locales steeped in mystery or latent magic.

What gripped him most was the idea that powerful beings—ghosts, in particular—could shift between worlds by force of will or sheer desperation.

The idea seized Rad's imagination.

Could he tap into such a power?

The prospect was equal parts thrilling and terrifying.

But if he was going to uncover the truth of his condition, experimentation was necessary.

In keeping with his charade, "Xavier von Schule" awarded the grand prize to the team behind *The Compendium* for their vivid and compelling accounts of the undead.

Rad penned a formal thank-you note on his stepfather's letterhead, a sheet he had pilfered from the study. He sealed it with the von Schule wax signet, the heavy impression lending weight to the lie.

To the other team, he sent a similar note—along with an extra gold coin for each participant, a nod to their meticulous efforts.

The contest was over.

It had cost him more gold than he liked—but he hadn't slogged through three million books alone, either.

He had used his imagination, his wits, and the resources of others to reach his goal.

That counted for something.

Rad allowed himself a brief moment of pride, then pushed it aside.

There were other tasks ahead.

And before he could face them, he needed answers—answers only Hadley might help him find.

Chapter Eighteen

∞

At Peace

Abby,

I miss you very much and hope to see you soon.

I have a theory.

The place where you are trapped is called the Ethereal Plane—a world of ghosts, spirits, and shadows. You and Ma are ghosts, for what reason, I can't fathom. I will figure this out.

I went to the Ornst Library.

Have you ever gone all the way up to the top?

I met a girl, Karin, and I used math to convince her to take me on my own tour of the observation deck.

Imagine that—math.

I saw *Château Saignoral*, the warehouse where I helped Tristin, and The Sweet Hatchet where Rosamund is.

I wish I could have stayed up there for an hour.

There's this woman, Ragna, who's almost as smart as you. She helped me organize a contest, even though she knew I was up to no good.

I talk to her anytime I'm at the library.

Aldric Thorne is like a walking history book, and he knows so much about magic and magic runes, as well as Elves.

(I think he speaks all Elven dialects.)

I don't know why he isn't one of the scholars, but he helped me figure out that my sword is named *Stalker* and is probably thousands of years old.

I went to this magic shop to see what they had there—everything costs too much. The wizard did give me these mints that make you stay awake. I dissolved them into that bourbon I nicked for Wilkins. If he drinks all of it, he might be awake for two weeks. Otherwise, he'll find it hard to sleep!

Well, I'll get this figured out.

I'm going to see Hadley.
I'll see you soon.
Love,
Rad.

Back at the estate, Rad tucked the treatises into the hidden compartment in his closet, confident they would remain undisturbed until he needed them again. With the task complete, he set off on a leisurely walk down to the temporary stables to see Hadley.

The crisp air carried the earthy scent of the estate, but Rad's mind was elsewhere. As he strolled, his mind turned over the logistics of crossing into the Ethereal Plane.

Could he summon the willpower necessary to step into the realm of the dead?

Or would desperation—a deep emotional trigger—be the key?

Questions swirled without answers, yet there was a flicker of determination. If his condition linked him to the Ethereal Plane, he would find a way to traverse it—and perhaps uncover the secrets his Ma had promised him.

Hadley stood by Moonsilver, nibbling on his well-worn pipe, the scent of spent tobacco faint in the cool air.

His strong, calloused fingers worked through the mare's mane, smoothing her striking gray coat adorned with its unique dapples.

Moonsilver stood serene, her temperament as balanced as her appearance, an elegant contrast to Hadley's rough demeanor.

Rad approached with a wave and posed his question.

"What do you know about will?"

Hadley turned, his face folding into a puzzled scowl. "Will? Who's Will?"

Rad chuckled.

"Not who—what. Willpower, like... forcing yourself to do something even when it feels impossible. I think that's what I need. That part of me that makes things happen."

Hadley considered this, stroking Moonsilver while he thought. "Willpower, eh? Hm. Tell me, lad—how do you throw a knife?"

Rad blinked.

"What do you mean?"

"Throw. How did you get so good at throwing knives?"

"Practice," Rad replied, not yet seeing where this was headed. "You mean I have to practice my willpower? That doesn't make any sense."

Hadley clapped him on the shoulder, the weight of it grounding Rad in place.

His gaze was sharp but kind.

"Listen. When you practice your throwing, what are you really doing? You're learning the moves, the rhythm, the 'dance' as you say. You know your knives—their weight, balance, and sharpness. You've trained your eyes to pick the target, your breathing to stay calm. By now, throwing is second nature to you. When you need to hit a target, your body obeys your mind's will without you thinking about it. That, lad, is willpower in action."

Rad frowned in thought, rolling the idea over in his mind.

"I guess it makes sense," he admitted, though it still felt abstract.

How could he practice transporting himself to the Ethereal Plane? How could willpower alone achieve something so impossible?

"So I just need to practice."

Hadley nodded. "Practice. Discipline. Both help. You hone it all like a blade. But tell me, what exactly are you trying to do?"

Rad hesitated, the weight of his secret pressing against his tongue.

"Trying to be better with weapons," he said at last, skirting the deeper truth. "When I turn sixteen, I'll have to leave. I need to be ready."

Hadley snorted, amused. "You're already an expert with knives. Blades too. Your sword work's coming along fine. Keep at it. Stick to those weapons, and you'll do well enough when you're out on your own."

Rad tried to soak in the praise but couldn't suppress the nagging uncertainty gnawing at his chest.

"You think so?"

"I know so," Hadley replied. "You're as deadly as any bowman at a good distance. You don't need long-range nonsense, not with your skill. Keep honing what you already know. Your willpower's there, lad—you just need to trust it."

Hadley's words settled in Rad's mind, heavier than he expected.

This would work.

Practice—focused, relentless practice—would unlock the willpower he needed to confront the impossible.

Rad nodded, murmuring agreement, his thoughts already slipping beyond the conversation.

He realized, with quiet relief, that Hadley wouldn't press further or offer unsolicited advice. It was better this way. Hadley's trust would keep his real purpose hidden—right where it needed to stay.

Still, Hadley's words lingered.

He was right about one thing: Rad needed to make traveling to the Ethereal Plane natural and effortless. His first crossing had been an accident, triggered by the curse—or sickness—left by the decrepit hand.

The other times had come in dreams, chaotic and unbidden, when his subconscious had been immersed in terror and confusion.

If his unconscious mind could pull him into the Ethereal Plane, then there had to be a way to consciously mimic the state of dreaming while awake.

But how?

It was a bold idea—bizarre, but worth attempting.

He decided he would try tonight.

"Thanks, Hadley," Rad said aloud, snapping back to the moment. "You're right. Swords and knives are second nature. I'll keep working on those. But I do want to improve with swords, hone my skills further. You up for it?"

"Aye," Hadley grumbled. "It'll sharpen you up, like I've been telling you."

Rad agreed with a small tilt of his head, filing the promise away for later.

After a moment, he said, "When I was at the library, a curator helped me figure out the runes on my sword. Its name is *Stalker*."

Hadley grunted, unimpressed.

"I like *Vanguard* better," he muttered.

Rad chuckled, the corners of his mouth lifting in a faint, fleeting smile.

"Me too," he admitted.

Rad recalled a passage from a book on enlightenment—meditation—bringing deep relaxation and heightened awareness. Seizing on the idea, he positioned himself in the center of his room, cross-legged on the wooden floor. He began with deliberate, rhythmic breaths, letting his chest rise and fall in a steady cadence.

His goal was simple yet profound: to empty his mind of all distractions and will himself to the Ethereal Plane—to pry open the elusive door between worlds and step through.

Despite his earnest efforts, nothing happened.

The stillness of the room mocked him.

Undeterred, Rad tried again the following night.

And the next.

And the one after.

Night after night passed, Rad seated in determined solitude, his breaths steady, his focus unwavering.

Each time, he hoped for a breakthrough.

Each time, only silence answered.

Frustration gnawed at him.

Rad was determined to solve the puzzle.

His evenings became a ritual of trial and error, his mind reaching inward to prod whatever latent force the decrepit hand had awakened in him.

Yet the stubborn barrier remained in place, immovable.

Meditation, he found, had other unexpected benefits.

It eased his tensions, sharpened his focus, and lent him a sense of clarity. But those small victories were dwarfed by his utter failure to travel to the Ethereal Plane.

What was missing?

A crucial piece of the puzzle remained out of reach.

A new idea began to coalesce at the back of his mind.

During his fleeting experiences with the Ethereal Plane, Ma and Abby had been present, their voices calling to him from the void.

Could it be his connection to them was the trigger he sought?

He spent subsequent nights weaving memories of them into his meditation, summoning their faces, their laughter, their warmth.

But the door remained shut.

In a moment of grim inspiration, Rad dredged up a darker memory—the bloodied bodies sprawled lifeless in the breakfast nook.

The scene blazed vivid in his mind, every detail sharp and nauseating. The anguish, the fury, the unbearable grief rose in his chest, a tidal wave threatening to consume him.

He recoiled from the mental image—but in doing so, he felt it: the first flicker, a shift, subtle but undeniable.

The key was pain.

The world dulled around him, colors bleeding into gray and muted tones, though everything still looked solid to his eyes.

A peculiar weightlessness overtook him, unfamiliar and disorienting.

He smelled nothing—not the faint scent of dust from his room nor the trace of wax from the candle he'd extinguished earlier.

The floor no longer pressed against his feet.

When he waved his hand, there was no resistance, no whisper of air.

It was as if every sensation tethering him to the material world had been stripped away.

Then came the voices.

Distant and indistinct at first, they grew sharper with every heartbeat, calling to him in an eerie chorus—each voice unique, yet blending into a singular presence.

They knew he was here.

The denizens of the cemetery had been waiting.

Rad stepped forward, his movements effortless and fluid, as if gravity no longer bound him.

His footfalls were silent, his balance steady, as if walking on a soft cushion of air.

When he reached the door, he instinctively reached for the handle—only to watch his hand pass through it as if it wasn't there.

Startled, he tried again, and once more his fingers traveled through the surface without resistance.

For a moment, he stood frozen, staring at his hand buried halfway through the door, caught between disbelief and awe.

But rather than pulling back, he steeled himself—and stepped forward.

The door yielded without resistance, and Rad stepped through, unscathed—and somehow invigorated.

Rad moved with purpose now, willing himself toward the staircase.

Each step was more thought than action, his body flowing down the stairs like a stream following its course. He moved faster than he expected, unbound by the usual constraints of muscle and effort.

A surge of exhilaration coursed through him.

He wasn't just walking—he was gliding, navigating the world as a ghost, not flesh and bone.

The distant voices grew louder as he approached the outer door, carrying with them an unmistakable pull.

His heart swelled with anticipation.

Outside.

That was where Ma and Abby would be waiting.

The thought of seeing them again—not as echoes of memory but as something real and present—filled him with joy. He pressed onward, his resolve growing stronger with every silent step.

Rad's concentration faltered.

A stray thought broke his focus—and an unnatural wave of nausea surged through him.

The solid feel of wood beneath his slippers snapped him back to the material world—and before he could react, he slammed into the door.

The impact sent a sharp crack echoing down the corridor, loud enough to still the air.

Panic clutched at his chest, hot and sudden.

With the estate on constant alert since the Black Storm attack, even the smallest noise drew scrutiny.

A single clatter could bring footsteps.

A thud like that might bring guards.

The outdoors beckoned—if someone caught him heading toward the stables, it could pass as routine.

He took a step, then saw his feet.

Slippers.

His heart sank.

No one wore slippers outside.

Not this late.

Not in this weather.

He pivoted, scanning the room for cover.

There.

An overstuffed chair stood like a sentry, its broad back casting a deep shadow.

Rad moved fast and quiet, slipping behind it. He folded himself into a crouch, limbs tucked close, spine curved like a bowstring.

Breath shallow.

Muscles tight.

The nausea pulsed at the edges of his awareness, but he buried it—stillness was all that mattered now.

Seconds stretched.

Every creak in the walls, every soft footfall in the hall became a threat.

He pressed himself deeper into the shadows and waited.

Rad's pulse held steady as the footsteps grew louder, their echoes magnified by his sharpened senses.

He braced for discovery, each breath slow, every movement honed to silence.

The clop of boots rang in his ears—Wilkins.

The valet's measured gait gave him away before his voice confirmed it, edged with suspicion.

"What are you doing here?"

Rad tensed, every muscle drawn tight. Wasn't he still hidden? Had he made a mistake?

Tristin's voice cut through the moment.

"I heard something. I was in the pantry looking for cheese. Sounded like a door banging shut. Did someone go in or out?"

More footsteps joined the fray—heavier, purposeful.

Guards.

Their boots thudded like a storm gathering around Rad's hiding place.

He held his breath, ears tuned to every voice as four men began to discuss.

"Could've been a door," one guard offered.

"Back door's locked," said another.

"It's undisturbed. What if someone unlocked it from the outside, slipped in, shut it too hard, and relocked it?"

Rad rolled his eyes.

Idiots.

No thief smart enough to pick a lock would be dumb enough to slam the door behind them.

"Doesn't make sense," Tristin cut in, echoing Rad's thoughts. "Why would a thief be that careless? And why the back door? This time of night, people are still awake. When Ma and Abby were killed, it was the dead of night."

Wilkins sneered. "What made the noise, then? Perhaps it was your sneaky little brother."

Fear lingered.

If they decided to search the lounge, they'd find him. No question.

The thought seized him.

His instincts screamed—run.

Bolt from the hiding place, crash through the door, flee into the night, no matter where it led.

But he didn't.

Not now.

Not like this.

Rad held still, white-knuckled fingers digging into the frame of the chair.

He slowed his breathing, forcing calm into his limbs. Every muscle remained coiled, ready to strike or flee.

Images of Ma and Abby surged forward, cruel and vivid—slit throats, pale skin, blood pooled beneath them.

The memory was a knife to the gut.

Nausea clutched him hard, and he swallowed it back, jaw clenched tight.

Then the world tilted.

A sickening rush of detachment swept over him.

Color drained from the room.

Sound dulled.

His body lightened.

The nausea dissolved—replaced by the ghostly silence of the Ethereal Plane.

Soundless and unseen, Rad slipped from behind the chair, each movement fluid and unstoppable.

He reached the nearest wall, his ghostly form passing through the plaster without resistance.

He emerged into the kitchen, where warm lantern light gilded clean counters and orderly tools.

Relief surged through him as he shed the Ethereal Plane—his body solid once more.

He stepped lightly, passing the butcher block, his slippers silent against the cool stone floor.

His target: the smaller pantry cloaked in shadow.

He slipped inside, crouching low, breath steady.

From there, he crossed into the vacant dining room, moving along the walls, careful to avoid the tall-backed chairs that loomed like silent watchers in the faint light.

From his shadowed vantage, Rad spotted the grand staircase framed by an archway to his right.

Beyond it, Wilkins, Tristin, and two guards prowled the floor, searching for any sign of an intruder. Their backs were turned—a slim window of opportunity.

He removed his slippers and held them in one hand. He padded up the staircase, his stockinged feet silent on the wood.

Step by step, floor by floor, he climbed—silent and unseen.

No one glanced up.

No one noticed.

At his door, he eased it shut behind him and exhaled slowly, a breath he'd been holding since the lounge.

He'd been careless.

He wouldn't make that mistake again.

Tomorrow, he'd try again—smarter, sharper.

He had to master the Ethereal Plane.

It was the only way to reach Ma and Abby in the world of the dead.

Weeks slipped past, blurring into months.

Rad discovered summoning the grim memories of his Ma and Abby's murders elicited an anguish deep enough to trigger his ability to travel to the Ethereal Plane.

Though the trips were brief, lasting only a few minutes at most, they were far from wasted.

Each visit to the gray, insubstantial realm was spent learning—observing his surroundings while avoiding contact with the dead.

The more time he spent there, the more attention he drew from the spirits of the Ethereal Plane.

He realized this attention intensified near cemeteries or burial sites.

When he ventured into the city, far from *Château Saignoral* and its cemetery, he found he could explore the plane for longer periods without drawing unwanted notice.

This newfound freedom proved invaluable.

He discovered that traveling through the Ethereal Plane granted him access to the most secure locations.

Rad honed his ability until he could use it with precision.

By briefly slipping into the Ethereal Plane, he could pass through walls. He would reappear just long enough to interact with objects in the material world, then vanish back into the gray realm to escape.

With that skill, he could steal almost anything he desired. Through careful practice, he determined he could carry about fifty pounds—enough to lift a gold bar or other valuable items—and still have the energy to phase back and forth.

This skill wasn't limited to theft.

He realized he could eavesdrop on private conversations, using the plane as both a hiding place and a gateway to rooms sealed from prying eyes.

Every night, Rad practiced in secret, refining his talent—shaping it into a tool that gave him an edge in the city soon to be his home.

The shadow of his sixteenth birthday loomed, a constant reminder of his precarious future. When it arrived, he would be turned out into a harsh and unforgiving world.

But now, with his talent growing sharper each night, he was determined to be ready.

In the Ethereal Plane, the world was a strange fusion of surrealism and tangibility. The spectral landscape exuded a sense of both familiarity and alienness.

Shadows stretched unnaturally long, and faint glimmers of mysterious lights occasionally danced in the gray mist.

Tonight, Rad moved through the otherworldly domain, his steps fueled by an unrelenting desire to find the spectral forms of his mother and sister.

The night was deep and cold, the heart of winter pressing down hard.

Rad's breath crystallized in the air, but his heart burned with the need to see Ma and Abby.

He hurried through the snow, his boots crunching with each step, leaving a trail of prints he couldn't avoid.

The faster he moved through the material world, the less time he would need to risk in the Ethereal Plane before finding them.

Ahead lay the cemetery, glowing with an unearthly luminescence. It stretched out like a solemn congregation of gravestones, the winter mist swirling among them.

He imagined ghostly figures hovering above the earth—ethereal beings caught between the worlds of the living and the departed. He couldn't see them, but he knew their movements—slow, languid, and devoid of purpose—mirrored the sorrowful stasis of death.

At the cemetery gates, he drew a deep breath and steadied his mind.

The familiar shift overtook him—his body shimmered, ghostly and transparent, as he stepped into the Ethereal Plane.

The chill of winter dissipated, replaced by the eerie stillness of the spectral realm.

His surroundings softened, the gravestones and trees blurring as if seen through a veil of mist.

And there they were.

Ma and Abby stood amidst the mist, their translucent forms distinct and shimmering in the dim glow of the plane.

Ma's expression was a bittersweet mixture of longing and sorrow, her eyes fixed on him with a depth of emotion that pierced his heart.

Abby's face was marked with sadness, her usual vibrance muted but not gone.

Rad drew closer, his heart both aching and swelling with an impossible sense of reunion.

The air around them was alive with a bittersweet energy, a tug of connection and separation he couldn't explain.

For a moment, he felt as though he were home—the three of them together again in this strange place between worlds.

He ached to touch them, to reach out and grasp their hands as he once had in life.

But he reminded himself of the rule he dared not break.

To touch them was to court disaster; he did not know what it would do to them—or to him.

He made a silent vow to maintain his distance, though the yearning threatened to overwhelm him.

"Ma," Rad began, his voice a whispered echo in the spectral silence of the Ethereal Plane.

Ma's translucent gaze met his, her eyes glimmering with bittersweet recognition.

"Radcliffe," she murmured, her voice carrying the soft resonance of a distant memory. "Have you come to join us?"

Beside her, Abby's form flickered faintly, her expression etched with grief and resignation.

"I don't want to be like this," Abby confessed, her voice trembling with sorrow. "I miss everything… our life. We're dead, yet we aren't."

Rad's chest tightened at the sight of his half-sister's anguish.

"Abby," he said, his tone tender. "I promise. I'll help you find peace—so you can rest."

A faint glow of maternal warmth emanated from Ma's spectral form, and for a fleeting moment, Abby's sorrow eased.

Ma stepped closer, her voice heavy with unspoken truths.

"Radcliffe, there's something you need to know," she said.

"I already know," Rad interjected, his voice steady. "I know my real father is Lanny Zeh."

Ma floated closer than he liked, her diaphanous presence unsettling, though he sensed affection beneath it.

Abby recoiled, caught in an invisible current, her translucent form shivering with unease.

She drifted away from them, her face twisted with hurt and confusion, as if the truth itself repelled her.

Ma lifted a ghostly hand, pointing toward the distant manor.

"I loved him," she said, her voice tinged with yearning. "And he loved me. We saw each other in secret, and I was ready to leave Xavier for Lan. I was going to take you, my unborn child, and start over. But he disappeared, Radcliffe. He abandoned me. My heart has never known greater sadness."

"Xavier killed him," Rad said, anger tightening his voice. "He trapped him in a collapsed tunnel beneath the manor. I found his remains. I'll bury them out here, next to you and Abby, so you can be at peace with his death. So he can be at peace."

"Xavier," Ma's spectral form hissed. "Xavier murdered him?"

"Yes," Rad answered, his voice soft. "He didn't abandon you. Take comfort. He loved you."

"How did he die?"

"Poison," he replied.

Rad felt the spectral air shift—subtle, but undeniable.

"I don't have much time," he said, searching for the source. "Tell me what he was like."

Ma's gaze flickered with fondness, warmer than her spectral form.

"He was everything I wanted in a man," she said with a wistful smile. "Charming, passionate, and daring. He promised to take care of me, of us, and to give us a new life. He was admired and feared in Leskaré, known for his schemes and his willingness to risk everything. He loved to fight, and he moved like he was born with a blade in his hand. There was beauty in the way he did it. But more than anything—his heart was mine, and mine was his. You, Radcliffe, are the proof of our love."

Rad's heart surged with tangled emotions as her words sank in.

He opened his mouth to press for more—but the air rippled, a tremor sharp and wrong, crawling across his skin and freezing him in place.

The cemetery grew darker, the mists thickening as new figures emerged.

Other ghosts coalesced from the gloom, their flickering forms heavy with malevolent intent.

They moved toward Rad with chilling purpose, their presence bearing an unmistakable threat.

Fear shot through him like ice.

He understood their intent with crystal clarity—they sought to take his life in this plane, to extinguish his existence in both worlds.

His resolve flared, and he began to back away.

"I can't stay," he told Ma, his voice edged with panic. "They're coming for me."

"Radcliffe, remember this," she called after him, her voice a fading echo as he willed himself back to the Material Plane.

Cold enveloped him as the ethereal world dissolved.

He stumbled back into the snowy cemetery, the night's chill biting into his skin.

The moonlit silence of the physical world offered a brief respite, but the air carried a strange unease.

Snapping around, he scanned the grounds, half-expecting a ghost to cross into the Material Plane in pursuit.

The moonlight shimmered—and Ma appeared again, her spectral form cloaked in mist. Her eyes bore into his with an intensity that sent shivers down his spine.

"Remember who you are," she said softly, her words carrying a weight he didn't yet understand.

Before he could respond, she vanished, leaving only the silent, snow-covered cemetery in her wake.

Later that week, Rad buried the bones in the cemetery beside Ma and Abby, marking the grave with a flat stone etched simply: 'L.Z.' It wasn't a grand memorial, but it was dignified—fitting for a man who had lived a shadowed life and met an unjust end.

Parting words were hard to find; speaking of a father he had never known felt almost insurmountable.

This man, Lanny Zeh, hadn't lived to see his son born or to fulfill the promises he had made to Ma.

"I hope this brings you peace," Rad whispered, "and I hope it brings her peace too."

He stepped back, letting the silence speak for what he couldn't find the words to say.

The following nights, Rad ventured to the Ethereal Plane with cautious optimism.

Ma appeared to him, her form radiating a calm he hadn't seen before. She was more at ease, her gaze no longer shadowed with longing or regret.

Though their conversations were brief, she often thanked him, her gratitude as soothing as her presence.

Abby, however, remained hesitant.

She hovered at the edges, her spirit too skittish to draw close, retreating when the restless dead began to gather.

Rad didn't press her, sensing it would only cause her distress. He focused on Ma, treasuring their moments despite the growing interference from the other spirits.

But as the restless dead became bolder, their interruptions grew more dangerous.

One night, after summoning Ma and Abby from their graves, he was met instead by a horde of malevolent specters, their intentions clear as they surged toward him.

Escaping back to the Material Plane left him shaken and drained.

Three more attempts yielded the same result—restless spirits arriving in droves, while Ma and Abby stayed absent, their peace untouchable now that Lanny Zeh had been laid to rest and the truth laid bare.

Rad, understanding the finality of it, stopped calling for them.

He told himself it was for their sake, though part of him ached with the loss of their brief reunions.

What mattered most was that they were at peace.

The connection may have faded in the ethereal, but it lived on in his memories—and in the truths they had shared.

He knew now who his father was—a man once feared and admired within Leskaré.

After all these years, someone in that dastardly organization had to remember him.

One day, when the time was right, he would find them.

He would ask about the infamous Lanny Zeh.

Abby,

I've stopped visiting you and Ma in the cemetery. I'm sorry—it's too dangerous now.

I don't know what would happen if the malevolent spirits caught me, much less touched me.

But I think about you both often.

I know you're at peace, and that brings me some comfort.

I'm sorry about the truth Ma revealed.

I understand now why you recoiled, why you stayed on the edges and watched instead of speaking. It wasn't me you were avoiding—it was the weight of what Ma said.

For her to admit she would have abandoned you, Tristin, Bella, and Marie for me and my father... it must have broken your heart all over again.

Even in death, it must still hurt.

I want to tell you about my real father, Abby.

Why I am who I am.

When I spoke with Ma afterward—those few times before it grew too dangerous—she told me things she hadn't said in life. She said Lanny Zeh used to leave her wildflowers hidden around the estate. Not bouquets—just small, scraggly things tucked into corners only she would find.

She said he called her his better life, not just his better half.

She said he laughed like a free man, even when he was hunted.

I don't know what kind of man my father was beyond the stories she gave me—charming, dangerous, daring.

But Ma believed in him.

And she believed in me.

She told me she carried me with pride, even when she was trapped here, even when she thought hope was lost.

I hold onto that now.

My focus has to be on surviving the world I'll face when Xavier finally turns me out.

Hadley's training is intense, but it's keeping me sharp.

I'm pushing myself every day.

The Ornst Library has become my haven—Xavier allows me that much, at least, on my day off.

I miss you, Abby.

I'll keep writing until the day I die and can finally join you in the beyond.

For now, I'll hold this journal close to my heart, and treasure every memory I have of you, my wonderful sister.

I don't know where this path will lead.

But wherever it does, you'll always be part of it.

With love,

Rad.

Chapter Nineteen

∞

Gone and Forgotten

Abby,

The snow is deep this year.

The boys sled down the hills, and I joined them for once.

It was like being free again, like when we were kids.

Hadley pulled long sleds with the horses. Groups of little ones took turns riding around the estate—they were so happy.

It meant extra work cleaning up, but it was worth it.

On the way back, a snowball fight broke out.

Wilkins stormed in to stop it, but I couldn't resist—pegged him right in the head.

You would've laughed so hard.

Best of all, I didn't get caught!

Wilkins has been complaining that he can't sleep—the wakeful mints are working. He's grumpy and tired—that lout deserves it.

Love,

Rad.

Abby,

The snow's gone, but the cold lingers.

A shipment of artwork came for Xavier—paintings, pottery, musical instruments. I caught a glimpse before it was locked away with the rest of the treasures in the cellar.

How much of it is real, I wonder—or are these, like the Sonner wine, more fakes for him to profit from?

I overheard guards talking about strangers spotted near the southern edge of the estate.

I had to see for myself.

There's a hidden entrance to the sewers there—stone walkways, almost like it was made for smugglers, not just to carry water and waste.

I wondered if that was how the Black Storm got onto the grounds without being seen by the guards.

I investigated, but the smell was unbearable. I didn't get far.

I chained the door shut.

No one's sneaking onto the estate, not while I'm here.

Love,

Rad.

Abby,

Happy Birthday!

You would have been eighteen today.

I'm sorry you're not here.

It was my fault.

Spring is here, and everyone's leaving except Tristin.

Bella and Marie left for Haddensack with Gabrielle and Xavier to go to court, along with an army of escorts. They took Jamie to manage the horses along the road, so it's just me and Hadley now.

Wilkins went with them.

I hope he finds a new home in Haddensack.

Maybe King Eldric will be so impressed by how he kisses arse, he'll keep him.

I wish you could've gone—you were supposed to.

I noticed Xavier packed the full set of armor with the falcon crest that used to be locked in the vault.

I'm guessing it's tied to the Haddensacks, given their sigil is the falcon.

He also took a bunch of the fake wine—crates of it—no doubt to sell.

Love,

Rad.

Abby,

With everyone gone, I've been spending a lot of time in the city.

Hadley and I finish our work and head into the city for a drink now and then.

I see Rosamund whenever I can. We talked about the future—about us. She laughed when I said we'd be together, but I meant it.

I don't think she was expecting me to feel this way.

She cried—happy tears—when I told her I meant it. I've never seen her cry before. It made me feel... something I can't describe.

I wish you could meet her. She's wonderful.

You two would be best friends, I'm sure of it.

Love,

Rad.

Abby,

They're back from their long trip. Bella and Marie are full of stories about Haddensack's court—the King's decadence, the wealth on display.

Prince Haden was quite the charmer, but no marriage proposals—no Princess Bella or Princess Marie.

Jamie practically ran to Florence.

I didn't have the heart to tell him what Tristin's been up to with her.

I wish Xavier would put a stop to it.

Poor Jamie.

He doesn't have a clue.

Love,

Rad.

Abby,

It's unbearably hot.

The grasses are yellow and brittle. Open flames are banned for fear of fire, and Hadley keeps extra barrels of water near every building—just in case. The whole estate feels dry enough to burn with a single spark.

Tristin left for Pehrone with a guard entourage. They say he'll be gone for months. I heard whispers it's not just for politics—there's talk of a match being arranged. Some girl from a good family I suppose.

Maybe he's lucky, getting out of here with a future waiting for him.

Suitors are already circling Bella and Marie. Xavier keeps turning them away, saying they'll wait a few more years yet.

They aren't happy about it.

But what they want doesn't matter here.

Sometimes it feels like we're all waiting—for something to happen, for something to end.

Love,

Rad.

Abby,

I turned fifteen.

One year left.

Hadley took me to The Sweet Hatchet again. Rosamund and I spent time together, talking about the future.

I miss your birthday gifts, especially the chocolates.

I went to the library and found books on druids—fascinating stories about their connection to nature.

Did you know they can cure blight in trees? And they carry these special staves to measure trees—and they can walk right into one tree and step out miles away through another! All because of The One Tree.

(Just like me, ancient and wise.)

Magic is so incredible.

Love,

Rad.

Abby,

Xavier threw another gala—not for wine this time, but for his Elven art collection.

He sold some pieces to eager patrons who got into a bidding war. I've never seen Xavier so smug.

Bella and Marie stole the spotlight as usual, entertaining suitors.

One of them, Beck Hogarth, was an oaf, rude to a servant. He needs a swift kick in the arse.

Tristin's back from Pehrone.

He's... different.

There's talk he met someone there—but knowing Xavier, it was probably planned all along.

Love,

Rad.

Abby,

I visited your grave and Ma's.

Left flowers for you both.

It felt like so little. Two bouquets for two lives.

But it's all I have to give you now.

The orchard is half gone—blight took the trees. I pleaded with them to find a druid—someone who could heal it. They ignored me. Scoffed at the idea of calling anyone to help.

Now the bonfires burn day and night as they clear the dead wood.

It's hard to watch.

The air stinks of smoke, and there's an emptiness spreading through the fields where the orchard used to stand.

I'm sure they'll replant it eventually.

But some of those trees had to be a hundred years old.

You can't just replace something like that.

Not really.

(Maybe magic could.)

Love,

Rad.

Abby,

I went to a celebration at the library. Brought a bottle of bourbon—figured I should contribute something.

Jamie came with me, though I wish I could've taken Rosamund instead.

The party was modest, but good. I'm starting to like wine, believe it or not. Hadley would call me a show-off if he saw how much I've learned about it from the books I've been reading.

I spent a good part of the evening teasing Karin about math. She's hopeless at it, but she takes it well—usually with a shove or a threat to make me shelve books all night. There are times I think Karin is a long-lost sister.

It's nice, having someone to joke with.

(One day, I think she'll surprise everyone.)

There was an interesting discussion too—about an old Elven place called Suriharon.

Aldric Thorne said it was a city of knowledge.

Others said it was a shrine, guarded by a Watcher who knew more than any Elf alive.

No one at the party could agree exactly what happened there—whether the Watcher was honored or betrayed.

But the way they spoke about it… it made you wonder if the place still exists.

And if it does, what secrets it's keeping.

Ragna was in rare form—sharp as ever.

She even challenged me to invite her to a gala at my house someday.

I told her I would.

And I meant it.

Maybe not today.

Maybe not tomorrow.

But someday.

When I see Rosamund these days, we hold hands and talk about our future. It's comforting to know we'll be together, even if I haven't figured out exactly how yet.

Love,

Rad.

Abby,

The snow's heavier than last year. There's so much you can't see any of the pathways or roads.

It's like the whole city's been smothered under a dirty white blanket.

Nobody knows what to do with it.

The city's a mess.

The estate's no better.

I'm stuck inside most days, waiting for it to melt, watching the same walls close in tighter.

Xavier's barely pretending to work.

He spends most of his time with Gabrielle now—she's not the governess anymore, of course.

We don't *need* one.

Yet he hasn't married her. Or if he has, no one's bothered to tell the servants.

Tristin's in the study more than Xavier these days.

I've never seen him open the vault door, though. So that secret hasn't been passed on yet.

Sometimes I think about stealing from Xavier. Taking back something—anything.

But I can't bring myself to do it.

His money's filthy.

He killed my father.

I don't want anything that carries his stink.

I just want out.

I can't wait to be away from this place—away from the rot, away from the lies—on my own, making my way with Rosamund by my side.

Soon.

Soon.

Love,

Rad.

Abby,

Hadley and I visit The Sweet Hatchet often these days.

Xavier doesn't care.

Somehow, I think Gabrielle's been a positive influence on him.

Perhaps.

Hadley's arms have fully healed, but he's slower now. He won't admit it, but I see it.

I see him tiring faster.

I see him standing still longer.

He won't leave the estate with me when the time comes. He's too loyal—stubborn as an old mule. It makes me mad, knowing he's resolved to stay behind, like he still owes Xavier anything.

He promised to join me one day.

But I'll believe that when I see it.

Still—Hadley gave me his word.

When the day comes, he'll be there. He'll walk me out of this place himself. Guard me one last time.

I hold onto that.

Love,

Rad.

Abby,

Six months.

Six months and I'm out on the streets.

Time feels like it's slipping away.

Hadley's teaching me even more about swordplay.

He says I'm improving, but I lack aggression.

He doesn't understand—I don't want to lose control.

He says sometimes I'll have to. That losing control is the key to survival.

He asked me, "How many swordfights can you lose?"

I shrugged.

I wasn't sure.

He said, "None. Lose one and you're dead."

That rattled me.

To think Hadley never lost a swordfight all these years.

I took it to heart.

Next time we train, I'm going to let go of my restraint.

(If I don't write, it's because Hadley killed me.)

(Accidentally.)

Love,

Rad.

Abby,

I found a place to rent above JP's locksmith shop in the city. It's small, but it's mine. Once I turn sixteen, I'll be able to move in and work for him full-time.

It feels strange, having a plan.

A real plan.

No more guessing where I'll sleep or how I'll eat.

No more skulking these halls full of hollow people and liars.

Just work. Just earning my way.

JP's teaching me the locksmith trade already. He says I've got good hands for it—quick, steady, careful. Maybe it's in the blood.

Turns out he knew my father.

Knew Lanny Zeh from his old days in Leskaré.

He said Zeh was cold, calculating, and fearless. That he could steal anything from anyone—but it wasn't the stealing that made him dangerous.

It was the way he saw people.

Saw through them.

And didn't bow to anyone's idiocy or whims.

JP said that's why Zeh made so many enemies—and fiercer friends. He wouldn't play dumb for anyone, and he let everyone know it. Wouldn't bend the knee, even when it would've been smarter—or safer.

I listened without saying much.

He sounds a lot like me.

(I don't know if that is good or bad.)

You're the only one who knows the truth.

I didn't tell JP who I really am.

Not yet.

Maybe not ever.

Hearing about Lanny Zeh makes me feel closer to him. But it also makes me miss Ma even more. She loved him, flaws and all.

Sometimes I wonder if I'm chasing devils all the way to the Nine Hells by asking about him.

Looking for answers to questions I can't even name.

There must be others who knew him, who loved him—or hated him.

Others who could tell me more.

But I don't know what good it would do me.

Knowing won't bring him back. It won't change anything.

Maybe it's better to let the past stay buried—and forge my own path.

Love,

Rad.

Abby,

Your birthday passed.

You would have been nineteen.

I left flowers on your grave and thought about who you might've been—a shining star at every gala, at court, wherever you walked.

I'm sure you would have ended up with Robert Ruud. He adored you even back then. And if you had married him—I could have worked for you.

At your home.

Not as a servant, not really—more like family.

I imagine it sometimes. Rosamund could have been your governess, helping raise your children.

We'd steal Hadley away from Xavier, have him running the stables like they were the king's own.

Jamie could have been your valet, loyal and proud.

We would've built a house full of laughter and loyalty.

A place without cruelty. Without fear.

(With lots of chocolates.)

It would have been a good life.

(With even more chocolates.)

A real life.

(And those sugar cookies that I got sick on when I threw up in that vase.)

I didn't realize it until now—how close I might've been to something better.

How much you would have saved me, just by being alive.

It's getting harder, Abby.

Harder to pretend it doesn't hurt.

Harder to pretend it's only the past.

I miss you.

Always.

(To be honest, you've saved me anyway.)

Love,
Rad.

Abby,

The starlings came back—you know what we must do.
Hadley and I took care of them—twenty in total.

Xavier's talking about building a second stable now. Raising horses as a business. Getting richer. Expanding.

But it doesn't matter to me.

I don't care.

Not one bit.

Let him build his empire of rot.

In two months, I'll be gone.

I'll walk out of this place and never look back.

I won't have to breathe the same air as that vile man ever again.

(But sometimes I wonder—what about Bella and Marie?)

(What if the rot spreads to them too?)

(What if Tristin turns out worse than Da?)

(I won't be there to protect them.)

(Who will protect them... from themselves?)

Love,
Rad.

Abby,

Two months.

The nights are restless, and sometimes I can't eat.

I'm not worried—just anxious.

To start my new life.

(Or that's what I keep telling myself.)

Meditation helps a little.

But the thought of leaving keeps me awake more nights than not.

My clothes are tight now—not because I'm fat, but because I'm stronger. I actually have muscles.

Not that I've been admiring myself in the mirror or anything.

(Only Tristin does. He probably kisses his reflection goodnight.)

Love,

Rad.

Abby,

I spoke with Aldric Thorne again. I asked about the *Librums*—not directly, just enough to get him talking. I think he knew I'd ask eventually.

He didn't say much, but what he did say... it confirms a few things.

The Mages didn't just shape the world—they tore it apart. The *Librums* were how they did it. Not wands or staffs or grand rituals. Books.

Aldric thinks some of the *Librums* still exist. Not in plain sight. Hidden. Lost. Guarded. Maybe even still working.

He said, "Some books don't want to be read, Rad. Some read you back."

That stuck with me.

I know there are nine of them. Each does something different. One can build anything. One unravels what's been built. One trains warriors. Another heals—or harms—depending on the hand that opens it.

And one... one walks between worlds.

I don't think people really understand what they are. Even now.

Aldric told me to be cautious. That things written in the time of the Mages don't always stay written. Some books change when you open them. Others change *you*.

I haven't stopped thinking about them. If even one *Librum* still exists, I want to find it. Not for power. Just to understand.

Maybe that's how it starts.

Love, Rad.

Abby,

It's almost time for me to go.

The next time I write to you, I'll be on my own.

I've been doing work for JP—stealing jewelry and trinkets.

I know what you're thinking. But don't be ashamed of me.

It's a living. It will keep me out of the gutters. JP says to keep the jobs small.

Stay unnoticed.

Stay safe.

Stay away from the militia—and from Leskaré.

I'm ready now. Ready to make my own way. Ready to live my life. But I'll never forget you.

I'll keep writing to you—always.

I miss you more than words can say.

The time has come.

Soon, I'll be <u>gone</u> and <u>forgotten</u>.

And I'm at peace with it.

You should be too.

Love,
Rad.

CHAPTER TWENTY

∞

Ruminations

The feeling Rad experienced wasn't dread. It was a blend of curiosity about what lay ahead—and a spark of excitement for the future. It was his sixteenth birthday, and he had no illusions about what the day meant. He imagined Xavier von Schule storming into his room to declare the time had come—*Get out. Never come back.*

Despite the sweat and effort he'd poured into *Château Saignoral,* nothing could extend his stay past this day.

He was ready.

A simple canvas bag, packed with his few belongings, sat waiting upstairs.

His true treasures—the black armor and his sword, *Stalker*—were hidden safely in Ornst, tucked away in the flat above JP Locksmith.

The flat wasn't just a hideaway.

It was a haven.

A place tied to Rosamund, who he hoped would one day share it with him.

He wasn't sure when that day would come.

But he hoped it would be soon.

Once he was free of Xavier, he could finally figure out the path ahead.

Jean-Pierre, the locksmith, was an older man with a storied past inside the ranks of Leskaré. Once a thief himself, he now walked a finer line—running a legitimate locksmith shop while discreetly fencing stolen goods.

His connections in the underworld kept the trade subtle, safe from prying eyes—particularly those of Leskaré.

In a way, Jean-Pierre wasn't much different from Xavier. He moved stolen goods too—just on a smaller, quieter scale.

Rad mulled over his future as he stared out his window overlooking the southern stretch of *Château Saignoral.*

It was clear his life likely wouldn't involve honest labor. With JP's encouragement, he had already honed his thieving skills to a proficiency far beyond a beginner.

Just like Hadley, JP reminded him not to show off.

Being a master thief took patience—and the ability to go unnoticed. Drawing attention was a mistake.

Always.

Jean-Pierre's quiet warnings about Leskaré echoed in his ears. If they grew too bold, too noticeable, Leskaré would find them.

Their survival depended on staying small.

Insignificant.

Beneath notice.

Yet Rad felt a pull he couldn't ignore—an itch of curiosity about Leskaré's world.

If they ruled the shadows, he needed to understand how.

As he stepped out of his room, Rad's thoughts drifted over the moments that had reshaped his life.

Being cast out—stripped of his name and forced into servitude—had been the beginning.

Then came the gala.

The night he uncovered his true heritage amid the lies and luxury of counterfeit wine.

The path had opened, and there was no going back.

There was Rosamund—warm, sweet—he could still feel the first time they had been together.

The warehouse.

Saving Tristin.

Losing Ma and Abby to the Black Storm's brutal retribution.

That night was seared into his mind.

The loss had nearly undone him.

Then the cursed hand—a relic of an unknown undead entity.

Its touch had almost ended him.

Yet the strange curse it left behind had become... a gift.

He had learned to project himself into the Ethereal Plane—a ghostly mirror of the living world.

Walls became meaningless.

Doors, mere suggestions.

With practice, he had mastered the ability—keeping his excursions brief, wary of the dead who watched too closely.

Those journeys had given him answers he once thought impossible.

His mother's ghost had painted a different picture of his father, Lanny Zeh—a man far from the heroic figure Rad had once dreamed.

A thief.

A leader of Leskaré.

A man of daring—and deep flaws.

The truth was sobering but not unwelcome.

Rad had faced it with clear eyes.

If his father had been a thief—then so was he.

His boots scuffed against the stone path, each step pulling him further from the weight of memory and closer to the present.

The past still clung to him—faintly, like the scent of smoke long after a fire—but he let it settle at the edges of his thoughts.

There would be time for reflection later.

For now, there was Hadley.

And the Sweet Hatchet.

The front gate rose ahead, and waiting by it was Hadley—arms crossed, looking about as fresh as a man like him could.

Hadley nodded to the guard, who opened the gate without question.

He studied Rad, reading the weight behind his eyes.

"Whatever ghosts you're dragging, leave them here with Xavier and the lot," Hadley said. "This celebration's for me and you."

Rad blinked, caught off guard. A small smile broke through.

"Right."

"Happy birthday, lad," Hadley said, clapping him on the shoulder.

"Thanks, Hadley."

"You're getting sturdy. Been putting on some muscle, have you?"

The gate shut behind them with a metallic clang—the scraping and banging of locks filling Rad's ears as the guards secured the protections.

"I have," Rad answered.

At sixteen, he stood a lean six feet, his wiry frame honed by years of labor and training. His muscles, bulkier now, held deceptive strength, and his agility set him apart. His throwing knives flew true to their marks, and *Darter*, his piercing blade, never wavered in his hand.

"It's noticeable," Rad added, "when I handle *Stalker* at my flat. Feels like nothing."

"Good," Hadley grunted. "Keep your strength. Work those arms. Don't get soft and lazy like old Hadley."

"Old and slow," Rad corrected, grinning.

Hadley smacked Rad on the shoulder with a lazy backhand.

"We can catch a ride. Don't feel like walking all the way anyhow."

"Let's head to the market," Rad said. "Someone's always coming and going from there."

They walked in companionable silence for a moment.

Hadley's gait was slower than usual—a telltale sign his aging body was starting to betray him. Yet there was still resilience in his movements. His shoulders, once so stiff they were useless, had recovered.

The wide-brimmed hat shading his weathered face was tilted back far enough for his sharp eyes to scan the street. The thin, gray hair he had left was tied into a makeshift ponytail that bobbed with each step.

"He's really going to do it, isn't he?" Rad asked quietly.

"Aye," Hadley said. "Tonight, you'll be excused from *Château Saignoral*. And I'll be right there, every step of the way, so there's no deception."

He rolled his shoulder with a grunt.

"I may not be as mobile as I once was, but I can still cause mayhem. Xavier knows it. I'll strap on my sword for the occasion—to remind him."

"The old, rusted piece of shit?"

"That piece of shit saved my life plenty of times," Hadley growled. "*Bloodspite* never let me down. Not once. It's got a few slashes left in it—enough to carve you into pieces if you get mouthy."

"You couldn't carve a ham, old man," Rad teased.

Hadley snorted. "I've seen crippled girls handle knives better than you."

"Oh, is that right?" Rad shot back, grinning. "At least I don't need a nap after swinging a blade twice."

"Wouldn't take more than two swings to take you down anyway."

Both erupted into laughter, their sides aching from the shared mirth. This was their world—bonded by a constant volley of barbed insults, a language more intimate than kindness.

Rad's smile faded as a thought crossed his mind: *If only he could convince Hadley to come with him.*

The flat above JP's Locksmith would be cramped, sure, but they'd make it work. It was bigger than Hadley's old shed, if smaller than Rad's plain room at *Château Saignoral.*

At least it would be theirs.

The loud clop of hooves drew their attention as a wagon rolled up behind them.

The horses were stout, massive beasts built for heavy loads. The wagon itself was tall and long, with wooden sides and a roof— more a house on wheels than a merchant's cart.

Unlike most merchants, there were no markings.

No banners.

No indication of who owned it—or what was inside.

Hadley waved at the driver.

"Aye, friend—fine-looking shires you've got there. Don't see many of them in Ornst."

The driver reined in the horses with a practiced hand.

"You've got a good eye," he said. "You know shires?"

"Enough to wish I had a pair of 'em," Hadley answered, grinning. "You wouldn't happen to know The Sweet Hatchet?"

The driver nodded. "Climb onto the tailboard. You can jump off when you like."

"Much appreciated." Hadley turned to Rad and muttered, "Stop staring. They're just big."

"Biggest horse I've ever imagined," Rad said, still wide-eyed.

They climbed aboard, and the wagon jolted into motion, settling into a bumpy rhythm that was anything but comfortable.

"Imagine the *chevel merred,*" Hadley said dryly.

"Big piles of it, I'm certain," Rad said, smirking.

He paused, glancing at the walled estates flanking the road. The grand homes loomed like silent sentinels, indifferent to his troubles.

"Are you sure you can't come live over JP's Locksmith?" he asked quietly. "We could work out the details after I get settled."

"For now, I need to stay with Xavier," Hadley said, dipping his chin. "One day you'll understand. I still owe the bastard for saving my life. My service to him isn't done yet."

He gave Rad a sideways look.

"Besides, you probably snore and leave the windows open so it's freezing. We'd be yelling at each other like some old broken-down married couple."

Rad chuckled, though the ache lingered in his chest.

"Fair enough." After a beat, Rad said, "Did you know JP used to work for Leskaré? He's retired now."

Hadley's smile faded.

"Careful, lad. Don't get mixed up with those louts. You remember the Black Storm. Leskaré's not much different."

"But they're everywhere," Rad said, frustration edging his voice. "They have their tendrils in everything. I saw one of Xavier's ledgers—they move all kinds of goods, and the scale is enormous."

He pointed at the towering estate walls they were passing.

"It's no wonder everything's locked up around here."

"Best avoid them," Hadley said, his voice low and certain. "It'll be hard enough, working with JP. Trust me—it'll happen. One day, they'll come knocking. And if you're not careful, they'll be the end of you."

He gave Rad a long, hard look. "Or worse—you'll end up becoming one of them."

Rad didn't answer.

Hadley's voice softened, almost like a prayer: "But that's the beautiful thing about life, isn't it? We have choices. And consequences. I'm still paying for mine. I'll be paying until the day I die. You remember that."

Rad acknowledged the statement with a nod, understanding that everything he did—or didn't do—carried a consequence.

"Did you know Leskaré has a full leadership structure?" he said. "It rivals any duchy or barony. Different roles, different responsibilities. Their Grand Master Thief is Bruno DuPont—"

"Stop admiring them," Hadley cut in, sharp and low. "Leskaré's full of bad men and women—like me. Like your real father."

Rad stiffened, but Hadley pressed on.

"He wasn't the princeling you made him out to be, was he? And now he's dead. Just like your Ma. Just like Abigail."

He let the words hang heavy between them.

"And what do they all have in common?" Hadley said quietly. "Xavier von Schule."

The barb stung—but it was true.

Hadley would never use their memory lightly.

He was making a point.

Rad drew a slow breath.

"I understand your... unique insight," Rad said, patting his chest—a gesture that was less than convincing, even to himself.

The plans he'd had—to tell Hadley everything he knew about Leskaré, to share his half-formed dream of joining them—fizzled in his mind.

Maybe it was time to reconsider. But the appeal lingered, stubborn and tempting.

They rode in silence after that.

The wealthy estates thinned, giving way to tighter streets and worn buildings.

The atmosphere changed—the smell of woodsmoke and fresh bread replaced by the sharper scents of tannery and iron. The sounds shifted too, from the hush of distant laughter to the clatter of carts and shouting hawkers.

Hadley chewed on the stem of his pipe, then tucked it away into his pocket, silent and thoughtful as they rolled deeper into the city.

"Ah, you smell that?" Hadley asked.

"Garbage?"

Hadley laughed. "No, lad. The smell of opportunity. Filthy, rotten opportunity."

He paused, gesturing at the bustling streets and crooked buildings. "The city's alive. Always shifting, always scheming. It's your birthday— let's go have some fun."

Without warning, Rad jumped off the tailboard, landing soft and balanced on his feet. He pivoted in time to see Hadley slip down, his body at an uneven angle.

Hadley caught the heel of his boot on the cobblestones.

He jolted awkwardly, stumbled a few steps before finding his footing, then dusted off his leather coat as if nothing had happened.

Rad crossed his arms, watching Hadley straighten himself.

"Stumbling, and you're not even drunk," he said. "Old man."

Hadley pointed at him. "Young and dumb."

Behind them, Rad heard the horses.

On instinct, he stepped aside just in time to avoid the oncoming wagon by a hair's width.

The driver bellowed a curse at them as he passed.

Hadley bounded to the side with ginger steps, his movements fluid but tight with pain.

"You all right?" Rad asked, genuine concern in his voice. "You nearly planted your face in the street."

"Aye," Hadley grunted, brushing himself off again.

He threw an arm around Rad and gave him an affectionate shake.

Together, they strolled down the bustling avenue under the warm glow of the midafternoon sun.

The city unfolded around them—street vendors shouting to passersby, the occasional clamor of hooves, the distant clang of a blacksmith's hammer.

The air was thick with a mess of smells—roasted nuts and sharp spices tangled with the stench of unwashed bodies and refuse piled in alleyways.

The heat sat heavy on Rad's shoulders, soaking his white shirt with sweat.

But despite it all, he felt at ease.

The day felt right.

Rad glanced sideways at Hadley.

"You know, Hadley... you've been instrumental in my growth. And I'm grateful. You stuck by me all these years—what's it been, six years now?"

"You helped heal my arms," Hadley said. "It made all the difference in our training. Healed up, I could train you properly. We both made out on the deal, don't you think? You're an expert with knives and swords."

He jabbed a finger at Rad.

"But don't get too smug. You haven't been in a real fight yet."

"I took down those two Black Storm assassins," Rad said.

"Shut it," Hadley growled. "Don't mention them. You surprised them, lad. That wasn't a fight—it was a slaughter. And those are the best fights, if you catch my meaning."

He leveled Rad with a look.

"Don't go seeking violence. It'll find you soon enough."

"I'll be ready," Rad said.

A long pause stretched between them.

"There's something I need to tell you, lad," Hadley said quietly. "Something I need to get off my chest."

"Can we save the sentimental bullshit for later?" Rad asked. "Can't have you crying on my sixteenth birthday."

Hadley didn't react.

He stayed solemn, relaxed.

"Do you remember the day Xavier wanted to talk to me, right after Ma and Abigail died?" he asked. "When I told you to stay in your room and not come out unless it was me at the door?"

"I do," Rad said. "You said everything was fine. Told me not to worry."

Hadley's voice dropped.

"He wanted to throw you out."

Rad came to a halt on the sidewalk.

He had spied on that conversation—he knew exactly what had happened. But he hesitated, then played along for Hadley's sake.

"What?" he asked, feigning surprise.

"He was considering it," Hadley said. "After Justine and Abigail passed, he wanted you gone. I threatened to strangle Xavier in his sleep if he didn't hold to his promise to Justine."

"You threatened Xavier von Schule?" Rad said, blinking.

Hadley gave him a sidelong glance.

"Aye, I did, lad. He knows what I'm capable of. Or what I was capable of."

He flexed his fingers slightly, as if remembering the strength he once had.

"He agreed to keep you until you were sixteen, as promised. Then he went on about me going after those responsible for Justine and Abigail's deaths."

Rad shook his head.

"It would have been futile. You wouldn't have come back."

Hadley grunted.

"Aye. Same thing I told him. I said revenge on an organization like the Black Storm would only invite more death. Yours. Mine. Maybe others too. I said it for your sake... and for mine."

He exhaled, long and slow.

"You're right. I wouldn't have come back. And we would've angered them further."

"Thanks for sticking up for me," Rad said. "You must be the only person to threaten Xavier von Schule and live to tell the tale."

"I'm sure there are a few others he fears."

"Thanks anyway," Rad said again, quieter. "I'm lucky to have you, Hadley. You're not bad at this friendship thing."

"Don't go thanking me too much," Hadley grumbled. "I did it for myself as much as you. Knew without you, the stables would fall apart. If he'd tossed you out back then, you might not have survived. Probably would've sent me after those assassins—and we'd both be dead."

Rad shrugged. "I get it. I can't blame you for using me. I'd have done the same in your situation. Thanks for telling me. It makes sense now."

Hadley grunted, then gestured down the avenue.

"The Sweet Hatchet awaits, lad. Let's celebrate. I only brought enough coin for one drink—and one drink only."

Rad laughed. "I brought a few silvers. I'm feeling magnanimous today—this glorious day of my birth."

He raised his fist into the sky in mock triumph.

Hadley barked a laugh as they resumed walking.

"Bastard. Fancy words for a fancy prick. *Magnanimous*—those books are making you soft."

They walked in companionable silence for a stretch before Hadley spoke again.

"I've got a present for you," he said. "For your birthday. Something... unique."

"You certain it's a gift?" Rad teased. "You've been whispering about it for weeks, dangling it in front of me. My first birthday gift was

Rosamund, and I don't know how you're going to top her. What is it, anyway? Not that rusted sword of yours, I hope. Come on—is it truly a gift?"

Hadley grunted. "I don't know," he said. "Depends on what you do with it. I kept it to myself for a reason. But I'm done holding onto it. It needs to be passed on."

Before Rad could press further, Hadley pointed ahead.

"Ah, there she is. The Sweet Hatchet. If I'm going to die, I want it to be in a place like this."

Rad chuckled.

The crooked sign of the tavern and brothel swung lazily in the warm afternoon breeze, the sugar-dusted hatchet badly in need of fresh paint and an artist's touch.

The usual guards at the door were absent—a small detail Rad noticed but didn't linger on.

Whatever Hadley's mysterious gift was, it could wait—at least for one drink.

Before they reached the entrance, Hadley clapped Rad on the shoulder.

"Come on, lad," he said, grinning. "Let's see what mischief we can avoid."

Rad snorted.

"Don't worry. It'll find us."

- 426 -

Chapter Twenty-One

∞

Atonement in Steel

The Sweet Hatchet was alive with its usual mix of raucous laughter, murmured conversations, and the occasional clinking of mugs. As Rad and Hadley approached, Rad's eyes swept over the building with practiced ease. He had mapped every inch of the place in his mind— from the inviting double doors to the hidden alcoves in the back.

He traced the escape routes he'd committed to memory: up the narrow stairs, out the second-story window, across the slanted rooftop, and onto the adjacent building. A ten-second sprint to freedom, if ever the need arose. He hadn't needed it yet—but he kept the skill sharp, just in case.

Inside, Glenys greeted them, her smile genuine as she directed them to a communal table in the center. It had higher chairs Hadley liked, and it offered a view of the other seating areas.

"Hadley, good to see you again!" she teased. "You've been in here so much, I'm tempted to add your name to the ledger."

"Don't tempt me, Glenys," Hadley replied with a grin. "You'll be regretting me the moment my tab starts collecting dust."

Rad chuckled at their banter as they settled into their seats.

Glenys returned a moment later with their drinks—a tumbler of stiff liquor, Stagwater, for Hadley, a cup of red wine for Rad.

Rad swirled his wine absentmindedly.

Over the past two years, his preferences had solidified.

Ale, while refreshing on a hot day, dulled his senses.

Hard liquor hit too fast, too hard.

But wine—wine offered a gradual, steady numbness, leaving him functional yet detached.

He was careful to keep his consumption modest, stretching it out over time. Too much, and his judgment blurred—he couldn't afford that.

He sipped, his eyes drifting over the bustling room. What had started as casual people-watching had become instinct.

His gaze swept across the patrons, assessing faces, body language, posture—mentally cataloging potential threats and opportunities.

The Sweet Hatchet teemed with its usual crowd: laborers unwinding from the day's toil, regulars whose postures spoke of comfort and familiarity, mercenaries nursing their cups while keeping one eye on the exits, couples leaning close in whispered conversation.

A table of scruffy Dwarves laughed, their thick beards bobbing as they leaned into their drinks.

But among the crowd moved the quieter currents of Leskaré.

They were here—he could feel it.

He couldn't pick out specific faces, but the signs were there: the subtle signals, the way certain patrons watched the room without appearing to.

Patterns he'd learned to recognize.

For a moment, he wondered if others looked at him the same way now—if he had already become something sharp and silent without even realizing it.

Leskaré's reach was extensive.

That much was clear.

And the more time Rad spent in the city of Ornst, the clearer it became.

Their grip extended into every corner of life—from gambling dens and brothels to legitimate businesses. Xavier von Schule facilitated their smuggling and fencing operations, while counterfeit documents, illicit goods, and clandestine deals flowed through the city's many trade routes.

Roads ran west through Conwich, northeast to Haddensack, east to Biggs, and ships sailed from the port to cities across the world. Ornst was an ideal locale for a thieving organization.

Not even the cooperage trade was free from Leskaré's grasp—a fact Rad had uncovered during one of his secret investigations into Xavier's affairs.

Every barrel and cask in Ornst bore Leskaré's silent mark. Their control was total, eliminating competition before it could sprout.

And if they controlled something as basic as barrels, what else did they own? How deep did the roots go?

Rad sipped his wine again, the bitter tang a match for his thoughts.

Leskaré's influence was a labyrinth of mysteries.

Beyond theft, smuggling, and counterfeit trade, Rad was certain they trafficked in something even more valuable: information.

Spying. Secrets. Blackmail.

Not just tools—but an empire built on what other people didn't want known.

In a city like Ornst, gold could buy much.

But secrets...

Secrets could buy everything.

And here he was—running a modest operation with JP, right in the heart of Leskaré's shadow.

It was a precarious game.

Their small-scale thefts were insignificant now, but that wouldn't last forever. Leskaré would notice, eventually.

With his eviction from *Château Saignoral* looming, Rad's focus sharpened. He would devote himself to becoming the most skilled thief in Ornst—a shadow in every alley, a ghost in every marketplace.

He would leave no trace.

And that's how they would know it was him.

It was a bold ambition.

But Rad was certain he could achieve it.

He envisioned a future where Leskaré not only noticed him—but respected him.

Feared him.

He wouldn't merely join them.

He would dominate them.

He would rise to Grand Master Thief and seize control of Leskaré itself.

And when that day came—his stepfather, Xavier von Schule, would pay for every slight.

Every scar.

Every ounce of blood Rad had ever bled.

The world would remember his name.

Rad's darker musings were interrupted as his gaze swept the room—and settled on her.

Rosamund.

She remained as captivating as the day they'd first met, two years ago, right here in The Sweet Hatchet on his birthday.

She had a presence that drew attention—a blend of confidence and warmth that made her stand out against the noise and chaos of the tavern.

Her beauty was undeniable.

Her charm, magnetic.

The age difference didn't bother Rad in the slightest.

She was at least six years his senior, but in her, he saw not only companionship—he saw a partner.

A future.

The thought of a life with her drove him harder than anything else.

To work.

To fight.

To become worthy of her attention.

When she caught sight of him, her face lit with a smile that melted whatever bravado he wore. Rad raised his eyebrows in playful challenge—their silent exchange.

As always, it worked.

Her laughter cut through the tavern's din like a melody meant just for him.

Hadley leaned forward, his voice low and edged with concern.

"You know she's a whore," he said, rolling his small glass of liquor between his gnarled hands. "She's paid to like you. Surprised you haven't realized it yet."

Rad shrugged, unbothered. "I know."

Hadley blinked, caught a little off guard. "And that doesn't bother you?"

Rad swirled his wine, watching the slow current in the cup.

"Might, one day," he said. "But not now. I'm not jealous. Not angry. She does what she has to, same as me."

Hadley chuckled dryly. "You're a cold bastard, that I can attest to. Never seen anyone so detached from the people they supposedly love. Something's wrong with you, lad."

Rad's smile faded, but his voice stayed even. "When Ma and Abby died, so did the part of me that trusted everything would turn out fine."

He set the cup down gently.

"I'm not as cold as you think."

A thin smile touched his lips.

"I have plans," Rad said. "And they include Rosamund. One day. When things are right."

Hadley grunted, neither approving nor disapproving.

The tavern's noise swelled around them, but Rad barely heard it.

He could wait.

He could build.

He could *earn* the right to ask her for more.

That was how the world worked.

And he was ready, he would offer her more than survival—he would offer her a life worth living.

A lifetime together.

Hadley stared into his glass, swirling the remnants of the amber liquid before downing it in one rough gulp.

He signaled for another.

"Best of luck to you, lad. And Rosamund." He set the glass down with a thud. "And best of luck to us both. I'm going to miss you terribly."

His voice softened, and he glanced at Rad, a rare vulnerability flickering in his eyes.

"Don't tell anyone I said so," he muttered. "But you know it's true. You saved me, lad. If Xavier turns me out too, I'll join you in whatever shithole you're living in. As long as Rosamund agrees, of course."

Glenys brought another drink, sliding it across the table.

Hadley's hand was steady as he caught it.

"You're going to miss the horses, aren't you, lad?" he asked, voice gruff again.

Rad leaned back in his chair, swirling the wine in his cup.

"I'll miss some of it," he admitted. "Moonsilver's a fine mare. And I liked working with Vanguard when we had him."

He shrugged. "But the rest? The mucking, the early mornings, the routine? No, I won't miss it all."

Hadley chuckled, shaking his head.

"You'll miss it more than you think. There's a quiet kind of satisfaction in taking care of those animals. They're honest creatures— not like people. You give them kindness, they give it back. You're going to miss that trust."

Rad shrugged, sipping his wine. "I suppose it was comforting, knowing they didn't have ulterior motives. But horses won't get me where I'm going."

"Wherever that is," Hadley muttered.

He studied Rad, the sharpness in his voice giving way to a quieter reflection. After a moment, Hadley asked, "You think you'll get to say goodbye? To your sisters? To Tristin?"

Rad leaned back, casual on the surface, but the tightness around his mouth gave him away.

"I don't know. Wouldn't bother me if I don't. As far as I know, they'll toss me out the second I come back."

Hadley raised a skeptical brow.

"Not Marie? Bella? They're your sisters, after all."

Rad snorted.

"Sisters? Hardly. They treated me like I didn't exist—or like I wasn't worth the air I breathe when they did." He set the cup down, voice steady. "No. I won't miss them. And I doubt they'll miss me either."

Hadley nodded, his face unreadable. "And Tristin? You've had your differences, but he's not all bad. Certainly not as bad as Xavier."

Rad hesitated.

The bite in his tone faded, replaced by something heavier.

"Tristin's... complicated. I guess I owe him a word or two before I go."

Rad leaned forward again, resting his elbows on the table. "But Xavier?" The contempt returned, sharp and final. "Not a chance. I'll leave without saying a thing to him. He doesn't deserve my time."

Hadley huffed a dry laugh, taking a sip of his drink.

"Don't reckon he'd be too eager to hear a sentimental farewell speech either. And I'll be right there with you, remember. But it doesn't give you permission to mouth off."

"I'll stay calm," Rad said, lifting his cup. "I'm not looking back, Hadley. My focus is ahead—I'll make Xavier von Schule regret every decision he ever made. You'll see."

Hadley sighed, setting his glass down with a quiet clink.

"Remember this: life'll point you in directions you think you want to go— but you ought to take the path you need."

He met Rad's eyes.

"You've got fire in you, lad. I just hope it doesn't burn you up before you get where you're going."

Rad raised his cup in a mock toast, a wry smile on his face.

"If it does, at least I'll burn brighter than him. And I will get there."

They shared a quiet moment, the noise of the tavern dulling around them. Two men, bonded by the weight of survival and the certainty of change.

Rad drummed his fingers lightly on the table.

"So, what's this gift you've been teasing for weeks? I'm half-expecting it to be a legendary artifact that makes sunshine beam out of my arse." He grinned. "Is it real, or did you dream it up?"

Hadley threw back his head and downed the last of his harsh liquor in a single fearless gulp—his hat slipping off and landing awkwardly behind him.

He grumbled, snatched it back, and jammed it onto his head.

"Oh, it's real," he said, voice low.

Rad leaned forward now, the grin fading into real curiosity.

"Let's see it. Go on. Hand it over."

Hadley's voice dropped to a whisper. "Back in my shed, there's a wood carving of a barn owl. You've seen it?"

Rad frowned, searching his memories.

"Yes. I've seen it."

"It's hollow. Inside, there's a map. That's your gift."

Rad blinked. "A map? To what? Treasure?"

Hadley nodded once, slow and deliberate, the gravity in his expression leaving no room for teasing.

"Aye. Treasure. But before I tell you anything more, you need to make me a promise." He leaned in, voice barely above a murmur. "This isn't for my conscience, lad. It's for your survival. I've never steered you wrong, have I?"

Rad raised a skeptical eyebrow. "What's to stop me from taking the owl when we get back and figuring it out myself?"

"I'd burn it first," Hadley said, his jaw tightening.

Rad laughed, shaking his head. "You? Burn it? Fight me for it? In your condition?"

Hadley's eyes hardened, and his voice turned cold.

"Teeth and nails, lad. I'd find a way."

Rad straightened, the humor slipping from his face. He heard the edge in Hadley's voice—and knew better than to push.

"All right, old man," Rad said more seriously. "What's this promise you want?"

"When the time comes," Hadley said, voice low, "you'll take at least half a dozen strong, fierce men with you. And if you can find one—bring a wizard."

He leaned in.

"You promise me that. Don't even *think* about going alone. You do, and your life will end."

Rad's brow furrowed. "What's so dangerous about it?"

Hadley's hand trembled slightly as he reached for his empty glass, tapping it once on the table.

His voice dropped, hollow and haunted.

"I went with mates of mine. Hard bastards—killers, every one. We had blood on our hands and fire in our bellies."

He shook his head slowly.

"But it wasn't enough. Not for what we found."

Rad's stomach tightened. He leaned in, his voice steady despite the unease knotting in his gut. "And you?" Rad asked.

Hadley's eyes darkened.

"I barely made it out. Injured. Bleeding. Half-dead—but alive. Don't know how I managed it. Luck. Blind, bloody luck. I never went back."

Rad absorbed the weight of the words, then asked, quieter now, "If it's so dangerous, why give me the map at all?"

Hadley held his gaze.

"Because you're not like me, lad. You're not like them."

He tapped the table lightly for emphasis.

"You're smart—smarter than we ever were. If anyone can make it there and back, it's you."

He straightened slightly.

"But *not alone*. Never alone."

Hadley's voice lowered to a rasp, rough with old fear.

"That's why you must promise me, Rad. You go by yourself—you'll be as dead as my mates."

Rad sat back, letting the weight of Hadley's words settle.

He studied the old man's face—the tremor he couldn't hide in his hands, the haunted look clinging behind his eyes.

This wasn't a challenge or a test.

It was a warning—one born from experience and loss.

"I promise," Rad said, his voice steady. "When the time comes, I'll take fighters and a wizard. I won't go alone."

Hadley's shoulders sagged with relief, though his grip on the glass remained tight.

"You keep your promise, you hear? You're all I've got left. When you get the treasure, I want to hear what you find."

Rad nodded, the weight of it settling in his chest—but alongside it, excitement thrummed.

"I'll let you see it."

"Good lad," Hadley said, patting Rad's shoulder with a heavy hand.

He gave a small, crooked smile.

"Still planning to ruin your family? Put me out of a job?"

The tension between them eased, the old familiar banter slipping back into place.

"That's the plan," Rad said, tapping the table. "Ruining you will just be a bonus. Take heed—I'm going to bring Xavier von Schule to his knees. By the time he realizes what's happening, it'll be too late. *Château Saignoral* will be mine, and I'll turn him out into the streets. Wilkins too."

Hadley chuckled, low and dry. "Ambitious bastard, aren't you?"

Rad leaned closer and whispered, "Tell me about this tomb."

"When I give you the map, I'll explain," Hadley said. "All you need to know now is this—there's a map, and you'll need a *formidable* group when the day comes. Promise to keep, lad. Don't forget."

They fell into a comfortable silence, each turning over their own thoughts.

Rad signaled to a passing server, but when she didn't respond, he stood to catch her attention. As he stood to request another drink for Hadley—the atmosphere shifted.

Two men wove through the crowded room, their movements deliberate, their eyes scanning faces as they advanced.

Rad froze mid-gesture, his focus snapping to them.

"I think I've seen them in here before," he muttered under his breath.

Hadley turned, following Rad's line of sight. His face darkened instantly.

"Shit," he hissed.

Rad shifted, instinct pulling him to position himself between Hadley and the danger—but Hadley's hand clamped down on his arm, firm and unyielding.

"No," Hadley said, his voice a gruff whisper. "Whatever happens, you stay put. Right there in your seat. You don't know me. Look the other way, lad. Pretend you don't know me."

Rad hesitated, jaw tightening, but he knew Hadley wasn't wrong. Not this time.

"These two," Hadley continued, his voice dropping even lower, "nasty killers. As bad as me back in my prime—Hadley the Pillager, the man who killed a village without blinking."

He shook his head once, sharply.

"These men? They'll kill us both and sleep soundly after."

Rad swallowed his anger and settled back into his chair, forcing himself into stillness.

His mind was racing, but his hands stayed relaxed on the table.

Without thinking, he cataloged the weapons on him: eight throwing knives hidden in their sheaths. *Darter* strapped against his hip.

He could pull them and throw—but not without drawing every eye in the room.

Not without risking Hadley's life.

He turned his back on the approaching threat and focused instead on the inattentive server.

Rad raised his hand again, feigning impatience, tapping two fingers sharply against the table to mask the tension thrumming through him.

The air thickened with each step the two men took, pressing closer.

A bead of sweat traced the back of his neck.

Not from fear—he told himself—but from awareness.

The last time he felt this—this tightening in the chest, this sharpening of the senses—he had been staring down the Black Storm assassins.

Men who would kill without a word, without hesitation.

These two felt the same.

He counted the steps behind him without turning.

Twelve feet. Ten. Eight.

Still too far to strike first—too close to run without drawing *Darter*.

No good choices. Only bad ones, measured in heartbeats.

The first man halted near Hadley, his presence heavy with menace.

His beady black eyes, devoid of warmth, gleamed with cruelty.

"It's been a long time, Hadley. It is you, isn't it? Finally. I thought we'd run into you one day at The Sweet Hatchet."

His voice was gravelly, carrying a smug edge.

"Been watching this place ever since Glenys mentioned you were a regular."

He wasn't as old as Hadley, but the rough roundness of his face bore the scars of a hard life. A red slash across his neck marked a wound that had nearly ended him. His patchy black-and-gray hair looked like it had been hacked short with a dull blade.

His clothes—an oversized white tunic and loose brown trousers—masked his bulk, but the power in his frame was obvious.

A short sword and knife hung from worn belts at his hips.

Rad's eyes caught the rumpled fabric around his ankles: he usually wore tall boots, but today he'd swapped them for sturdy leather shoes.

It didn't soften the air of violence around him.

Nothing would.

The other man approached, a stark contrast to his burly companion.

He was tall and wiry, his movements fluid and intense. Aquiline features gave his face an edge of cruel elegance, and his sharp gray eyes sparkled with intelligence, though there was an unnerving hardness behind them. His unkempt dark hair framed his face, and there were hints of Elven blood in the angles of his cheekbones and the slight taper of his ears—likely a quarter-elf.

Unlike the first man, this one bore no scars, but his gear told a story of a dangerous life.

A short sword and knife mirrored his companion's weapons, while a short bow and a full quiver slung low across his back showed signs of regular use. His white shirt was open at the chest, revealing a feather necklace swaying against his pale skin with each step. His turquoise coat, once vibrant, had faded with years of hard living, its tattered hem brushing against his weathered blue trousers. Tight-laced knee-high boots completed the look—sturdy, practical, worn.

Rad's pulse quickened as he studied them.

These weren't ordinary thugs. They moved with the confidence of men who had seen—and survived—countless battles.

Their armaments were no accident. Every weapon was positioned for quick draw and brutal use.

And the quarter-elf's kit, in particular, told Rad everything he needed to know—his kit spoke of the harshness and violence of his life, a careful balance of steel meant for killing swiftly whether at distance or up close.

Rad's instincts screamed for him to act, but logic overruled them.

They couldn't risk a public killing here—not in a tavern full of witnesses, not without inviting retaliation.

No, this would be threats first.

A warning.

A flex of muscle to rattle Hadley—or to judge how much fight he still had left.

Still, Rad stayed on edge.

Threats were safer than blades... but not by much.

And if something went wrong—if the men decided to make an example after all—Rad would be ready.

"Blackjack, thought you'd be visiting a farm instead of a brothel," Hadley said, voice dry as dust. "You don't have to pay the sheep."

"Ha! Same old Hadley—Hadley the Pillager." Blackjack's voice rose, thick with mockery. "The man who killed hundreds thinks he's funny. Hadley the Pillager."

He said it louder, daring heads to turn—and a few did, curious or wary at the name.

Rad angled himself away from Hadley, sinking into his seat, his posture lazy and disinterested. He toyed with his wine cup, but his sharp eyes stayed locked on the two men through the corner of his vision.

The wiry one—Marlow—stepped closer, his movements loose but predatory, like a cat that had already decided it would pounce.

Hadley snickered without humor.

"Marlow. Still scrounging scraps with this whoreson?"

He tipped back his empty glass, forgetting it was drained. Frustrated, he banged it lightly against the table, trying to catch a server's attention.

Marlow laid a hand on Hadley's shoulder—heavy, deliberate, a warning in the touch. His scarred fingers pressed down, a reminder that he wasn't here for talk.

"It's a living," Marlow said, his voice casual, almost amused.

Rad's eyes flicked to the hand. Scarred, knuckles gnarled—a man who had lived by brawl and blade.

Hadley didn't flinch. "Get your hand off me," he said, voice low and dangerous, "or I'll shove it—"

He never finished the threat.

A sharp gasp tore from him instead. His empty glass slipped from his grasp, spun across the table, and shattered on the floor.

Hadley's body locked rigid, his face twisting in sudden pain.

Rad's attention snapped to Blackjack, who now stood on Hadley's other side, his hand hidden—causing Hadley's sudden agony.

"Let's go outside," Blackjack said. His tone was firm, almost pleasant, but the malice behind it was unmistakable.

The flutter in Rad's chest tightened into a knot.

They were going to kill Hadley.

Why? Because he was Hadley the Pillager?

Rad forced a steadying breath, keeping his face a mask of lazy disinterest even as his mind raced.

They hauled Hadley upright, Blackjack's knife pressed into his side.

Rad caught a glimpse of the blade, buried nearly to the hilt.

Hadley's breath came in short, shallow gasps as they dragged him toward the side door.

No one in the tavern noticed—or cared. At The Sweet Hatchet, such scenes weren't uncommon.

Rad's fingers brushed the hilt of *Darter* as he stood.

The blade was small but deadly, its weight a familiar comfort.

He resisted the urge to charge after them. Recklessness would get them both killed.

Instead, he slipped through the crowd, fast but deliberate, heading for the front exit.

The evening air hit him like a slap, cool against the sweat clinging to his back.

The streets of Ornst were already draped in shadow as the sun slid below the horizon.

Rad kept to the building's edge, circling toward the alley.

Blackjack and Marlow wouldn't waste time.

And Hadley was running out of it.

The odds spun in his head—either he'd come up behind them, or he'd run straight into them.

If he flanked them, Blackjack would go first—the blade in Hadley's back made him the greater threat. Marlow, wiry and fast, could wait half a second longer.

But if he faced them head-on...

Rad's grip on *Darter* tightened.

He spun around the corner—then slowed, cursing under his breath.

Shit.

He was in front of them.

No advantage.

No surprise.

Suppressing a surge of panic, Rad kept moving, feigning indifference.

Ahead, Blackjack strangled Hadley with his left arm while his right hand twisted a knife into his back.

Rad stopped twenty feet away, lazily sheathing *Darter* with a dramatic flourish.

His face wore a smirk of mock surprise, even as his fingers slid two throwing knives into his palms.

"This is none of your concern," Marlow snapped, waving him off. "Bugger off."

Blackjack shoved Hadley to his knees. The old man fell hard, a wet grunt escaping him.

The knife flashed in the dim alley light, slick and dark.

Hadley braced himself on shaking thighs, blood dripping from his mouth.

A cough racked his body, spraying crimson across the cobblestones.

"Lad," Hadley gasped, his voice a whisper.

Blackjack cuffed him hard across the head. The sound was dull, ugly.

"So now you're ready to talk?" Blackjack said.

Marlow's gray eyes flicked over the alley, checking for witnesses. His hand settled on his sword.

"Bugger off, boy," Marlow warned again, blade hissing free. "Or die with him."

Hadley's head sagged, his shoulders trembling.

Still, he lifted his face to Rad, blood streaking his battered features.

"Lad," he rasped again.

Another stab.

Hadley grunted but stayed upright, refusing to fall.

Steel rasped as Marlow leveled his sword at Rad, stance tight, precise. "Last warning."

Hadley coughed once more—then smiled.

A broken, bloodied smile.

"Rad."

The knife pulled free.

Hadley's voice was faint but clear.

"Show off."

Lightning-quick, Rad moved, fueled by a rage he hadn't felt since Ma and Abby were taken from him. The knife in his hand blurred through the air—and so did he.

Before Marlow could react, Rad's blade pierced his eye, the sickening impact sending the wiry man crashing to the ground, his good eye wide in unseeing shock.

Rad's gaze snapped to Blackjack.

The big man raised a hand instinctively to deflect—and the second knife struck his palm.

He staggered, but did not fall, tearing the knife from his hand.

Drawing *Darter* in one fluid motion, Rad twisted and flung yet another throwing knife—not caring whether it hit.

The blade clattered wide as Blackjack dodged, cursing as his sword cleared the scabbard, fury flashing across his scarred face.

Hadley, bloody and swaying—not with strength or speed—by sheer stubborn will, lashed out with his fist, crashing into Blackjack's knee.

Rad saw it then—the old man was done. With the last of his life, Hadley gave him the only thing that mattered—a chance—a split second.

The larger man stumbled sideways, off balance as Hadley went face-first to the ground.

Rad pounced.

Blackjack's sword came slicing down, the tip nearly catching his leg.

Rad stabbed *Darter* deep into Blackjack's thick neck, the blade sinking to the hilt, severing flesh, muscle, and windpipe.

Blackjack thrashed, gurgling, one hand clawing at Rad, the other struggling to bring the sword around.

The air was thick with the stench of blood.

Rad seized Blackjack's greasy hair with his left hand and slammed him face-first onto the cobblestones, jabbing *Darter* with brutal precision again and again.

He dropped his knees to Blackjack's back, pressing his full weight down, pinning him against the filthy stones.

Blackjack kicked once, twice, boots scraping weakly.

Rad shoved *Darter* deep into the back of his skull.

The big man jerked—and then went still, the death rattle bubbling in his throat.

Dead.

Rad wrenched *Darter* free, blood sluicing down the blade.

For a single heartbeat, he hovered there, every nerve strung tight, every instinct screaming for another strike.

But there was no need.

Both men were dead.

And Hadley—Hadley needed him.

Rad staggered off Blackjack's corpse, *Darter* still clenched in his blood-slicked hand, and rushed to the older man's side.

Desperation clawed at his chest, but the moment he reached Hadley, he knew.

The old man's battered body lay crumpled in the alley, his life already fled.

There were no last words.

No parting wisdom.

Only the ghost of a bloody smile—and the memory of a voice, stubborn to the end.

Rad… show off.

The weight of the moment pressed down on Rad, but he didn't break.

The alley was a slaughterhouse, blood slicking the stones, bodies scattered like loose hay in a storm. It wouldn't be long before someone stumbled onto the carnage.

He couldn't stay.

Not with blood staining his hands.

Not with three dead men cooling in pools of congealing blood around him.

Forcing his breath steady, Rad moved.

He snatched up his throwing knives, wiped them clean on the dead men's tunics, and stowed them away.

Hadley's *Darter* caught his eye—the name still etched into the handle, a quiet echo of the man now lost to stillness.

Rad picked it up.

The blade was cold.

Without hesitation, he drove it into Marlow's ruined eye, then into Blackjack's back, leaving it buried there.

Let them think it had been some drunken brawl gone wrong, or a robbery.

No ties. No witnesses.

Every move mattered.

One mistake, and it would all come undone.

His mind raced.

He could slip onto the Ethereal Plane and reappear elsewhere—but if someone saw him materialize, it would only raise more questions.

He could hide inside The Sweet Hatchet, but the blood on his clothes, on his hands, on *Darter*...

It would be seen.

Fleeing would make things worse.

There had to be a way.

Rad drew a long, steady breath.

Then he turned from the alley and walked, head down, to the kitchen entrance of The Sweet Hatchet. At the threshold, where the shadows were thickest, he willed himself onto the Ethereal Plane—and vanished.

In this state of nothingness, where cold and heat no longer touched him, Rad let the queasy pit in his stomach and the sting of sweat in his eyes fall away for a moment.

The hazy, distorted world around him solidified.

He crouched low near the threshold between the kitchen and the common room.

He stood, stooping slightly to shield any bloodstains, and moved to the bar.

He wanted to mutter *cup of that brown shit*, but caught himself.

Instead, he tossed a copper onto the counter without meeting the barkeep's eyes.

"Cup of brown," he muttered.

The barkeep, busy wiping his hands, barely glanced at him.

"Stagwater or Redmark?"

Rad dropped another copper onto the counter with a soft clink. "Whatever this buys me."

The barkeep grunted, grabbed a thick, imperfect glass, and sloshed a measure of dark liquor into it, and pushed it across the bar. Without looking, he scooped up the coins and dropped them into his apron.

The smell hit Rad's nose—sharp, sour, and oily.

Rad's gaze swept the room, dreading the drink already.

There—Rosamund—laughing with a group of men, her red dress catching the light, her black hair cascading down her back in soft waves.

When she caught his stare, he lifted a finger, gesturing toward the stairs.

Rosamund nodded once, said her goodbyes, and moved toward the steps, graceful even through the drunken noise of the room.

For a moment, Rad watched, forgetting everything else.

Rad grabbed the drink, eyed the contents with contempt, and downed the fiery liquid in one rough gulp.

It clawed its way down his throat, and for a heartbeat, he thought he might spit it back up.

He swallowed hard, blinked the burn out of his eyes, and said, half-hoarse, "Have you seen Hadley? Gruff old man. Comes here a lot."

The barkeep, already reaching for another patron's order, shrugged.

"Not for a while. Thought he was over there earlier, downing a few. You a friend of his?"

Rad shrugged, casual.

"We work the same stables. It's my birthday. We were meeting for a drink, but..."

He glanced around as if just noticing Hadley's absence.

"You sure you saw him earlier?"

The barkeep nodded vaguely.

"Might've seen him. Might be upstairs with one of the girls. Don't know for sure. Busy night. You can ask Glenys if you can find her."

"Don't bother," Rad said quickly. "Just thought I'd say hello and have a drink."

He gave a crooked, slightly sloppy wink.

"Need to find Rosamund. Birthday tradition."

The barkeep chuckled, already turning to the next shouting patron.

Rad slipped through the crowd, the fiery liquor burning a hole in his gut. Each step up the stairs felt heavier, like he was dragging his own grave behind him.

His legs were leaden, weighed down by more than fatigue.

It wouldn't be long before someone stumbled into the alley—the bodies of Hadley, Marlow, and Blackjack lifeless and bloodied.

Questions would follow, spreading like wildfire through the tavern and beyond.

Sooner or later, they'd come for him—a known associate of Hadley, a familiar face at The Sweet Hatchet.

He reached the third floor.

Without knocking, he pushed open Rosamund's door.

The familiar space hit him like a warm tide—the scent of her perfume, the soft glow of candlelight, the heavy shutters muting the outside world.

It should have been comforting.

Instead, it made the storm inside him worse.

Rosamund stood near the bed, her clingy dress hiked up to her hips, ready for a different kind of night.

"*Stop.*"

The word snapped from him, colder than he meant it.

Rosamund froze.

Slowly, she tugged the dress back down, smoothing the fabric with both hands.

Confusion flickered across her face, replacing the practiced warmth she'd worn a moment before.

"What is going on?"

"Grab another basin of water for me," he said, walking past her without hesitation.

He could feel the tension between them—thick, heavy, undeniable.

Her hand reached toward him, brushing his sleeve.

Her fingers came away sticky with blood, stained dark.

"Please," he said, as he dumped his throwing knives and *Darter* into the basin of water. "Another basin of water."

The water turned a sickly shade of pink.

Rad heard her shuffling away, followed by the creak of the door opening and closing.

He took a long, steady breath, his emotions swirling inside him.

Hadley was gone.

His closest friend—dead in an instant.

Sorrow, regret, guilt—they swelled inside him, a storm he couldn't let break loose.

He replayed the fight again in his mind—the knives, the blood, the final blow—and knew, with bitter certainty, he had managed the best outcome possible.

Once Blackjack had stabbed Hadley in the back, there had been no saving him.

The door creaked open again.

Rosamund stepped inside and barred it with the small metal slide.

She set the second basin on the table without a word.

Rad was stripping off his clothes—shirt already off, inspecting his pants for blood.

There was a dark patch near his right knee.

"Rad," she said softly, "what is going on?"

He met her gaze, the coldness in his eyes freezing her words before she could say more.

"Rosamund," he said, drawing in a slow breath. "A terrible thing happened today."

"Rad…"

"Rosamund, I trust you with my life. Nothing's changed between us. I still want us to be together—the flat above the locksmith's, the life we talked about. It's ours. But right now, I need to know… Can you cope with the truth?"

Rosamund's face twisted with confusion. "You aren't making any sense, Rad. What happened?"

Rad sat on the edge of the bed and started unlacing his boots.

Rosamund interceded, steering his blood-smeared hands aside, and pulled off his boots while waiting for his response.

"Can you cope with it?" he asked again, voice rough. "My truth. The truth of my life."

"You're asking me to handle something I don't even know!" Her voice cracked. "Talk to me, Rad. Please."

Rad heard the strength in her voice.

It wasn't anger—it was an earnest plea to be trusted, to understand. With understanding would come pain—an inevitability he was prepared to face.

"I'm the bastard son of a Leskaré thief," Rad said. "Today—on my birthday—Hadley was murdered. Two thugs came for his treasure.

Their blood is on my hands. I killed them both. I couldn't save Hadley."

He dropped his head, voice breaking.

"I couldn't save him."

Rosamund moved closer, her presence steady against the rising storm in his chest.

"Rad, I don't even know what you're asking. If it's silence, you have it. But I need to understand."

Rad, half-naked, strode forward, brushing past her. He dipped the bloodied parts of his clothes into the fresh basin, scrubbing the stains from the fabric and his hands.

He sensed her behind him—a quiet, steady presence—then felt her hands settle on his shoulders.

Soft.

Warm.

Her thumbs worked into the knots beneath his skin.

Her breath was hot on his neck as she whispered, "I want a future for us, like we always talked about. But sometimes... sometimes I can't see it. I'm getting older, Rad. I can't do this forever. I don't want to waste my life here and be... forgotten."

Her chin rested lightly on his right shoulder, her nose nuzzling against his neck.

"Talk to me."

Rad swallowed hard.

"You're not staying here," he said, voice low. "No more men. No more Sweet Hatchet. I'll find you something better. The library... I know people there. They'll give you a chance."

Rosamund laughed softly against his skin.

"Oh, they would love me there. I can barely read!"

"You can learn," Rad said. "I'll teach you. Remember how I taught you math? I can teach you to read too."

He turned slightly, his voice rough but certain.

"It'll be my purpose in life."

Rad, his face lit by a nervous smile, slipped into her arms and kissed her—soft, desperate.

He drew back, searching her eyes.

"Talk to me," she demanded.

"The truth is, I've done terrible things. And that won't change—it can't. I can't undo what's been done. From this day forward, I'll be tied to shady people. Dangerous people. I'll disappear for days. You won't know where I am. You won't know if I'm alive or dead."

He swallowed hard.

"No cottage in the country. Just a flat in this stinking city. Tell me, Rosamund—what is our future?"

Rosamund took a slow, steady breath.

"It's you and me. Laughing. Finding whatever happiness we can. I know it'll be hard. But right now, I barely get by. Together, we have a chance. Rad, I will never betray you. Tell me what to say! Part of me wants to know everything. The other part... doesn't."

She looked into his eyes.

"You decided to do these terrible things?" she whispered.

"Not entirely. Out of necessity. I'm not a murderer, Rosamund. But I am a killer. I need to know—do you want the unfiltered truth? Can you live with the consequences?"

Tears welled in her eyes.

Her voice broke.

"I adore you. I don't want to live in a world without you. You make me laugh. You make me smile. You respect me... even when others don't."

She dipped her head, ashamed.

"You may as well make me cry, too. I want to know everything. The good and the bad."

"So be it," Rad said. "Tonight's your last night at The Sweet Hatchet. Take your things to JP Locksmith. You know it?"

"I've walked by it a hundred times. Of course I know it."

"The upstairs flat above the shop is mine. Ours. The entrance is around back—up the stairs, not through the store. JP isn't expecting two of us, but he's reasonable. I'll explain it to him. Spare key's in a false plank near the door. I've already outfitted the place. No need to worry about chairs or a bed."

"It'll definitely need a woman's touch if you've been decorating," she said, smiling. "It might take a few trips to move everything. Can't you help me?"

"I can't," he said. "After we're done here, I have to go back to *Château Saignoral.* Retrieve my things. I'll meet you tonight. We'll celebrate—with the best bottle of wine you've ever tasted. I'll tell you my truths... and you can tell me yours."

He kissed her—deep, desperate.

For the first time that night, he felt something ease inside him.

"I love you," she whispered. "Truth or no truth, I love you."

"And I love you," he said, voice steady. "I've loved you since the moment I first saw you—two years ago. I've never wanted another woman, and I never will. Not for as long as we live and breathe."

They held each other in silence, time slipping by in soft, lingering heartbeats.

Eventually, they broke the embrace.

There were still things to do.

Together, they cleaned the blood from his clothes and hung them to dry.

They wiped down his weapons.

The towels—stained and wrung out—were burned in the stove.

The basin water, thick and murky with evidence, was poured out the window.

The room, at last, was restored—ordinary again.

They slipped into bed and curled together, their bodies drawn tight with exhaustion and quiet resolve.

Beneath the cover of darkness, the dam inside him finally broke.

Rad buried his face against her shoulder, shaking.

Silent tears soaked her skin as she held him, stroking his hair, whispering nothing at all.

No demands.

No questions.

Just warmth and steady hands while he wept for Hadley, for himself, for the life that would never be the same.

When the storm passed, he stayed close, breathing her in like the only thing left worth saving.

He nearly drifted off, safe and warm in her arms.

But peace didn't last.

An hour later, a sharp knock rattled the door.

Glenys stood outside with two members of the Ornst militia, their expressions grim.

They were looking for Hadley's companion—Radcliffe von Schule.

KEEPER OF THE DEER   THE SERVANT

CHAPTER TWENTY-TWO

∞

Severance

Château Saignoral was quiet in the dark, its silhouette sharp against the star-scattered sky. Rad navigated the secret paths with silent precision, slipping unnoticed past the towering walls that had once confined his life.

He felt the cool night air on his face, crisp and biting, carrying with it a strange finality.

His path took him near the graves of Ma and Abby. He stopped, standing with reverence over the hallowed ground. Just hours before, in Rosamund's arms, he had let it break. Here, he would carry it silently— he would bear the anguish.

The air around him was heavier, a tangible reminder of all he had lost.

This would be his last visit.

He bowed his head, words unspoken but suffered.

Nearby, his gaze fell on another marker—the corroded flat stone etched with 'LZ.' His real father, Lanny Zeh, rested there now beside Justine.

"Goodbye," Rad murmured to all three.

As his eyes shifted toward the stables, he saw the faint glow of a lantern. Beyond it lay Hadley's shack, now as cold and lifeless as its former occupant. A pang of sorrow struck him, but he stifled it as quickly as it surfaced.

He had shed his tears already, buried them in her arms.

Here, he gave Hadley a warrior's farewell: quiet, unfinished.

Approaching the shadowy figure near the stables, he called out, "Come to say my goodbyes."

Jamie turned, his face lighting up before pulling Rad into an embrace.

"Figured you'd come here, so I waited after supper. You and Hadley have been gone all day. I managed without you. Where is that gruff old man?"

One last lie, to finish the night.

Rad hesitated a beat longer than usual.

His voice came out steady.

Too steady.

The ease of it unsettled him, a sharp crack splintering inside his chest.

"Hadley was murdered in the city," he said.

Jamie froze.

The smile slipped from his face as if yanked away. Disbelief overtook him first—then pure shock. He stared at Rad, searching for something—denial, a lie, anything to grab onto.

Rad didn't move.

Didn't blink.

He let the silence stretch, letting the weight of the truth sink deep.

Jamie's voice finally came, raw and small.

"How? What happened?"

Rad swallowed, his mouth dry.

"We went to The Sweet Hatchet for my birthday. Like usual. I spent time with Rosamund. The militia questioned me after they found the bodies."

Jamie blinked.

"Bodies?"

Rad nodded, keeping his tone measured. He stuck to the story the militia had already corroborated: he'd been with Rosamund the entire time.

The barkeep's confirmation had been invaluable—no further questions.

And Glenys, heartbroken, had said nothing.

Nothing about serving them earlier.

Nothing about their conversation.

She'd protected him.

Protected Rosamund too, though she didn't know it.

"He got into a tussle with two thugs," Rad continued. "Managed to kill them, but his wounds were mortal. I didn't recognize the men, but the owner said they'd been asking around about Hadley. Unlucky. On my birthday, no less."

Jamie's face crumpled, grief washing over the shock. He turned slightly away, like he didn't want Rad to see it.

Rad reached out and placed a hand on his shoulder. It was all he could offer.

"I thought he'd die of old age," Jamie whispered. "Didn't think anyone could hurt him. Not Hadley. He knew how to fight. He was invincible."

"I thought he had more time too," Rad said, voice breaking. His throat tightened—and this time, he didn't stop the tears.

They stood in silence, the weight of Hadley's absence settling between them like a third body in the room.

Rad stepped back, breaking the moment before it dragged him under. Both of them wiped at their cheeks—quick, ashamed movements, like they didn't want to be caught crying.

"I'm leaving tonight," Rad said, sniffing. He paused, steadying himself. "After I grab my extra knives from Hadley's shack, I'll head to the manor for the rest of my things."

A beat passed.

Quieter, Rad added, "Doubt I'll ever come back. Probably wouldn't be allowed to anyway."

Jamie nodded, blinking back fresh tears.

"Good luck. You've been my best friend. I know we haven't spent much time together lately. Florence—"

"We'll always be friends," Rad cut in, his voice firm. "Forever."

He said it for Jamie's sake, hoping the words would bring him comfort, even if they rang hollow in his own heart.

To Rad, true friendship was deeper—reserved for those who had changed him:

Rosamund.

Hadley.

Abby.

They had meant something.

Jamie didn't.

Not really.

And now, with Hadley gone, all he had left was Rosamund.

"Yes, friends," Jamie said, reaching out his hand.

Rad didn't reply.

He turned away before Jamie could say anything else—before he could change his mind and stay.

There were things to do.

And no time for falling apart.

Rad lifted a lantern, its warm glow casting long, flickering shadows along the path to Hadley's modest shack. The walk felt longer than usual, burdened with the weight of finality, as though the small, weathered shed held what remained of Hadley's life.

Inside, the space smelled of wood shavings and pipe smoke, a lingering memory of the man who once called it home.

Hanging on a rack was the old blade, *Bloodspite*, never to be used again. Rad hoped they would bury the blade with Hadley. The horse-master deserved it.

His eyes landed on the wooden owl, perched on a nearby shelf like a silent guardian. It was the same size as its living counterpart, its glossy surface etched with black lines to define its features. Time had left its mark—edges worn smooth from handling, tiny nicks marring the otherwise polished finish.

Lifting it, Rad tested its weight, feeling the faint shift of something hidden inside. He shook it gently, confirming Hadley's instruction, and brought it closer to the lantern's glow. His fingers traced a faint seam near the base, and with a firm twist, it loosened.

A rolled piece of parchment tumbled free.

Rad caught it before it hit the floor.

He checked the hollow interior to be sure nothing else was concealed, then twisted the base shut and returned the owl to its place.

He stared at the map for a long moment, his pulse ticking in his throat.

This was it—the thing Hadley had never talked about. A path marked by one of the hardest, cruelest men he had ever known.

Hadley feared nothing—but he hadn't gone back.

Not once, though he'd known about it for years.

He held the map between his palms, wondering what was within.

This was the thing Hadley couldn't keep any longer—the secret that haunted him, the one he'd rubbed smooth like the wooden owl that hid it.

And now Hadley was dead.

Killed by men who had come looking for the treasure.

Rad's pulse quickened.

This wasn't just a gift—it was a burden, a thread in a web of danger he couldn't yet see the edges of.

Doubt crept in.

He wasn't so sure.

Not about the map.

Not about himself.

All his training, the bravado, the bluster—it felt thin now.

Like old cloth stretched over something hollow.

He clenched his jaw, steadying his breath.

The fear didn't vanish, but he tucked it under his belt along with the map.

He couldn't linger.

Grief—and everything tangled up with it—would find him soon enough.

After collecting the extra roll of knives stored in the shack, Rad stepped outside and closed the door firmly behind him. A small gesture—but it felt like goodbye.

He turned to Jamie, raising the roll of knives in a silent farewell.

Without waiting for a response, he started toward the manor, where lanterns and candles cast golden pools of light onto the darkened grounds.

His boots creaked on the wooden deck—too loud in the stillness of night. Cursing his carelessness, Rad veered off the noisier path, melting into the shadows. He chastised himself—not for the noise, but for letting memory dull his edge.

In places like this, being loud didn't just get you caught.

It got you killed.

At the manor's entrance, two guards stood posted, giving him a passing glance—but something in their eyes lingered a second too long.

Not suspicion.

Not respect.

Something colder.

Rad returned their gaze with a curt nod—confident, familiar, unthreatening—masking the flicker of unease tightening in his chest.

He stepped inside, merging with the lanternlight of *Château Saignoral* like he still belonged there.

The scent of the manor enveloped him: familiar, layered, bittersweet. The aroma of the evening meal still clung to the air— savory mutton and the sharp tang of red onions, strong enough to taste. Beneath it, a trace of sweetness lingered.

Cookies, likely—dusted in sugar and cinnamon. The baker still had a soft hand in the kitchens.

For a fleeting moment, the house almost felt like it had years ago.

Warm.

Alive.

But warmth had never lasted here.

Not for him.

At the threshold, Rad slipped off his boots and moved forward in stockinged feet. Every step placed with purpose—the way Hadley had taught him—toes first, heel last, weight forward.

He drifted through the lounge like a wraith, soundless, invisible.

Not a servant.

Not a son.

Not tonight.

A shadow with a purpose.

He stood there for a moment, absorbed by silence.

No one noticed his presence.

No one greeted him.

No one stopped him.

As he climbed the stairs, memories surged—sharp, uninvited.

He smirked, recalling the time he'd crammed a muffin into Tristin's smug face. That small act of rebellion had gotten him—*the bastard*— expelled.

Maybe it was the best thing that ever happened to him.

The grand gala flickered through his mind—opulence and lies, where the secrets were as real as the guests. It was the night he had first seen Xavier for what he was: a cruel, manipulative man. Later, he'd learned the rest—his true heritage.

The darker memories crept in.

Two assassins—dead by his hand.

Vanguard's last scream in the fire.

Ma and Abby, lifeless in the breakfast nook, soaked in blood that never dried in his mind.

His fists clenched.

Jaw tight.

There was no time to be soft.

He had chosen this path—a hard path.

And it was almost time to see it through.

He reached his room—his sanctuary for so many years.

Stepping inside, he felt a flicker of solace. The air was heavy with the familiar scent of worn linens, old books, and the faint must of dust.

Safe.

Still his.

For a few more minutes, at least.

He placed his boots down quietly and went straight to the packed canvas bag on the floor.

Two-thirds of the contents were dumped onto the bed.

Moving with practiced precision, he rearranged it all—wrapping his coins in grimy stockings and tucking them deep inside.

His savings were modest, but hard-earned.

He wasn't about to let the last of it slip away now.

The roll of knives went next.

Then the folded shirts.

From the back of his closet, he retrieved a bottle of *Maitrasse Cru Bonnage*—one of the few genuine vintages he'd managed to liberate from Xavier's collection, swapping it with a counterfeit.

The other real bottles were locked away in Xavier's study vault, waiting for the day Rad came back for them.

But this bottle?

This one was for tonight.

For Rosamund.

He stuffed the last of his clothing and tested the balance of the oblong bag.

It felt right—weighted, but not slow.

Ready to move.

At the top, he added a stained coin purse filled with silvers Abby had given him, along with a few stray coppers.

He cinched the bag shut.

His preparations were complete.

He should have felt relief. But something was wrong.

No one had stopped him.

No one had called out.

Not even a curious glance on the way in.

And the guards at the back entrance? They had looked at him like he was already dead.

A chill ran up his spine.

He didn't like it.

The door swung open.

No knock.

No pause.

No pretense of respect.

It slammed against the wall hard enough to make Rad flinch and rattle the lantern hanging on the wall.

Rad didn't turn.

Only Wilkins barged in like that—as if he owned every room in the house.

He froze as the man stepped forward, ego filling the space long before his voice did.

"Xavier is looking for you," Wilkins said, his voice soaked in disdain.

Rad, his canvas bag slung over one shoulder, adjusted the strap and grabbed his boots in his left hand. "Let's go. Is he in his study?"

But Wilkins wasn't here to be helpful. His face hardened, and with a swift motion, he yanked the bag from Rad's shoulder.

"Not so fast."

Rad tensed, letting the strap resist just enough to make Wilkins work for it. He could have put the bastard on the floor—and he wanted to—but he kept his tone calm.

"It's just my clothes."

Wilkins loosened the rope closure and peered inside.

Rad noticed his search was cursory at best.

His fingers barely shifted the garments, his eyes skimming rather than seeing. Wilkins's hand closed around the battered coin purse, and he pulled it free, weighing it in his palm with a smirk.

"Well, well," he said. "How'd you come by this?"

"That's all I have!" Rad snapped. "I need my coin!"

Wilkins didn't blink at the emotional protest.

He tossed the canvas bag back at Rad and slipped the purse into his coat pocket with a lazy shrug.

"This is mine now. Say anything, and I'll deny it."

Rad's blood boiled, fists clenching around the bag's strap.

Wilkins jerked his thumb toward the hallway.

"Get downstairs. Your father's waiting. Time for you to leave." Then, with a sneer, he added, "I should lock you in your closet one last time. Make sure you remember your place."

Rad shoved past him hard enough to make the man stumble.

Behind him, he heard the smug jingle of stolen silver.

Rad stormed down the stairs, fury pulsing through him.

His mind spun, hot with rage and cold with control.

He didn't see the grand staircase, the accent table where he'd once hidden the shared journal, the polished banister, or the warm glow of the lanterns lighting his way.

This was it—the final act in his long, bitter stay at the manor.

What would Xavier say? Would it be a drawn-out lecture? A curt dismissal?

Part of him, deep and animal, stirred uneasily.

Xavier didn't do things cleanly. There was always a catch.

His boots remained in his hand until he reached the bottom of the stairs.

Before stepping to the study doors, he paused to slip them on.

He could sense Wilkins trailing close behind, reveling in his small victory.

Drawing in a deep breath to steady himself, Rad lifted a hand and knocked.

"Enter," came the voice from within—sharp, commanding.

Rad strode into the study, boots clicking on the polished wooden floor, Wilkins trailing behind with an arrogant grin.

The room was the same: dark-paneled walls, shelves lined with books Rad doubted Xavier had ever read, and the imposing desk where his stepfather and Tristin conducted their business.

This was also the room where unimaginable wealth lay hidden within the magical vault.

Since the day he had touched the undead hand, Rad had only ventured inside the study once—to glimpse the fortune stored within.

Stacks of platinum.

Piles of gold.

Treasures beyond reckoning.

He had fantasized about relieving Xavier of it all, once.

But the thought had been fleeting.

No amount of money would bring back Ma or Abby.

No treasure could undo their deaths.

Now, his heart ached anew.

He would have given anything to have Hadley at his side.

What he wanted wasn't wealth.

It was revenge.

He would ruin Xavier.

Take Leskaré for himself.

Leave the von Schule patriarch destitute—groveling in the streets.

"Hand over the bag," Xavier ordered.

"Wilkins already searched it," Rad replied, voice steady.

He slipped the canvas bag from his shoulder, holding it casually in one hand. He made it appear lighter than it was, masking the weight of the wine bottle and the coins hidden in his stockings.

The air in the room grew heavier.

"Is this true?" Xavier asked, sharp eyes darting to Wilkins.

Rad's face remained impassive—a mask of calm.

He was ready for this.

If Wilkins denied searching the bag, Rad would expose him as a thief—pointing out the missing coin purse with its distinctive dark stain.

He was certain Wilkins hadn't discarded it yet.

Proof of his meddling.

If Wilkins admitted the search, Xavier would likely drop the matter.

Rad stood silent, letting the tension thicken.

Waiting.

"Nothing in there," Wilkins said, waving his hand dismissively. "Clothes and shoes. Daresay the lad's destitute—didn't find a stray copper. Dumped all of it out on the floor, found nothing to his name."

Xavier's expression didn't shift. He motioned toward the door with a flick of his hand.

"Wait outside."

Wilkins hesitated, nodded, then obeyed.

The door shut softly behind him, leaving Rad alone with his stepfather.

The tension between them crackled like lightning.

Xavier leaned back in his chair, cold gaze locked on Rad.

"Your mother made me promise to keep you here until you were sixteen," he said, voice measured and razor-sharp. "I should have thrown you out the day she died. But I kept my word. And now—you are sixteen."

He let the words settle between them.

"You will leave this estate and never return. If you are caught here again, I will have you beaten to death and buried beside your mother. Do you understand?"

Rad didn't flinch.

His voice was calm, his expression unreadable.

"I expected empty threats. Don't worry—I won't be back. Jamie and I were close; I'll miss him. Tristin, Marie, Bella? They never spoke to me. I'm better off without them."

He paused.

"Hadley is dead. So I have no reason to return."

Xavier's eyes narrowed—a flicker of something crossing his face. Uncertainty. Maybe fear.

"What do you mean, Hadley is dead?"

"In the city. Today."

Rad recounted the same story he'd told Jamie, voice flat, devoid of emotion.

"I'm sorry. I know he was your horse-master, and your horses were important to you."

He let the cut sink deep before continuing.

"I also know he stopped you from getting rid of me. He told me—if you broke your promise to Ma, he was going to strangle you in your sleep."

Xavier's mouth tightened in recognition of the truth.

His knuckles whitened against the arms of his chair.

"He told you that, did he?" Xavier's voice strained, brittle. "What else did he say? Did he tell you why they called him Hadley the Pillager?"

Rad shrugged, indifferent.

"I don't care about Hadley's past. He's dead. What's done is done."

He let the silence stretch.

"No, he didn't tell me anything. Said I wasn't ready to hear his story. Now we'll never know."

Xavier sneered. "He was a murderer, saved by my kindness. It's no wonder you admired him. You're scum—like he was."

Rad shook his head slowly, voice calm and steady. "He taught me how to fight. How to survive. I'll be able to defend myself because of him. So... thank you. Kicking me out of the family gave me a trade. Turns out I'm a natural with horses."

Xavier's frustration cracked through his veneer. His jaw clenched. Nostrils flared.

"You're a bastard—sired by the garbage of this city. You're lucky to be alive. Lucky I didn't strangle you the day you were born."

His voice dropped, quiet and cutting.

"You don't have Hadley to protect you any longer. If what you say is true."

Rad refused to bite. His face remained impassive.

"Jamie will do a decent enough job for you," he said. "Is there anything else before I get on the road?"

Xavier's face flushed with anger.

"Didn't you hear me? You're a bastard! Your father was a nobody—scum!"

The tension thickened, suffocating.

Rad stood in the study, surrounded by dark wood, silence, and venom. Inside, his mind was a storm—truths he could unleash, insults that would cut deeper than any knife.

He knew about the affair with Gabrielle, the governess.

He knew Tristin visited Florence's bed far too often.

He knew his real father, Lanny Zeh, had once ruled Leskaré—and was murdered beneath this very house.

He knew Marie and Bella had secrets of their own.

And most of all, he knew Ma and Abby had died because he had saved Tristin.

But he said nothing.

Xavier didn't deserve his words.

Words would only feed him.

What Xavier deserved was ruin.

He deserved to see the boy he had hated rise to lead Leskaré—and destroy him piece by piece.

Hadley's voice echoed in Rad's mind.

Show off.

Hadley had spent years warning him not to.

Stay quiet. Stay unseen. Stay alive.

But that wasn't what he meant at the end.

Not anymore. It was a final command.

Rise. Be everything they feared you could be.

Rad exhaled slowly.

"Nothing to say?" Xavier snapped. "I see you are as cold as your dead mother."

Rad's gaze flicked to the door.

Something crawled at the edge of his awareness—the way the guards had looked at him… the too-easy silence of his walk inside… the way Xavier had dismissed Wilkins from the room.

Something was wrong.

Rad steadied himself.

Masked his breath. Turned his eyes back to Xavier with calm precision.

"One thing."

He raised a finger and let the pause linger.

"If I see you outside these walls, I will not be cordial. There is no peace between us."

He took a step forward.

"I will ruin your family. I will reclaim this fortress—Souterrain Hall. I'll bring you to your knees, and I will piss on your ashes."

Xavier shifted in his chair, the mask of control slipping.

"Your threats are as hollow as your mother's promises," Xavier said, voice sharpening. "You come near me, and I'll make sure you're buried beside her. It's only because of her—and Hadley—that you're not already in the ground. And because I'm a man of worth, you will be allowed to leave tonight. Unmolested."

His mouth twisted into a sneer.

"Be careful. These may be your last words."

Rad's gaze burned with cold fury.

"Generous of you to offer me a free burial," he said. "But I won't bury you."

He took another step closer.

"I'll leave you destitute. Begging for death."

Rad let the words carve into the silence.

"That's your future. Etch it into your memory."

He leaned forward, voice cold, certain: "I'm a man of my word."

Xavier's temper snapped.

"Wilkins!"

The door burst open.

The valet strode in, face lit with eagerness.

"Escort him from the estate. Now. Before I change my mind and bury him next to his mother."

Wilkins lunged for Rad's arm, gripping hard—but Rad didn't flinch.

He shook the man off and walked forward, steady and unstoppable.

Wilkins scrambled to catch up, pushing toward the rear of the manor with a sneer.

"Out the back. Don't come around. Ever again."

Rad adjusted his bag and kept walking, ignoring the taunts.

He didn't look back as he breached the threshold.

Behind him, the door locked with a sharp snick.

He was free.

Wilkins entered the study after a sharp knock, the faint stink of bourbon clinging to him.

Xavier sat at his desk, inspecting a ledger with the focus of a man whose world revolved around numbers, profit, and the next grand scheme.

"Sir," Wilkins began, clearing his throat, "there's been... an incident in the city."

Xavier didn't look up.

He continued making notations with precise, deliberate strokes.

"If it's some petty crime or drunken squabble with the staff, handle it. I'm not interested in the trivialities of your responsibilities."

"It's Hadley," Wilkins said, urgency creeping into his voice.

Xavier paused.

He set the quill down with a faint click and steepled his fingers.

"Go on."

"The Ornst militia brought his body to the gates this evening."

Xavier's expression didn't shift. But his eyes narrowed faintly, like a man calculating a loss.

"Dead, is he?"

Wilkins nodded.

"Knife to the back—must've nicked the heart. Another to the shoulder. Two assailants, both dead by his hand. One dagger to the eye, one to the neck. They think it was a robbery gone wrong. Witnesses say the men escorted him from The Sweet Hatchet into the alley."

"He was with Radcliffe today, wasn't he?"

"I believe so," Wilkins replied, stiffening.

"Well?"

"No word of the boy. The militia didn't mention him. I can inquire—"

"Don't bother."

Xavier leaned back in his chair, his expression unreadable. But his mind moved swiftly, coldly.

Hadley was gone.

The boy would follow soon enough.

Both replaceable.

But not without cost.

Finding a stablemaster as capable as Hadley would be tedious, costly, irritating.

And the horses—his true investments—deserved better than fools and peasants handling them.

Still, Hadley's death cleared a path.

No one left to shield Radcliffe now.

No one to bargain on his behalf.

No one to stand in the way.

Xavier exhaled through his nose—a sound of mild irritation, not grief.

"A shame," he said. "Hadley was masterful with my horses. Efficient. And he kept the boy in line." His mouth tightened. "Now both are gone."

Wilkins hesitated.

"Out with it," Xavier hissed.

"The boy—Radcliffe—he may not know yet. Or he's being detained while they investigate. He hasn't returned."

Xavier nodded, jaw tight. His gaze drifted toward the study's closed door.

"The militia wants to speak with you about claiming the body. They're expecting compensation for transporting it."

Xavier waved a hand. "Pay them. Handle it quietly. No need for a scene."

His voice turned colder.

"Burn the body in the blighted orchard. He won't need a grave. Empty the shed tomorrow."

Wilkins blinked, then nodded.

"Yes, sir."

Xavier tapped a finger against the desk, lost in thought.

"Radcliffe may not know... But what if he does?"

"Sir?"

"If he knows Hadley is dead, he'll try to sneak out tonight."

Xavier's gaze darkened.

"I want you to watch for when he returns to his room. Confront him. Bring him to me." Xavier's lip curled. "I'll throw him out myself—but you make sure he leaves through the back of the manor."

He paused.

"The shadows are deep there."

Wilkins swallowed. "Yes, sir."

"And Wilkins—send the guard captain here. You handle the Ornst militia. Deal with Hadley's body."

Wilkins bowed—but hesitated, lingering at the threshold.

"You have more to say?" Xavier asked.

Wilkins met his eyes. "Silence doesn't come without cost, sir. Silence is like loyalty."

Irritation flickered across Xavier's face.

He exhaled sharply.

"Ever the opportunist. You'll be rewarded. Now go."

Wilkins turned on his heel and left without another word.

He knew what Xavier had just done.

He'd signed Radcliffe's death warrant.

Rad stepped off the back stoop, the night air cool against his face.

For the first time in years, he felt relief.

It was over.

The confrontation, the exile, the suffocating weight of *Château Saignoral*—he'd left his old life behind. Whatever came next, at least it would be his.

He adjusted the bag on his shoulder and took a slow breath.

His chest felt lighter.

No more stables before dawn.

No more bowing and scraping for people who despised him.

No more biting his tongue just to survive the day.

Waiting for him were endless possibilities.

His life. His future.

For a moment, he allowed himself to believe it.

But—

Fear tugged at the edge of his thoughts.

Why had Wilkins locked the door behind him?

Rad slowed as he crossed the back deck, the wooden boards creaking under his boots.

A glance to either side showed empty corners, empty shadows.

No sentries along the manor's edge.

No lanterns, only darkness.

No distant murmur of voices or shifting armor from the roving guards.

The back lawn stretched out in pale moonlight, untouched.

Too untouched.

The guards were gone.

He stopped, listening.

The breeze whispered through the trees.

No footsteps.

No warning.

But the hair on his arms stood on end.

It was all wrong.

For a lingering moment, he stood there, eyes sweeping the lawn. Then he jogged down the steps without a sound.

Rad adjusted the canvas duffle on his shoulder and slipped a throwing knife into his hand.

His boots crunched against the gravel path—too loud, every step a flare in the dark, announcing his presence.

To either side, the grassy lawn stretched out—familiar, haunting. These were the places he'd played as a child, before truth and tragedy carved his innocence away.

Far to the left, the carriage house stood dark and silent.

Straight ahead, the stables loomed—solid, familiar.

Off to the right, the gardens and gazebo where he and Abby had once hidden the shared journal.

And beyond them, catching the pale moonlight—Hadley's shed.

A pang of regret caught him as his gaze returned to the stables. He'd say goodbye to the horses—for himself, and for Hadley. They deserved it.

For a moment, he considered taking Moonsilver.

She could carry him far, fast—one last insult to Xavier.

But practicality won out.

There was no place for her in the city.

And stealing her would only invite more wrath.

Better to leave her behind.

Thoughts of Rosamund steadied him. She was waiting. A quiet life was waiting—far from this madness.

Rad stepped off the gravel, absently twirling the knife in his hand.

His boots brushed through the short grass, the sound softened by habit. A lesson from Hadley—always step quiet when you can.

The night wrapped around him—cool, still—as he moved toward the stables.

When he reached the back of the property, he'd pay his respects to Ma and Abby.

One last time.

A sharp *clink*—like glass on stone—shattered the quiet.

Rad flinched. Something small struck his shoulder and stuck with a faint hiss. He looked down.

A glowing sphere—no bigger than a coin—clung to his coat, pulsing green.

A second one struck near his boot.

A third missed, rolled across the grass, and dimmed.

He tore the glowing tag from his shoulder, but another landed— this one clinging near his hip.

His blood ran cold as the realization set in.

They were tagging him.

Arcane markers.

Ambush.

He turned just as figures emerged from the dark.

Three shadows—closing fast. Swords drawn.

From the gardens behind, more boots thundered—cutting off his escape.

"Get him!" a voice bellowed.

Rad bolted, darting toward the stables.

The gravel exploded under his boots, each breath tearing through his lungs.

Another figure stepped into his path—a bulky shape with a curved sword glowing faintly blue.

An enchanted blade.

Rad didn't slow.

A knife flashed—struck the man's thigh. He staggered, snarling.

Rad hurled a second knife—struck the opposite leg. The man crumpled to his knees.

Rad swerved around him, sprinting hard.

More footsteps behind—closer now.

A flicker caught his eye—*another sphere* arcing toward him. It skipped once across the grass.

Rad kicked it like a ball.

It bounced straight into the legs of the pursuing group.

Blue light exploded waist-high.

Tiny spheres erupted into a freezing mist.

Men screamed—three of them collapsing in shock as frost raced up their limbs.

The chill wasn't deadly—but it was enough to incapacitate.

One of them fumbled another rune in his hand.

Rad flung a knife, fast and low.

The man jerked backward, and the rune slipped.

It burst at his feet.

A column of cold engulfed him, driving him to the ground.

Three knives. He had nine remaining. Another slipped into his hand.

Rad kept running.

The shed was close now.

Too close for them to catch him.

A last figure lunged from the shadows—but Rad faked left, then cut hard to the right.

He reached the door, flung it open, and slammed it shut behind him.

The bar dropped with a thud.

His chest heaved. He turned, eyes scanning the space.

The sword.

He crossed the shed in two steps and unsheathed Hadley's blade.

Moonlight kissed the edge.

Rad stared at it, then slammed it point-first into the floorboards.

A farewell. A refusal.

Hadley would've appreciated the insolence.

The door shuddered as boots crashed against it.

"Come out, boy!" someone shouted. "You're delaying the inevitable!"

Rad didn't answer.

He drew in a breath.

Steadied himself.

Reached inward.

The world blurred.

Color drained.

The Ethereal Plane took hold.

Weightless. Dim. Silent.

He passed through the wall as oil splashed behind him.

Torches flared.

In the ghost-gray haze of the Ethereal Plane, the fire bloomed—like pale flowers opening in reverse.

"Come out!" a voice snarled. "We'll make it quick. Burning's cruel."

Rad drifted, spectral, across the estate—over lawn and gravel and the memories buried beneath them.

Through the great hall.

Past the front gate.

To the tree line where shadows lingered.

There he emerged—solid again, breath catching in his chest.

The canvas bag still clutched in his hand.

Behind him, the manor stood dark against the firelight—the shed now a pillar of flame.

He stared for a moment.

His prison. His battleground. His home.

Now ash and memory.

Rad turned away.

Somewhere in the city, Rosamund waited.

And Rad—Rad was finally free.

EPILOGUE

∞

The Maw of Darkness

Bastien awoke in near darkness. He lay chained to a cold, damp slab of stone, stripped of all but a blood-soaked cloth wrapped around his waist. The faint flicker of a candle was somewhere in the distance, but he couldn't see it.

His wrists ached where rusted shackles bit into the skin, and his back burned with raw welts. The air was thick and wet, reeking of rot and old iron.

In the blackness, water dripped in slow, mocking rhythm.

Drip.

Drip.

Drip.

The last thing he remembered was the sanctuary—the gasps of the other disciples, the voice of High Priest Casten condemning him for sacrilege, for abandoning the Oath of Tidall. The man he had refused to heal had died calling out for mercy. Bastien had watched the light fade from his eyes and whispered one word:

"Endure."

They whispered of betrayal.

A healer who turned away from mercy.

Not a heretic—at least not at first—but a danger to the Order.

There was no trial. No farewell. Only silence, and the slow, dawning horror in their eyes.

He fled before they could bind him, robes still damp with the blood he refused to stop.

He told himself he had no choice.

That mercy had become weakness.

But when the forest closed behind him and the stars offered no comfort, he began to wonder if they were right.

Not all lives could be saved.

Not all deserved to be.

Perhaps not even his.

He tried to sit up but couldn't. His body trembled from thirst, and his ribs ached with every breath. Shapes loomed on the crypt walls—crude murals daubed in flaking red.

Horned demons, bodies flayed open, skulls weeping vines of black rot. Beneath the madness, he made out patterns—loops and spirals, circles drawn over and over again.

Voices echoed beyond the stone.

Screams—human, or so he thought.

Footsteps approached.

Two figures emerged from the gloom, their robes of crimson and black trailing behind them like smoke. One was tall, skeletal beneath his wrappings, with a chilling voice.

"I am Arnaud," the man said. "Master of the Pale."

The woman beside him—light-haired, sharp-eyed—smiled without warmth.

"And I am Odette," she said with a purr. "We are your salvation."

They said nothing of why he had been taken. Nothing of where he was.

"You must learn to suffer," Arnaud said.

The first days—or what he thought were days—were spent in silence and pain.

They began with cold water and chains, with lashings across his back until he bled. Then came the branding, the deprivation, the hunger.

They denied him sleep, waking him with pain if he began to drift. Once, Odette whispered chants in the Abyssal tongue while slicing the flesh between his fingers with a thin, curved blade.

Another time, Arnaud held a candle to his bare feet and simply watched.

Each torment came without explanation.

There was no promise of release. No bargain offered. Only the endless ache of torn flesh and the gnawing hunger that hollowed out his thoughts.

But he did not scream. Not at first.

Instead, he tried to remember the Oaths—the sacred words of Tidall—using them to shield his mind. But they unraveled, syllable by syllable, until they meant nothing.

Protected nothing.

The god of healing had abandoned him. Or perhaps he had never listened at all.

When the screams did come, they were his own.

He lost count of how many times he woke in a pool of his own blood, his body broken anew.

They left him alone in the dark for what felt like days.

He dreamed of his old life—the white halls of the temple, the smell of herbs, the warmth of healing light. But those dreams curdled into nightmares, always ending with the face of the man he'd let die.

Endure.

The word haunted him, and the irony was not lost on him.

At first, he thought it a memory—his own voice, echoing backward through time. But it came again. And again. In dreams, in moments of drifting fever, in the gaps between pain and numbness.

It came colder than he remembered. Older.

Endure.

The presence that spoke it was not Tidall. It was vast, unfeeling, and deeply wrong. It watched him from beyond the veil of death. It made no promises. It offered no comfort.

Only that one word.

Endure.

The days blurred together.

Pain lost its novelty. Hunger, its urgency. Bastien no longer flinched when the lash came. His body, flayed and broken, became nothing more than a vessel—emptied, restored, emptied again.

He had begged once.

"Please… kill me."

It was the only thing he had said aloud in days.

Odette had smiled then—not her usual cold smirk, but a reverent grin. She knelt beside him, her fingers brushing the matted hair from his face with unsettling tenderness.

"You're beginning to understand," she whispered. Her hand rose, not to strike, but to heal. A soft incantation slipped from her lips, and warmth spread through Bastien's ribs. He could feel the bones knitting, the torn flesh sealing. The bruises faded. The fever cooled.

Then came her dark blade.

They began again.

Each time he healed, the pain returned, worse than before.

And with every cycle, they spoke to him.

Not in riddles, but in mantras. Simple. Repeated. Inescapable.

"To give pain, you must first receive it."

From the onset, he refused. He bit his tongue to keep from echoing the words.

But the silence earned him worse.

A knife between his toes. A brand pressed against the inside of his thigh. Salt poured into open wounds, just before Odette kissed the edges clean.

"Say it," Arnaud demanded. "Say the creed."

His voice came hollow. "No."

Odette touched the blade to his belly, just above the navel. "Say it."

He didn't.

She carved a single, elegant line, and walked away.

The next day, they brought parchment. Ink. A crude desk.

"You will write," said Arnaud. "Write until your hand fails."

The chant was already burned into his mind. He scratched the words over and over, his blood darkening the parchment where ink ran dry.

To give pain, you must first receive it.

His hand trembled. He kept writing.

Mercy is weakness. Suffering is truth.

He didn't know when he began to believe them. Maybe it started the day he was left alone in the dark and caught himself whispering the words just to feel like someone else was still there.

He chanted in silence.

When no one was watching.

The walls wept and the floor grew slick with condensation and his blood.

He repeated the phrases not to appease them—but because the silence felt colder without them.

Then the voice returned.

Not Odette. Not Arnaud. Not his own.

It filled the crypt like a thick fog. No direction. No center.

Only intent.

This is the truth.

You were chosen because you endured.

Bastien opened his eyes. He wasn't asleep. He wasn't awake. The boundaries had long since blurred.

He saw himself—naked, scarred, arms stretched out over an altar of obsidian. But he was not bleeding. He was… content.

His eyes glowed with a pale, violet light.

"Who are you?" he whispered.

The air answered in his bones.

I am hunger.

I am cold.

I am the master of the threshold between breath and stillness.

The presence leaned in, vast and unknowable.

You are nearly ready.

Bastien woke.

His wounds were healed. No magic. No potions. No bandages.

The flesh had sealed without help.

When the cultists came, they said nothing.

They knelt.

He was given a black tunic. The same red sash Arnaud wore was draped across his shoulders.

That evening, he was moved to the common cell.

Ten other initiates huddled in the dim stone room, each with a small cot and a bowl of brackish water. Most were young. Some were old. None looked up.

A few rocked and whispered. One scraped his nails into the stone wall, carving a circle again and again.

Another looked up and saw the brand on Bastien's collarbone. His lip twitched.

"You're going to live," he muttered. "That's worse."

Bastien sat cross-legged on the floor, and in a low, calm voice, he began the chant:

To give pain, you must first receive it.

The others joined in. The cell echoed with quiet, rhythmic voices— like waves against the shore of madness.

Bastien's eyes closed, his face slack with peace. The presence in his dreams stirred once more. And filled him with pain.

Endure.

The summons came at dusk.

Two robed cultists entered the cell without a word. One pointed to Bastien. The others looked away. No one dared speak.

He followed them down twisting corridors slick with lichens and decay, past rows of iron-barred cells, empty now, but echoing with old screams. The scent of tainted blood and filthy stone grew stronger with every step. At last, they reached a sealed archway flanked by sconces made of human skulls. The guards withdrew.

The door opened on its own.

Beyond lay a crypt chamber built of ancient black stone. The walls curved inward toward a central dais, where a single obsidian altar rose from the floor like a tooth. Braziers burned low, casting slow-turning shadows that danced along the high vaulted ceiling. Crimson light shimmered across the wet stone.

Bastien stepped forward. He knew this place.

He had seen it before.

In his nightmares.

Arnaud stood behind the altar, his gaunt hands folded before him. His mask was off—his face was pale and angular, sunken at the cheeks, but his eyes were alive with cruel intelligence.

"You remember this place," Arnaud said.

Bastien nodded slowly. "In my… dreams."

Arnaud gestured to the altar. "Kneel."

Bastien obeyed. The cold stone kissed his knees.

"You've passed every test. The flesh has broken and mended. The mind has bent and refused to shatter. You have learned the chant. You have borne the brand. You have endured." His voice lowered. "But there is one sign we cannot fabricate."

He circled the altar slowly, his bare feet silent on the damp stone.

"Many survive the blade. Fewer accept it. Only a handful hear the voice beyond." Arnaud came to stand before him. "Tell me, what was your first breath?"

Bastien didn't hesitate.

"Innocence stolen. My life for the Prince."

The silence that followed was absolute.

Arnaud stepped back, lips parting in reverence. "Then it is true. He has marked you."

From beneath his robes, he produced a small satchel and withdrew a curved dagger with a hilt of bone and dark iron. Bastien recognized it at once—it was Odette's ceremonial blade. Its edge had flayed him. Carved him. Rewritten him.

It was beautiful.

Arnaud held the dagger flat across his palms and bowed.

"You are to build a dominion of your own. That is his will."

He set the blade on the altar.

"There is a place in southern Haddensack. Bacani. A city full of life and promise, where the ancient cemeteries have grown deeper than the roots of the trees. Whispers still haunt the tombs. You will go there. You will call the lost. You will build your house in darkness and fill it with their cries."

Bastien took the blade.

"And what shall your sect be called?" Arnaud asked.

The name came to him with ease, as if whispered by that cold, watchful presence coiled behind the veil of his thoughts.

"The Maw of Darkness."

Arnaud smiled. "Then go, Master of the Pale. Feed the earth. Sow despair. Call them."

Bastien rose, eyes aglow with purpose.

The next day, Arnaud said nothing. He only pointed.

Two guards escorted Bastien through the winding crypts, past screaming cells and sacrificial alcoves, until the stench of blood began to fade. The walls shifted from jagged rock to polished stone. The torches burned cleaner here. The silence was deeper.

They brought him to a door—carved, fitted with iron hinges, and locked from the outside.

When it opened, Bastien stepped into a room far removed from the filth he had known. It was modest by noble standards, but luxurious compared to the cold floor and chains of the cells. A bed with a frame. A basin of clean water. A desk with parchment and ink. Even a simple wardrobe of black tunics folded neatly on the shelf.

The door shut behind him.

Bastien stood still, half-expecting a blade from the shadows. Was this another test?

None came.

He raised his hand and snapped his fingers.

The pillar candles on the desk flared to life, their flames dancing low and steady.

For a moment, he simply breathed.

Then he crossed the room, sat on the edge of the bed, and allowed his weight to sink into the mattress. His limbs trembled from the luxury of it.

He slept.

He dreamed of vast caverns lined with skulls, of oceans filled with blood that bubbled and whispered secrets. He wandered through fields of bone where no wind blew, where the sun hung frozen in a black sky.

Things moved at the edge of his vision—staggering shapes with hollow eyes and claws like rusted hooks. Creatures with red eyes and fangs stalked him.

And then came the Prince.

He did not walk. He did not fly. He emerged.

A horned figure, goat-legged and vast, with skin like rotted parchment stretched too tight over the frame of something larger. His crown was a wreath of bone. His eyes burned with frozen, crimson fire. In his hand he carried a mace tipped with a skull that was… alive, eyes with pinpoints of white.

He looked down on Bastien—not with rage, nor warmth, but recognition.

A clawed hand reached out. The air bent around it.

You are the vessel.

You are the hunger.

You are the mouth through which I will speak.

Then came the scream—not Bastien's, but a world's. It rose from the fields, from the blood sea, from the depths of every dying star. It clawed its way through his ears and filled his mouth with ash.

He awoke gasping.

The room was silent. The candles had gone out.

And yet he felt no fear.

Only purpose.

Bastien stood, dressed in fresh black, and fastened the red sash over his shoulder.

He found a satchel prepared for him—rations, maps, coin, and a bone-handled blade.

No one waited in the halls.

He passed through the last door of the Crimson Shroud's dominion, alone.

The road ahead led southeast, toward Bacani.

Toward his dominion.

Toward the Maw of Darkness.

***

The long road to Bacani was quiet.

Dust clung to Bastien's boots as he walked, the late summer heat thick with gnats and the smell of dry grass. His tunic stuck to his back. The red sash lay coiled in his satchel—unworn for now.

He kept to the shade where he could, watching the trees bend beneath the weight of unseen crows. One dropped from the branches in a sudden swoop, landing just ahead of him on the path. It bobbed up and down, cawing sharply—once, twice, *thrice*—then turned and shrieked at the trees.

The forest answered. A hundred wings burst skyward in a black rush, the murder taking flight as one.

The crows vanished into the sky, leaving behind a stillness more complete than before. No branches creaked. No insects called. Only the hush of the forest and the distant beat of wings fading into nothing.

Bastien kept walking.

The road was uneven, littered with ruts and errant stones, but it wasn't the terrain that troubled him. It was the space above. The sky stretched wide and empty, blue as a wound, and the sun seared against his brow like it might consume him. After so long underground, the open world felt too large, too bright, too *uncontained*. There were no walls to lean against. No ceiling to stop the sky from swallowing him whole.

He breathed through his teeth, keeping his head down, moving from one patch of shade to the next. Still, the pressure built.

Once, when no one was near and the wind had stilled, he stopped beside a gnarled stump and stretched out his fingers.

Dark threads of energy unwound from his hand—thin, wispy ribbons, black as smoke and cold as grave water. They twitched like snakes in the air, searching… searching for breath.

He watched them drift, weightless, for a long while before curling his fingers closed.

The shadows obeyed.

A hare froze in the brush, twenty feet away—ears perked, body tense.

Bastien whispered an incantation in the Abyssal tongue, a language rarely heard on the Material Plane.

The ribbons surged.

They lashed forward without sound, slicing through the air, piercing fur and flesh. The hare spasmed, eyes bulging, mouth gaping in a silent scream. It writhed in the dirt for a heartbeat more—then went still.

Bastien lowered his hand. The ribbons slithered back, vanishing into his skin.

He stared at the small corpse, waiting for guilt. None came.

"This is the way of it," he murmured. "Our Lord of Withering Rot does not forbid. He enables."

He knelt beside the hare, but did not touch it. The air around the body was colder now, as if the dead thing had left more than flesh behind.

This was not cruelty. It was understanding.

He had studied healing once—stitched wounds, poured tinctures down dying throats. But mercy had limits. He had seen them. Felt them. All that kindness, and still they died.

Maybe, in this—this unraveling—he would finally reach the root of what he'd always sought.

Not power. Not escape.

The last fragment of the man he used to be.

He rose without another word and left the hare to rot, a gift for his master—The True Cure.

By late afternoon, he spotted the wagon up ahead—half-sheltered beneath an old poplar where the road dipped low.

A man stood by the horse, adjusting the tack. A woman sat on a blanket in the grass, nursing a babe in the shade. Nearby, a toddler chased bugs with a stick, his babblings echoing over the hill.

Bastien slowed.

His fingers twitched.

The boy saw him first and ran to meet him, fearless and grinning.

Bastien crouched as the child approached.

"Well, hello there," he said, ruffling the boy's sun-bleached curls.

The boy giggled and darted away, calling for his mother.

The man turned, resting a hand near the hatchet looped on his belt. The woman, startled, shifted her shawl to cover herself—but relaxed when she saw the stranger's face.

Bastien smiled—warm, open, disarming.

"I don't mean to startle," he said. "Long road. Thought I'd greet the only friendly faces I've seen all day."

The man eyed him for a moment, then nodded. "Road's empty lately. You heading north or west?"

"Southeast," Bastien said. "Bacani, if my feet hold out. Name's Bastien."

"I'm Tarnik," the farmer said. "Mara, my wife. Jonrel, my son. And the babe is Cally."

"Pleasure," Bastien said with a curt bow.

"I've never heard of Bacani," Mara added, adjusting the baby. "It must be far away from here."

She tried not to stare, but failed. Bastien caught the glance, then looked politely away. She blushed and turned her gaze back to the infant, brushing a loose curl from her cheek.

"We're headed to our village of Viercourt," Tarnik said. "Back from my cousin's wedding. You're welcome to ride with us—if you don't mind the little ones. We'd like to hear news of where you've come from."

Bastien dipped his head. "I'd be grateful."

Tarnik gave a sharp whistle, herding the boy back to the wagon. Jonrel climbed aboard with his father's help. Mara wrapped the baby tight and shifted to make room beside her husband on the bench.

Bastien waited, then stepped up into the back.

The cart rocked under his weight. The smell of old hay and wood oil clung to the air.

He noticed a faint bloodstain across the floorboards—likely a deer from the summer hunt.

He leaned back against a crate and stretched his legs.

Then, without sound, he drew the wicked blade from his pack.

It gleamed in the shadows—curved, black-edged, and hungry.

Hungry for innocent blood.

The True Cure.

Here ends Book One of the Keeper of the Deer series:

The Servant

Rad will return in Books Four and Five:

Master Thief
and
Forsaken Fate

Follow his rise to fame in Leskaré, surviving the Black Storm invasion, and a confrontation with the Skull Lord.

The search for Hadley's treasure begins. Assassins and treacherous creatures lurk in the shadows, stalking him at every junction. When he returns home, betrayal.

The Keeper of the Deer series continues with Book Two:

The One Tree

We begin Heather's journey within the magical realm of druids, her destiny tied to The One Tree, and the discovery of an ancient relic, a Mage-Gate.

DRAMATIS PERSONAE

A

Abigail von Schule — Youngest daughter of Xavier von Schule, bright and quick-witted.

Alden Fairmont — Ornst nobleman, known for his prowess judging wines and hosting cotillions.

B

Bastien — Cult leader of the Maw of Darkness, follower of the Demon Prince of Undeath.

Bella von Schule — Eldest daughter of Xavier von Schule.

Brak — Mysterious wizard, searching for relics.

C

Chilcott — Also known as "Puzzle Boy," runs errands for Leskaré, ally and friend to Radcliffe.

D

Duwy — Black Storm representative, operating in Ornst.

F

Florence — Housemaid at *Château Saignoral*

G

Gabrielle — Governess to the von Schule children, known for her stunning beauty.

H

Hadley — Horse-master at *Château Saignoral*, also known as "Hadley the Pillager."

J

Jamie — Young stable hand at *Château Saignoral*, friend to Radcliffe.

Justine von Schule — Matron of the von Schule family, wife of Xavier.

K
Killigrew — Longtime friend and business partner of Xavier von Schule.

L
Lanny Zeh — Former business partner of Xavier von Schule and ranking member of Leskaré.

M
Marie von Schule — Middle daughter of Xavier von Schule.
Merrow Keff — Renown scholar present at the founding of the Ornst Library. After two years of dedicated work, he was promoted to the Assistant to the Assistant Head Libarian. Known for spilling soup and collecting sketches of dryads. *(deceased?)*

R
Radcliffe von Schule — Youngest son of Xavier von Schule.
Robert Ruud — Young nobleman of Ornst, known to have admired Abigail.
Rosamund — Young woman who works as a prostitute at The Sweet Hatchet.

T
Tristin von Schule — Eldest son of Xavier von Schule, heir to *Château Saignoral*.

W
Wilkins — Household valet to the von Schule family; precise and formal.

X
Xavier von Schule — Master of *Château Saignoral*, powerful and calculating.

TIMELINE

Era	Years Ago	Key Themes
Primordial Age	???–4000	Wild magic, flourishing of ancient races.
Age of the Bloodlords	4000–3000	Human dynasties thrive; coexistence with elder races.
The Bloodletting	~3000	Collapse of Bloodlords; chaos, wars, ruin.
Age of Quiet Expansion	3000–1100	Gradual rebuilding; early libraries; cautious magic.
Rise of the Mages	1100–1000	Mage domination, obsessive chronicling of knowledge.
Sundering	~1000	Mage downfall; global collapse.
Age of Recovery	1000–700	Survival, preservation of knowledge.
Age of Rising Kingdoms	700–300	Human duchies rise; Elves retreat into isolation.
Reign of Haddensack	300–Present	Human stabilization; ancient secrets stir anew.

"The Sundering unmade the world that gave the Mages power."
—Archivist Revalan

"In those years, we did not chase glory—we chased memory. Every scrap of parchment, every whispered tale, every half-burned tome was a lifeline to who we once were. To preserve knowledge was to preserve hope."
—Archivist Temen Drel, Master Scribe of the Ashen Hall

"Never trust a city without a library—or a scribe who isn't tired."
—Old Archivist's Saying

UNDEAD

Summarized from the treatises commissioned by Xavier von Schule. *A Treatise on the Undead: Characteristics and Known Environments*
A Treatise on the Undead: A Compendium of Fiends

General observation taken from the treatises: all undead shun sunlight, as it is deadly to them in extended exposure.

B
Blightghouls – Ghouls with toxic spores, variant of a ghoul, fungal in origin, highly contagious. Will hide in groups during the daylight.

D
Dread wolves – Undead beasts, fast and powerful, often found near vampire lairs, eyes glow red, claws poisonous.

G
Ghosts – Remnants of profound trauma, not aggressive unless provoked, may be reasoned with, exist in the Ethereal Plane and can cross over into Material Plane.
Ghouls – Undead warriors, mindless servants, agile and quick, can climb, hunt all living things, follow instructions of their master. Will hide in groups during the daylight, but will brave the sunlight if provoked.

L
Liches – Undead wizards or magi, bound to phylacteries, destruction of physical form does not end them. Dangerous planners, near immortals. Perfected by the Mages.

M
Mummies – Desiccated undead, tied to unholy rituals practiced upon the living, carry curses, best to avoid. Often found in tombs.

S

Shadow-fiends – Giant extraplanar undead, extremely rare, used as guardian-hunters, vengeful, survivors, cataclysmic??? Only suspected vulnerability is sunlight.

Shadows – Vitality draining entities, may be controlled with wards or runes, susceptible to holy or consecrated light.

Skeletons – Animated bones, mindless warriors, controlled by necromancers, often massed to overrun the living. Only undead able to survive daylight for a few hours.

Specters – Vengeful incorporeal spirits, drawn to places of violent death.

U

Umbrals – Intelligent shadow-born undead, stronger than ghosts or specters, maybe necromantic spell casters or soul-drainers. Often created by liches to collect souls to feed their hunger.

V

Vestiges – Location-bound spirits, seek living or undead hosts, undying, extremely difficult to destroy, exist in the Ethereal and Material Planes. Often thought of as neither good or evil. A living host allows them to move in sunlight.

Vampires – Cunning, intelligent, blood-feeding, retains intellect and spellcasting, master manipulators, used at times as forever guardians. Create their own vampire spawn and dread wolves, avoid sunlight (deadly to them). Vampires can have necromancer abilities to create ghouls and blightghouls.

Vampire spawn - stealthy undead, corrupted victims of vampires, skulk in ruins, hunt at night, avoid sunlight (deadly to them).

W

Will-o'-wisps – Lure travelers to ruin, feed on fear, appear in regions where there has been ancient death or tragedy, often found in deep forests and known to hunt Fey.

Wraiths – Powerful spirits, often can command lesser undead, often born from rituals, avoid direct confrontation. Difficult to destroy.

Wights – Intelligent undead, often bound to ancient oaths and burial grounds, possess martial skill and will, dangerous in small numbers. Can wield weapons.

Z

Zombies – Rotting corpses, mindless but relentless, decay slows reactions, carry disease. Mildly resistant to sunlight.